T0356345

BRIDAL SHOWER MURDER

Books by Leslie Meier

MISTLETOE MURDER
TIPPY TOE MURDER
TRICK OR TREAT MURDER
BACK TO SCHOOL MURDER
VALENTINE MURDER
CHRISTMAS COOKIE MURDER
TURKEY DAY MURDER
WEDDING DAY MURDER
BIRTHDAY PARTY MURDER
FATHER'S DAY MURDER
STAR SPANGLED MURDER
NEW YEAR'S EVE MURDER
BAKE SALE MURDER
CANDY CANE MURDER
ST. PATRICK'S DAY MURDER
MOTHER'S DAY MURDER
WICKED WITCH MURDER
GINGERBREAD COOKIE MURDER
ENGLISH TEA MURDER
CHOCOLATE COVERED MURDER
EASTER BUNNY MURDER
CHRISTMAS CAROL MURDER
FRENCH PASTRY MURDER
CANDY CORN MURDER
BRITISH MANOR MURDER
EGGNOG MURDER
TURKEY TROT MURDER
SILVER ANNIVERSARY MURDER
YULE LOG MURDER
HAUNTED HOUSE MURDER
INVITATION ONLY MURDER
CHRISTMAS SWEETS
CHRISTMAS CARD MURDER
IRISH PARADE MURDER
HALLOWEEN PARTY MURDER
EASTER BONNET MURDER
IRISH COFFEE MURDER
MOTHER OF THE BRIDE MURDER
EASTER BASKET MURDER
PATCHWORK QUILT MURDER
BRIDAL SHOWER MURDER

Published by Kensington Publishing Corp.

BRIDAL SHOWER MURDER

LESLIE MEIER

Kensington Publishing Corp.
kensingtonbooks.com

This book is a work of fiction. Names, characters, businesses, organizations, places, events, and incidents either are the product of the author's imagination or are used fictitiously. Any resemblance to actual persons, living or dead, events, or locales is entirely coincidental.

To the extent that the image or images on the cover of this book depict a person or persons, such person or persons are merely models, and are not intended to portray any character or characters featured in the book.

KENSINGTON BOOKS are published by:

Kensington Publishing Corp.
900 Third Avenue
New York, NY 10022

All Kensington titles, imprints, and distributed lines are available at special quantity discounts for bulk purchases for sales promotion, premiums, fund-raising, educational, or institutional use. Special book excerpts or customized printings can also be created to fit specific needs. For details, write or phone the office of the Kensington Special Sales Manager: Attn. Special Sales Department, Kensington Publishing Corp., 900 Third Ave., New York, NY 10022. Phone: 1-800-221-2647.

Library of Congress Control Number: 2024949729

ISBN: 978-1-4967-4924-6
First Kensington Hardcover Edition: April 2025

ISBN-13: 978-1-4967-4926-0 (ebook)

10 9 8 7 6 5 4 3 2 1

Printed in the United States of America

Chapter One

Lucy Stone, intrepid part-time reporter for the *Courier* newspaper in the quaint coastal town of Tinker's Cove, Maine, recoiled and took a deep breath to steady herself. "What are those things? Medieval weapons?" she asked. *Those things* were several long poles with very nasty-looking hooks on the end, and they were on display in the hallway of the 1789 Jacob Pratt House, headquarters of the Tinker's Cove Historical Society.

"Oh, no," said Hetty Furness, shaking her head. "They're peaveys, and they were invented right here in Maine."

"Uh, how do you spell that?" asked Lucy, opening her reporter's notebook. Lucy had interviewed Hetty, who was chairperson of the historical society's board of directors, plenty of times before and knew that if she didn't get every detail absolutely right, Hetty wouldn't hesitate to demand a correction. She was well into her sixties, with a head of curly, permed, white hair, bright blue eyes, and rosy cheeks. Today, in honor of the display that Lucy was previewing, an exhibit documenting the logging industry in Maine, Hetty was wearing a plaid flannel shirt tucked into a roomy pair of pull-up corduroy pants.

Hetty spelled *peavey* for her, and went on to explain that the peaveys were used by lumberjacks in two ways. "They helped them balance on floating logs, and they also used them to break up logjams when they were moving the logs down rivers. Come on into the parlor, as the spider said to the fly," giggled Hetty, leading the way. "Here we have old photos from the days when the river, our river here, was packed with logs from shore to shore every spring."

"Oh, my, that looks like dangerous work," said Lucy, leaning in to study the old sepia-toned photos showing the lumbermen precariously balanced on floating logs, peaveys in hand. She shivered despite the fact that she was dressed for the weather in her work uniform of jeans and boatneck tee, topped with a warm flannel-lined windbreaker. Ocean breezes kept things chilly in Tinker's Cove well into May, but today's brisk weather was nothing compared to the primitive conditions the loggers had to endure.

"Oh, it was dangerous," admitted Hetty. "Every part of logging was dangerous. Cutting down the trees, dragging them to the river, then moving them down to the sawmills. That's why exhibits like this are so important, so people understand our history and the struggle it took to get us to where we are today."

"There's a lot of romance about lumberjacks," said Lucy. "Pancakes, plaid shirts, and Paul Bunyan with his blue ox, Babe."

"As you can see," said Hetty, nodding at several photos pinned to a movable display board, "they did wear a lot of plaid shirts and I imagine they ate plenty of pancakes and lots of other food, too." Hetty pointed to another photo depicting a lumber camp kitchen, where several cooks were manning a couple of cast-iron stoves set up in a three-sided makeshift shelter with their stovepipe chimneys poking through the roof and puffing away. "If you didn't feed the workers, they weren't likely to stay."

"Who were the workers?" asked Lucy, as she moved along from photo to photo. They were mostly posed, due to the long exposure time the earliest cameras required, typically showing a group of lumbermen gathered in front of a tent or cookhouse. There were a few of loggers cutting down massive trees with long two-man saws, and others of the felled logs ready to be moved by teams of oxen using chains. Views of the frozen river in winter showed it packed with logs waiting for the thaw, and then after it melted in spring there were photos of the men on top of those slippery logs, floating along with their peaveys in hand.

"Mostly young men, I imagine. It was seasonal work; they'd cut the trees in winter, when the ground was frozen and they could get the logs to the river. Probably local farmers, and migrants who came down from Canada. It was hard work, and very risky, but gave them much-needed income."

"And all the pancakes you could eat," said Lucy.

"Right," agreed Hetty, with a laugh. "In fact, we're going to kick off the exhibit with a pancake breakfast."

"Now you're talking," said Lucy, jotting down all the details. Then tucking her notebook in her tote, Lucy said good-bye and headed back to the office. Her walk took her a few blocks along Main Street, where the white clapboard Community Church with its tall steeple stood at one end, and the white clapboard Baptist Church with its tall steeple stood at the other, right by the town's only traffic light. Country Cousins, the famous e-commerce giant, with its folksy old-time country store, was also at the far end, next to the Community Church. In between were the town hall, the police and fire stations, post office, hardware store, several shops mostly catering to tourists, and the *Courier* office. If you continued on through the traffic light, which marked the intersection with Sea Street that led downhill to the harbor, you'd pass Jake's Donut Shack. A bit farther along you'd find the luxurious and expensive Queen Victoria Inn, the town's finest hotel. On the very outskirts, approaching Route 1, was St. Brigid's Catholic Church, which was brick, and instead of a steeple had a skinny metal superstructure topped with a cross and was surrounded by a huge parking lot.

Pausing at the office door, Lucy took a moment to survey the town she'd been covering for a couple of decades. It was calendar and picture-postcard ready, she decided, noting that the trees had just leafed out and the Chamber of Commerce had filled the barrels that dotted the sidewalk with red and white geraniums accompanied by American flags. Tinker's Cove was all gussied up, ready for the summer tourist season. She shook her head and smiled ruefully to herself: Picture perfect could cover up a lot of, well, a lot that wasn't photo ready. She yanked the door open, setting the little bell to jangling, and went in.

Phyllis, the receptionist, was at her desk behind the counter where she'd placed a vase of purple and white lilacs that filled the office with fragrance. Lucy immediately buried her nose in a feathery plume and breathed in. "I love lilacs," she sighed.

"Me too," said Phyllis, who had dyed her hair lilac-purple and was wearing a lavender track suit. "This is the last of them, I'm sorry to say."

"My lily of the valley is coming along," said Lucy. "And

soon we'll have roses. It's almost too much, all my favorites all at once."

"That's spring for you," said Phyllis.

"Yeah," agreed Lucy, noticing that their boss, Ted's, rolltop desk was empty. "Where's his nibs?" she asked.

"Over in Gilead," said Phyllis, with a disdainful snort. Ted had taken to spending most of his time in the modern Gilead office, which he'd acquired when he bought the *Gilead Gabber* and combined it with his *Pennysaver* to create the county-wide *Courier*.

"Can't blame him," said Lucy, casting her eyes around the office, which boasted crooked, scuffed wood floors, dingy paint, ancient Venetian blinds, and a Simon Willard clock that had been ticking off the minutes to deadline since 1840.

She settled herself at her desk, a heavily shellacked wood model with drawers that stuck, and powered up her computer. As she expected, Ted had sent her an email with the week's story budget, which was heavy on local government committee meetings. She could cover those with her eyes closed; sometimes she actually did, dozing off as the selectmen or the Fin Com members endlessly debated increasing the school budget, raising the price of dog licenses, and cutting back trees along the power lines. With nothing breaking at the moment, she decided to expand her preview of the logging exhibit into a feature story. Hetty would be so happy!

But after she went over her notes, she decided she had more questions than answers and decided to do a bit of research. She knew the lumber industry had once been a major part of the Maine economy but now played a much smaller role. There were still plenty of trees—what happened? She flitted from file to file, learning that in its beginning, back in the 1820s, the industry had operated statewide, carried on by small, independent outfits owned by individuals or partners. That eventually became financially unsustainable and the independents formed cooperatives, which by the 1880s were themselves unable to compete with the large paper companies. Nowadays, those once dominant companies were faced with rising fuel and equipment costs and supply chain delays, as well as an aging workforce. Timber stands were being replaced with solar farms, and most of the lumber jobs had drifted to foreign competitors.

Times change, thought Lucy, as her cell phone announced a call with a jaunty little ditty. "Hi, there," she said, with a smile in her voice. The caller was her daughter Zoe, who rarely called, and Lucy was eager to catch up on her news. "What's up?"

"Something big!" crowed Zoe. "Frank's retiring and I've been named communications director for the Sea Dogs." Zoe had moved to Portland a few years earlier when she was hired as assistant communications director for the AA minor league team.

"Wow, that's great!" enthused Lucy. "Does it come with a big raise?"

Zoe sighed. "Well, eventually. It's kind of conditional, like I'm on probation for three months. Joe, you know he's the team's CEO, he said he wanted to give me a chance, said Frank had strongly recommended me to succeed him, but I definitely got the feeling that he's doubtful I can do the job."

"Because you're a woman?" asked Lucy.

"Well, yeah. Baseball is pretty much a man's world."

So what's new? thought Lucy, who sometimes felt as if she'd been fighting an uphill battle to gain journalistic credibility for her entire career. Ted was nice enough, but she knew he took advantage of the fact that she loved her job to offer ridiculously low pay and no benefits at all. His thinking was that if she didn't like it, she could go home and bake pies or do whatever women did; he wasn't convinced he actually needed the Tinker's Cove office and was only keeping it going for Lucy and Phyllis out of the kindness of his heart.

"But you've done such a good job," said Lucy. "You're the one who set up the Home Base Fun Zone for kids on the concourse, you brought in entertainment for the seventh-inning stretch, not to mention the healthier meal options. You've sent the players out for community events. It's a whole new ball game!"

Zoe laughed. "I think there's a feeling that I kind of pushed Frank out with all my new ideas."

"Did anybody say that?"

"Well, the word *ambitious* was mentioned, and not in a good way."

"That's so unfair. As a woman you have to work twice as hard to gain any recognition at all and then they say you're pushy and ambitious."

"I thought I was making Frank look good. I mean, I really did try to be supportive and a team player and all that. And he seemed to like my ideas—I mean, he went along."

"Probably thought you'd fail and fall flat on your face," guessed Lucy. "Gave you enough rope to hang yourself."

"Well, that didn't happen and now Frank is retiring. Honestly, from the way Joe was talking you'd think the guy was dying or something instead of taking off with his wife on a cross-country RV trip."

"Do you think he has somebody in mind, a son-in-law or somebody like that, that he wants for the job?"

"Could be, I don't know." Zoe sighed. "All I do know is that I love working for the team, and I'm going to do a fabulous job for them."

"You need to think about corporate politics, though," advised Lucy. "Doing a good job isn't enough. You need to build up a base of support with the other execs, and especially the board of directors. Is there a board?"

"Oh, yeah. I'm going to be introduced to them in a week or so."

"Well, do some research ahead of the meeting. Find out who they are and what they're involved in. You can build on that, especially if there are a couple of women. Get to know them, meet with them, and get them on your side."

"That's great advice, Mom."

"Well, it's easy to give advice. I can't say my career has taken off. I'm still here in Tinker's Cove plugging away on selectboard meetings."

Zoe laughed. "You're underestimating yourself. You've won lots of awards and broke stories that went national. You're the voice of Tinker's Cove!"

"A big frog in a small pond . . ."

"I'm going to tell you what you always told us kids: Stop feeling sorry for yourself. You can find sympathy in the dictionary."

"Nothing worse than your own words coming back at you," said Lucy, laughing.

"Well, I'm coming back myself this weekend." Zoe paused. "And I'm bringing someone I want you to meet."

"Who?"

"His name's Chad."

Lucy had a million questions. Like was this a serious relationship? What did he do? Where did he come from? What was his family like? What did he look like? And what was his last name? But before she could utter another word, Zoe said, “See ya soon,” and ended the call.

Typical. “See ya soon.” Like when? she wondered. It would certainly be nice to know, so she could plan meals. Should she expect them Friday afternoon? Evening? Or maybe Saturday morning? Lucy shrugged her shoulders, resigned. Better plan for Friday, just in case.

Chapter Two

"What was that all about?" asked Phyllis, peering over the polka-dot cheaters perched on her nose.

"Zoe's bringing a boy home for us to meet," said Lucy, still in shock.

"Wow, that's big," said Phyllis. "They must be serious."

"Maybe, maybe not. She's brought boyfriends home before, but last I knew she was having a ball dating every player on the team. Kind of a revolving door; they came and they went."

"Well, it sounds like somebody struck a home run," said Phyllis, terribly pleased with herself. "What did she tell you about him?"

"Practically nothing. The call was all about her promotion. She's been named communications director for the team."

"That's terrific," said Phyllis, brushing aside this news. "Did she mention his name by any chance?"

"Yeah. Chad."

"That's it?"

"I told you. She actually seemed more excited about the promotion."

"You're a reporter, Lucy. Use your reporting skills and see what you can find out about this mystery man. He's probably on the team."

Phyllis was right. The Sea Dogs website listed bios of all the players, including Chad, written in Zoe's unmistakable style. "Okay," began Lucy, peering at her screen, "Charles 'Chad' Nettleton . . ."

"Nettleton?"

"Yeah, Nettleton. He's a Virginia native, a Union College honors graduate. . . ."

"No dummy then," observed Phyllis.

"It doesn't mention his major, but I think Union has a lot of phys ed majors."

"We can't all be physicists, Lucy. What else does it say?"

"Um. He played on the college team and for the Cape Cod League, summers."

"Cut to the chase, Lucy. Is there a photo?"

"Oh, yes."

Phyllis popped up and crossed the office in a flash to peer over Lucy's shoulder. "Oooh," she cooed. "That is one very good-looking young fellow."

"Photos can be doctored," said Lucy, staring at wide-set brown eyes that looked right back at her, a straight nose, dimpled chin, and wide smile featuring a perfect bite. We don't know how tall he is, after all."

"It's right there, Lucy, in his stats. He's six-two."

"He could have premature baldness under that cap."

"Give it up, Lucy. He's tall, handsome, intelligent, and athletic. I'd say he's quite a catch, ticks all the boxes. What's not to like?"

"Bill will find something, he's pretty protective of his girls," confessed Lucy. "He's never really gotten over Elizabeth going off to France, where he can't keep an eye on her," she said, naming her oldest daughter. "And he worries about Sara, living in the sinful city. . . ."

"Boston?" asked Phyllis, eyebrows raised.

"In Bill's eyes, the Museum of Science is staffed with a bunch of sex maniacs, all panting after Sara. And Zoe's his baby. He never approved of her going to work for the team. The way Bill sees it, this guy is only going to confirm his worst suspicions about baseball players. Poor Chad won't be able to do anything right." She sighed. "It's going to be tense."

Phyllis patted her shoulder. "Good luck to him. If they're really in love, nothing's going to keep them apart. Not even Bill."

"That's not what I'm worried about," said Lucy. "I'm worried about him creating a rift and alienating Zoe. I don't want to lose my daughter."

"I'm pretty sure Zoe knows the score. And you can act as a buffer and make the lad feel welcome."

"Right," said Lucy, checking her calendar. It was already Thursday afternoon, and if they were coming Friday evening, she didn't have much time to get the house ready for company. "I'm going to have to take tomorrow off. . . ."

"Ted won't like it," said Phyllis.

"There's no way around it. I've got to clean and shop, put fresh sheets on the beds."

"Beds? I think you only need to do one, Lucy."

"Oh, no. Bill will insist on separate rooms." She smiled. "Of course, what happens after the lights go out is up to them." Lucy closed out Chad's bio and took another look at her story budget for the coming week. The selectboard wasn't meeting until Monday, Fin Com was on Tuesday, she'd already written up the highway superintendent's retirement, which left only the story about Hetty's exhibit at the historical society. She opened a new file, flipped open her notebook, and got to work.

That evening, after giving Bill his favorite meat loaf dinner, she casually mentioned in an offhand way that Zoe was coming home for the weekend, with a friend. She didn't want to give him time to fret, which he would certainly do, so she didn't mention that the friend was male. Intent on watching the Bruins get one game closer to the Stanley Cup, Bill merely said, "Oh, that's nice," before heading into the family room.

Lucy immediately swung into action and loaded the dishwasher, then scrubbed the countertops and the cabinet fronts. She cleaned the insides of the toaster oven and microwave, polished the round golden oak table where she and Bill had just eaten dinner, and wiped down the stovetop. She peered inside the oven, discovered it needed a cleaning, but settled instead on polishing up the door. What are the chances he'd look in the oven? She swept and Swiffered the floor, then she slipped into the guest bath and gave the sink and toilet a scrub, emptied the wastebasket, and put out fresh soap and towels.

By then the game was going into overtime and she hurried upstairs, where she quickly stripped off her clothes and ran herself a bath, confident that Bill would be none the wiser when he came to bed. He'd assume she'd spent the evening as she usually did, watching a movie on the small TV in the bedroom or reading one of her favorite mystery authors. He'd never dream she'd spent it deep-cleaning the kitchen, much less wonder why.

Next morning, after Bill left to work on his latest antique home restoration, which happened to be one of the multimillion-dollar "cottages" overlooking the Atlantic on Ocean Drive, she poured herself a second cup of coffee and planned her menu for the weekend, and her shopping list. It was a daunting task, since she didn't know Chad's food preferences, or even if he had food allergies. What if he was vegan, or on a gluten-free diet? A lot of people had shellfish allergies, so she better avoid that. In the end, she figured it was unlikely an athlete would be vegetarian and went with pork chops and rice pilaf for Friday and steak and potatoes on Saturday. Then she was off to the IGA where she grabbed bouquets of carnations and mums, loaded her cart with dinner fixings plus plenty of snacks and cases of flavored seltzer. Back home, she unloaded the groceries, arranged the flowers, and vacuumed and dusted the living room, dining room, and family room. Fueled by a quick peanut butter sandwich lunch, she then lugged the vacuum upstairs to change the sheets in son Toby's and Zoe's old rooms, where she noticed the windows needed a clean. When she took the curtains down she decided they could use a wash, so she dashed down to the cellar and tossed them in the washer, along with the sheets. While they sloshed around in the washer she zipped upstairs and washed the bare windows, and started dusting. Then it was back down to the cellar to switch the wash into the dryer, up again to finish the dusting, vacuum the bedrooms and scrub and polish the bathroom. Then it was back down the two flights to retrieve the clean curtains, permanent press thank Heaven, and hang them back up. She folded and put the clean sheets away in the closet, vacuumed the hall, and, checking her watch, realized they could arrive at any minute and what was she going to wear?

Too tired to give the matter any serious thought, she grabbed a fresh shirt and was pulling it over her head when she heard a car beep, announcing Chad and Zoe's arrival.

No time to change her pants, so she quickly ran a comb through her hair and slapped on some lipstick before rushing downstairs to greet them. They were still in the car, a massive four-wheel-drive pickup truck, when she opened the door to welcome them.

The truck looked brand new and Lucy wondered if minor league baseball players made much money. She rather doubted it; in fact, she'd heard that even if they went to the majors, rookies didn't begin to command the million-dollar deals offered to star players. She knew oversized trucks like Chad's went for at least fifty thousand dollars, which made her suspect that Chad probably had some family money to subsidize to his earnings. Maybe even a trust fund?

What was she thinking and why was her mind going down this particular path? she wondered. Was she a modern-day Mrs. Bennet, panting to marry her daughter to a man with a healthy income and a stately home? She vowed to banish such mercenary thoughts from her mind and waited with a smile on her face as Chad jumped down from the cab and went around to the passenger side to help Zoe exit the truck. Polite and gorgeous, oh my. It was almost too much to bear, she thought, as the couple made their way up the path and climbed the steps onto the porch. "Hi!" Chad declared, sticking out his hand and preparing to grab Lucy's. "Nice to meet you."

She was reaching for his hand when he suddenly exclaimed, "Oops! I forgot!" and ran back to the truck, returning with an enormous bouquet of lilies and roses, wrapped in paper from Portland's most expensive florist. "Zoe said you like flowers," he said, presenting them to her. Zoe's eyes met her mother's, and she burst into amused laughter.

Lucy took the flowers and inhaled their gorgeous scent.

"It's great to meet you, Chad, and thank you so much for the flowers. Come on inside." She stepped aside, and as the couple passed she noticed the air was filled with a fresh and lovely fragrance. The flowers? Or was it something Chad was wearing?

Chapter Three

There was an awkward moment as they stood in the kitchen. "How was traffic?" asked Lucy, to break the ice. "Any tie-up in Wiscasset?"

"Smooth sailing the whole way," said Chad.

"It's still early in the season," commented Zoe, going on to explain her mother's question to Chad. "Wiscasset's a real trouble spot when the tourists start coming."

"I can see why folks want to come," said Chad. "This is a beautiful area."

"Well, I want to get these flowers in water. Why don't you bring in your stuff and get settled. Zoe, your room is ready for you, and, Chad, I've put you in Zoe's brother's old room. I think you'll be comfortable there."

"That's fine," said Chad, heading out to get their bags.

"Toby's room?" demanded Zoe, when the door closed behind him.

"It's because of your father," explained Lucy. "I don't care what you two do, as long as you don't frighten the horses, as my Aunt Fredi used to say."

"You mean frighten Dad," laughed Zoe.

Lucy nodded. "Just keep it cool, okay?"

"Got it," said Zoe, as Chad returned with a duffel in each hand. "We're upstairs," she said, leading the way up the back staircase.

Lucy had just finished arranging the flowers in her best vase when Bill arrived, hanging up his jacket and putting his lunch bag on the counter. "Nice flowers," he said, giving her a peck on the cheek. "Who are they from?"

The moment of truth had arrived. "From Zoe's friend, Chad. He brought them."

"Chad?" he asked suspiciously.

"Yeah, he's one of the Sea Dogs. Seems like a nice boy."

"Do you think they're serious?" he asked, grabbing a beer from the fridge.

"Well, she brought him home to meet us."

Bill popped the tab on the can. "Hmph." He took a long swallow from the can, then looked up, hearing them clatter down the back stairs.

"Hi, Dad," said Zoe, giving him a hug. "This is Chad."

"Pleased to meet you, sir," said Chad, extending his hand.

Bill gave Chad the same look he might have given Al Capone, if he were still alive and Zoe had brought him home. "Yeah," he said, narrowing his eyes.

"I bet you guys are thirsty," said Lucy. "What can I get you? There's beer, wine, seltzer."

After Chad had chosen beer, and Zoe asked for seltzer, Lucy asked Chad to stay in the kitchen to help her and shooed Zoe and Bill into the family room. Lucy fixed the drinks on a tray, she set Chad to work pouring some chips into a bowl, and together they went into the family room to face the music.

"So, Chad, I understand you play for the Sea Dogs?" asked Bill.

"That's right, sir. I'm on first base."

"Really," said Bill, refusing to be impressed. "How's your hitting?"

"Pretty solid," admitted Chad.

"Chad's one of the team's top players, Dad," said Zoe. "I wouldn't be surprised if he gets moved up to the Boston Red Sox."

Bill fixed a beady eye on Chad, awaiting the answer.

"I'm taking it one day at a time. My focus is on the team. We're number one in the league right now."

"That so." Bill reached for a handful of chips. "What about your family? Are you a Mainer?"

"I'm from Virginia, but I do have some local family ties I hope to explore while I'm here."

"Really?" asked Lucy. "Who are they? Do I know them?"

"Maybe," replied Chad. "The family name is Logue, but that's all I know. We've kind of lost touch."

Lucy recognized the Logue name and wanted to learn more, but Bill interrupted. "And if the baseball doesn't work out, what then?" he demanded.

"My dad has a pharmaceuticals business. I could go into that, I guess." Chad set down his beer on the coffee table. "It's not my first choice. I love baseball."

"C'mon, Chad," said Zoe, getting to her feet. "Let me show you the garden. Mom's got lettuce coming up. . . ."

"I love lettuce," said Chad, taking her hand. Lucy suspected that if Zoe expressed an interest in dust bunnies, Chad would, too.

"I'll call you when dinner's ready," promised Lucy, relieved. She turned to Bill. "Do you want to help me with dinner, or have another beer and watch the news?"

"I'll watch the news," growled Bill. "And I'll take you up on that beer."

Dinner was more of the same, as Bill glowered across the table at Chad and peppered him with questions that Chad answered diplomatically.

"So who's your favorite team?"

"Sea Dogs, by far," said Chad, piling rice pilaf on his plate.

"Politics?"

"I'm an independent."

"Are you a churchgoing man?"

"Not so much. Sunday practices, you know."

"Did you play in college?" Bill scratched his chin. "Where'd you go?"

"Union. I played varsity all four years. And summers I played in the Cape Cod League."

Grudgingly, from Bill, "I heard that's a pretty good league."

"It's hard to beat Cape Cod in the summer."

"You know what we call folks from Massachusetts?" asked Bill.

"Uh, delicious dinner, Mom," said Zoe, cutting him off before he could say *Massholes*. "But I think Chad and I will skip dessert and head out to the roadhouse."

"The roadhouse?" Lucy was disappointed, but also relieved.

"Yeah. Zeke and Marcy and who knows all from high school will probably be there."

"Okay by me," said Chad, pushing away from the table. "Thanks for dinner, Mrs. Stone."

"Oh, please call me Lucy," she said, as they disappeared into the kitchen. After she heard the door close and the truck roar into action, she turned to Bill. "Jeez, Bill. Couldn't you have been a little nicer?"

"What do you mean? I was nice."

"No you weren't. You were confrontational, and I was terrified you'd ask him what his intentions are."

"Well, I'm pretty sure they aren't good. And speaking of that, I hope you put them in separate rooms."

"Of course I did. But I'm pretty sure . . ."

"I don't want to hear it, Lucy. I can't control what Zoe does in Portland, but when she's in my—"

"Our house, Bill."

"Yeah."

Lucy took Bill's hand. "I know it's hard, but Zoe's all grown up. I think she really likes this guy, so let's give him a chance. Okay?"

Bill's eyebrows shot up. "You really think they're serious? Did she say anything to you?"

"Not in so many words, but she's glowing. Did you see the way she looks at him?"

"It's not the way she looks at him that I'm worried about. It's the way he looks at her."

Lucy squeezed Bill's hand. "The way you used to look at me?"

Bill finally cracked a smile, even adding a chuckle. "Yeah."

Next morning, Lucy and Bill were up early to get a head start on their weekend errands, but the doors to both Zoe's and Chad's rooms stayed shut, a fact that Bill did not fail to notice as he sat down at the golden oak table and began eating his usual bacon and eggs. "Pair of lazy-bones, sleeping in," he grumbled. "I wonder what time they got in."

"I think I heard them around midnight," said Lucy, placidly digging into her black cherry yogurt.

"Well, I hope they don't expect you to cook up a big breakfast for them, when they decide to make their appearance," said Bill, picking up a piece of bacon and waving it around. "Pretty inconsiderate, if you ask me. You can't be expected to spend the entire morning waiting around for them."

"I don't actually have much on tap, today," admitted Lucy, who didn't need to do her usual Saturday housecleaning and grocery shopping since she'd done those chores in anticipation of the visit. "I thought I'd go to the farm store and get some plants for those big pots on the porch. That's about it."

"Put them to work," suggested Bill. "They could rake the driveway, get that gravel the snowblower sent onto the lawn back where it belongs."

"Great idea," said Lucy, who had no intention of doing any such thing.

Bill used his last piece of toast to mop up the egg yolk on his plate, drained his coffee cup, and stood up. "Well, I'm off," he said, bending down and kissing the top of her head. "Time and tide wait for no man."

"Or the guys at the hardware store?" asked Lucy, who knew Bill's weekend always began at the local contractor's rendezvous at Slack's. "See you around lunchtime?"

"Yeah." He put on his barn coat, slapped a faded blue Red Sox cap on his head, and headed out the door.

Lucy got busy emptying the dishwasher so she could start filling it up again, which got her thinking that the task served as a metaphor for much of her life. Her work was never done, it was simply repeated. Dinner had to be cooked every night, the bed had to be made every morning, the selectboard meeting had to be covered every week. She paused, a dish in her hand, and looked out the window. The seasons made a change, she thought, looking forward to filling those pots with geraniums, or maybe something different this year. Petunias? Nasturtiums? Maybe a colorful mix . . .

"Morning, Mom," said Zoe, bopping down the stairs, followed by Chad. The pair were fully dressed, and said they didn't want breakfast. "We're going to Jake's. Chad wants donuts."

"That's the place," said Lucy, smiling. They looked so cute together, she thought. They made a really handsome couple. "Are you going to show Chad all the local sights?"

"What there is," said Zoe. "And that's not much apart from the lighthouse."

"I'd really like to track down those relatives," said Chad, taking her arm and pulling her close. "I'm hoping to find them and make their acquaintance."

"Logue's their name, right?" asked Lucy, eager to help. "There's Logue Log Homes. Zebulon Logue is the owner. He's active in civic affairs. I've taken his photo plenty of times, handing over a check in a grin-and-grab shot."

"Yeah. That's him. I've got his name and address, too," admitted Chad. "That's not the problem. It's a bit awkward, family stuff, you know? There was a divorce, plenty of bad feelings. But I want to reach out to them. If they're still mad, well, at least I might get a look at them, right?"

"Yeah. And while you're at it, ask about their medical histories," teased Lucy. "Cancer, heart problems, obesity . . ."

"The only one I'm really worried about is baldness," confessed Chad, with a grin and ruffling his thick black hair.

"Well, have fun, kids. Back for dinner?"

"Uh, no, Mom. Chad got reservations at the Queen Vic."

"Oh, okay," said Lucy, somewhat disappointed. What was she going to do with that gorgeous three-pound steak she had the butcher cut specially for her?

She put it in the freezer, that's what she did, and had Bill cook up a nice piece of salmon on the grill. They were eating ice cream and watching Logan Roy thwart yet another of his children's schemes to take over his company in an episode of *Succession* when Zoe and Chad returned. Lucy and Bill heard the kitchen door shut, and Lucy rather expected them to go directly upstairs, but instead they bounced into the family room, brimming with excitement.

"We're engaged!" announced Zoe, flashing a ring containing what seemed to Lucy to be at least a two-carat diamond, maybe even bigger.

"Oh! That's wonderful!" Lucy was on her feet, hugging Zoe and Chad and Zoe again. "And the ring is beautiful! And, oh, I'm so happy for you," she exclaimed, bursting into tears of joy.

Bill rose slowly from his seat, clicking off the TV with the remote, and advancing across the room. He stuck out his hand and shook with Chad, locking eyes. "You're going to take good care of my little girl, right?"

"Absolutely, sir," Chad responded, man to man.

"Such big news," said Lucy, her hand on her chest. "Are you going to tell the others? I think it's too late in Paris, but perfect timing for Toby and Molly in Alaska. And Sara's sure to still be up."

"I don't know," said Zoe, looking to Chad. "I think we kind of want to wait a bit. What do you think?"

"Up to you," said Chad, with a shrug.

"Well, I'd like to wait until we set a date."

"That makes sense," offered Bill, with an approving nod. "Take some time to get used to the idea and feel your way into this new relationship. There's no rush. . . ." His eyebrows shot up and he turned to Zoe. "Is there a need to hurry?"

"No, Dad," laughed Zoe. "I'm not pregnant, and even if I were . . ."

"If you were, you'd be going straight to the altar, no detours."

"Hopelessly old-fashioned," said Lucy, shaking her head.

"No shotgun needed, sir," said Chad, wrapping his arm around Zoe's waist and pulling her close. "I can't imagine spending my life without Zoe."

"Well, then," said Bill, humphing, "that's all right."

"More than all right," said Lucy, grabbing both of them in her arms, "it's absolutely wonderful."

Chapter Four

On Sunday mornings Bill liked to cook a big breakfast, and the happy couple was unable to resist the scent of bacon wafting up the kitchen stairs. They appeared, along with their appetites, eager to dive into scrambled eggs, blueberry muffins, fresh fruit salad, and locally made sausages along with the crispy bacon.

"Mmm, great sausage," said Chad, helping himself to seconds from the generously filled platter in the center of the golden oak table.

"A fellow down the road makes it, raises the pigs, too," offered Bill, in a display of geniality that stunned Lucy.

"Poor little piggies," said Zoe, nibbling on a strip of bacon.

"Well, as the farmer says, they have one really bad day in what is otherwise a great life, rooting around in the woods and taking mud baths," said Lucy.

"That's one way to look at it," said Chad, pausing to spear a piece of sausage. "I can't argue with the product." He chewed thoughtfully. "Say, babe, maybe we can pick some up on the way home. Whaddya think?"

"Sure," said Zoe. "We can even pick up stuff for a picnic lunch to eat on the way home."

"I hope you're not in a rush," said Lucy.

"No, we can take our time," said Zoe, gazing lovingly at her handsome fiancé.

"No rush at all," said Chad, returning her gaze.

Bill shoved his chair back from the table and got up. "More coffee, anybody?"

"Sure," said Chad, holding up his mug.

"You mentioned you were hoping to find some relatives around here," said Lucy. "Any luck?"

"Yeah, I found my grandfather. My mom's dad, actually."

"You hadn't met your grandfather until now?" asked Lucy, puzzled.

"No. I know it's crazy, but my mom was estranged from him, and her mother, my grandmother, too. Old Zeb, that's his name, Zeb Logue, didn't approve of my dad, or something, not sure exactly what caused the rift. When she and my dad married, they moved to Virginia and never looked back. Turns out I even have a half brother, Chris, who was raised by Grandpa Logue and my grandmother, Margery. She's passed, so I couldn't meet her."

"You have a half brother that you never met?" asked Bill, furrowing his brow.

"Yeah. He's older than me. I know my mom was married before—my dad is her second husband—so I guess Chris was from that first marriage."

"She left her child when she married your dad?" asked Lucy, somewhat appalled.

"I'm sure there's a story there," said Chad, with a shrug, "but I don't know what it is." He pushed a bit of sausage around with his fork. "It really seems out of character. She's a great mom."

"What are they like?" asked Lucy. "Your grandfather and Chris."

"Really nice," said Zoe. "They live in this big mansion, really, and they were very welcoming."

"That was because of you," said Chad. "Old granddad there took a shine to Zoe."

"That's not hard to do," said Bill. "And the fact you play pro baseball probably impressed them." Lucy was dying to hear more about this family reunion, but Bill was more interested in baseball than family dynamics. "Say, what do you think about the Red Sox this year? That new pitcher, the thirty-million wonder kid, is already on the DL."

"They did get off to a slow start," admitted Chad, who seemed rather relieved at the change of subject. "They've won the last three games, though, so I think they're finally starting to click."

"They've got a lot of ground to make up, if they're going to get in the playoffs," observed Bill, pushing his plate away and leaning back, settling in for a chat.

"There's time, more than a hundred games left in the season. . . ." said Chad, warming to his favorite subject.

Lucy glanced at Zoe, then stood up. "I guess I'll just clear away these dishes. . . ."

"I'll help, Mom," said Zoe, picking up a couple of plates.

Together they cleared the table and loaded the dishwasher, then went upstairs to tidy the bedrooms. "Do you want me to strip the bed?" Zoe asked, when they reached the upstairs hall.

"Just one bed?" asked Lucy.

"Just one," said Zoe, giggling.

"So what's the story with the half brother, and the grandpa?" asked Lucy.

"I'm not sure," said Zoe, with a shrug. "This was all new to me. Far as I knew, Chad had a perfectly normal life in Virginia with his mom and dad. He's mentioned cousins and grandparents, all his dad's folks. The Nettletons seem pretty well off, his dad has some sort of specialized pharmacy business. They go to church, he played Little League, was a Boy Scout, all that sort of stuff."

Lucy couldn't quite wrap her head around the situation. "But his mom left her firstborn? And never looked back? Were they surprised to see Chad? Was there tension when you showed up at the Logue mansion?"

Zoe leaned her back against the wall and stared at the display of family photos on the opposite side of the hall. There were pictures of Lucy holding each baby as it arrived, snaps of toddler Toby pushing a truck in a sandbox while his sister Elizabeth blew bubbles. Sara was caught chasing a puppy, Zoe was showing off her pet turtle. There were graduation photos, high school and college, and the latest photo, which showed the whole family together, including Toby's wife Molly and son Patrick, at what was supposed to be Elizabeth's wedding in France.

"Family stuff doesn't always work out," said Zoe. "Like Elizabeth's wedding."

"True," admitted Lucy. "But we're still a family, we still talk to each other. What was it like, when Chad finally met his relatives for the first time?"

"A bit awkward at first," said Zoe. "As you'd imagine. But Dad's right, when they learned that Chad is a pro baseball player things definitely warmed up. The grandfather, especially, is a big fan. He watches all the Red Sox games on TV."

"What about the half brother?"

"He was really shocked, you could tell. He didn't have a clue that he had a half brother, and neither did Chad, for that matter. They kind of stared at each other, and after a bit Chris took off—he didn't stick around."

"It would be a lot to process," said Lucy. "How does Chad feel about it all?"

"He hopes to get to know them better, he's kind of pumped about having a brother. He says he always wanted one, he didn't like being an only child." She grinned. "Doesn't know how lucky he was!"

Hearing footsteps on the stairs, the two women parted. Lucy went into the master, where she began making the bed. From the hall, she heard Chad's voice. "We should probably get going, if you want that picnic. I've got a practice later this afternoon."

"Okay. I'll just finish packing," said Zoe, which was followed by the click of the bedroom door closing behind them. Some time later, rather longer than it would take to pack a couple of weekend bags, they appeared, looking relaxed and glowing with happiness, ready to hit the road.

"Before you go," said Lucy, remembering that this expansion of their family circle entailed some social responsibilities, "I need your details, and I really should send a note to your mother, so I'll need her address, too."

Chad obliged, providing names and addresses, and even his birthday, which Lucy especially requested and jotted down in her address book. Then there were hugs and good-byes, as the happy couple drove off to begin this new phase of their lives. Waving them off, Lucy and Bill shared a smile. "Cute, aren't they?" asked Lucy.

"He's okay," mumbled Bill, which Lucy thought was the highest praise he was likely to offer regarding a future son-in-law.

With the rest of the day ahead of her, Lucy planned to do some yard work. Weeds were already springing up in the vegetable garden among the lettuce, radishes, and other early crops that were almost ready for harvesting. She clapped a hat on her head, grabbed some gloves, and headed out to the backyard shed for the hoe. It was pleasant in the backyard, she thought, as she scratched at the dirt between the rows. The sun was out, there was a nice breeze, and birds were flitting about, busy feeding their nestlings. As she worked, she thought of Zoe and Chad, wondering when they would start their family. But that was jumping ahead; a lot could happen between an engagement and a wedding, and once they were married Lucy knew there would be even more challenges. A surprisingly large number of marriages ended in divorce. Chad's dad, for example, was his mother's second husband. Did she divorce her first husband, Chris's dad? Did divorce run in the family?

With that rather upsetting thought, Lucy put the hoe back in the shed and went back in the house, determined to learn more about Chad's local ties. She set her laptop on the kitchen table, sat down and clicked on Google, typing in Zebulon Logue's name. Her search turned up a rather old story in the now defunct *Maine Business Quarterly* that listed him among the state's wealthiest citizens as the owner of Logue Log Homes. After Googling that business, she doubted very much that it was the actual source of his purported wealth. A bit more digging revealed that earlier Logue family members had owned huge stands of timber, which they opportunely sold off when that business began to decline, in favor of real estate and energy investments. All very interesting, and certainly impressive, but not exactly the information she was looking for about the Logue family.

On Monday, back in the office, she had more luck digging through old newspapers stored in the morgue. There she found the wedding announcement for Zebulon and

Margery's only daughter, Penelope, to one Samuel Taylor, complete with a photo of the happy couple. Penny, as she was known, bore a strong resemblance to Chad. Leafing through subsequent issues, she found the birth announcement of their child, Christopher. She found additional mentions of the family, and the business, too, as she flipped through the dry, yellowed pages. Even back then the Logues were involved in many community projects and frequently made contributions to worthy causes. Margery, in particular, was often among the sponsors of fund-raising events and was regularly pictured in an evening gown at some gala, or posed among a group of smartly dressed Women's Club members. And then, turning to the last issue in the bound volume for 1998, a front page story announced Sam Taylor's tragic death in a construction accident. The family, it was mentioned, was devastated, with the accident occurring so close to Christmas.

Well, not a divorce, concluded Lucy. But something had happened that caused Penny's estrangement from her parents, so Lucy pulled down the volume for 1999 and continued her search. A few months later, in April, she hit pay dirt when Penny Taylor's marriage in Virginia to businessman Nate Nettleton was announced. Fast work, she thought, so maybe the Taylor marriage hadn't actually been all that happy. On a hunch, she flipped to the August issues, looking for Chad's birth announcement, but didn't find anything, which struck her as odd because she knew he was an August baby. It wasn't until January of 2000 that she found it, precisely nine months after the wedding. How odd, thought Lucy. In this day and age people weren't so concerned about the arrival of a baby soon after a wedding, before a wedding, or without a wedding. Unless, she thought, that baby was the result of an extramarital affair. Was that the reason for the family estrangement? And what about Sam? Was his conveniently timed death truly an accident? And why was Chris left with his grandparents? What sort of family were these Logues?

Lucy emerged from the morgue, eager to discuss these discoveries with Phyllis, but found that she was busy taking a birth announcement from Janice Oberman. Janice was apparently on her way to the gym, her workout clothes revealing an extra thirty pounds or so. "Oh, Lucy, there you are. I just popped in with that birth announcement I'd warned you was coming: my third grandchild! And more on the way! Morgan's pregnant, and Chelsea has told me she and her husband Todd, he's a doctor, you know, are trying. He's from a very wealthy family, and the in-laws are absolutely panting for a grandchild." She paused to press a thoughtful finger on her chin. "Oh, Lucy, you have one, right? Just one little lone chick, and he lives so far away, in Alaska. Any progress on that front? What's going on with Elizabeth? She's not getting any younger, now."

Lucy and Phyllis exchanged a glance, and Lucy sighed, promising herself that she would not rise to Janice Oberman's challenge. "Elizabeth's very happy in France," she said, with a serene smile.

"I'll never understand why anyone would go to live there. The French are known for being rude and there's the language barrier. That would make dating very problematic."

"Well, Elizabeth's fluent in French, but it just so happens she's dating an American."

"An expat?" Janice's eyebrows rose in indignation. "Why, the very word indicates he's anti-American. What on earth does she see in him?"

"Love is very mysterious," said Lucy, wishing Janice would magically disappear. Poof!

"And there's Sara, too. Is she still working in that dismal museum?"

"The Museum of Science, in Boston. She loves it there."

"But what about marriage prospects?" demanded Janice.

"Sara plays her cards close to her chest," offered Lucy, refusing to take the bait Janice was dangling in front of her. True, the woman had five daughters, all married, and now apparently busily reproducing. And it was apparently Janice's mission in life to make her feel inferior, what with her three girls who were all still single. Except for Zoe, she realized, brightening up. "A bit of progress," said Lucy, with a sly smile. "Zoe's engaged."

"Really!" shrieked Janice. "How wonderful! And she's no spring chicken. You must be over the moon!"

"Zoe's in her early twenties," said Phyllis, rising to Lucy's defense. "I'm guessing this is the fellow she brought home for the weekend? Chad?"

"Yeah," said Lucy, beaming with pride. "They told us Saturday night. . . ." That's when she belatedly remembered that the engagement was supposed to be secret. "Oops! Actually, forget I said that. They don't want to announce it until they decide on a date; they want to take some time to get used to the idea."

"Well, I call that very odd," said Janice, pressing her lips together. "Did he give her a ring?"

"A lovely ring," admitted Lucy.

Janice pressed on. "I suppose he's one of those baseball players? A Sea Dog?"

"First base," admitted Lucy.

"Well, I hope you know that minor league players rarely make it big. And what do they do when their careers peter out? I mean, it's not like being a lawyer, or a doctor, now is it?" Janice, of course, was referring to two of her sons-in-law. "And most of those baseball players come from nothing, growing up in some teeny little southern town in Arkansas, places like that," she concluded, with a shudder.

The words just flew out of Lucy's mouth. "Actually, it just so happens that his family is quite well off."

Janice was thoughtful. "Lucy, there's no time to lose. You don't want him to change his mind: A bird in the hand is worth two in the bush. You don't want him slipping away over some little quarrel. What you need to do is to get busy planning the wedding right away. It just so happens that my daughter, Taylor, is a wedding planner. I'll have her get in touch with you. I'm sure she has lots of ideas."

"No need," protested Lucy, feeling the ground beneath her shifting and slipping away.

"Nonsense, there's no time to lose," declared Janice. "But don't worry, Lucy, just leave it to me. Taylor and I can take care of everything." And with that, she bustled out the door, leaving the little bell jangling behind her.

Chapter Five

"Ohmigod!" exclaimed Lucy, realizing what she'd done. "I can't believe I did that. The engagement's supposed to be a secret."

"The cat's well and truly out of the bag," observed Phyllis. "You know Janice. She'll tell everyone she meets."

Lucy shook her head. "Zoe will kill me, and I don't blame her. I don't know what came over me." In truth, Lucy knew only too well what had happened and was deeply ashamed. She'd given in to the temptation of getting one up on Janice Oberman.

"Don't feel too bad," advised Phyllis, shoving her zebra-striped cheaters up on her nose. They coordinated nicely with her leopard-print leggings and, a subdued choice for her, tan safari shirt. "Janice should work for the CIA; they wouldn't need waterboarding anymore. Trust me, she could get the most hardened terrorist to tell all his secrets, plus the marriage status of every one of his children."

"And offer to plan their weddings, too," added Lucy, glumly. "How am I going to fend her off? She's even going to sic Taylor on me."

"Well, remember, you've got to run interference and

block the woman. Whatever you do, don't give her Zoe's phone number."

"My lips are sealed," said Lucy, making a zipping gesture. "Sealed," she muttered, powering up her computer and getting busy on a story about the recently renovated fish ladder, which saw record numbers of the migratory fish. She'd just finished interviewing fish warden George Waterman when her phone's ring tone went off and the screen showed Janice Oberman's name.

"Hi, Janice," she said, locking eyes with Phyllis, who gave her a sympathetic smile.

"Well, Lucy, good news! I've talked to Taylor and she's ready, willing, and able to help out. She's got loads of ideas about showers, wedding ceremonies, receptions, the whole kit and kaboodle. You're in good hands."

"Like I told you, Janice, Zoe isn't ready to announce the engagement. They haven't set a date for the wedding. It's not on her radar."

"Well, that's fine. Taylor is very discreet. She just needs to know a little bit about Zoe, the sorts of things she likes. It's a question of style. Is she country? Modern? What sort of music is on her playlist? Does she have a favorite color?"

"I have no idea," said Lucy, wondering if she was really a terrible mother. Was she supposed to know these things? "Well, just guessing, but I think Zoe likes to keep things simple. I don't imagine she wants a big to-do."

"Oh, Lucy, that's where you're wrong. Trust me. Kids today want all the bells and whistles." Janice paused to let this sink in. "And the sooner we get started, the better. That's why I need some information from you. Like Zoe's phone number, and some parameters for a budget. Doesn't have to be anything firm, just ballpark, pun intended! Ha-

ha! So Taylor can get started, I know she'll come up with lots of ideas that Zoe will absolutely love."

"Ohmigosh, Janice, breaking news, I've got to go. . . ." said Lucy, hitting the red button.

At her desk, on the other side of the office, Phyllis gave Lucy an approving nod. "Nicely done."

Lucy was already thinking ahead. "What other excuses can I come up with, now that I've used breaking news?"

"Kettle's whistling, nature's calling, bad connection."

"Those are great. I'm writing them down so I'll have them handy. I think this is going to be a siege. What else have you got?"

"Building collapse, gas explosion, earthquake, cyclone, power failure."

"I don't think she'll believe those. Besides, the phone is battery powered."

"Battery dying, use that. Down to your last bar and it's shrinking fast. And there was that car that drove into the beauty salon over in Salem. . . ."

"Yeah, that would work. I see an SUV coming through the window, gotta run," said Lucy, breaking into a fit of the giggles.

"Desperate times call for desperate measures," said Phyllis, before breaking into laughter herself.

By the time Thursday rolled around, the day that Lucy met her friends for breakfast, she had used up every excuse to end Janice's calls, except those requiring natural disasters. Janice didn't take these heavy-handed hints, however; they only seemed to make her more determined.

"I'm in big trouble," Lucy sighed, sinking into a chair at Jake's Donut Shack and joining the group of women who had begun gathering regularly every week when their kids went off to college and they no longer ran into each other at school events and team practices.

"What's the problem?" asked Rachel Goodman, her big brown eyes expressing concern. Rachel, who had majored in psychology and never got over it, was married to the town's top lawyer, Bob Goodman.

"Well, Zoe's engaged. . . ."

All three erupted in whoops and applause.

"Big news!" exclaimed Sue Finch, the group's most fashion-conscious member, whose husband Sid insisted he got started in the custom closet business in order to keep up with Sue's ever-expanding wardrobe.

"Fantastic!" enthused Pam Stillings, a former cheerleader who was married to Lucy's boss at the paper, Ted.

"Details!" demanded Rachel. "Why is this a problem? Don't you like the, well, boy? Girl? Trans-person?"

"He's a boy, a man. A straight male. He's on the team. His name is Chad Nettleton and he's absolutely adorable."

"I don't see a problem here," said Sue. "He sounds perfect."

"He is. He's not the problem. The problem is that they want to keep the engagement secret for a bit, to get used to the new relationship. . . ."

"Very wise," said Rachel, looking up as the waitress, Norine, approached.

"Hey, congratulations, Lucy. I hear Zoe's made quite a catch. Got herself a Sea Dog."

"Ohhh," sighed Pam, suddenly understanding the problem. "It's supposed to be a secret but . . ."

"I told Janice Oberman," confessed Lucy.

"Wasn't Janice who told me," said Norine. "It was Lydia Volpe, she was in here on Tuesday. She said she actually saw a really cute guy propose to Zoe at the Queen Vic, and Zoe must have accepted because he put the ring on her finger. Word's out, Lucy, everybody seems to know and they're all happy for Zoe." She pulled the order pad out of her ruffled apron and licked her pencil. "Regulars all round?" Receiving nods, she went off to place the orders, then returned with a fresh pot of coffee. "And it's all over social media that one of Janice's daughters is planning the wedding," she said, filling Lucy's mug. "Which one is it? I can never keep them all straight."

"Social media? This is crazy. Nobody's planning any wedding, yet," declared Lucy, exasperated. "This is all Janice's fantasy." She took a sip of coffee. "Chad and Zoe want time to enjoy their new relationship. They're engaged, they're not ready to get married."

"As I started to say," began Rachel, "I think that's very wise. Marriage isn't all about parties and presents, it's about building a life together, and they need time and space to explore what they want their marriage to be. Do they want kids? What about careers? Where do they want to live? Rent or buy? Joint bank accounts or separate? Those are the building blocks of a strong foundation."

"Not according to Janice," said Lucy. "It's all about color schemes, playlists, and budgets. She says the sooner we get started the better."

"That's true," observed Norine, arriving with their orders. "If you want to have a reception at the Queen Vic, you've got to reserve the space at least a year in advance," she added, setting down Rachel's sunshine muffin, Pam's yogurt parfait, and Lucy's hash and eggs. "And for you, madame?" she asked, glaring at Sue. "Just more black coffee?"

Sue smiled sweetly. "Thank you, Norine."

"One of these days," replied Norine, eyes narrowed, "you're going to break down and have a chocolate-topped Boston cream."

"In your dreams," said Sue, lifting her mug in a toast.

They all knew that Sue existed on a diet of black coffee and white wine.

"So what's this dreamboat like?" asked Pam, digging into her yogurt.

"Pretty dreamy," admitted Lucy, poking the corner of a toast triangle into an egg yolk. "He's from Virginia, so he's got that southern-boy polish. Very polite. And smart—he graduated from Union."

"What about his folks?" asked Sue. "Have you met them?"

"Not yet. I wrote a note to his mom, but she hasn't replied yet." Lucy took a bite of eggy toast. "He's got family around here, too," she said, quickly adding, "but they're not close."

"Well, in due course, I'd love to host a shower for Zoe," said Sue, getting approving nods from Pam and Rachel. "No rush at all. Whenever Zoe's ready."

"Thanks," said Lucy, giving her friend a big smile. "That's sweet of you. And I know it's going to be lovely. All your parties are perfect."

"Something to look forward to," said Pam.

"We're all happy for you, Lucy," said Rachel, raising her mug. "Here's to Zoe."

They all joined in, raising their mugs. "To Zoe and Chad!"

"And maybe grandkids," added Pam.

"Hear, hear!"

Lucy felt lighter on her feet as she left Jake's and headed across the street to the office. She could always count on her friends to give her loving support and good advice. And the fact that Lydia had broken the story about the engagement meant that, even if she'd managed to resist Janice Oberman's probing, everybody would know anyway. It wasn't entirely her fault that the news got out. She knew only too well that everybody in Tinker's Cove knew the news before it appeared in the *Courier*. Even the online edition was always a beat behind the local grapevine, no matter how hard she tried to be the first to deliver breaking news.

She was thinking along these lines as she neared the office, wondering if she'd taken the wrong approach in her efforts to learn more about Chad's family. Instead of clicking her way through Google and digging into old newspapers, she ought to have consulted the town's wise old oracle. People joked that Hetty Furness had likely forgotten more local history than anybody else remembered. Hetty was the one to talk to and, since it was Thursday, when the historical society was open, she would probably find her there.

Lucy continued on past the newspaper office to the Jacob Pratt House, where a colorful flag flapped in the breeze announcing it was open. Stepping inside, Lucy inhaled the lingering smoky scent from the wood fires that had once burned constantly for cooking and warmth. Hearing her footsteps in the tiny hall, Hetty popped out from the keeping room to greet her, feather duster in hand. "Lucy! Thanks for the story! We had quite a turnout for the exhibit opening."

"Happy to be of service," said Lucy, continuing, "but now I hope you can help me. I'm after some information. . . ."

"Oh, Lucy, let me congratulate you. I hear that Zoe is engaged."

Lucy gave a rueful chuckle. "It was supposed to be a secret, but it turns out that everybody knows."

"That's a small town for you." Hetty stepped closer and lowered her voice. "I heard he gave her a huge diamond. A real whopper."

"The ring is lovely," admitted Lucy. "And I don't know if you know this, but Zoe's fiancé, Chad Nettleton, is actually Zebulon Logue's grandson."

"No! I had no idea." Hetty paused, wheels turning. "I remember, it was a bit of scandal, back in the day. They were Baptists, just like me, and their daughter Penny was the talk of the church. It seemed that they hadn't even got little Chris baptized when Penny's marriage to Sam Taylor began to falter. She was often seen at that notorious roadhouse on Route 1," said Hetty, emphasizing the point with raised eyebrows and pursed lips. "People were not kind, you see. Terribly judgmental, as church folks can be when others fall into sin. They seem to forget about the forgiving part of the prayer."

"So true," said Lucy, resting her back against the wall.

"Oh, what am I thinking. Come on in and sit down." Hetty led the way into the keeping room, where a couple of rocking chairs were set in front of the enormous hearth. They each took one and Hetty continued. "Looking back, I think Penny was simply overwhelmed, maybe even suffered from that postpartum depression. And she didn't get much support from her family, or from Sam. Zeb and Margery were rather cold and stiff at the best of times, and Sam was working hard to get the log home business off the ground." She paused and sighed. "The funny thing is that the guy she started carrying on with was also a member of the church, Nate Nettleton. He was a student at Winchester and sang in the church choir. Lovely baritone. The two knew each other and when they encountered each other at the roadhouse . . ." Hetty gave a resigned shrug. "Human nature being what it is, they gave in to temptation and began an affair."

"And everybody knew this?" asked Lucy, somewhat uneasily.

"Not at the time. It came out later, after she and Nate ran off together and settled in Virginia. She filed for divorce, but then poor Sam died in that horrible accident, lost control of a truck carrying a load of logs."

"Oh, my," said Lucy.

"Indeed." Hetty gave a sharp nod. "But that wasn't the end of the story. Penny had left little baby Chris behind with his father. . . ."

"Really?" Lucy was appalled.

"Really. You can only imagine how that went over among the Baptists. So when Sam died, Zeb and Margery immediately sued for custody of Chris. Penny fought it, but didn't stand a chance since she'd already deserted the poor little mite."

"That's quite a tale," said Lucy. "But maybe there's a happy ending. Chad and Zoe went to see Zeb while they were here. Chad met his grandfather and half brother, too. I think some sort of reconciliation may be in the works."

"That would be wonderful," said Hetty, smiling at the idea. But then her expression changed, almost like a cloud crossing the sun. "But I have to say unlikely. Zeb is not the forgiving sort."

"Well, people change," said Lucy, reluctantly rising from the comfortable rocker. "And I'm afraid I've been neglecting my job."

"Consider this background for a future story," said Hetty, struggling a bit to get out of the chair. "Knees," she said by way of explanation. "Both fake; they stiffen up on me."

"Well, thanks for the conversation. It's been most enlightening."

"If it's dirt you're looking for, I'm your gal," laughed Hetty.

"Hardly," said Lucy. "See you around."

Back on the sidewalk, Lucy walked along briskly, feeling somewhat guilty. She'd shirked off work, and she'd perhaps learned more about Chad's family than she ought to know. If these were family secrets, which they certainly seemed to be, she really had no business digging them up. It was old history, water under the bridge, and she mustn't roil the waters by digging up old muck. She'd resolved to keep all that she'd learned from Hetty under lock and seal when her cell phone produced its chirpy little ring tone. It was Zoe.

"What's up?" asked Lucy. "Still engaged?"

"Definitely," replied Zoe. "And guess what? Chad's folks are going to be in Tinker's Cove next weekend and want to meet you."

Chapter Six

Lucy hadn't expected this, at least not so soon. Somehow she'd pictured meeting the Nettletons in a restaurant, somewhere neutral, preferably in Portland. But here they were practically on her doorstep. What was she expected to do? "Why in Tinker's Cove? Why not Portland?" she asked.

"Not sure. Renewing old family ties, I guess. I said you'd be happy to have them over for dinner one night."

Lucy felt the sidewalk reeling beneath her. What was her daughter thinking? She hadn't given a dinner party since, well, she didn't remember when. She and Bill had a lively circle of friends, but gatherings tended to be informal, backyard affairs with paper plates and beer straight from the bottle. Sure, she had inherited silver flatware and fine china, even some Waterford crystal, but she hadn't actually used them in ages. "You've kind of caught me flat-footed," she confessed. "I don't even know what they like. Do they have food allergies? Are they vegan? Gluten free?"

"No, Mom. They're just regular. You can feed them anything."

"And when am I supposed to have this shindig?"

"Well, we thought Saturday would be nice. And don't worry, Chad and I will be there, too. It's going to be fun."

It was obvious to Lucy that Zoe had never hosted a dinner party, because fun was not what dinner parties were, at least not for the hostess. Dinner parties were high-pressure events that involved a lot of planning and polishing and fingers crossed that there'd be enough wine, but not too much because you didn't want people getting sloppy, and then there was the juggling between cooking and hostessing, and always the worry that you'd got the recipes right and they turned out the way they were supposed to.

"Mom, are you still there? Can you hear me?"

Lucy sighed. "I'm here."

"Good. So we're all set? You can expect us around six."

Lucy was doing a quick calculation in her head. It was almost noon on Thursday; that gave her two and a half days to get ready. "I think we should go to Cali Kitchen. I'll make a reservation. . . ."

"No, Mom! They're Southerners, they entertain at home. That's what they'll expect."

Lucy knew when she was defeated. "Okay, okay. See you at six." She dropped her phone in her bag and yanked open the office door so hard that the little bell jangled furiously.

"Hi," said Phyllis, giving her a puzzled look. "Something the matter?"

"You bet. Zoe called and announced she's bringing Chad's folks to dinner on Saturday."

"Oh, boy," said Phyllis, commiserating. "Better call Sue for advice."

"Good idea!" Lucy resurrected her phone and called her friend, who really didn't see the problem.

"A dinner party! How lovely!"

"Sue, I haven't given a dinner party in a thousand years. Just polishing the silver will take me days."

"So, don't. Go casual. Throw some lobsters on the grill, pick up a blueberry pie at the bakery, eat on the deck. Don't forget the sauvignon blanc, I recommend a New Zealand and plenty of it."

Lucy grabbed this like a drowning man reaching for a bit of flotsam. "Good idea. You're a genius. Checkered cloth and napkins, Bill can string up some lights, we'll have a heater in case it's chilly. Thanks."

"No problem," replied Sue. "Kim Crawford, Oyster Bay, those are the ones I recommend."

"Sure," said Lucy, not quite sure what Sue was talking about, but feeling the need to buckle down and get to work. The sooner she finished her stories the sooner she could start ordering lobsters and blueberry pies.

Saturday arrived right on schedule, and Lucy had poured herself a glass of Kim Crawford, which turned out to be a sauvignon blanc, in an attempt to steady her nerves when her guests arrived, also right on schedule. Hearing the crunch of gravel in the driveway, she quickly tossed down the wine and went to the door. Chad and Zoe were first to park under the maple tree, followed by Nate and Penny in a separate car, a sleek Acura sedan. She slapped a smile on her face, watching as Chad helped his mother from the car and the four proceeded up the walk to the porch.

"Welcome!" exclaimed Lucy, exchanging air kisses with Penny. Nate came in for a real lipsmacker, but she turned her head just in time and got a wet one on her cheek. Smiling, she gave her face a quick wipe and led the way through the house to the deck.

"What a lovely home you have," exclaimed Penny, taking in the cozy country kitchen and the comfy family room, which now sported a fresh set of throw pillows on the aged sectional sofa that Lucy hoped would distract from its shabby condition.

"Thanks. We're on the deck tonight," said Lucy. "Don't worry, it's not the least bit chilly out there. We have one of those propane heaters." She pushed the sliding door aside, revealing a lovely outdoor scene illuminated by a string of trendy Edison bulbs. The wicker furniture offered comfortable seating for a welcoming round of drinks, and the long table was set with super-sized, super-sturdy, lobster-ready paper plates and a generous selection of nutcrackers and picks.

"Nate, darling, would you get my sweater?" requested Penny, who was a tiny little size two. Maybe zero, dressed in what seemed to be brand new resort casual slacks and shirt. Her hair was sprayed into a helmet shape, and she spoke with a slight Southern accent.

"Sure thing, honey," he said, turning to go when Chad spoke up.

"Never mind, Dad. I'll get it." He hurried off on his errand, while Zoe invited Penny to take the seat closest to the heater.

Bill took drink orders, gin and tonics all round, and Lucy passed traditional Yankee appetizers: a bowl of Goldfish crackers and a plate of Triscuits topped with thin slices of cheddar. Lucy was trying to think of a conversation starter when Nate dove right in. "Whaddya think of these kids?" he demanded, slapping Bill on the back when he arrived with the drinks, almost causing him to spill them. "Pretty fantastic, hunh? Chad got himself the prettiest little girl in Maine!"

Nate struck Lucy as a born salesman, always ready to

joke and laugh. He was a big guy, but kept himself in shape despite the gray at his temples.

"Chad's a wonderful young man," said Lucy, plucking a Goldfish from the bowl. "You should be very proud of him."

"I am," drawled Penny, as Chad draped her sweater, a white cardigan dotted with navy blue anchors, over her shoulders. She passed on the snacks, but drained about half of her gin and tonic in one long swallow. "When I think of that itty-bitty baby, it's hard to imagine this handsome fella is the same person."

"Don't forget, hon, he's quite the athlete," offered Nate. "All-State in high school, NCAA champs twice in college, and now, well, if those Red Sox don't pick him up they'll be making a big mistake."

"We'll see, Dad," said Chad. "There's no rush. I'm enjoying the Sea Dogs."

"He's too modest, isn't he?" Nate asked Zoe, reaching around and giving her a hug. "What do you think of the team's prospects?"

"I'm always positive about the team," said Zoe, extricating herself from his grasp and passing the cheese and crackers.

"Well, I'm going to heat up the grill for the lobsters," said Bill.

"Now this is something I gotta see," announced Nate, rising. "Do you put 'em on live? Do they wiggle and jump around?"

"Uh, no," Bill was quick to answer. "I kill them just before, a little poke in the back of their heads."

"That's terrible!" exclaimed Penny, horrified. "Poor things."

"They're pretty low on the evolutionary scale," said Bill, with a shrug, as the men gathered around the grill.

"They don't have much in the way of a nervous system, no brain at all, really."

"And they're very delicious," said Zoe. "Mom, why don't you chat with Penny while I get the rest of the meal on the table?"

"That would be great," said Lucy, realizing that escape had been cut off and turning to Penny, who was sitting beside her on the outdoor sofa. "I'm so glad we have this chance to get to know each other."

"Thank you for having us. I know it was rather last-minute and I apologize. Zoe insisted that you wouldn't mind."

"Of course not. We've been looking forward to meeting you."

"We're family now, so we really wanted to meet y'all, get acquainted, you know." She ran a finger around the rim of her glass. "I do have to say you have the most wonderful daughter. Zoe is absolutely lovely. If I dreamed up the perfect girl for my Chad, well, that girl would be exactly like Zoe."

"We're very happy for her and Chad," said Lucy.

"O'course, I don't know why they want to keep this engagement a secret. I told them I wanted to have a big engagement party for them, back at our home in Virginia. We have a very nice place, in horse country, you know. Several acres, with a pool and all. And I had the loveliest gathering in mind, but they said no, it's too soon. But I just don't understand. If you've made up your minds and got engaged, why not tell the world?"

Lucy was about to answer when a big fat raindrop plopped on her hand, followed moments later by several more. "Oh, dear, I think we better go inside. Everybody grab something."

There was a flurry of activity as the rain began falling

steadily and they transported the table settings inside, back through the family room to the kitchen and on to the dining room on the opposite side of the house. The transition had not worked to Lucy's advantage; paper plates and a picnic cloth looked incongruous on her inherited mahogany table in her pretty, wallpapered room lit by mirrored candle sconces.

It was one thing, Lucy thought, to do battle with a lobster on a picnic table, where flying bits of shell and dripping melted butter didn't matter, but rather a different proposition on a highly polished table over a carpeted floor. Lucy, Bill, and Zoe were lobster pros, who knew exactly where to place the nutcracker to break open the claws, and how to neatly separate the tail meat from the rest of the beast. The Nettletons found it tough going, despite the Stones' instructions, and Penny gave up entirely after she followed Zoe's demonstration of how to separate a claw from the lobster's body and got squirted in the eye. Bill obliged, and cracked the critter open and extracted the meat for her.

"Oh, dear, it is fishy, isn't it?" she said, after taking a bite.

The lobster was clearly not a success, thought Lucy, noting that the Kim Crawford went down well and consoling herself with the thought that there was blueberry pie with ice cream for dessert. And after that, the Nettletons would depart, leaving her and Bill to do a quick cleanup, which she planned to follow with a long, relaxing soak in the tub.

That plan went awry, however, when Penny insisted on helping with the dishes. "There's really not much to do, since we used the paper plates," protested Lucy. Penny, however, insisted that she couldn't possibly leave Lucy with the entire job and followed her into the kitchen helpfully carrying her wineglass and the remaining half-full bottle of wine.

As Lucy suspected, Penny's idea of helping involved sitting herself down in one of the kitchen chairs, along with the wine, and watching as Lucy dumped the empty lobster shells and dirty paper plates into the trash bin, loaded the dessert plates, flatware, and glasses into the dishwasher, and finally wiped up the counter. "All set," she announced, resisting the temptation to sarcastically thank Penny for her help.

"Do sit down and join me," invited Penny, patting a chair and sounding a bit like Hetty's spider inviting the fly in for a visit.

"It is getting rather late," hinted Lucy.

"Tomorrow's Saturday, we can all sleep in," said Penny, once again cutting off any chance of escape. The woman was amazing, thought Lucy, a steel magnolia for sure.

"I'm a reporter," Lucy reminded her. "I'm on call twenty-four/seven, weekends included."

"Oh, my, that's terrible. I hope there's no, what do you call it? Breaking news?"

"Unfortunately, that's what we live for," said Lucy, who had remained on her feet. "I wonder what the men are up to."

"Oh, men," said Penny, with a resigned sigh as she refilled her glass. "I imagine they've found some sport to watch on TV. It seems that there's always something. Nate's particularly fond of golf. If he's not playing, he's watching it. He'll even watch replays of old Masters tournaments."

"My goodness," replied Lucy, impatiently drumming her fingers on the kitchen counter.

"Do sit down," invited Penny, once again. "I know how

exhausting a dinner party can be, even if you don't make everything from scratch, like I do."

Lucy realized that resisting Penny was only going to prolong the evening. "Okay, but just for a minute," she said, taking the indicated chair. Once seated she gave a big yawn, followed by a sigh.

Penny smiled and leaned forward, lowering her voice to a whisper. "Now don't say a word to Zoe, but your good friend Janice has contacted me and invited me to hostess a surprise shower for Zoe. Isn't that fabulous?"

Lucy didn't think so, not at all. "That's very generous of you, but my dear friend Sue Finch has already offered to hold a shower, which is more appropriate, I think. Perhaps I'm old fashioned, or perhaps you do things differently in the South, but here in the North it isn't usual for a family member to host a shower. It's considered a bit"—she paused, struggling for the right word—"well, grasping, if you get my drift. Not at all the done thing."

"Lucy, you are so quaint. I'm sure Janice knows what's proper and what's not, after all she's connected through marriage to the Wentworths of Fairfield, Connecticut, and the Wentworths are connected to the Bush family. If you remember Barbara, she was very socially polished, always knew and did the correct thing. And Janice's daughter Taylor certainly knows what's done and what's not. She's a pro and she's planning the whole thing. Here"—she whipped out her cell phone—"let me show you some of the events she's planned."

Penny held out her phone, flipping through the photos on Taylor's website. "Here's a tea party brunch; nothing could be more proper than a tea party, right?"

Lucy took in the table covered with flowers and mixed vintage china, the enormous pile of presents, the balloons. "Very pretty," she admitted.

"Of course, this one, I believe Janice called it boho, would be a bit more lively. It's a Moroccan theme, but I do have my doubts about the food. Not that it has to be authentic Moroccan food. I suppose it could be rice pilaf and things on sticks, something like that."

"Perhaps with belly dancers," suggested Lucy.

She meant it to be outrageous, but Penny seized on it. "Wonderful idea! I'll pass that on to Janice!" She swiped at her phone. "Look at this: a bounce house! Wouldn't that be fun?"

Lucy stared at the bounce house, a turreted white version appropriate for weddings, rather than the usual red, yellow, and blue model. But even so, perhaps not actually appropriate. "I'm not sure about the bounce house. Liability issues."

"Well, I'm sure Taylor will come up with some smashing ideas. She's asked me to consult with you about Zoe's tastes, favorite colors, just to get her started."

It was now or never, decided Lucy, if she was going to squash this outrageous plan. "I'm sure you mean well," she began, "but it's way too soon to even think about a shower. As you know, they haven't even announced the engagement, and they certainly haven't set a date for the wedding."

"I know, Lucy, and this silly reluctance simply won't do. I declare I've never heard of a bride who wasn't ecstatic at the idea of a wedding, with the presents and flowers, and the dress! It does make me wonder about Zoe, just a teeny bit."

"It's not just Zoe, it's both of them. They want time to enjoy getting to know each other better. I think it's very wise."

"Lucy, I think we can be candid with each other, don't you?" She leaned forward and grabbed Lucy's hand. "Is money an issue? Is that why Zoe is delaying the wedding?"

"Not at all," snapped Lucy, pulling her hand away. "It hasn't even come up. Zoe has not even mentioned the word *wedding* at all, much less how to pay for it."

Penny nodded sympathetically and covered Lucy's hand with her own. "You don't need to worry about the money at all," she said, speaking in honeyed tones. "Nate and I will take care of everything."

Lucy really felt her hackles rise. She'd fed them lobster and wine from New Zealand, and Penny thinks they can't afford to give Zoe a wedding? "I assure you," she said, "that Bill and I are perfectly able to give Zoe the wedding she wants."

"Don't get me wrong. I'm sure you could. But Nate's business—it's a compound pharmacy—is doing terribly well. Actually, he's got a chain of pharmacies. They prepare medicines that treat rare diseases, meds that aren't economical for the big pharmaceutical companies to manufacture. There's quite a lot of money in that line, and he's got some terribly clever people working for him. Not to mention that he can charge whatever the market will bear, which turns out to be quite a lot for people who have these rare diseases that can be fatal if not treated."

"So he takes advantage of seriously ill people?" asked Lucy.

"No, Lucy. He helps them. He's a pharmaceutical angel."

"Right," said Lucy, thinking that she never heard of an angel charging anyone.

"And like I said, honey, we're more than happy to give those kids the wedding they've always dreamed of. It would be a privilege, an honor. Who else are we going to spend our money on?"

Maybe underprivileged children, thought Lucy. "Well, since you've asked, my friends and I have started a little fund to make sure local kids have warm winter clothing and school supplies. You can make a check out to the Hat and Mitten Fund."

"How sweet of you," cooed Penny. "I'll certainly keep it in mind. And don't worry about the wedding plans. I'm going to be on hand to help with all the preparations. Nate and I found this terrific VRBO, right in town. . . ."

"VRBO?"

"Haven't you heard of VRBOs? It means *vacation home rented by owner*, something like that. It's a great place, out on Shore Road. I'm calling it Wedding Headquarters."

"Great," said Lucy, fearing she might be losing this battle. But she wasn't going down without a fight. She stood up. "Let's go see what the others are up to. I think the game must be winding down."

Penny also rose, wobbling a bit on her feet, which Lucy thought wasn't surprising since she'd drunk a couple of gin and tonics, followed by most of a bottle of wine, which seemed to have suddenly gone to her head when she stood up. Stretching out her arms, she collapsed against Lucy in a hug. "We're going to be such good friends, Lucy. We'll be a team. BFFs," she added, giggling.

Not if I see you coming, thought Lucy, guiding her unsteady new best friend into the family room.

Chapter Seven

It was a long good-bye, but Nate finally helped his unsteady wife to the car, and Lucy and Bill waved them off from the porch. "Is she drunk?" asked Bill.

"She polished off the Kim Crawford in the kitchen, while you guys were watching the game."

"Probably just nerves," said Bill, turning to go back inside.

Lucy didn't answer, but followed Bill into the kitchen where she found Chad and Zoe foraging for a bedtime snack. They finally settled down at the table with bowls of cereal and Lucy and Bill headed upstairs to bed. Lucy realized she was too tired to take a bath, opting instead to peel off her clothes and slip into a nightie, then collapsing into bed.

"The Nettletons seem okay," said Bill, joining her underneath the covers.

"Are you kidding? She's trouble," said Lucy. "She's rushing Chad and Zoe, pushing them to announce the engagement. She's even planning a shower."

"That's nice, isn't it?"

"No, Bill!" What was it with men? wondered Lucy. Why were they so thick? "Chad and Zoe want to take their time. They know they love each other, but they're not ready for marriage. There's no rush, you know. They've only been engaged for a week or so, but Penny can't wait to get the show on the road. She's even offered to pay for everything!"

"Well, good for them," said Bill. "Lets us off the hook."

"No, Bill. You don't get it. It's insulting. They're riding roughshod over us and Zoe and Chad. Penny just assumed we don't have any money, after we gave them a lobster dinner. And she criticized the pie, mentioning that it wasn't homemade!" She punched her pillow a few times. "I have a job. I don't have time to make everything from scratch like Lady Ladidah!"

"Lucy, I think you may be overreacting."

"No, Bill. I'm not. These are danger signals. Trouble ahead. Mark my words."

Bill shrugged. "I kinda like Nate. He and Chad have a nice relationship."

"Do you know how he makes his money? Of which, she says, they have more than they know what to do with. He sells overpriced meds to people with rare diseases!"

"It's a messed-up system," admitted Bill. "But you can't blame a fellow from taking advantage, as long as he follows the law."

"You say that, but you don't really believe it. You operate your business ethically. You could charge rich clients who are renovating million-dollar mansions more than the going rate, but you don't. You don't take advantage of others." She paused. "They have a different value system; it's all about showing off, letting everyone know that they're better than the rest of us. That's not what Zoe wants. I know my girl and she likes to keep things simple. She's never liked a lot of fuss."

"She didn't mind accepting that big diamond ring," said Bill. "It didn't have to be quite so large."

"My point exactly. They're show-offs, even Chad, although I do like him. And Zoe's much too polite to criticize a gift," said Lucy, defending her daughter. Then she sighed and turned to face him. "The worst part is, Sue's already offered to give Zoe a shower. How am I going to tell her that Penny has hijacked the shower?"

Bill patted her hand. "Sue's a big girl. She can take it."

Lucy shook her head. "No, Bill. No." She let out a sigh. "Why does Sue have to back down? Why does Penny always get her way? I don't like it, and I see trouble ahead."

Bill responded with a snore. Her complaints had fallen on deaf ears; he was already asleep.

When Lucy got to work on Monday morning, Phyllis was eager to hear all about the future in-laws. "So how did the summit meeting go?" she asked, as soon as Lucy stepped through the door.

"Nightmare," said Lucy, noticing that Ted was seated at his desk, the antique rolltop inherited from his father, a noted regional journalist.

"Oh, dear," said Phyllis, commiserating. "That bad?"

"She's a bully, she's trying to take over the entire wedding. And Janice Oberman is her accomplice. They're already planning a shower, even before the kids have officially announced the engagement."

"She's just looking for work for Taylor," said Phyllis, with a knowing nod that sent her polka-dot cheaters sliding down her nose.

"So what's this all about?" asked Ted, puzzled.

"Didn't Pam tell you? Zoe's engaged."

"Nope. As it happens, she's away for a few days, catching some Broadway shows with her mom. Congratulations, Lucy." He paused. "Or not. Weddings are expensive."

"No worries there," exclaimed Lucy, sarcastically. "Chad's family, the Nettletons, want to pay for it all. They've just assumed we're swinging on the poor house gate, as my mother used to say."

"Well, that's understandable," observed Phyllis. "Considering what Ted pays us."

"Good news, ladies. I hear minimum wage is going up."

"Very funny, Ted," snapped Lucy. "For your information, Bill and I could easily afford the sort of wedding Zoe wants—well, what I think she would want, anyway. We haven't even talked about it. But when you get into wedding planners and fireworks and pony rides. . . ."

"Pony rides?" asked Phyllis.

"Actually, pony rides didn't come up. But she did show me a bounce house. A wedding white bounce house."

"Those are expensive," volunteered Phyllis. "Elfrida looked into getting one for little Alfie's birthday but decided it cost too much. She went with a pirate theme instead and the kids had a great time tearing around the backyard and chasing each other with water pistols and foam sabers."

"You could have a pirate wedding," teased Ted, just as sirens were heard and the town's two police cruisers raced past the windows, lights flashing.

Phyllis flicked on the scanner, and they all listened to the staticky voices. "I think it's the historical society, Lucy," said Ted, deciphering the garbled messages.

"I'm on it, boss," said Lucy, turning on her heels and dashing out the door. She didn't have far to go as the Jacob Pratt House was only a couple of blocks down the street, and she could see a crowd had already gathered. Moving closer, she realized a demonstration was taking place, protesting the logging exhibit. The department's two cruisers were parked, blocking the street, and she saw that Officers Barney Culpepper, Sally Kirwan, and Todd Kirwan were already on the scene, assessing the situation. Nodding their heads in agreement, they took up watchful posts on the perimeter of the crowd, which was noisy but peaceful.

Lucy duly noted down the size of the crowd, about twenty people, some of whom were dressed in Native American clothing and beating drums. Spotting Bear Sykes, who she knew was president of the Metinnicut Tribal Council, she approached him. "Do you have a minute?" she asked.

Bear was a big man, sporting an untamed head of flowing white hair, dressed today in a tweed jacket over a flannel shirt, and wearing an impressive strip of blue-and-white wampum draped over his shoulder.

"Sure, Lucy. Thanks for being here. We're protesting because this exhibit, which celebrates the Maine logging industry, doesn't include mention of the many Native American and French Canadian workers who were exploited by their corporate masters. It wasn't just pancakes and parties in the woods, you know. It was dangerous work and many were maimed by axes and saws, or died horrible deaths, crushed and drowned in logjams on the river. They often didn't have adequate clothing; there was no such thing as protective gear back then. They were confined to these remote camps, were poorly paid and usually ended up owing the company store that sold them necessary gear like boots and long johns. This exhibit glamorizes what was basically a system that profited hugely from the exploitation of minority workers."

"So what's the answer? What do you want?"

That question was answered by Bear's son, Skye, whose long black hair was tied back with a rawhide strip adorned with a striped turkey feather. He was a handsome kid, taller than his father, dressed in jeans and sweatshirt, with fringed moccasins on his feet. "We want some changes. We want displays that tell the whole story. Let's see photos of the owners in their top hats, driving around in their carriages, getting together for twelve-course dinners. Contrast that with the actual living conditions of the workers, and the families they were trying to support. Let people know that a lumberjack took home five dollars at the end of the season, while Mr. Gotrocks spent five dollars for a top hat to wear to the opera."

"Point taken," said Lucy, who had recorded it all on her cell phone. "You got a nice turnout today."

"It's not just today," he said, in a slightly threatening tone. "We're not going to stop until we get the changes we want."

Lucy noticed the police officers were beginning to take action, moving demonstrators who had stepped into the road back onto the sidewalk. It was peaceful, there was no resistance, but the atmosphere was beginning to change as protesters grumbled and even argued with the police.

"Thanks to you both," said Lucy. "I see Hetty at the window. I'm going to get a statement from her."

"Go in peace," said Bear, raising one hand.

Lucy made her way through the crowd to the front steps, waving to Hetty, who quickly disappeared from the window and opened the door, letting her in. "Goodness, Lucy, this is the last thing I expected. Our problem is usually getting people to come to our exhibits, which mostly go unnoticed."

"Well, you've got quite a crowd today."

"Yes, we do." She glanced out the window uneasily. "Do you know what they want? The signs say *unfair* and *no representation.* I don't understand . . . it doesn't make any sense because the photos include plenty of Native Americans."

Rather than try to explain, she thought it better if Hetty heard from the protesters directly. "I spoke to Skye and Bear Sykes and recorded them. You can listen."

Hetty agreed and Lucy played the two men's statements for her, which she listened to very carefully, head tilted to catch every word. When it ended, Hetty took a moment to process their allegations, then nodded. "They've definitely got a point. It certainly wasn't intentional, but I guess we unwittingly presented a privileged white interpretation of the timber industry. We were looking top down and these folks see it from the bottom up."

"So what are you going to do?" asked Lucy.

"I'm going to ask the board to close the exhibit temporarily while I do some more research. I see now that I should have included the Tribal Council from the beginning." Hetty straightened her back and made her way to the door, a slight limp betraying her recent knee replacement. She pulled the door open and stepped onto the porch, where she was greeted with an expectant silence.

"Thank you all for coming," she said, getting a roar of approval, and a drum staccato.

"As of today, I am closing the exhibit," she began, getting more applause. "With the approval of the society's board of directors, I intend to conduct more research and I hope that the Metinnicut Tribal Council will help me rework the exhibit so it more accurately represents the logging industry."

"Happy to help," said Bear, waving his arm.

Then Officer Barney Culpepper joined Hetty, grabbing the railing and hoisting himself up onto the steps. "I think we're done here," he announced, in his policeman voice. "Time to move along, clear the street and sidewalk so folks can get around."

A couple of young male demonstrators, Skye and another young man, faced off against Barney, but Bear was quick to intervene. "We got what we wanted," he told them. "We don't want any trouble. This was a peaceful demonstration and let's keep it that way."

Skye and his partner backed off, somewhat grudgingly, and Bear thanked Barney for keeping the peace without resorting to force. "It's all a matter of balance," said Barney, adjusting his utility belt over his large stomach and stepping down from the front steps. "You got rights to demonstrate, Mrs. Applegate has a right to walk down the sidewalk to the general store."

"Well said," agreed Bear. "Want a cup of coffee?"

"Wouldn't say no," replied Barney, falling in step beside Bear and heading down the street to Jake's.

"A win-win situation," said Lucy, turning to Hetty. "You handled that very well."

"People believe that as you get older you get more rigid in your thinking, but I think it's the reverse. I'm more open-minded than ever. It seems to me we were taught a sort of fairy story—Pilgrims and Native Americans eating turkey at the first Thanksgiving. You don't hear so much about the massacres and forced marches, relocations, and broken treaties. I'm glad they reminded me." She lowered her voice, watching Bear and Barney walking along together. "And I don't mind telling you, Lucy, that Bear Sykes is one very handsome man. You don't happen to know if he's married?"

"Why, Hetty! Aren't you the one!" exclaimed Lucy, thinking that Hetty was a far more complicated person than she'd realized. "Far as I know, he's single."

"Well, I am looking forward to working closely with him," replied Hetty, adding a little giggle. She suddenly lifted her head, as if receiving a transmission from a distant sender. "Oh, my. I forgot. Your Zoe's engaged! Congratulations, Lucy."

"Thanks." Lucy paused, wondering if there was some invisible news service she was unaware of broadcasting breaking news. "They haven't officially announced it. How did you hear?"

"I got a lovely invitation to a shower for Zoe. Janice Oberman dropped it off when I opened up this morning. She said she was on the way to the post office to mail the rest, but since she saw me she might as well save a stamp. I have it in my purse. Do you want to see?"

Lucy was momentarily speechless, then found her tongue. "I certainly do," she said, following Hetty into the society headquarters. Hetty's purse was on a table in the entry hall, and she promptly produced a fill-in-the-blanks invitation on heavy card stock, decorated with umbrellas and bows.

"Isn't it lovely?" cooed Hetty. "Weddings are so beautiful, and it's been years since I've been to one. Though I know being invited to a shower doesn't mean you'll get an invite to the wedding. I'm just tickled to pieces to be invited to the shower. Now, what do you think I should get Zoe? Any ideas?"

Lucy was staring at the invitation, which specified the shower would take place at Janice Oberman's house in about three weeks, hosted by Janice herself and Penny Nettleton. Boy, those two worked fast, she thought, picturing the two writing the invitations on Sunday afternoon. She wondered who else was invited, and if she'd find an invitation in her mailbox when she got home this afternoon.

"Any ideas, Lucy?" asked Hetty, bringing Lucy back to the here and now.

"I don't know," admitted Lucy, thinking back to the shower her college friends gave for her, eons ago. "Dish towels, grapefruit knife, vegetable peeler, any of those would be great."

"I think I can do better than that, Lucy," protested Hetty, as Lucy's phone tinkled through the ring tone.

Lucy glanced at the screen, seeing Zoe's name, and hit answer. "I've gotta take this, keep me posted," she said, stepping outside. She knew she had a lot of explaining to do to her daughter.

She was worried that Zoe would be upset that wedding plans were already in motion and probably blamed her for leaking the news. But Zoe's voice was cheerful, announcing that she'd moved in with Chad.

"Believe it or not, Mom, he lives in that ritzy apartment building that Leanne and her gang are in. Remember how they didn't want me to join them in their apartment?"

As she walked along the street, phone pressed to her ear, Lucy did indeed remember how hurt Zoe had been when her best friend from high school, Leanne, had changed her mind about sharing an apartment with her in Portland and instead moved into the expensive rehabbed loft building with Jenna and Lexie, who were also former classmates. The three had claimed to be doing her a favor since, they said, she wouldn't be able to afford the rent. Zoe had taken the supposed favor as a backhanded insult. "How do you feel about being neighbors with them?" asked Lucy.

"It's fine. Forgive and forget, that's what I say. Besides,

they couldn't be nicer. I mean they've been knocking themselves out to be friendly."

"Well, seeing how you're engaged to a Sea Dog, maybe they think you can introduce them to some hot prospects."

"That could be it," admitted Zoe, laughing. "I don't know, I think they're planning something. Maybe a housewarming or something?"

Lucy stopped in front of the Carriage Trade boutique, realizing it was time to bring Zoe up to speed. She knew it wasn't a housewarming, it was a shower, and it seemed that the girls knew all about it. Janice must have been deploying her many contacts, which included among them her four daughters who had also graduated from Tinker's Cove High School, some of whom were certainly friends with Leanne, Jenna, and Lexie. And with Zoe, for that matter. This thing was bigger than she imagined; she was up against a formidable network of females who were determined to participate in Zoe's wedding. It was like a monster octopus with many tentacles, and Janice was the mastermind behind it.

"Uh, Zoe, I have a confession to make. I accidentally slipped and told Janice Oberman about your engagement. . . ."

"Oh, Mom, it's no big deal. I know the news is out. You can't keep an engagement secret, especially if you're wearing a honking big two-carat ring. It was a big giveaway for sure, and Mrs. Volpe's eyes were practically falling out of her head at the Queen Vic. She saw the whole proposal."

"Well, I'm glad you're not upset. I felt terrible about it. Janice wasted no time. I don't know how she did it, but she got in touch with Penny. . . ."

"Probably from Jordan's sister-in-law, Missy Wentworth. She's at Southern Maine University here in Portland

and she's dating Joe Zapata—he's Chad's best buddy on the team."

"Well, brace yourself. Penny and Janice are already making plans and have sent out invitations for a shower in three weeks."

"It would have been nice of them to check with me," said Zoe. "Just to make sure I don't have other plans that day."

"If you ask me, all this has a lot more to do with Janice and Penny than it does with you and Chad." She paused. "Or the rest of us. Before this goes any further the rest of the family needs to be informed. Elizabeth, Sara, Toby and Molly haven't got a clue. And Grandma Stone, she'll be over the moon! Do you want to tell them, or shall I?"

"I'll text them. I'll include a photo of the ring. Elizabeth might actually be jealous—it's bigger than that antique Jean-Luc gave her."

"I wouldn't count on it," said Lucy, thinking of her oldest daughter, who lived in Paris and had broken off her engagement after wedding plans went awry. "She seemed happy enough to return it. But Molly might be a bit envious," she added. Her son Toby had eloped with Molly, skipping the preliminaries, including an engagement ring, and Molly only had a thin gold wedding band. "Or Sara." She sighed, thinking of Sara, who worked at the Museum of Science in Boston. "You'd think the place would be packed with eligible young scientists, but Sara doesn't seem to catch even one's interest."

"I think Sara's got more going on than she admits," observed Zoe.

"Well, I certainly hope so, just so I can tell Janice Oberman!" exclaimed Lucy. "So what's the apartment like? Is it roomy? Do you have closet space?"

"It's real nice, Mom. A one-bedroom, but it does have a

walk-in closet that is mostly empty apart from baseball stuff."

"He'll have to get that stuff out."

"There's no rush. I'm keeping my old place. I don't want to leave Charlie in a bind so I'll keep paying my half of the rent. Chad says there's no need for me to chip in on the rent with him, so it's no hardship for him and, well, it's kind of nice to know I've got a place just for myself. I like being independent; I'm not going to be one of those clingy women who depend on their husbands for everything."

"Good for you," said Lucy, determined to support her daughter. But Zoe's declaration also gave her pause and she wondered if her daughter truly understood that a successful marriage required a great deal of compromise and mutual consideration. "How does Chad feel about that?"

Zoe didn't answer, but said instead that she had to go, she had a meeting. Maybe she did, thought Lucy, but she probably didn't. She just wanted to avoid answering an awkward question.

Chapter Eight

Lucy dropped her phone in her bag and continued on to the office, lost in her thoughts and walking slowly. She was relieved that Zoe wasn't angry with her; truth be told, nothing seemed to upset Zoe these days. And why should it? Everything was going great for her. She was in love, she was engaged to a wonderful man, and on top of all that, she got the job she wanted. They said you couldn't have it all, but right now, Zoe seemed to be the exception that proved the rule.

"What are you smiling about?" asked Phyllis, when Lucy returned to the office. "You look like the cat who got the cream."

"That would be my daughter," laughed Lucy. "I hope she knows how lucky she is."

"Unlikely," observed Phyllis. "It seems to me that kids today take for granted the stuff that we had to work hard for." She added a disapproving sniff. "And they have absolutely no shame. It's perfectly okay to be a single mom, marriage optional. They run around in leggings with their bums hanging out, and nothing is private. Just this morning a girl passed me on the sidewalk arguing with herself. I thought she was having a nervous breakdown, hearing voices or something, but she was wearing earbuds and informing her mother that she couldn't control her, she needed to self-actualize and discover her own truth."

"I can only imagine what my mother would have said, if I'd tried that," laughed Lucy, sitting down at her desk and powering up her computer.

"I would have gotten a smack, that's what would have happened to me," admitted Phyllis. "I don't know what's worse: what they say or the way they say it. Where do they get these words? *Self-actualize?*"

"I do worry," confessed Lucy, as her computer emitted a series of groans and clicks, eventually producing a blue circle on the screen. "Zoe's so happy but . . ."

Phyllis interrupted. "You're afraid there's a worm in the apple?"

"I know there's a worm, two in fact, and I know their names!" The computer had finally produced Lucy's emails and she was clicking down the list, moving most of them to trash while saving a few that were possible story leads, when Sara called.

"Mom! It's so exciting! Zoe and Chad are engaged! And I'm going to be her maid of honor!"

"Were you surprised?"

"Not really. I met Chad a few weeks ago, and the way he looked at her, well, it was pretty obvious he was head over heels with her."

"And what about Zoe?" asked Lucy.

"She was playing it cool, but when we were alone she told me she was sure he was the one."

"You never told me," complained Lucy. "Not a word."

"You're the one who always said not to count those chicks before they hatched!"

"Nothing's worse than having your own words thrown back at you!" Lucy had paused at a press release from the water department announcing it was time for the annual system-wide hydrant flushing. "I'm a little worried, though. Did Zoe tell you she's keeping her old apartment? What do you think about that?"

"Pretty smart, if you ask me. Chad's not her whole life, you know. He's important, for sure, but she's really focused on succeeding in her new job. Keeping the apartment will give her a place to concentrate on work without distractions, you know?"

Lucy didn't know. She'd always juggled her job and family responsibilities, keeping all her balls in the air simultaneously. She'd conducted interviews in the supermarket, ticking items off her list while discussing the town meeting agenda with the selectboard chairman, she'd written story leads in her head while driving the dog to the vet, and on one memorable occasion she'd pulled off the road with a carful of Little League players to cover a helicopter crash. "What if Chad gets called up to the majors? She won't be able to keep her job then."

"Sure she will, Mom. People work remotely all the time now. And she's not going to give up a career to follow a man around, no way."

"Shouldn't her marriage come first?" asked Lucy. "She'll need to take care of Chad. . . ."

"Ohmigod, Mom. That's so dated. Chad can take care of himself. Zoe's really excited about her new job and she's really focused on succeeding. That means Chad's going to have to give her the space she needs."

"Do you think he's really okay with that? And her keeping the apartment?"

Sara's voice was firm. "He'll have to be."

Lucy was thoughtful as they ended the call, thinking that while Chad might be okay with Zoe's independent spirit, his mother certainly was not. She'd already complained to Lucy about the couple's reluctance to announce their engagement and seemed hell-bent to begin the festivities, with or without their cooperation. This became even clearer that afternoon when Penny called to inform her that plans for the shower were coming together thanks to Janice's daughter, Taylor.

"Such a lovely girl," enthused Penny. "They haven't even been married for two years and she's already got a little tyke. Janice showed me pictures, so cute! And now she's starting up this event-planning business, which is ideal because it's only part-time and it doesn't conflict with her family responsibilities." She paused. "That's something Zoe should really consider."

"Becoming an event planner?" asked Lucy.

"Well, now that you mention it, it's not such a stretch. She already organizes events for the Sea Dogs. But what I meant was working part-time. She could be a consultant, for instance, and pick occasional work."

Lucy knew exactly how Zoe would react to that idea and it wasn't pretty. "Uh, Penny, it's nice to chat and all, but I'm at work and—"

"Work. Poor you. Well, I'll get right to the point. Janice tells me the shower invitations are in the mail and the excitement is already building! We've decided on a Tuscan wine tasting for the shower, such a fun idea! There'll be long tables outdoors with wildflowers and that colorful Italian pottery. It'll be just like a trip to Italy. The sommelier will explain the various vintages, but this is why I called you: We're not sure about the main course." Penny's voice became very serious. "Now, honestly, tell me what you think: would Zoe prefer chilled beef tenderloin or should we go with wild boar sausage, which is more authentically Tuscan?"

Lucy was genuinely rendered speechless. Tenderloin or wild boar? How on earth would she know about that? And did she even care? Would Zoe care? Here these women were springing a huge event on Zoe, and herself, an event that neither of them actually wanted, and now they were asking for her advice. Well, that simply wasn't going to happen. "Gosh, Penny, gotta run. Breaking news."

"What was that all about?" inquired Phyllis.

"The groom's mother, Penny. She's planning this huge shower. Hetty Furness has already gotten her invitation."

"I haven't," said Phyllis, pouting for effect.

"It's probably already in your mailbox. I think they're inviting the whole town. I mean, I like Hetty, but we're hardly what you'd call close friends, and I don't actually think she could pick Zoe out of a line-up. But Janice hand-delivered her invitation on her way to the post office, and Hetty's thrilled that she was invited." Lucy shook her head. "I'm really embarrassed. People we hardly know are going to be expected to bring gifts. It's so tacky, and people are going to think I'm okay with it."

Phyllis was thoughtful, twirling a lock of freshly dyed blue hair on her finger. "I can see why you're upset, but just for the record, what's the theme of the shower?"

Lucy glared at her office mate, then laughed. "Tuscan wine tasting."

"Oooh, nice."

"Traitor," accused Lucy, reaching for her phone to call someone who would be more sympathetic: Sue.

Sue listened patiently while Lucy explained the situation, occasionally offering a supportive comment. "I agree with you, those two are absolutely awful," she said when Lucy had run out of steam.

"I feel terrible about all this. I know you wanted to give Zoe's shower, and it would have been lovely."

"I suppose I still could. . . ."

"Everybody in town's going to be invited to this one. I don't think we can ask people to come to a second one."

"You're right," said Sue. "I could do the bridesmaid's luncheon."

"That would be nice," agreed Lucy. "I'll tell Janice and Penny you've got first dibs."

"It is crazy. I guess these women have nothing better to do. But face it, Lucy, you're up against an unstoppable force: the Wedding-Industrial Complex. If I were you, I'd relax and go along for the ride."

"I have no choice," grumbled Lucy. "To be honest, I don't have the time, or the interest, to get involved." She paused. "But it all seems such a waste of time and money. This Tuscan wine tasting is going to cost a fortune, money that the kids could use for a down payment on a house, or a graduate degree. And all those gifts, things they don't need and probably won't use. As my Aunt Helen used to say, 'It's all so unnecessary.' "

"Lucy, you are a Puritan at heart," said Sue. "It's okay for people to have fun—you know that, right?"

"Fun doesn't have to cost a lot of money," countered Lucy. "It doesn't cost much to toss a ball around in the backyard, or play a board game."

"I give up," said Sue. "What are you going to wear to this Tuscan wine tasting?"

"What do you think? My Tuscan wine-tasting outfit, of course," laughed Lucy, ending the call. A glance at the clock indicated she really needed to buckle down and write up the demonstration so it could be posted on the *Courier*'s online edition. Ted would be calling any minute, asking for it, so she opened a file and started reviewing the photos she'd taken. She chose two: one of Bear and Skye Sykes, as leaders of the protest, and an overview that included the demonstrators and their signs. After nailing down the basic facts she began reviewing Bear's and Skye's comments, which struck her as being thoughtful and well-expressed. Hetty was also well-spoken and Lucy was impressed by her decision to close the exhibit while doing more research on the story. She'd almost finished when Ted called; she just needed to add a headline and captions for the photos. That done, she sent the story, then decided she'd only scratched the surface of a bigger issue.

Acting on impulse, she called Bear Sykes and arranged to interview him at the Indian Meetinghouse in the northmost corner of Tinker's Cove. It seemed to her that a new sense of purpose and activism was brewing among the Metinnicut people that deserved a second look. What did they want? How did they plan to achieve their goals? How would the larger community respond? Lucy Stone, girl reporter, was on the job!

The Indian Meetinghouse was a simple clapboard building, constructed in the mid-nineteenth century as a church to serve the spiritual needs of the Native American community, which had fallen into disrepair as individual Metinnicuts gradually shed their tribal identity and were assimilated into the larger white community. Bear had attempted to halt that trend some years ago by successfully applying to the national government for tribal recognition, which would allow them to build a gambling casino. When plans for the casino moved ahead, however, the tribe ran into opposition from Tinker's Cove locals. Excavations had actually begun but were abruptly halted when archaeological remains, including graves, were discovered and the site was preserved, ending the matter. Thwarted on that front, Bear and other Tribal Council members turned their attention to restoring the old meetinghouse, which became a museum celebrating the tribe's heritage.

Lucy arrived a bit early for the interview, which had been scheduled a few days later, with an eye to checking out the museum's exhibits. It was still a work in progress, with display cases and movable partitions scattered about in the large space that had once served as a chapel. The pews were gone but the traditional twelve-pane windows that were common to New England churches still remained, as did a mini steeple on the roof. That steeple was open to the space below and Lucy could see the bell it contained, and the rope that dangled down so it could be rung. As she wandered among the displays, which included bits of pottery, war clubs, wampum belts, and other artifacts, Lucy felt the past was a heavy presence in the old building. She was pausing to examine some old photos dating from the early 1900s that were taken in a place called Pine Tree. They seemed to have been taken at a picnic, as people were dressed casually for the times. The men had rolled up their sleeves and were pictured playing horseshoes, the women were hatless but wore blouses with leg-o'-mutton sleeves and long skirts.

"Hi, Lucy," said Bear, announcing his arrival. "What do you think of our museum?"

Lucy smiled at him, noticing that today he was wearing a fringed deerskin shirt, which was not his usual attire. She knew he was a smart promoter of the tribe's interests and he'd most likely worn the shirt with an eye to being photographed. It would be good publicity, probably on the front page of the *Courier*.

"It's fascinating," said Lucy, answering his question. "The exhibits are great, but there's something about this building that speaks of the past. The old floorboards, the wavy glass in the windows, the bell . . ."

Bear nodded toward the photos she'd been examining. "Those are the people who came here, to pray and sing. To be together."

"Here?" asked Lucy. "It says Pine Tree."

"This area used to be called Pine Tree. It was a flourishing village mostly inhabited by Metinnicut people along with descendants of fugitive slaves who had escaped to the north. The village was named for a stand of old-growth pine trees, some so old that they bore the king's mark."

Lucy knew that in colonial days British agents had roamed the woods, claiming trees suitable to be made into masts for the king's ships with a mark. Those trees could not be cut except for that purpose. But she had never heard about the town of Pine Tree. "What happened to the town?" she asked.

"It was taken by the state and razed. This building is all that's left."

Lucy was amazed. She'd never heard of this and couldn't understand why it had happened. "Why would the state do that? And when did it happen?"

"1913," answered Bear. "Eugenics was a popular theory then, and the white race was believed to be superior. Folks like these"—he pointed to the photos—"were considered inferior, prone to disease, dirty, and unhealthy. State health inspectors came and condemned the village. . . ."

Lucy was incredulous. "The whole village?"

"Yup. They claimed people were living in primitive and

squalid conditions and the whole thing had to go." He paused. "Except for this building here."

"What about the people? What happened to them?"

"Some were taken into state custody and committed to insane asylums, and the children were taken to boarding schools. A handful simply dispersed into local communities where they settled, others picked up and moved far away."

Deeply shocked and disturbed, Lucy's eyes wandered over the photos of the once vibrant town, landing on one that pictured a distant view of the surrounding forest. "The trees? What happened to the trees?"

"They were cut down by whites, the ones who take everything," said Skye, who had joined them, arriving silently in his soft deerskin moccasins.

Bear gave his son a disapproving glance. "Lucy, I apologize for my son. He's young and hotheaded." Turning to Skye, he continued. "Lucy is here to learn about our people, and how we have played an important part in our town's history." He indicated a table and chairs in a corner of the room. "Let's all sit down and you can tell her what you're working on."

When they were all seated Lucy got out her phone, as well as her notebook, to record the interview. When she was ready, Bear began speaking, explaining that Skye was a student at local Winchester College, where he was majoring in political science.

Getting a nod from his father, Skye took up the thread. "I'm working on an independent project researching Metinnicut history and hopefully developing a legal case so we can sue for reparations. I guess Dad has explained how Pine Tree was seized and destroyed by the state, people were confined to mad houses, kids were taken away from their parents and put in boarding schools that claimed to civilize them. All that had terrible cultural and economic consequences for our people."

Lucy nodded. "As a white person I'm deeply ashamed. It's absolutely awful, but for a case to be brought in court you'd need to prove individual damages, right? How can you do that when everyone was scattered to the four winds?"

"That's where genealogy, especially the developments with DNA, come in. It's now possible for people to prove their ancestral heritage. Not to mention social media. It's easy now to get the word out and encourage people to trace their ancestry. We don't need everyone, we just need a few folks willing to make their case in court."

"It doesn't have to go to court. It could be a bill in the state legislature," said Bear.

"For reparations?" asked Lucy, pressing him. She knew that would be a tough sell in the current political climate.

"That's what we want," affirmed Skye. "And an apology."

"And you?" Lucy directed her question to Bear.

"Like Skye said, the state must acknowledge what it did to us, the injury it caused, and make amends. I would prefer for the state legislature to act, but if that doesn't happen, we will file a suit in court for damages. Reparations doesn't necessarily mean payments to individuals, it could be a scholarship program for Metinnicut descendants. Or subsidies for mortgages, for example."

Lucy thought those things might be slightly more acceptable. "Are you okay with those ideas?" she asked Skye.

"I haven't decided," admitted Skye. "Right now I'm interested in doing the research and getting the story out. That's why I'm excited to be working with Hetty Furness at the historical society. She has access to documents and materials that are going to be very useful in reassessing and amending our town's history. We, the Metinnicuts, were here long before the whites came, and we've been here through everything—the Revolution, white settlement, industrialization, the Civil War, the World Wars—we were part of it all and we're still here. I am reclaiming our past, our heritage."

The interview was over, but as Lucy gathered up her things and prepared to leave she found herself lingering, troubled about what she'd learned. Bear and Skye were escorting her to the door and she knew she didn't want to leave without expressing her feelings, but that was the problem: her emotions were in turmoil and she hadn't had time to process them. She didn't know what to say, so that's what she told them.

"This has been eye-opening," she began. "I'm at a loss for words, but I'm very grateful to you for sharing this with me. Everyone, the whole community, needs to know our shared history. We all need to know what really happened, especially the difficult parts."

"Thanks, Lucy," said Bear, holding his hand out to her. "I trust you to tell the truth."

Skye, beside his father, nodded. "I'll let you know what Hetty and I discover."

"And I'll be digging, too," promised Lucy, squaring her shoulders and heading to her car. She had a lot to think about, and a lot more to discover. The truth, the facts, that's what she was after, and she was determined to give this story its due.

Chapter Nine

Back at the office Lucy wrote up the Pine Tree story she'd learned from Bear and Skye, but noting only that the exhibit at the Indian Meetinghouse included photos of the now vanished town since she knew she needed more sources to confirm their claims about the state takeover. She knew it was an accepted fact that the state did evict an interracial community from the island of Malaga in 1912, but questions remained about the destruction of Pine Tree. It would certainly have been big news at the time, so why wasn't it known? That was the question she was struggling with, and doubted that readers who thought they knew their town's history would believe it. In the end, she wrote a separate, longer story that included Syke's claims to Ted, but knew in her heart that he wouldn't agree to print it.

"We've got to stick to what we know," he told her. "We'll report the facts as we know them, that the logging exhibit remains closed pending further research, and you can give a plug to the Pine Tree exhibit at the Old Indian Meetinghouse."

"Can I include Skye's request that people with information about Pine Tree contact him?"

"Sure. Public service, that's our middle name."

"I thought it was advertising," quipped Lucy, getting a groan from Ted.

"Actually," he said, "I'm pretty sure you'll be interested in our latest promo. I've talked to Corney at the Chamber of Commerce and we're doing a special advertising supplement featuring Tinker's Cove as a destination for weddings. There's a lot of interest in weddings."

"Don't I know it," moaned Lucy. While she wasn't making much headway on the Pine Tree story, she was certainly getting plenty of attention from the Wedding-Industrial Complex, which had switched into high gear. These days her phone and email were filled with questions from Penny and Janice, as well as from friends and family who had been invited to the shower. "What should we wear? What can we give Zoe? Is it really outdoors, and what if it rains? I don't drink, will there be mocktails? Gluten-free options? Vegetarian options? Can I bring my sister/daughter/husband/boyfriend/nursing baby?"

Lucy didn't actually know the answers to most of these questions, but she felt duty-bound as the mother of the bride to respond. That meant contacting either Taylor or Penny or Janice to get the necessary information. These calls tended to become long conversations in which various options were discussed at length and rarely resolved. Lucy found herself turning to Sue more and more, as she always seemed to have a sensible answer.

"So, Lucy, what are you going to wear to the shower?" asked Sue, changing the subject when Lucy called her one Saturday morning.

"I haven't given it much thought," admitted Lucy.

"Well, I have and I don't think you have anything suitable in your closet."

This was shocking news to Lucy, who had a lovely walk-in closet chock-full of clothes. "I'm sure I've got something," she insisted, conducting a quick mental review of her wardrobe. "What about that Pucci-style shift dress?"

"Good idea," began Sue, "except that it's twenty years old and the hem sags."

"I can fix it."

"It's also rather tight," added Sue.

"I've been dieting," said Lucy, who hadn't.

"We're going shopping," Sue informed her. "I'll pick you up in ten."

"But I need to get groceries, mail a package, pick up six bags of mulch. . . ."

"That can wait. Ten minutes. Bring your charge card."

Lucy knew resistance was futile. Someone, probably Zoe, had enlisted Sue to whip her into shape. The shopping was just the beginning, she suspected. Next stop would be the hair salon, the day spa for a mani-pedi-facial combo and, knowing Sue, a reviving glass or two of wine on the porch of the Queen Vic, the town's poshest inn. Oh, well, she sighed, she might as well enjoy it.

The day of the shower dawned bright and sunny, the temperature was predicted to hit the mid-70s, with a gentle breeze off the ocean. Lucy took her time dressing, admiring the brand-new lacy underwear Sue had insisted she buy, and slipping into the silky boatneck jersey and midi-length patio skirt with its colorful Riviera print. "Perfect for a Tuscan wine tasting!" Sue had exclaimed, spotting the skirt in the Carriage Trade, which was the town's most exclusive boutique. Twisting back and forth in front of her full-length mirror, Lucy enjoyed the way the skirt swished against her legs, which was a sensation she hadn't felt in a very long time since she was usually either in jeans or shorts. Sue had also insisted she buy a coordinating pair of espadrilles, and the cloth flats felt light on her feet as well as adding a touch of Mediterranean flair.

She also quite liked her new hairstyle, a looser, layered cut that framed her face with wavy locks. The facial had done wonders, and she'd followed up faithfully with the skincare routine recommended by the facialist; she'd even been applying sunscreen every morning. Her fingernails were painted a light coral shade, as were her toes, but they were hidden by the espadrilles. All in all, she decided, after applying a coat of coral lip gloss, she looked pretty good.

"Wow," said Bill, looking up from his laptop when she appeared in the kitchen. "You look great."

"Thanks," said Lucy, hoping he wasn't reviewing their charge account. Her transformation had not come cheap. "What'cha doin'?" she asked, leaning over his shoulder.

"An estimate," he answered, sniffing at her neck. "You smell good, too."

"Well, as Sue pointed out, we Stones have to hold up our end. We don't want people to think we're the poor relations."

Bill furrowed his brow. "You do look like a million dollars," he said. "I hope all this didn't cost a million."

"Not close," said Lucy, tucking her brand new straw clutch bag under her arm. "Ta-ta!" she said, with a smile and a wave as she slipped through the door.

She felt quite pleased with herself, and was bursting with expectation as she drove the short distance to Janice's house, a spacious ranch perched on a hill overlooking the town cove. She knew from the endless consultations that no detail had been overlooked by Janice and Penny, and while the shower wasn't the sort of thing she would have organized, she had to give them credit where credit was due. Turning into the Obermans' drive and discovering the jauntily striped tent in the backyard, Lucy was reassured that Taylor had thought of everything, including Maine's fickle weather.

Reaching the end of the drive, Lucy was directed by a teenage kid hired for the day to oversee a part of the lawn designated for parking. More proof, if it was needed, that Taylor knew her stuff, decided Lucy, observing the neat rows of cars as she walked up the hill to the tent.

There she was greeted by Penny, who grabbed her by the shoulders and delivered air kisses on either side of her face. "That's what they do in France," she exclaimed, causing Lucy to wonder if she'd gotten Provence confused with Tuscany. Then she reminded herself that it wasn't nice to be catty, especially when you were a guest, and resolved to get in the spirit of the thing.

Next thing she knew Zoe and Sara had swept her up, giving her a tour of the promised long tables, which were indeed loaded with flowers and the promised Italian pottery. "Isn't it all gorgeous, Mom?" Zoe asked, indicating the festive scene and the view of the cove with a wave of her arm.

"If this is the shower, what do you think the wedding will be like?" mused Sara, who was wearing a summery little sundress.

"I really can't imagine how they'll top this," said Lucy, hugging Zoe, who was radiating happiness in a full-skirted white eyelet dress. "You look very bridal."

"That's the idea," said Zoe, as Pam, Sue, and Rachel joined them, offering hugs and compliments. Sue, however, soon cut to the chase: "We should have a celebratory toast to the bride."

"I think that's coming right up," said Zoe, as Taylor invited everyone to find their place cards and take a seat so the wine tasting could begin.

There were two long tables, each seating about twenty people, which meant there were forty guests. Lucy knew them all; they were women she'd interviewed for the paper, women she went to church with, women who'd joined her on committees devoted to worthy causes. She saw Franny Small, who'd turned a little hobby making jewelry out of hardware into a million-dollar business, and Lydia Volpe, who'd taught all Lucy's children in kindergarten. There was police officer Sally Kirwan, out of uniform for once, and Dottie Halmstead, a fixture at the Country Cousins general store, and real estate agent Frankie LaChance. Corney Clark from the Chamber of Commerce was there, and so was Ellie Martin, whose hand-made dolls had been the subject of one of her feature stories. Miss Tilley was there, too, seated alongside Rachel, who was her volunteer caregiver. And of course, the gang from the Portland condo: Leanne, Lexie, and Jenna. One seat, however, was vacant. Who was missing? Lucy quickly scanned the women, who were now all seated, and realized it was Hetty. What a shame, she thought. Hetty had really been looking forward to the shower; she'd been so delighted to be invited. Lucy hoped she wasn't sick, resolving to give her a follow-up call, when her attention was claimed by Penny, who was tinkling a glass.

"As the mother of the groom," she began, "I am so delighted that y'all came to our little shindig in honor of my daughter-to-be, Zoe Stone. You're all in for a treat, we're going to have a lovely time, with plenty of Tuscan treats and"—she paused, dramatically—"lots of wine!" This was greeted with polite, ladylike applause. "So to get things started, I'm asking you to raise those glasses of sparkling Asti Spumante in a toast to our lovely bride, Zoe."

"To Zoe!" they all chorused, raising their flutes and drinking her health.

"I wonder how long this ladylike politeness will last," whispered Sue, in Lucy's ear.

"Probably through the second glass of wine," predicted Pam, seated on her other side.

It was true that conversation became livelier. The group was definitely noisier as they worked through an antipasto containing grilled zucchini with fresh thyme, marinated baby artichokes, sautéed red peppers, and olive tapenade accompanied, as the sommelier explained to them, with a dry, red Dolcetto d'Alba. This was followed by a *zuppa di cozze*, a spicy mix of tomatoes and mussels, accompanied by a Tuscan white, Bianco di Toscano.

Conversation was definitely becoming freer and looser as the traditional pasta course, a penne with vodka tomato-cream sauce was served, accompanied by a Chianti Classico. "I'm full already," was heard around the table, as women patted their tummies and took small bites of the delicious dish.

A pause in the action was suggested by the sommelier, who happened to be a vivacious brunette borrowed from Antica Trattoria, the top-rated Italian restaurant in Portland. She invited the ladies to take a moment to savor the Chianti and discuss the various flavor notes while the chef put the final touches on the wild boar entrée.

Hetty's place was still empty, so Lucy took advantage of the pause in the action to give her a call, but the phone rang unanswered. Lucy left a message, saying she was missed, adding that she hoped everything was okay. "Checking in with Bill?" asked Sue, noticing the phone.

"No. Hetty. She isn't here and she was really excited about coming."

"She was," added Pam. "She was at my yoga class the other morning. She mentioned she was really looking forward to it."

"Maybe she got a touch of flu," suggested Sue. "We could take her some leftovers, for when she feels better."

"Good idea," said Lucy, turning to Miss Tilley.

"Oh, my," sighed Miss Tilley, whose cheeks were quite pink. "Wild boar. That's a first for me, and I've been eating for quite a while!"

"How old are you, if you don't mind my asking," queried Penny, who had left her seat and was working the table, chatting with the guests.

"Old enough to know not to answer that question!" joked Miss Tilley, at least that's how Penny took it. Lucy knew that Miss Tilley's age was a closely guarded secret, but most everyone suspected she was close to a hundred, if not actually older.

"Well, it's clear you have great genes," offered Penny.

"Have you ever had your DNA tested?" asked Janice. "I did, and you'll never guess what I learned! I always thought my family was Swedish, but guess what, we're actually Norwegian!"

"Shocking," muttered Sue, under her breath.

"I am jealous," declared Penny. "I've always wanted to do it. Wouldn't it be exciting to discover you're descended from Shakespeare, or related to royalty?"

"I did it and guess what?" said Franny, blushing. "I'm actually descended from William Bradford, who came over on the *Mayflower*."

"That's fantastic!" enthused Penny. "I'm so jealous. I just feel this strong connection to Marie Antoinette. I'm sure I have a bit of her DNA, but my husband won't let me do it. He's absolutely against it."

"Perhaps he's worried he's got some pirate or Gypsy blood," suggested Miss Tilley, rather naughtily.

"No, that's not it," continued Penny. "He says your DNA is your most private, precious possession and you don't want the Deep State getting ahold of it."

"What would the Deep State want with our DNA?" asked Pam. "What would they do with it?"

"I don't know," admitted Penny, breaking into a giggle. "You'd have to ask my husband."

The sommelier had returned, holding a bottle of dark red wine as if it were a newborn baby. "If I could have your attention, I would like to introduce you to our next wine, a fabulous Brunello di Montalcino, which can certainly stand on its own, but which will enhance your enjoyment of the wild boar entrée. *Salute!*"

The guests seemed somewhat uneasy about the boar, but the wine went down very well. And after a few bites, and sips, so did the boar, which was rich and meaty and served in a sauce that seemed to capture the essence of the forest itself. Lucy found herself imagining wild boars snuffling and rooting beneath decaying wood and leaves for roots and fungus, with, she decided, top notes of thyme.

"I'm woozy and I think I'm going to burst," declared Rachel. "But I want more. This is all so good."

"I think that's all you get," said Lucy, perusing the menu card. "Next up is *insalata misto,* which sounds to me like salad."

Lucy was right, as they were all presented with plates of baby salad greens tossed with oil and vinegar. No wine was offered, but bottles of plain and bubbly water were served.

"There is dessert," said Penny, getting groans from the women. "Fear not, y'all," she said, raising her hand. "After this delicious salad, we're taking a break for some fun games. We'll have some delicious espresso while Zoe opens her presents, and that will be followed by tiramisu, fresh fruit, cookies, and if you're up to it, a delicious *vin santo.* But before we adjourn, how about a round of applause for our wonderful sommelier, Lucia Antinori, and Chef Dina Busatti from Antica Trattoria."

They all clapped heartily for the two women. Then the table broke up as the overstuffed women stood up and made their way unsteadily to the porta-potties placed discreetly behind the Obermans' garage, or gathered in groups to chat and admire the view. Servers cleared the tables, whisking away the dishes, glassware, and silver, and setting out tiny espresso cups.

The lines at the porta-potties eventually dwindled, conversations began to flag, and Taylor called everyone to seat themselves for Bridal Trivia. Lucy hadn't been consulted, and had no idea where Taylor got her information, but the game revealed things even she did not know about her daughter. Zoe had gone skinny dipping at a Girl Scout campout? And she'd had a crush on her chemistry teacher, Mr. Bryan?

That news had just been revealed when Chad himself showed up, along with his half brother Chris. "I'm a little uneasy," he declared. "I hope I can stack up favorably against Mr. Bryan."

"No question," said Zoe, as he embraced her and delivered a long kiss. Blushing when he finally released her, she gave Chris a hug.

The women were tittering at this development, beaming at the handsome groom and his half brother. Chris was not as tall as Chad, and had the gaunt appearance of someone recovering from a serious illness, but the two young men bore a definite family resemblance. Chris, however, had dirty blond hair in contrast to Chad's almost black hair, and had a slighter build.

"Aren't you boys naughty, crashing our party," teased Penny, giving them each a hug and a peck on the cheek.

"We just want to be part of the fun," said Chad, as his mother slipped her arm around his waist. "Isn't that right, Chris?" he asked, tactfully bringing him into the family group.

"Yeah," agreed Chris, who seemed uncomfortable. "Looks like you had quite a party."

"Well, it's not over," said Penny, in a mother voice. "But, Chris, I think you would be bored with all this lady-stuff. . . ."

"Penny, Penny," said Taylor, intervening. "Did you forget? It's time. We have that something special you planned for Chad and Zoe."

Penny immediately brightened. "That's right."

"And then we can move on to the presents." Taylor clapped her hands and one of the servers appeared holding a gigantic white balloon, decked out with ribbons and fake flowers.

"What's this?" "Isn't it pretty?" "I saw this at another shower." "So did I. It's fun."

Taylor summoned Zoe and Chad, standing between them with the balloon and providing each of them with a hat pin. "Careful now," she joked. "I hope I'm not in danger."

"No way, ma'am," Chad said, reassuring her.

"On the count of three, I want you to pop the balloon. Got it?"

Zoe and Chad nodded.

"Now let's count together," she urged, as they all joined the chorus. "One," then a higher pitched, "Two," and finally, a big "Three!" The balloon popped and a long banner floated into the air. Chad grabbed it, holding it out for everyone to see. *June 20* was written in silver letters, along with their names.

"We have a date!" announced Taylor, as everyone clapped and cheered.

Lucy managed to smile and clap along with the others, but she was stunned. Zoe hadn't mentioned a date to her. As far as she knew the couple were still planning to take their time and hadn't chosen a date. Studying Zoe's expression, Lucy was no wiser. If the date announcement was a surprise to Zoe she was hiding it well, smiling and laughing along with Chad.

Then Penny, with a big smile on her face, linked arms with Chad and Zoe and led them along to two chairs set up on the lawn, beside the pile of presents. Chris, she saw, was standing awkwardly, as if at a loss of what to do with himself, thought Lucy. He stood for a moment, observing the scene, then turned and shambled his way across the lawn, back around the house to the driveway. For a moment she considered running after him and inviting him to join them for espresso and dessert, then decided against it. He was the odd man out and there was no point in embarrassing him further. As she went to join the others, she heard a car roar into life before zooming down the drive, brakes squealing.

There was quite a pile of presents, which Chad and Zoe took turns opening while Sara carefully logged each gift and the donor so Zoe could thank them with handwritten notes. That was one tradition that Lucy was not going to let slip away. Dessert and espresso coffee was served to the guests while the presents were opened, and some guests took advantage of the distraction to discreetly slip away. Lucy was tired and had eaten too much; she wished she could go home and take a nap. Instead, she did her duty and thanked Penny for what she had to admit was a lovely afternoon—with a big surprise.

"This was really a marvelous event. I think everyone, myself included, had a wonderful time." She took a deep breath. "But I was shocked when the date was revealed."

"Really?" countered Penny, coolly. "It's more than a year off. Plenty of time for them to get to know each other," she said, adding air quotes.

"Did Zoe even know or did you surprise her?"

"Well, Taylor and I decided to take a risk and go ahead with a date. It's just impossible to make arrangements without a date positive. And I did mention it to Zoe just before the shower and texted Chad, too."

"And how did she react?"

"She was thrilled, Lucy. Absolutely thrilled." Penny paused to smooth her helmet hairdo, which was sprayed into submission. "I do think it all went very well. Everyone enjoyed the Tuscan food." She sighed. "I do wish Nate had come, he would have loved the wild boar."

"He might have felt a bit out of place among so many women," suggested Lucy, feeling a bit as if she was losing her grip on reality. She'd never really encountered anyone quite like Penny before, someone who was so involved with her own agenda that she remained completely unaware of others.

"That's what he said. He went off to play a round of golf," she said, teetering a bit as her high heels sank into the grassy lawn.

Lucy grabbed her arm, steadying her. "Heels can be

tricky," she said, thinking they were a bad choice for a lawn party.

"Well, they can be hazardous to your health, especially after a wine tasting," confessed Penny, and for the first time Lucy felt a tiny bit of connection. The woman was clearly trying her best to welcome Zoe into her family, even if she was using a bulldozer to do it. Realizing she couldn't continue to pretend that Penny was an irrelevant annoyance but instead a force she would definitely have to reckon with, she decided her best plan of action was to get to know her better. Acting on that realization, Lucy issued an invitation.

"Would you and your husband like to join me and Bill for dinner tonight? I'm thinking of getting a light dinner at Cali Kitchen. It would give us a chance to get better acquainted."

Penny was quick to respond. "Why, Lucy, that would be lovely. Say eight o'clock?"

"Eight o'clock," said Lucy, straightening her shoulders and preparing to go into battle.

Chapter Ten

After the shower, Zoe and Chad, along with Sara, stopped by the house to drop off their presents, which filled the entire porch. Zoe and Chad didn't plan to linger, however, opting to go for a swim at Blueberry Pond. When Lucy asked if they'd like to join both sets of parents for dinner at Cali Kitchen they demurred, planning instead to eat at the Schooner where there was music and dancing. "I've gotta work off that enormous meal at the shower," declared Zoe. "I'm gonna have to fit into a wedding dress."

"You look just fine," said Chad, slipping an arm around her waist.

"And you have a year to get ready," said Lucy.

"We'll see about that," said Zoe, venting. "Penny and Taylor chose that date, not us. It came out of nowhere and we're certainly going to be taking another look at it. Right, Chad?"

"I don't know," he said, nuzzling her neck. "Does it matter so much? Maybe we should just get it over with."

"I don't really trust your judgment on this," said Zoe, rolling her eyes. Unwilling to press the issue further, she grabbed his hand. "C'mon, let's go cool off."

Lucy and Sara watched them go, then got busy snooping around in the pile of presents. "Ohmigosh, look at this," laughed Sara, holding up an elaborate silver candlestick with four arms that was designed to impress on a twelve-foot table.

"Right out of somebody's closet," suggested Lucy.

"But this is nice," declared Sara, pointing out a teak cutting board.

"It's really a lot of stuff," observed Lucy, wondering where Zoe was going to stow all this stuff since apartments, even fancy loft renos, didn't usually have a lot of storage space. "Are you coming to dinner with us?"

"I don't think so," said Sara, making a face.

"I'll need moral support," said Lucy, her earlier determination fading. "I don't know what possessed me to suggest it. I'm not exactly comfortable with the Nettletons."

"All right," said Sara, giving in with a sigh. "I can use a free meal."

"Thanks," said Lucy, with a yawn. She wandered into the family room where she settled down with a new magazine and soon fell asleep. She woke when Bill came home, dusty and dirty from helping Sue's husband Sid unload and stack a cord of firewood. She wasn't entirely confident that he'd approve of the dinner plans she'd made, but he surprised her by announcing that going out with the Nettletons was a fine idea and jumped in the shower. While he showered, Lucy changed into pedal pushers and a French terry top against the evening chill. Sara had also changed out of her summer dress, opting for the jeans and oversized button-down Oxford shirt that had lately become her favorite outfit, and they drove off together to the restaurant.

The Nettletons were waiting outside Cali Kitchen, seated

on a bench that offered a calendar-ready view of the cove, and the lighthouse beyond.

"This is such a beautiful little town," said Penny, who was still in the Chanel-style suit and heels she'd worn to the shower. "I could just sit here for hours, gazing."

"We like it," said Bill, shaking hands with Nate. "Did you go to the shower? I hear the food was great."

"Nope. I played eighteen over at Gray Owl. Discretion, my papa used to say, is the better part of valor."

"You wouldn't have gotten in trouble at the shower," teased Lucy. "We ladies are pretty harmless."

"And who is this pretty young lady?" inquired Nate, indicating Sara, who bristled at the familiarity.

"Now, Nate, you've heard me mention Sara, Zoe's sister," said Penny. "She was such a help at the shower today."

"It was fun, I had a great time," mumbled Sara, as they all proceeded into the casual restaurant.

The manager, Matt Rodriguez, greeted them at the door and led them to a round table set in a front corner of the restaurant, next to two big windows. "Is this okay?" he asked, giving Lucy a big smile. He was a handsome guy with coal-black hair and skin that seemed permanently tanned. "I don't want to get a bad review in the *Courier.*"

"No chance of that," said Lucy. "This is our favorite restaurant."

"Your server will be over in a minute," promised Matt, stepping away to greet a couple of new arrivals.

"This is the best table in the place," declared Penny, seizing the seat that gave her the clearest view of the picturesque harbor. "Y'all get to see this lighthouse all the time," she said, defending her choice.

"Now, sweetie," observed Nate, seating himself beside

her, "you're going to be here all summer. You'll see it so much you'll probably get tired of it."

"No way," declared Penny. "This is such a pretty area. Everywhere you look there are gorgeous views."

"We've got pretty scenery in Virginia, too," said Nate.

"He's right," said Penny. "And I hope y'all will come and visit us soon."

"All one big happy family," added Nate.

As promised, the server soon appeared to give them menus and take their drink orders. When she'd gone, Nate turned to Bill. "Is that guy, the guy who greeted us, is he one of them Metinnicut Injuns I'm hearing so much about?"

Lucy and Sara exchanged a shocked glance, while Bill attempted to tactfully set Nate straight. "The Metinnicut people were here long before any of us, and they're valued members of our community."

"Uh, well, sure, I didn't mean anything," replied Nate, with a shrug.

"Matt Rodriguez, the manager, is Latino," said Lucy. "He's the son of Rey Rodriguez, the famous TV chef. Rey actually owns the restaurant."

"And the Rodriguez family go way back," said Sara. "They're actually descended from the conquistadors who arrived in the New World sometime in the fifteen hundreds."

"My goodness," began Penny, in a wondering tone of voice. "We just don't realize. I like to watch that show about famous people finding their roots, you know the one?"

"I watch it, too," offered Lucy, who was wondering whether she wanted something from the appetizer menu like fish tacos or maybe just a quesadilla. She really didn't have much of an appetite after eating so much at the shower.

"Well, the other night," continued Penny, "there was this Black woman, who it turned out was descended from somebody who came on the *Mayflower*. Imagine that!"

"Actually Black?" asked Nate, sounding doubtful.

"Yes. With the big Afro do and everything," she said, waving her hands over her head. "I don't quite see how it could be true, but they say DNA doesn't lie."

"It doesn't," offered Sara, perhaps a bit too firmly.

"Sara would know," trilled Lucy, trying to smooth things over. "She's a scientist and works at the Museum of Science in Boston."

"So, Sara, you're a pretty girl and you have a lovely figure," began Penny. "I suppose you're fighting off those brainy scientists. Do you have any hot prospects?"

Sara paused a moment, then took a deep breath, as if she was preparing to do something rather risky. Perhaps something she'd been planning to do for a long time. "Well, I actually do," she began, making eye contact with her parents. "I am in a serious relationship with someone, a colleague. Her name is Jodi."

Lucy looked at Bill, and Bill looked at Lucy as they processed this news. Nate spoke right up. "So you're one of them queers?" he asked.

"I sure am," declared Sara. Her words were a real conversation stopper, hovering in the air over the table.

No one quite knew what to say, but they were saved by the server's timely arrival with the drinks. They watched as he distributed a scotch and soda to Nate, a beer to Bill, white wine to Lucy and Penny, and sparkling water to Sara. Bill offered a tactful, inclusive toast: "To family!" They all clinked glasses, and Penny, who was at bottom a social creature, deftly changed the subject.

"I think the shower went rather well, don't you, Lucy?"

"It was a triumph," agreed Lucy, who was now thinking that she needed something a bit more sustaining than an appetizer. Shrimp Veracruz?

Later that night, when she and Bill were tucked in bed, Lucy asked Bill how he felt about Sara's announcement. It had come as a complete shock to her; she'd never considered the possibility that Sara was gay.

"I'm happy for her," said Bill. "What about you?"

"I'm still trying to get used to the idea," admitted Lucy. "It came as a complete surprise."

"Didn't you wonder why she never had any boyfriends?" asked Bill. "She's pretty and smart, she's funny, and Penny was right about her figure. I'm sure guys notice and are attracted."

"I did wonder," admitted Lucy. "It bothered me that she never seemed to have any serious relationships. She always came up with a date for big events, like the prom, so I figured she was just more interested in her studies, and then her job. A career girl."

"But she's always had a best friend," said Bill. "Always a girl."

"But girls are like that, Bill. I've always had a group of girlfriends, I still do. We just naturally seem to fall into groups."

"If you think about it, Sara was never much into groups. She never had a gang of friends. Usually just one best friend."

"And you think those were romantic relationships?" asked Lucy, eyes wide.

"I think it's likely," said Bill.

"And she kept them secret." The wheels were turning in Lucy's head. Bill could almost hear the gears grinding as she reviewed Sara's best friends. When the thoughts and images crashed to a sudden stop, Lucy turned to her husband. "Bill, do you think she was afraid we wouldn't approve? That we'd disown her or something like that?"

Bill took her hand. "I don't think it was that. I think she was probably just working it out, trying to figure things out for herself."

"I feel so bad," confessed Lucy. "I wish she'd trusted me, trusted us. We'd love her no matter what. Nothing she could do would make me stop loving her."

"Same with me," said Bill, yawning and reaching for the bedside lamp. He promptly fell asleep, but Lucy remained awake in the dark for quite a while. Her thoughts kept turning to Sara and everything she wanted to tell her. It wasn't until she resolved to express her love and approval to Sara, first thing in the morning, that she finally fell asleep. But as it happened, she never got the chance. When she woke, an hour later than usual, Sara had already gone. She did leave a note, however, explaining that she and Jodi had an appointment at an animal shelter to adopt a rescue dog.

Lucy immediately felt her spirits lifting. Adopting a dog was often a couple's first step toward building a family. Perhaps the pair would take the second step and adopt a child, a grandchild for her. Lucy found herself already warming to this Jodi and couldn't wait to meet her. She already had two things going for her in Lucy's book. First, she loved Sara, and second, she liked dogs. Lucy smiled to herself, thinking how amazed her friends would be when she announced this surprising turn of events. And she didn't have long to wait. They were getting together later this morning for brunch at Jake's, where they would conduct a postmortem of the brunch.

But when Lucy arrived at the coffee shop, which was

packed with the usual Sunday morning crowd, the three were sipping their first cups of coffee and already deep in a discussion of Penny's relationship, or rather the lack thereof, with her first child, Chris.

"She didn't seem to know him at all," mused Pam, who had an especially close relationship with her own son, Tim. "How could she abandon her own child? I don't get it. Ted and I went through some tough times with Tim, but it never, ever occurred to us to reject him, and in the end, it made us closer."

"That often happens," observed Rachel. "A crisis can bring families together, but it can also have the opposite effect. I guess that's what happened here."

"It isn't as if she's cold or distant, she seems to have a comfortable relationship with Chad. Why the one and not the other?" observed Sue, turning to Lucy. "Do you know what happened?"

"I did ask Hetty about her and got the whole story," said Lucy, looking around for Norine, the busy waitress, to get a cup of coffee. She was able to get Norine's eye as she delivered orders to a nearby table, and got a nod promising she'd get to her as soon as she could. "By the way, has anybody seen Hetty? I've called a few times, thinking she must be sick since she missed the shower, but got no answer."

"Maybe she turned the phone off, so she could rest," suggested Rachel.

"Yeah, I put mine on *do not disturb* when I teach yoga, and then three days later realize that's why I haven't gotten any calls," confessed Pam. "So what did Hetty tell you about Penny?"

"Right," said Lucy, turning to the subject at hand. "Hetty told me that she goes to the same church, the Baptists, that Penny's family does, the Logues. She said it all started with postpartum depression after Chris was born and the marriage to his father, her first husband, fell apart and she ran off with Nate, also a Baptist. He was a student at Winchester and sang in the church choir—that's where they met. At church! As you can imagine, it was quite the parish scandal. Her parents strongly disapproved of her behavior and got custody of little Chris. His father, the first husband, died in an accident, so he was out of the picture. By that time Penny was already pregnant with Chad and went off to Virginia to make a new start with Nate."

"That explains a lot," declared Sue. "Postpartum depression can be terrible, and I don't think it was taken seriously back then. You were just supposed to pull yourself together, and we know it's not that easy."

"It sounds to me like there were some long-standing family issues even before she had Chris," suggested Pam. "I bet they all could've benefitted from some family therapy."

"From what Hetty said," explained Lucy, "they weren't the sort of folks who went in for that sort of thing. Penny was judged to be a sinner, destined for hell and damnation."

"That must have been terrible for Chris," observed Rachel. "Not only did he lose his mother, but probably grew up hearing what a terrible person she was."

"And I bet they came down hard on him, desperate to save him from his mother's tainted blood," suggested Lucy. "Not exactly confidence building."

"It's classic textbook stuff," declared Rachel. "That sort of situation can lead to long-lasting consequences, including low self-esteem, difficulty maintaining relationships, depression, addiction, and even suicide."

"I saw Chris leave the shower, he kind of wandered off, like he knew he wasn't wanted," recalled Lucy.

"Enough! Time out!" declared Pam. "This is supposed

to be a happy time, getting ready for a wedding." She turned to Lucy. "Was Zoe pleased about the shower? It was quite the event."

"She's not terribly happy about the date reveal," reported Lucy. "Penny told her about it just before the shower, but. . . ." Lucy shrugged. "But honestly, she's so in love I don't think anything could bother her these days. Maybe there's trouble ahead but—" Lucy decided to change course. "But in other news . . ." She paused and tapped out a drum roll on the table. "Sara came out last night! She says she's in a serious relationship with a woman named Jodi. And they're adopting a rescue dog!"

"Sara came out?" asked Sue, perplexed. "You mean you didn't know she's gay?"

Lucy looked around the table at her friends, who were all looking at her. Even Norine, the waitress, who'd finally arrived to take their orders, was waiting for her answer.

"Uh, no, I didn't," she admitted, as a troubling suspicion took root. "Did you all know?"

"Oh, yeah," volunteered Norine. "She and her gal pals came here often."

Lucy looked from one friend to another, around the table. "You all knew but never thought to mention it to me?"

"I thought you knew," said Sue. "I figured you just weren't comfortable talking about it."

"I didn't think it was up to me. I was waiting for you to bring it up," said Pam.

"Many parents find it difficult to acknowledge their children's sexuality at all, whether it's hetero or binary, or whatever," said Rachel. "Good for you, Lucy. It sounds like you're quite comfortable with Sara's lesbian relationship."

"So what can I get for you, ladies?" asked Norine, impatiently tapping her pencil against her order book. "The usual?"

"Maybe not," said Lucy, thinking she didn't quite feel up to her regular order of two eggs over easy with hash and toast, washed down with several cups of coffee.

Sue reached over and patted her hand. "She's had a shock. I recommend tea and toast with jam."

Hearing this, Lucy rallied. "My regular. Of course," she said.

When she got back to the house, she found Chad and Zoe were in the driveway, getting ready to leave. "What about the gifts?" asked Lucy, with a nod to the porch, which was loaded with boxes.

"Can you keep them for us, just for a while," pleaded Zoe. "I don't know what to do with them all and I'll be busy enough writing thank you notes."

"Maybe Chad could help with that," suggested Lucy, unsure how he would react.

"Sure thing, babe," he said, surprising her. She was pretty sure Bill had never, ever written a thank you note.

"We're going to be in Boston next weekend for a team event and we're going to stop by at Sara and Jodi's to see the new dog," said Zoe. "Do you have anything you want me to take to her?"

"Just my love," said Lucy, suddenly curious about her daughter's relationship. "Have you met Jodi?"

"Oh, yeah," Zoe was quick to answer. "We hang out pretty often. Jodi's a lot of fun, and she gets Sara out of the house."

"Yeah," agreed Chad. "Jodi's even got Sara running. They're talking about trying to qualify for the marathon."

"Wow." Lucy was amazed at this news since Sara had always resisted exercise in favor of curling up with a book.

"I know they're adopting a dog, and sometimes that's a trial run for starting a family. Do you think they'll get married and adopt a child?"

"Oh, Mom," groaned Zoe. "I can't believe you're already campaigning for grandkids!"

"Why on earth not? I've only got the one, Patrick."

"Well, don't count on us," warned Zoe. "Chad and I are focused on our careers right now. We're not even thinking about starting a family."

"No?" Chad cocked his head and smiled. "It wouldn't be the worst thing, would it?"

Zoe rolled her eyes. "No kids! Not yet! Let's get out of here!"

"Okay," agreed Chad, giving Lucy an apologetic shrug. She stood in the driveway, waving, as they climbed in the Jeep and drove off down the road. Sort of a metaphor, she thought, for the life they were building together.

Chapter Eleven

When Monday rolled around Lucy found she was happy to fall back into her usual routine, driving the familiar route to the office. She could probably drive it blindfolded, she thought, though that was not a good idea. Sometimes she spent the drive planning her day, or even working out a story; other times, like today, she took her time on the road to sort out her feelings. It had been a rather intense weekend, what with the shower, the dinner with Chad's folks, and Sara's surprising revelation. Well, surprising to her, she admitted. Everybody else seemed to know. Did Bill? Somehow she doubted it. He wasn't one to look too closely at his children's love affairs. He did have a kind of primal male hostility to the girls' boyfriends, letting them know in no uncertain terms that they would have him to deal with if they mistreated his daughters, but that was about as far as it went. When it came to female hormonal surges and relationships, romantic or otherwise, he respected their privacy.

Lucy couldn't quite master a similar sense of detachment. She was always on the alert for emotional imbalances and upsets, and she was always ready with a shoulder to cry on and a large supply of tissues. The weekend had given her plenty to worry about, even though both Sara and Zoe seemed to be happily involved in romantic relationships. While she knew only too well that those relationships could often be the source of much anxiety and copious tears, she suspected that for her girls most of the challenges facing them would actually come from others outside the couple. For Sara there was still a definite bias in some quarters against homosexual relationships, and she and Jodi would have to deal with it. Zoe, on the other hand, would probably run into problems with Chad's family. His mother had failed in her first marriage, and also with her first child. Lucy hoped there wasn't some sort of emotional instability that Chad might have inherited. And then, she admitted to herself, she really didn't like Nate's values when it came to people of color, and unfortunately, LGBTQ people. People could change, however, and perhaps Nate's attitude would soften as he got to know Zoe's family and friends.

Those were her thoughts as she turned onto Main Street, preparing to look for a parking spot. That idea was abandoned, however, when she spotted the town's two police cruisers parked once again with lights flashing in front of the historical society. Oh, no, she thought, fearing that Hetty must have collapsed from some physical problem, perhaps a stroke, or a heart attack. Could that be why she missed the shower? Had she been lying there since Friday? Images from TV commercials of people who'd fallen and couldn't get up flooded her brain. What if Hetty had lain there, alone and unable to call for help, for the entire weekend? The weekend that her entire circle, all her friends, had been celebrating at Zoe's shower. The thought horrified her and she pressed her foot on the gas, speeding down the street and braking to a halt behind one of the cruisers.

Get a grip, she told herself, as she grabbed her bag and climbed out of the car. Maybe it had been a simple case of vandalism, or a break-in. That was much more likely. Hetty was probably relaxing at home, tucked up on her sofa with an afghan and a cup of tea. Lucy was planning to swing by her house later that day with the leftovers, and Hetty would undoubtedly want to know all about the shower that she'd missed. That was what Lucy was telling herself when she noticed Officer Todd Kirwan rushing out the door and bending over by the bushes, vomiting.

Well, perhaps he'd had a wild weekend and was suffering from a hangover. Or perhaps not, she thought, as Officer Sally Kirwan appeared in the doorway, white-faced. Lucy met her at the doorway, where Sally blocked her entrance. "You can't come in, Lucy."

"What happened?"

"It's Hetty. . . ." began Sally.

"Is she going to be all right?" asked Lucy.

Sally looked over Lucy's head, gazing at the milky sky. "I'm afraid not."

"Oh, no. A stroke? Heart attack?"

"No, Lucy. Much worse." Sally was agitated, clearly upset. She crossed her arms in front of her chest, hugging herself, and took a deep, quavery breath. "It's murder, it has to be. It couldn't be anything else. Hetty was impaled on one of the peaveys."

The ground seemed to tilt under Lucy and Sally grabbed her hands, steadying her. "Sit down, head between your knees."

Lucy obeyed, sitting on the steps, feeling as if she'd been punched in the gut. She couldn't catch her breath. She was panting and struggling to breathe, shivering despite the muggy June heat wave.

"You've got to move, Lucy. We're putting up crime scene tape."

Lucy raised her head to see Todd Kirwan standing in front of her with the roll of yellow tape in his hand. His usually ruddy face was pale, but expressionless. He'd gotten control of himself and was focused on doing his job.

"Sure," said Lucy, rising unsteadily and stepping aside. She also had a job to do, and she was going to do it. She pulled her notebook out of her bag and turned to Sally. "Have the state police been notified?" She knew the state police took charge in murder investigations.

"Yup." Sally nodded. "The medical examiner, too."

"And you're absolutely sure it's murder?" asked Lucy.

Sally and Todd shared an uneasy glance. "That's for the medical examiner to decide," said Sally, backtracking. There was an awkward silence. "Uh, that thing I told you, about the peavey?"

Lucy nodded.

"That's off the record. I never said it."

"Understood," said Lucy.

Lucy knew it was now a waiting game. She took a couple of photos of Todd putting up the crime scene tape, and Sally standing guard in the doorway. Then she sat in her car, waiting for the state police investigators and the medical examiner to arrive. She knew they wouldn't talk to her; she would have to wait for them to issue official statements. At most she'd be allowed to take a few photos of the gathered official vehicles, and perhaps a few snaps of the investigators entering the building. There was no need, no reason for her to stay. She could go back to the office and watch through the windows for the investigators' vehicles to drive past, but somehow she couldn't make herself leave. All she could do for Hetty now was to stay as a witness and report what had happened to her. How a defenseless woman had apparently been brutally attacked on an otherwise ordinary day in the quaint coastal town of Tinker's Cove, Maine.

People were already beginning to gather. Passersby on their way to work or to shop were pausing, curious as to why there was an unusual police presence outside the historical society. Their curiosity wasn't satisfied; all the two officers would say was that there had been "an incident." Some went on their way, others remained, waiting for developments. They didn't have long to wait. The state police crime investigation team soon arrived, giving credence to the idea that a major crime, perhaps a serious theft or hateful vandalism, had taken place. It wasn't until the medical examiner's van arrived that people began to suspect a death had occurred. That drew more people, and some began to wonder if the death was related to a theft. There was also a lot of speculation as to who the victim might be and the general consensus was that it must be Hetty, since she was at the historical society most days. One or two women who had been at the shower remembered her empty place at the table, and that seemed to some to be conclusive evidence.

All seemed to agree that whatever was going on inside the building was taking a very long time, but the watchers were finally rewarded when a stretcher was taken into the building and some time later came out with a black body bag. Everyone was hushed as the transfer from the building to the ME's van took place. The doors of the van were slammed shut, the driver and his colleague climbed in, the motor was started, and the van was driven away. "Nothing to see here, folks," declared Officer Todd Kirwan, and gradually, begrudgingly, people drifted away.

Spotting Lucy still sitting in her car, he approached her. "There'll be a press conference, probably later this afternoon."

"Thanks," said Lucy, starting the engine. "How are you doing?" she asked, genuinely concerned. "It isn't every day you have to deal with something like this."

"And that's a good thing. It's not too bad when I'm on the job. It's like playing a part. I know what to do, and I do it. But tonight, when I get home? Well, that's when it hits you, you know what I mean?"

"I do," said Lucy. "Take care."

"You too, Lucy." He banged the top of her car, sending her off.

She made a three-point turn, to go back to the office, and that's when she saw Sally, sitting in her cruiser. The officer had collapsed onto her steering wheel, shoulders heaving, as if she was crying her heart out. Lucy didn't want to intrude on her privacy, and she drove on, blinking back tears herself.

Phyllis looked up when she entered, expecting to learn what was going on down the street. She was dressed today in black and white stripes, with her hair dyed bright orange and held back with a polka-dot headband. Lucy found herself suddenly silent, as if by putting what she knew into words and speaking them aloud she would be making it true. This horrible thing that was hidden inside would now be out, released for all to know. It would become real, a fact that the whole town would have to deal with.

"What's going on, Lucy?" asked Phyllis, picking up on Lucy's distress and speaking softly. She stood up and came around from behind the reception counter, where she took Lucy's arm. "Sit down?"

"Sorry." Lucy knew she was a mess and apologized.

"It's okay," said Phyllis, swinging Ted's desk chair around and easing Lucy into it. "Do you want to talk about it?"

Lucy shook her head.

"I understand. It's Hetty, right? She wasn't at the shower." Phyllis paused. "Is she going to be all right?"

Lucy sniffled and Phyllis passed her the box of tissues. She pulled out a bunch and blew her nose. She took a deep breath. "She was murdered. Hetty was brutally attacked and killed."

Now Phyllis was plopping herself down in the chair Ted kept for visitors. "Murdered?"

"It was horrible."

"Of course it was horrible. The poor woman is dead. Was she shot?"

Lucy couldn't keep it in anymore. "A peavey."

"Good God," said Phyllis, letting out a long breath.

All the phones in the office, all tied into a single land line, had begun ringing. Phyllis grabbed the set on Ted's desk and answered it. Lucy could hear Ted's voice coming through the receiver. "What's going on?" he demanded. "A death at the historical society?"

"Hetty Furness was killed, with a—"

Lucy snatched the phone from her. "No details yet. There's going to be a press conference later."

"But it was definitely Hetty?"

"Not confirmed."

"But it was Hetty?"

"Yeah."

"You were there? What did you see?"

"Investigators. Crime scene tape. The ME took a body away in a black plastic body bag."

"Write that up for me, Lucy. Post it online."

"What about the press conference?"

"I can send someone else, Lucy," said Ted, in a rare moment of compassion. "Pete Popper's available."

"No. I want to go. I was there when she was discovered," said Lucy, wondering who had discovered Hetty's body, and when. She suddenly realized she had a lot of questions. "I want to stick with Hetty."

"No one better, Lucy," said Ted, making Lucy wonder if she had heard him correctly. Words of encouragement or praise from Ted were few and far between. "Keep me posted," he added, brusquely, sounding more like himself.

It didn't take Lucy very long to post the little information she was free to reveal on the *Courier*'s online edition. The breaking news item was a single paragraph, stating that police had discovered a body at the historical society that was now in the custody of the ME. Further details would be provided at a press conference, TBA.

While there was no official announcement of Hetty's murder, the grapevine was in overdrive. Plenty of people had seen the crime scene tape at the historical society, they'd seen the removal of the body, and what had been guesswork at the scene had become a seemingly inevitable conclusion as the rumors spread. The longer officials refused to provide information, the wilder the stories became. But all seemed to agree on two important facts: Hetty was the victim of a murder, and that murder had been particularly brutal.

Soon the phones, land lines and cell phones alike, were ringing. Texts and emails were pouring in. People even dropped by at the office, looking for information, and Lucy retreated behind the closed door of the morgue, the room where the old papers were stored. It was almost two o'clock and she was thinking that she really ought to eat something when the official announcement of the press conference came. It would take place at five o'clock in the emergency management headquarters located in the county seat, Gilead.

"I'm going to go home and try to eat something before I head over to Gilead for the press conference," she told Phyllis. "Can you hold the fort here?"

"Sure thing," promised Phyllis, as Lydia Volpe and Franny Small came into the office, all aflutter.

"You're not leaving, are you, Lucy?" asked Lydia, sounding disappointed.

"Afraid so," answered Lucy. Once she was behind the women she caught Phyllis's eye and made a zipping motion across her mouth. Phyllis nodded, signaling she'd got the message.

There was quite a crowd of media at the emergency management conference room when Lucy arrived, including a camera crew from the local TV station, a reporter from the Portland *Herald*, and Deb Hildreth, the stringer for the *Boston Globe*. Lucy chose a seat in the back, by herself, unwilling to indulge in small talk and speculation with her colleagues. DA Phil Aucoin entered the room at exactly five o'clock, accompanied by Tinker's Cove Police Chief Jim Kirwan and the state police commander.

"This is going to be brief," announced Aucoin. "I'd like to begin by expressing my appreciation for the cooperation of our local law enforcement officials, Jim Kirwan of the TCPD and Jack Flaherty of the Maine State Police. They have assured me that this investigation will be their top priority and will devote every available resource to bring it to a conclusion."

The two uniformed officers nodded their agreement, their expressions grim.

Aucoin, a slight man in a gray suit, squared his shoulders. "We are not taking questions today. We are simply issuing a statement. My assistant Beverly has copies for you all." He took a deep breath and began reading from his iPad: "Hetty Furness, sixty-seven, the volunteer head of the Tinker's Cove Historical Society, was found deceased, an apparent victim of homicide, in the society's headquarters, the Jacob Pratt House in Tinker's Cove, Maine, shortly after eight this morning. The state medical examiner is conducting an autopsy to determine the time and cause of death. We are asking the public for any information about persons who may have been seen in the vicinity of the Pratt house between noon Friday and eight a.m. this morning. Anyone with information can call or text the state police tip line: 1-800-CRIMEXX. We are also reminding the public to take basic safety precautions. Lock doors and windows. Pay attention to your surroundings and report any suspicious activity. If you see something, say something. Thank you."

Aucoin then turned to leave, accompanied by the two officers, ignoring the questions that were shouted at them. "Who discovered the body?" "Was she murdered?" "When will we get the ME's report?" "Is the public in danger?" Then, realizing the officials had gone, they began talking among themselves. "That doesn't sound good." "They don't have a clue about what happened?" "Is there some maniac on the loose?" "What are we supposed to do with this?"

Lucy had received her printout of the statement from Beverly and was heading for the exit when Deb tapped her on the shoulder. "Lucy, what's really going on?"

Others had paused, recognizing her as a possible source of inside information, and she chewed her lips uneasily. "Honest, guys, I don't know any more than you do. I saw a police presence at the historical society this morning, the ME took a body away, that's it."

"Who was this Hetty Furness?" asked the TV reporter, shoving a mic in front of Lucy, who found herself suddenly on camera.

"Hetty was the head of the Tinker's Cove Historical Society and was active in the community. She was well-liked and people in Tinker's Cove are shocked and upset by her sudden, unexpected death. She will be greatly missed." Lucy shook her head, indicating that was all she had to say.

Deb gave her hand a squeeze. "That was good, Lucy."

They were silent as they made their way out of the building, but once outside, Deb pressed her. "C'mon, Lucy, old buddy. What happened? Off the record."

Lucy made sure no one was in earshot, and lowered her voice to a whisper. "Off the record, and I mean it. You can't print this or I'll never get another word out of the police department."

Deb nodded and crossed her heart. "I promise."

"It's bad. Brutal. She was impaled on a peavey."

Deb swayed a bit on her feet and Lucy grabbed her arm to steady her. "Ohmigod."

"Yeah."

"Who would do such a terrible thing? And to Hetty?"

"I hope they find out fast and get 'em," said Lucy. "It's pretty scary, thinking there's some homicidal maniac running around killing senior citizens."

Deb's face was serious. "I suspect there's more to this than crazy. There was that protest, just days ago. I think somebody is sending a message."

Lucy found Deb's words troubling, and she mulled them over as she made her way to her car. If Deb thought the protest and Hetty's death were connected, it was more than likely that the police would think so, too. It would certainly be a starting point of their investigation; Lucy hoped it wouldn't be the end.

Next morning, Lucy got right to work writing Hetty's obituary. She began with her old friend, Miss Tilley, who had known Hetty longer than anyone else in town.

"Oh, Lucy, I remember when Hetty was born. Her parents were childless for the longest time and it was quite the happy event when she arrived. She was a bit of a miracle baby, a preemie, and it seemed like everyone in town was rooting for her. They kept her in the Portland hospital for a long time, and it was quite the celebration when she finally came home. This was back in the 1950s you know, when we didn't have the advanced care for premature babies that we have now."

"Was she always a fighter?" asked Lucy.

"I guess you could say that. She had a ton of energy. She was first in her class and went on to college, Simmons, I believe, in Boston. She married a young doctor, and I think they settled somewhere around Boston and started their family. They kept a place here, too, and when he died, shortly after retiring, she sold the Boston house and came back to Tinker's Cove. As you know, she became a full-time volunteer. She was active in the Baptist church, she helped establish the food pantry, she was fascinated by local history and was instrumental in getting the historical society to purchase and restore the Jacob Pratt House."

"I didn't realize that," said Lucy.

"Oh, yes. She'd also started writing a history of the town."

"Really?"

"I think it was almost ready to be published. What a shame. I doubt the society will go ahead with it, now that she's gone."

"That's too bad," said Lucy, wondering if she could get her hands on that manuscript. It might contain a clue to the reason she was killed.

"I imagine her funeral will be quite an event," predicted Miss Tilley, sounding as if she was looking forward to it. "Those Baptist women always put on a good spread; they're known for their church dinners."

Lucy interviewed several others for the obituary: the Baptist church minister, selectboard Chairperson Franny Small, and lastly Lydia Volpe, who was a member of the historical society's board of directors.

"Miss Tilley mentioned that Hetty was writing a history of Tinker's Cove. Do you know if the society is going to publish it?"

"I'd like to," replied Lydia. "It would be a fitting memorial to Hetty, but the entire board would have to approve it. I wouldn't put that in your story, not until we've come to a decision."

"Any particular reason?"

"Well, just between you and me, some members weren't happy about the book. Hetty had mentioned that she was going to expose the town, warts and all."

"Do you think that's why she was killed?" asked Lucy.

"By one of the board members?" Lydia was appalled. "Absolutely not. I admit I've had my differences with some of them, but there aren't any murderers among them."

"That's good to hear," said Lucy, who wasn't certain she agreed with Lydia.

Lucy got to work writing up the obituary, but the notion that Hetty might have been killed because of something she knew and was planning to reveal in her book stuck in her mind. Even the fact that she had responded to the Metinnicut's protest by agreeing to do more research into the town's treatment of minority communities might have angered some folks. But that hardly seemed a motive for murder. What if Hetty had discovered some long-hidden secret that had present-day ramifications? Something that would endanger someone, or shame them? Someone powerful? Lucy knew from her many years as a reporter that self-interest, whether for love or money, could be a powerful motivator. But the need to protect one's image, one's reputation, could be even stronger.

She typed the last sentence, reporting that funeral preparations were underway, then reread the obit, made a few changes, and finally hit send. Now she had time on her hands, and those nagging questions about Hetty's murder came front and center. Acting on impulse, she grabbed her phone and called Skye Sykes, wondering if Hetty had made good on her promise to dig deeper into the logging industry that had once been so important to the local economy.

The phone rang and rang and she was about to give up when she finally heard Skye's voice. "Uh, Lucy?"

"Yeah, it's me. I have a few questions for you about Hetty."

"That was terrible," he said. "She was a nice old lady. Why would anybody kill her?"

"That's what I'm trying to figure out," began Lucy. "I was wondering if you had a chance to talk to her about changes to the exhibit?"

"We had agreed to meet, but when I went to the Pratt house the door was locked, and nobody was there. I figured I had mistaken the date, or the time, or something. I called and got no answer, so I sent a text and went on my way."

"When was this?" asked Lucy.

"Sunday afternoon. I suggested Saturday but she said she was busy that day."

This reminder of how much Hetty was looking forward

to the shower brought up a whole mix of emotions that Lucy had been doing her best to control: sadness, regret, even guilt. She'd been having fun at the shower, being the mother of the bride, at the same time poor Hetty's body was lying lifeless on the floor of the historical society.

Skye's voice brought her back to the present. "I thought it was kind of odd, because I'm pretty good about keeping my schedule straight, but maybe she forgot. I kind of doubted it, though, because she'd seemed very eager to meet with me. She said she had found something that I'd find very interesting. She seemed real excited," he added, sadly.

Hearing this, Lucy was suddenly very interested herself. "Did she give you any clues?"

"No. She just said it was 'absolutely incredible.' Those were her exact words."

"I wonder. . . ."

"Yeah. Me too. I guess we'll never know," said Skye, ending the call.

Lucy sat, holding her phone, letting sadness roll over her. Poor Hetty. What could she have uncovered that was so dangerous that it got her killed? What could it be? Lucy was determined to find out, because uncovering the secret might reveal Hetty's killer.

Chapter Twelve

As she sat in front of her computer, staring at the blank screen, it occurred to Lucy that Hetty might have shared her discovery with another member of the historical society board. The person who immediately came to mind was Lydia Volpe, a retired kindergarten teacher who through her long years at the elementary school knew absolutely every family in town, back through several generations. She had once admitted to Lucy that little five-year-olds had absolutely no boundaries and shared everything with their teacher. And what the little ones didn't tell her was clearly evident from the state of their hygiene, their clothing, even the snacks they brought to school. If anyone knew what Hetty had discovered, it would be Lydia.

"Hi, Lucy," she said, skipping her usual cheerful greeting. After all those years in the classroom every day began with "good morning,"; after twelve she switched to "good afternoon." Evenings went unremarked as there was no evening kindergarten class. But today all she said was, "I suppose you're calling about Hetty."

"I am," confessed Lucy. "Do you feel up to talking about her again?"

"Why not? I might as well talk since all I'm doing is thinking about her and the awful way she died. I can't put it out of my mind. A peavey for gosh sakes."

"Me too," said Lucy. "Skye Sykes told me something interesting that might be a clue to why she was killed. He said that she'd discovered 'something incredible' when she started digging deeper into the town's history for the logging exhibit."

"Something to do with the tribe?" asked Lydia.

"Probably, but he didn't know. They were going to meet and she was going to share it with him, but she was killed first."

"That does sound suspicious," agreed Lydia, "but she never mentioned anything like that to me."

"What about that book she was writing?" suggested Lucy. "There must be a manuscript."

"The police have taped off the Pratt house, as well as Hetty's place."

"It must be in the papers she was using for research," suggested Lucy. "Where are they kept?"

"Good idea, Lucy! The historical society has a lot of stuff, but the library has a big local history collection, too, and Hetty must have consulted it. I bet the librarian will know exactly what she was examining."

That was a problem. "It's closed today, due to those budget cuts. Do you want to meet me there tomorrow?"

"Absolutely, Lucy. Let's go when it opens at nine o'clock. And you can tell me all about your kids. What are they up to? Is Toby still in Alaska? And what about Elizabeth? Are they coming to Zoe's wedding?"

"I don't know about either of them, but I do have some interesting news about Sara. . . ."

"I know! Isn't it great she finally came out!"

Lucy was stunned. She couldn't believe even Lydia knew and she didn't. "It seems I was the last to know," she admitted, "but Bill and I are both happy for her."

"Have you met Jodi?" asked Lydia.

Really? thought Lucy. Really? "Not yet but we're looking forward to it."

"You'll love her," predicted Lydia. "I ran into them both at an MFA exhibit in Boston a while ago and I was very impressed. They're absolutely great together."

"That's nice to hear," volunteered Lucy. "I'll see you tomorrow at the library?"

"Sure thing."

Lucy's phone announced an incoming text and she opened it, hoping for some good news. Anything, really, to distract her from thinking about Hetty's murder, but it was only Ted, reminding her that tomorrow was deadline day and he was expecting a story about the upcoming tourist season, which accounted for a major part of the local economy. Good old Ted, thought Lucy, staring at the message. Was he completely unaware that news of a gruesome murder might have a negative effect on the tourist trade? Would people really want to come to a town where some maniac was still at large, skewering folks with a peavey?

It seemed she'd been speaking out loud, because Phyllis answered her. "Lucy, it will probably bring them in droves. They'll want to see the place where it happened. They'll be taking pictures of their kids in front of the Pratt house. I bet Mel's Treasure Chest will be selling authentic peaveys"—she put the word *authentic* in air quotes—"in time for the Fourth of July parade."

"I'm afraid you're right," said Lucy, reaching for her phone to begin calling her usual business contacts. Were summer rentals up? What about the prices? How many inquiries had the Chamber of Commerce received requesting information? Boat charters? Hotel rooms? What about staffing? She could do it in her sleep, she thought. Maybe she could even rerun last year's story. Would anyone notice? Probably not, she thought, fighting the temptation to go home and take a nap.

She didn't do that; instead she plugged away, getting the predictable answers and writing it all up. After she finally hit SEND she shoved her chair away from her desk and stood up, feeling about a hundred years old. That's what depression did; it made you feel as if every little thing you needed to do was too much. She picked up her bag—it might as well have been filled with sand—and made her way to the door, her feet heavy as if slogging through ankle-deep water against an incoming tide. She reached for the doorknob and pushed the door open, thinking it was suddenly very heavy.

"See you tomorrow, Lucy," said Phyllis.

Lucy didn't answer. She was already out on the sidewalk, blinking in the bright June sunlight.

Next morning, fueled by three mugs of coffee and a sugar-filled donut, Lucy was sitting at her desk, preparing to leave for the meeting with Lydia when she got a text from Ted, advising her that the DA had called a press conference. She immediately scrolled back through her inbox and found the conference announcement, which included the information that a suspect had been arrested. She also learned she had no time to lose—the conference was to take place in half an hour, barely time to get over to Gilead. She called Lydia as she hurried out to her car.

"Hey, Lydia, I have to reschedule; Aucoin's holding a press conference. They've arrested someone. . . ."

"That's a relief." After a pause, she added, "I hope it's not one of my little kiddies, all grown up and gone bad."

"Me too," agreed Lucy. "So maybe tomorrow?"

"Actually, I was going to call you. I'm at the library, where it seems Hetty checked out a box of documents. She was going to take them to the historical society so she could work on them when the library's closed."

"And the society is now a crime scene. . . ."

"Right. It's off limits. We can't get in. I'm going to ask Chief Kirwan if he can get the box for us, but I don't have much hope." She sighed. "He always was a contrary little fella, very independent."

"Well, thanks anyway," said Lucy, who had now reached her car, parked in front of the office.

"Do me a favor? Let me know who it is."

"You got it," said Lucy, hitting the red button and slipping her phone into her bag.

Lucy yanked the car door open and slid behind the wheel, starting the engine. She shifted into drive, checked her mirrors and pulled out of her parking spot onto Main Street. The car seemed sluggish and she checked to make sure the emergency brake wasn't on. Nope, no little glowing red BRAKE light. Steering, maybe? Did she need fluid or something? She was mulling over that possibility when a flapping sound coming from the right front of the car provided the answer. She had a flat. Not a problem. Bill was working on a reno just down the street. He could change it for her and she'd be on her way in a few minutes. But when she made her slow, flap-flap way to the craftsman bungalow at the corner with School Street there was no sign of his truck. A phone call revealed he'd be back in "half an hour, tops" since he was at the lumberyard out on Route 1, too late for her to make the presser. There was nothing she could do—she'd have to call Ted.

"No problem, Lucy," he reassured her. "Pete Popper can go."

Lucy felt like punching the dashboard, or kicking the tire, or maybe shooting Pete Popper. Or Ted. But into each life a little rain must fall, she reminded herself; there was no sense going crazy over things she couldn't control. And since she was married to a contractor, nails were definitely a clear and present danger. She often found them in the driveway, or in his pockets, or in the little change dish on his dresser. At least she knew who she could blame for the flat. "Give me a heads-up, Ted, as soon as you know who's been arrested," she begged.

"Sure, Lucy. And I'll have Pete post it online right away."

So now she had to get her news like everyone else in town. It was a bitter pill to swallow, and all because of a nail. There was a poem about that, how some battle had been lost for want of a nail. She'd had to memorize it, long ago. Little did she know then that she would lose a breaking news story because of a nail.

Soon Bill arrived and put the little emergency tire on and sent her on her way to the tire store, where she learned the tire couldn't be fixed and, really, the other front tire was pretty bald so she'd better replace both of them. And while she was at it, an alignment would be a good idea. So Lucy sat fidgeting in the waiting room, reading old *People* magazines, while Pete Popper scooped her news. She kept checking her phone for his post and it finally appeared after her car was ready and she'd paid for the tires and was heading back to the office. Hearing the phone ping she pulled over to the side of the road and learned that Skye Sykes had been arrested and would be charged with Hetty's murder. Skye Sykes!

Lucy could hardly believe her own eyes, and Pete Popper's report wasn't giving her much to go on. He'd put a quote from DA Aucoin right up front in the post: "Sykes's fingerprints are all over that peavey and witnesses saw him at the crime scene."

Good old Pete. His story left her with more questions than answers. Like was Skye actually seen entering or leaving the building, or was he simply in the vicinity, caught on someone's doorbell video camera? And was Aucoin aware that exhibit-goers were encouraged to handle one of the peaveys, to hold it and feel it in their own hands? He could have touched it when he viewed the exhibit, before the protest demonstration. Was there more evidence against Skye, and if there was, what was it? Because she was finding it very hard to believe that he was the killer.

Lucy sat for several minutes, drumming her fingers on the steering wheel. If only she'd been the one covering the press conference! Pete, known for burying the lead, wouldn't challenge the official line. Whatever the DA or the cops said was what he'd write. He'd never think to get a reaction from Skye's family. . . .

Instead of heading back to the office, as she'd intended, she made a three-point turn and drove straight to the Old Indian Meetinghouse. There were always at least two sides to every story and she was going to get reactions from the folks who knew Skye best, the people in his community. When she arrived, she found Bear, sitting by himself in one of the pews that were lined up along the wall. He was slumped over, resting his elbows on his knees, looking at the floor.

"Hey," said Lucy, sitting beside him.

"What do you want?" he asked, in a rather hostile tone of voice.

"Your side of the story," said Lucy, wishing she could

make eye contact with Bear. His sadness was almost unbearable and she wanted to reach out to him, to give his hand a squeeze, but knew she needed to respect his boundaries.

"So you can mock it? Make me out to be dumb? Or worse? Sly, cunning, all the stuff they say about my people. We're Indian givers, you can't trust us. The only good Indian is a dead Indian."

"Not at all," said Lucy, understanding how the weight of history might make it difficult for him as a Native American to trust a white woman. "I have a lot of questions for the DA. I wasn't at the press conference, but from what I've read there are a lot of holes in the DA's case."

He turned to her. "I'm sorry, Lucy." He shook his head. "I didn't expect it. I thought the times had changed, but I was wrong. Skye was the prime suspect right from the beginning because he was the leader of the protest."

"When I spoke to him the other day, he had nothing but good things to say about Hetty."

"Yeah. He really liked her. He'd worked with her before; she helped him with research for his thesis."

"When I interviewed him the other day he told me he didn't go in the historical society building because it was locked. He just waited around for Hetty and eventually left, but Aucoin says they can place him at the crime scene."

"Like I said, he was at the Pratt house often, doing research on the tribe."

"Aucoin must have some reason for thinking he was there, inside, on the day of the crime."

Bear shrugged. "If he said he didn't go inside, he didn't go inside. He tells the truth."

"I can see why he might not want to admit something

that would make him seem guilty. Did he feel he was under suspicion?"

"Of course. He knew they'd be looking at him because of the demonstration. But there was no reason for him to kill Hetty—she was helping him." He stared at the floor. "It's racism. Rears its ugly head whenever we try to stick up for ourselves. As long as we keep a low profile, then folks love to say they're one percent Native American, or that Grandma was a Cherokee or something. But when push comes to shove, when we start asking for our piece of the pie, then all of a sudden we're not so popular."

"I think you may be right," said Lucy.

"There's no maybe about it."

"So look. You need to get a lawyer for Skye. But first, why not tell me about him. What was he like growing up? When did he become an activist?"

Bear didn't answer right away; he took his time, remembering, while Lucy waited patiently. Finally, he spoke. "It was just me and him, right from the beginning. His mom died when he was born; she was hurt in a car accident and went into labor. The doctor said it was touch and go for Skye. He was lucky to be able to save him."

"I had no idea," said Lucy. "It must've been hard being a single dad."

"I had help from my sister, Ellie. She stepped in, she was like a mother to him. He went to school, like all the kids, and there was no bigotry back then. He was a good athlete, he was popular, he had a lot of friends. He was actually voted prom king in high school."

"Have you got a photo of that?" asked Lucy, who was already putting a profile together in her mind.

"Probably. Ellie would, for sure."

"And then he went to college?"

"Full boat at Winchester. Turned out the founders of the college, way back in the 1700s, put in the charter that Native Americans could go for free." He sighed. "I think that's when the resentment started, that he was getting something that others didn't."

"How did anybody know about it?"

"The college's PR department made a big deal about it. It hadn't been used in years. Skye was one of the first in this century anyway."

"So that backfired on him?"

"You could say that. And that's when he got really interested in Metinnicut history. The college museum has a lot of stuff, war clubs and moccasins, wampum. He'd go and study it, started trying to make arrows, stuff like that."

"He told me that Hetty had discovered something incredible, something to do with the tribe, I think. Do you have any idea what it was?"

"No." Bear shook his head, then stood up. "I think I'm gonna take your advice, Lucy. I'm gonna get that boy a lawyer. Anybody you'd suggest?"

"I'd start with Bob Goodman," said Lucy, naming Rachel's husband.

"Bob Goodman. Thanks."

"Thank you," said Lucy, aware that the interview was over. "It will work out."

"I sure hope so, but I'm not as optimistic as you."

"I get it," said Lucy, dropping her notebook into her bag. She wasn't done; she was going to talk to Ellie Martin next.

Ellie's little ranch house wasn't far from the meetinghouse, and when Lucy pulled up in front she was relieved to see her little Toyota parked in the driveway. She'd written several features about Ellie, who was a skilled needleworker and made dolls that were highly appreciated by collectors and sold for hundreds, sometimes thousands of dollars. As it happened, she didn't even have to knock on the door since Ellie had seen her arrive and was standing to greet her in the open doorway. She was a bit on the plump side, with café au lait skin and a head of glossy black hair she wore in a braid down her back. Today she was in a chambray work shirt and jeans, little feather earrings dangled from her ears.

"Hi, Lucy. Terrible news."

"It really is," agreed Lucy, stepping inside.

"Let's talk in the kitchen. I just made some coffee."

That sounded good to Lucy as her mega-dose of caffeine was wearing off. "Thanks." She followed Ellie through her comfy, carpeted living room and seated herself at the wooden table she knew had been made by Ellie's grandfather.

"Here you go," said Ellie, giving her a hand-crafted pottery mug filled with coffee. A matching pitcher and sugar bowl were already on the table. Ellie poured herself a cup and sat across from Lucy, where she stirred some cream into her coffee.

"Thanks. I'm actually running on caffeine these days."

"Times is sure hard," said Ellie, intentionally ungrammatical. "I'm so sad about Hetty and now they've arrested Skye, well, it's really too much."

"Yeah. That's why I'm here. I interviewed Bear and he said you had some photos of Skye when he was prom king."

"Oh, yeah," said Ellie, brightening. "I've got a whole album full!"

"Can I take a look?"

Ellie bustled away, down the hall, and quickly returned

with a thick album. She set it on the table, pulled her chair around to sit beside Lucy, and opened it up. They perused the pages together, following the chronicle of Skye's life from babyhood, as a toddler with his go-kart, getting on the bus for the first day of school, and right on up to the prom and high school graduation, when the saga abruptly ended. "I've got more but they're all on my phone," explained Ellie.

"These are fine," said Lucy. "I'll just snap a few with my phone, the prom one for sure, and the graduation. His mug shot is going to be all over the news, and these will humanize him. They'll go along with the stuff Bear told me." She took pictures of the pictures, then turned to Ellie. "What can you tell me about Skye?"

"I can tell you one thing for sure and that is that he did not murder Hetty Furness. His whole life has been about kindness and fairness. He helps people, and he's heartbroken if he ever hurts somebody's feelings. He would never lift his hand against someone, even to defend himself. It's simply inconceivable to me that he would kill someone. Inconceivable."

Lucy nodded in agreement. She didn't believe Skye was a murderer, either, but how was she going to prove it?

Chapter Thirteen

When Lucy got to work on Thursday the fresh stack of *Courier*s was on the reception counter. She plucked two copies from the pile, one for her files and one to read, as was her habit. Phyllis was already studying her copy, crouched over her desk with a red pencil in her hand, searching for typos and corrections in the classified ads.

"Ohmigod, look at this." She pointed to an ad with her neon-green-tipped finger, which matched her freshly dyed hair. "Ira Richard's ad for a trailer hitch reads 'trailer bitch'!"

"I don't know what happens. We send perfectly good copy and it gets garbled. Gremlins in the computer?" Lucy was studying the front page, where she found Hetty's obituary sharing the top of the fold with Pete Popper's account of Skye Syke's arraignment. Each story was accompanied by a photo. The obituary had a file photo Lucy remembered taking some years ago of Hetty reading a story to a group of first-graders who were visiting the museum; she looked sweet and grandmotherly sitting in a rocking chair surrounded by the adorable little kids. The photo accompanying Pete's story was a sharp contrast: It depicted Skye in handcuffs, his long hair flopping over his face and an angry expression on his face. A reader only had to scan the headlines and look at the photos to get the whole story. Forget innocent until proven guilty, it was obvious to anyone that this angry young man had brutally assaulted a helpless senior. Why would he do such a dreadful thing? It didn't matter. There was really no understanding these things, but it was probably because of some long-simmering resentment against white people that had recently bubbled up. Wasn't there some protest at the historical society? Wasn't Skye part of it? And just look at him? Practically seething with testosterone-fueled rage!

"This isn't good," muttered Lucy, flipping through the pages in search of her profile of Skye and failing to find it. "My profile: it's not here."

Phyllis looked over her cheaters at her. "What profile?"

"About Skye," said Lucy, puzzled. "I interviewed Bear and Ellie. They told me his mom died giving birth to him. He's really smart, athletic, an all-around good guy."

Phyllis turned back to the front page, which she'd missed in her search through the classifieds. "That apparently didn't fit the narrative."

"I know Ted doesn't mind a bit of sensationalism, but this? It's yellow journalism."

"Well, in his defense, maybe there just wasn't room," speculated Phyllis, checking the page numbers. "Yup. We're down six. Ted's been complaining that the ad revenue's been slipping."

"So he chose a puff piece about a new sandwich shop in Gilead?" fumed Lucy, pointing out a quarter-page photo of the smiling proprietor holding up a foot-long sub.

In reply, Phyllis pointed to the full-page ad from Ray's Superior Subs on the following page.

Lucy groaned. "He could've run a smaller photo and had room for my profile. And he didn't have to use this one"—she paused and swiped her hand on the front-page photo of Skye—"that has guilt written all over it. Skye doesn't look like this, he doesn't glower, he was just caught at a bad moment. Face it, nobody looks good in handcuffs."

"They do it all the time, Lucy. Haven't you noticed how if it's a story about some corrupt official, they show an unflattering photo. But if the same guy helps out at the food pantry, then it's smiles, eye crinkles, and dental implants. And political ads! Those are the worst! They put the opponent in black and white, while the guy who's advertising himself is in color along with his adoring wife and smiling kids."

"Honestly, I don't know why Aucoin even charged him." Lucy was shaking her head. "Anybody who knows Skye knows he would never do such a thing."

Phyllis's voice was gentle. "He must've had a reason, Lucy. Aucoin's actually a pretty decent guy."

"I think it's pretty clear what the reason is," declared Lucy, angrily. "Anybody who stands up against the status quo, and also happens to have brown skin, must be guilty."

Phyllis shook her head. "I think there's more to it than that."

"Well, I'm going to find out," growled Lucy, plopping herself down in her desk chair and reaching for her phone. "Ted. It's me. What's up with my profile of Skye? Why isn't it in the paper? And that front page? Really, Ted. What are you trying to do? Incite violence against the Metinnicuts?"

Lucy put the phone on speaker mode, so Phyllis could listen. "Calm down. I think you're being a bit hysterical,

Lucy. Maybe it's one of those female things? Pam's been complaining about menopause. She gets these hot flashes. . . ."

Lucy and Phyllis shared an outraged glance. "For your information, this is not a hot flash, Ted," began Lucy, only to be interrupted by Phyllis.

"What you said is offensive, and inappropriate. Possibly actionable," she said. "I'm going to start keeping a record, Ted, so you better watch what you say to us."

"Okay, okay. I'm sorry. I didn't realize it was such a tender subject. I just thought that since Pam is going through some stuff, maybe you ladies are, too."

"We're not ladies, Ted," growled Phyllis. "That's a patronizing, patriarchal word."

"That's right," agreed Lucy. "And what's worse, you've been irresponsible. You skewed the story with those front-page photos. And believe me, you're gonna be sorry when the citizens start brandishing pikes and pitchforks and terrorizing anybody who isn't lily white."

"Ohmigod, enough. I've got better things to do than argue with my employees." There was a click, which Lucy suspected was Ted slamming the receiver down.

"He never answered my question," said Lucy.

"You don't think he put that menopause thing out there to distract us?" speculated Phyllis.

"You mean he played us?"

"Could be."

Lucy considered this possibility, then dismissed it. "Nah. He's not that smart."

"Not on his own," agreed Phyllis. "But he might've read it in a book or something."

"Like *Management for Dummies*?"

Phyllis liked that and began laughing. "Yeah," she finally said.

Lucy, however, didn't share her amusement and was saddened but not surprised when public sentiment began growing against Skye. When she arrived at the county courthouse to cover the arraignment that afternoon she found police had cordoned off an angry crowd of demonstrators. There were not a great many of them, perhaps twenty or so, but they made up for their small number by making a lot of noise. One, an extremely clean-cut fellow in a polo shirt and chinos, had a loudspeaker and was leading the others in chanting "Lock him up!" Lucy had covered similar protests in the past and recognized the leader as a member of a white nationalist group, and she noticed a number of that group's members among the protesters. All were identifiable by their matching polos and chinos, as well as their military-style haircuts. What shocked her, however, was the number of regular folks who had joined them. She recognized at least a dozen people she'd seen around town, including Geri, the friendly clerk at the Quik-Stop, and Hank Hogan, who sat on the town's finance committee.

The protest was getting plenty of media attention, too, from outlets that were covering the arraignment. The Portland TV news crew was there, as well as crews from two Boston stations, and reporters from all the local papers, including the *Mariner's Weekly*. Lucy snapped a few photos, then circled around behind the assembled demonstrators, looking for someone she might approach for a quote. Spotting Nora Keller, who was the assistant coach for the youth soccer league, she pulled out her notebook and went up to her. "Hi, Nora," she began, with a friendly smile. "What brings you here today? Can you give me a quote for the paper?"

"Pretty obvious, Lucy," she replied. "This guy, I mean,

stabbing a little old lady! With a peavey! He deserves to go to jail. And if you ask me, I'd like to see them bring back the death penalty, just for him. A life sentence is letting him off easy."

"But isn't he innocent until proven guilty? Doesn't he deserve a fair trial?"

Nora rolled her eyes. "Lucy, fair trials are a thing of the past. These days everybody gets off, especially if they're members of some minority that can claim they've been discriminated against. Thanks to affirmative action it's almost impossible for a white kid to get into college or get a good job. There's quotas, and whites are at the bottom of the list."

"Is that what this protest is about?" asked Lucy. "Quotas?"

"No. It's to let the DA know we support him, and to let the judge know we're watching."

"So you're going to attend the trial?"

"You betcha. We're gonna pack the courtroom every day."

"Well, thanks for your time," said Lucy, deciding that she'd better hustle on inside or there might not be room for her in the courtroom.

The courtroom was indeed packed; every seat was filled. She joined the group of reporters who were standing along the wall just as the court officers closed the doors, barring further entry. The bailiff ordered everyone to rise and Judge Francis Whelan took his place at the bench. He banged his gavel for order, seated the crowd, and gave the clerk a nod. She consulted a clipboard and called out a case number and Skye Sykes's name. A side door opened and he was brought in by two uniformed court officers, one on either side of him to prevent his escape. Not actually necessary, thought Lucy, noting that Skye was handcuffed and shackled. He held himself proudly, however, holding his head up and checking out the courtroom with a level gaze.

As soon as he appeared the guys in polo shirts leaped from their seats, screaming and growling. "Murderer! Killer! Lock him up!" Their angry outburst spread through the assembly like a contagion, and soon almost everyone was joining in, rising and adding their voices to the pandemonium. Skye didn't react, but merely followed the court officers' instructions and took his place before the judge's bench.

Judge Whelan banged the gavel, but the crowd ignored him. He gave it another try, banging harder. The noise subsided somewhat, and he ordered everyone to sit down. The arrival of several more court officers reinforced his demand, and people grudgingly took their seats, muttering.

Whelan's expression was stern as he gave the gavel another bang for good measure. "This is a court of law. Any further displays will be treated as contempt of court. If necessary, I will clear the court. I also will not hesitate to impose appropriate penalties to those who behave contemptuously, including jail time."

The room was silent.

"Mr. Aucoin, you may proceed."

The DA got to his feet and began reading from a sheaf of papers. "On or about the sixteenth day of June, we allege that Skye Sykes killed Hetty Furness, first beating and then stabbing her with a peavey."

An angry murmur arose from those seated in the courtroom, but was quickly silenced with a tap of the gavel. "Please continue," Whelan advised the DA.

"Evidence includes fingerprints and doorbell camera footage showing Skye Sykes on the scene at the Tinker's Cove Historical Society where the murder took place at a time coincident with the crime. Therefore Skye Sykes is charged with first-degree murder."

This was greeted with nods and a chorus of approval, again quickly silenced by the judge. "How do you plead?" he asked, turning to Skye and his attorney, Bob Goodman.

Lucy had been observing Skye, who was neatly dressed in a collared shirt, open at the neck, and gray slacks instead of the usual jumpsuit, his dark hair pulled back in a ponytail. Bob was clearly trying to influence public perception, refusing to allow him to be characterized as a prisoner. Skye stood, squared his shoulders, and made eye contact with the judge. "Not guilty, your honor," he declared, in a firm voice.

"So entered," said the judge, with a nod to the clerk and a stern look for those seated in the courtroom. "Are you requesting bail?" he asked.

"Yes, your honor," answered Bob.

"Mr. Aucoin?"

As Lucy expected, Aucoin was not in favor. "In light of the viciousness of the crime, and the risk of escape by the defendant, we request he be held without bail in the county jail until trial."

This was greeted with nods and a chorus of approval, again quickly silenced by the judge.

"In consideration of the current situation, and for Mr. Sykes's safety, I am inclined to agree. So ordered," he announced, with a tap of the gavel.

Bob conferred briefly with Skye, shook hands with him, and they all watched as he was led away, out of the courtroom.

"Next case," called the clerk, and almost everyone got on their feet and began making their way to the doors.

"Show's over," said Ed Maroney, the Portland paper's veteran reporter.

"Hardly," said Lucy. "It's just beginning. How much do you want to bet that Aucoin is at this very moment taking questions out front?"

"I'm not a betting man, Lucy," he answered, chuckling, "but I suspect you're right."

When Lucy and Ed stepped outside, they saw that the demonstrators had gone, leaving their signs behind. Aucoin had chosen a spot on the steps, where a mic had been set up and reporters were already gathering. Lucy was amused to see he was wearing an old gray suit, white shirt, and subdued blue-and-black striped tie. It was a change from the more sharply tailored suits he'd recently been wearing, often accompanied by colorful shirts, coordinating ties, and pocket squares. These days, everybody seemed to be experts at presenting images that sent a message, and today Aucoin was signaling that he was a hardworking, down-to-earth prosecutor, representing the people's interest and protecting them from those who would do them harm.

"Okay," he began. "Thanks for being here. As you know, my office today brought charges against Skye Sykes for the murder of Hetty Furness, and successfully argued against bail. Sykes will be confined to the county jail until his trial, at which time I am fully confident we will get a guilty verdict." He paused, surveying the clustered reporters. "Questions?"

"What did the video show?" asked a reporter from a Boston TV station. "Was there blood on his clothing?"

"What was the motive?" asked another.

"A history of crime? Past convictions?"

They were all shouting at once, so when Lucy spotted Bear and Ellie leaving the courthouse she abandoned the media crowd and followed them, catching up in the parking lot. "Have you been able to talk to Skye?" she asked. "How's he doing?"

"Hi, Lucy." Ellie didn't smile, she simply shook her head. "We weren't allowed to see him. We'll have to wait until he's processed and settled in the county jail."

Lucy glanced up and looked over the courthouse, to the jail that was located atop a hill. She could see the sunlight sparkling on the barbed wire atop the chain-link fence that surrounded the correctional complex. "I see Bob's defending him."

"Yeah, he's doing everything he can," said Bear, looking glum.

"He's really on Skye's side," added Ellie.

"That makes one," observed Bear.

"More than one," Lucy quickly added. "And from what Aucoin said in court, it doesn't seem as if he's got much of a case against Skye."

"He comes up for election in the fall, so he's playing to popular sentiment. Giving the folks what they want," said Bear.

"He's already sending out postcards saying he's tough on crime," added Ellie.

Lucy shrugged. "He's still got to prove his case to the jury."

"After today, Lucy, I don't think that's going to be a problem," said Ellie.

"They're ready to hang him," added Bear, shaking his head.

Bear was right, thought Lucy, making her way through the lot to her car. Aucoin seemed more interested in using this case to bolster his reelection efforts than in finding the truth. And the media, she was dismayed to see, was only too happy to help him. In the days following the arraignment Lucy was dismayed to see the local TV news running clips of the Indian protest that depicted Skye leading the demonstration, terming him a "radical agitator," and advising viewers that there were no new developments in the case whenever they had a slow news day. Other outlets picked up that thread. The Manchester *Union Leader* ran an opinion piece that asked if there was a rekindling of unrest among the local Native Americans, and the *Boston Globe* reprinted it, as did the *Globe*'s sister paper, the *New York Times. Fox and Friends* discussed "growing anti-American sentiment among Indian tribes," which set off the entire right-wing media. What Lucy didn't expect was to see Skye's face on the cover of *People* magazine when she was in line at the grocery store. WHEN ACTIVISM BECOMES VIOLENT was printed in large red letters, and smaller letters identified NATIVE AMERICAN PROTEST LEADER SKYE SYKES.

Chapter Fourteen

Motive. That's what Lucy was thinking about as she drove back to Tinker's Cove. Whoever killed Hetty must have had a reason. The very fact that she was beaten and then stabbed with the nearest weapon at hand, the peavey, seemed to indicate that the killer had been enraged and acted on impulse. As often happened when Lucy was driving a familiar route, she was operating on sort of mental automatic pilot. She didn't notice the woods, the horses grazing in pastures, the hay fields, or even, as she approached Tinker's Cove, the picturesque views of coves and salt marshes. Instead, she was picturing Hetty and her killer, confronting each other in the Pratt house. What could Hetty have possibly done or said that so angered her killer? What words so inflamed him, or her, to reach for the peavey and drive it into her body? And could Skye possibly be that person?

Try as she might, Lucy couldn't put him in the frame for the simple reason that Skye and Hetty had too much in common. They had a shared passion for local history: Skye was researching the Metinnicut's largely forgotten past while Hetty's passion had been discovering the true history of the town. They must have been excited to find each other and share the knowledge they'd each acquired in their separate areas to develop a more comprehensive and inclusive story. It would have been the meeting of two minds, both committed to searching out the truth. Hetty had certainly been excited; she'd told Skye she'd learned something "incredible," something she'd most likely found in that box of documents that she assumed he would be interested in learning. Perhaps even something that would cause people to see the town and themselves in a new way.

Did this backfire? Did this incredible bit of history anger Skye? That didn't seem to make sense, thought Lucy, signaling left for the turn that would take her into town. If her theory was right, and whatever Hetty had discovered had motivated her killer, it certainly didn't fit with what she knew about Skye. What could it be? she wondered. What kind of inflammatory information had Hetty found? If only she could get her hands on those papers, she might be able to discover the "something incredible," the what, that would lead her to the who. She had just parked the car in front of the office and was reaching for her bag when her phone announced a text had arrived.

It was from Franny, she noted. **Sorry. No-go on the docs,** she'd written. **Firm no from TCPD and DA.**

Lucy sat for a minute, staring at her phone. There was no way she was going to get her hands on those documents any time soon unless she broke into the Pratt house, or maybe the police station, and neither break-in was a good idea. But those documents had been in the library for years. Who might have seen them? Who might have stored stray bits of information in their brain? Her thoughts immediately turned to Miss Tilley, now retired, but who had been the town's librarian for many, many years. Miss T had a mind like a steel trap, she remembered everything, or so she claimed. No time like the present to put her to the test, Lucy decided, starting the car.

Miss Tilley, known as Julia only to an aging and sadly diminishing group of close friends, was the town's oldest resident and lived in an antique gray-shingled Cape Cod–style house a few streets over from Main Street. She had taken an interest in Lucy when she was a newcomer in Tinker's Cove, bringing her growing brood of children to Miss Tilley's weekly story hours. Miss Tilley had picked right up on Lucy's inquiring mind, suggested books she suspected would interest her, and encouraged her when she began writing for the paper. The two had become true friends, even though Miss Tilley was some forty or perhaps even fifty years older than Lucy.

These days Miss Tilley was almost always home, attended by Lucy's friend Rachel, who had taken on the role of home-care provider. Rachel did a bit of light housekeeping, cooked a substantial and healthy midday meal, and most importantly, provided companionship. It was Rachel who answered the door when Lucy knocked.

"Hi! Come on in! We're just sitting down to lunch."

"Funny about that, the way Lucy always manages to arrive in time for a meal," observed Miss Tilley, who had lately taken to using a cane to raise herself from her chair.

Looking at her, thought Lucy, with her aureole of fluffy white hair and pink cheeks, anyone would think she was a sweet old lady. That would be wrong.

"Well, I'd hardly come to see an old witch like you," said Lucy, giving her a hug and a peck on the cheek. "What's for lunch?"

"Shepherd's pie," said Miss Tilley, smacking her lips.

"With strawberry shortcake for dessert," added Rachel.

"Made with Rachel's biscuits," said Miss Tilley.

"There goes the diet," said Lucy, holding a chair for Miss Tilley.

Soon they were all seated at the polished table, which was set with Miss Tilley's Canton china and family silver, oversized starched white damask napkins on their laps. Rachel began serving the shepherd's pie and Miss Tilley turned to Lucy. "What really brings you here, Lucy?"

Lucy recounted the situation as she saw it: Hetty's death, Skye's arraignment, and the "something incredible" that Hetty had discovered in the box of documents.

"So you suspect Hetty was killed because of this information?" asked Miss Tilley.

"I do."

"Bob," began Rachel, referring to her lawyer husband, "Bob says the DA's case is pretty weak. He says Aucoin grabbed the first available suspect in order to calm folks down and reassure everyone that they're not in danger from a peavey-wielding madman."

"Aucoin said Skye was caught on doorbell video. . . ." began Lucy.

"Video can be cut and altered, bits taken out of context," said Rachel. "Bob has serious doubts about that video. He says it's so murky that the figure could be anybody."

"And Aucoin's looking to get reelected," added Miss Tilley, spearing a juicy piece of meat.

"What I'm wondering," began Lucy, turning to Miss Tilley, "is if you might have any idea what Hetty could have found."

"Well, if I do say so myself, the library has quite an extensive local history collection of its own, as well as the historical society's archives, which are stored there. It's especially rich in genealogical data, which is very popular these days. A lot of it came from the town hall, old tax records in particular, that they moved to the library when they needed more space. And a lot of families donated letters, old Bibles with lists of births and deaths, even photos. There's a lot there but it's rather hit or miss, it's not comprehensive in any way, and it hasn't been properly catalogued. That's what the historical society has been trying to do, to organize the collection, find the gaps and fill them."

"I think it must have had something to do with the Metinnicut Indians," suggested Lucy. "Hetty had promised to dig deeper into their participation in the logging industry. That's what the protest was all about, you know, the fact that they weren't included in the exhibit."

Miss Tilley put her fork down and adopted a faraway look. She was consulting the files in her head, the enormous amount of information she'd gathered and stored during her long life. "Indians," she said, raising one finger. "Logging," she added, raising another finger. "Pine Tree," she said, putting the two together. "It must be something to do with Pine Tree."

"Pine trees?" asked Rachel. "For timber?"

"No. The village of Pine Tree. It was part of Tinker's Cove, a long time ago. It's where the Indians lived, also some Blacks."

"I never heard of it," mused Rachel.

"That's because the state came and seized it, back around 1910, sometime around then."

"What do you mean?" asked Rachel. "Seized it?"

"I don't know much about it," admitted Miss Tilley. "It was before my time, but people did talk about it when I was a child. There was a big stand of trees there; I guess that's what they wanted. The state can take land by eminent domain, you know. For highways and such."

"Eminent domain," said Rachel. "That's what happened to my grandfather's farm when they built the interstate. They kept what they needed for the road and sold the rest. I think there's a motel there now."

"Was your grandfather upset about losing his farm?" asked Lucy.

"No, not at all," recalled Rachel. "Thrilled to bits. He was sick of cows, getting up at four every morning, never being able to leave the beasts. He took the cash, and even got a job working on the road crew that built the highway."

"But taking over a village and moving everybody out, that's a different story," said Lucy. "Ellie Martin told me it was pretty much the end of the tribal community. The state claimed the town was unhealthy, unfit for habitation, filled with half-wits and deviants. They actually put some people in institutions and packed the kids off to residential schools. Others kind of drifted off, to other places."

"There's usually at least two versions of any story, what happened and then the official explanation," said Miss Tilley, picking up her fork. "Sometimes it's hard to discover the truth."

"That's what I want to find out," said Lucy, scooping up the last bit of mashed potato.

When she got back to the paper that afternoon she was eager to start digging deeper into the Pine Tree story and called the Maine state archives, which would certainly have information about the seizure. Anything involving the taking of property would certainly require legal action of some sort, either from the courts or perhaps the state legislature. There would have to be a paper trail, she thought, but when she reached the state archivist's assistant, she was surprised to learn that there was not only no mention of such a seizure, there was no mention of Pine Tree at all.

"I'm sorry, but there doesn't seem to be anything. In Tinker's Cove, you said?"

"Yeah," confirmed Lucy, adding the name of the county.

"Gosh, this is odd," admitted the assistant, whose voice seemed to indicate she was a bright young thing, probably straight out of college. "All I can figure is that it hasn't been entered into the database yet. That's a work in progress, as you can imagine. We have boxes and boxes of stuff. Some of it's hundreds of years old and is just sitting there in storage."

"And not enough staff," offered Lucy, commiserating.

"You said it." She paused. "You know, something like a seizure would require legal action. You could try the attorney general's office. They're better funded, for one thing."

"Good idea," said Lucy. "Thanks."

"No problem. Let me know what you find out, okay? It sounds awfully interesting."

Lucy agreed, then called the attorney general's number. Again, her call was answered by an assistant secretary; this time the voice was male and sounded more mature. Or perhaps just tired.

"A land seizure?" he asked. "We've been getting a lot of calls about that lately."

Lucy felt her spirits rise; it seemed she was going to get some answers. "Really?"

"Yeah. Malaga Island. It's been rediscovered, thanks to some book."

"Malaga Island? I must've missed it," admitted Lucy. "Can you fill me in?"

"Sure. It's in Casco Bay, about forty miles north of Portland. There was a little community there of Blacks. . . . I guess freed slaves and their descendants. The state took it in 1912, declaring it unhealthy. The residents were moved away and the buildings cleared. Nowadays it's a nature preserve, open for recreation."

"Well, that's exactly what happened in Pine Tree," said Lucy. "The state came in and moved everybody out."

"I don't think so," said the assistant secretary. "Like I mentioned, there's been a lot of interest in land seizures since the Malaga Island book came out. I've had a lot of requests for information, and while the Malaga Island taking is well documented, I haven't discovered any others."

"But it happened—local people remember it."

"I don't know what to tell you. If it was done by the state, there would be a record, but I haven't found anything apart from Malaga." He sighed. "And believe me, I would have."

"Perhaps the paper trail was destroyed to hide what happened?"

"That's very unlikely. Looking back, a lot of people nowadays are unhappy about what happened to Malaga Island and the people who lived there. . . . If you ask me, it was shameful. But at the time people believed it was entirely justified because it was done for the public good. We still have the records. Nobody saw any need to cover it up. It's all there for anybody who wants to find out about it." He paused. "My advice is to check with the town itself. Most towns have archives, and maps, going way back to when they were founded."

"I'll do that, thanks," said Lucy, ending the call. She'd no sooner hit that red button when a text from Ted popped up assigning her to interview a high schooler who'd won an essay contest and had been invited to deliver an address at the upcoming Rotary Club state convention. Some nerve, she fumed, eyeing the clock, which told her it was after three. A new assignment at three in the afternoon on a Friday. She weighed her choices: spend the remainder of her work week talking to some nerdy kid, or catch the town assessor before town hall closed at four. It wasn't even close.

When Lucy arrived at the window of the assessor's office, in the town hall, she learned the assessor himself was gone for the day, but the clerk, Sandy Croy, was happy to help her. No wonder, thought Lucy, noticing a crossword puzzle book open on her desk. She'd been killing time until four, when she could begin her weekend, and was happy for a distraction. Sandy opened the door and invited Lucy into the office itself, and began pulling out some of the oversized drawers that were ranked along one wall in search of the relevant maps.

"Okay, here we've got 1910," she said, carefully laying the map, which easily measured three by four feet, out on a large table. She leaned over it, her long hair falling and hiding her face, studying it closely. "Here it is," said Sandy, pointing to a cluster of little squares, indicating plots of land, each occupied by the figure of a house. Various names were attached to each square, including several Sykes. There was also a church, along with a graveyard.

"So where exactly is this?" asked Lucy, not seeing any familiar landmarks. "Where was it located?"

"I'm not sure. . . . We're missing all the roads built since 1910, so it's a bit confusing. Let's take a look at the current map and compare it," suggested Sandy.

The present-day map was much more familiar; Route 1 ran along one side of town, the river followed a meandering course through the middle, the Atlantic Ocean served as the eastern boundary.

Sandy was leaning over the table, resting on her elbows, her fingers following new roads, and comparing them to the ones on the old map. "I've got it," she said. "This church"—she stabbed it with her finger—"is now the Old Indian Meetinghouse."

"Figures," said Lucy, feeling rather dumb.

"And here, where most of the houses were, well, now it's Logue Log Homes. See, it says, right here, Zebulon Logue. But it's not his house; that's right on the town boundary. This is his business."

"That's really interesting," said Lucy, wondering what possible connection the Logue family had to the little Pine Tree community. Chad wouldn't know, but perhaps his brother, Chris, might. But the person who most probably did know was their grandfather, Zebulon.

"I hope this was helpful," said Sandy, drawing Lucy back to the present moment.

"Oh, yes. I think so. Thank you."

"No problem, Lucy." Sandy began replacing the maps in their drawers. "Have a good weekend."

"You too," said Lucy, making her way down the vinyl-floored hallway to the exit. As she walked, it occurred to her that Chris bore a slight resemblance to Skye. They were both tall and slender, both had long hair, but there was one important difference. Skye was a well-balanced, high-achieving young man while Chris seemed to have some issues, judging from his behavior at the shower. The DA had cited doorbell camera video as evidence that Skye was present at the scene of the crime, but that sort of video tended to be fuzzy and was affected by outside light sources. As she went down the steps, crossed the sidewalk, and checked the street for traffic, she thought of the various grainy videos that were often shown on the morning news, asking viewers if they could identify "the person seen here." She often laughed, wondering if their own mother would be able to identify them, much less a casual acquaintance.

It was intriguing, thought Lucy, that the Logues' business was located on land that had been seized from Metinnicut families, but did that add up to a motive? A motive for murder? It was worth investigating, she thought, waiting for a chance to cross the street, but first she had to interview that kid who'd won the Rotary Club essay contest.

Samantha's mother assured her that her daughter was home and working on her speech, and invited her right over to interview her daughter. "No time like the present," she told her, since Samantha had a ballet lesson at five-thirty, followed by fencing at six-thirty. "It was the fencing that got her into Harvard, but she's going to Princeton because their program is more highly rated."

"That's very impressive," said Lucy, somewhat awed. She was also wondering what was wrong with her kids, who she'd thought had done rather well, going to college and on to successful careers. She was apparently mistaken; they were slackers compared to the amazing Samantha.

She decided to walk over to Samantha's house, estimating the twenty-minute walk would give her time to put together some questions, but found herself instead thinking about Chris. It struck her as odd that he was so different from Chad, but the two were actually only half brothers. Chad, like Samantha, seemed to have won the genetic lottery, while Chris lost out. Or was it that simple? Samantha certainly seemed to get a lot of support and encouragement from her Tiger mom, and maybe that was also the case for Chad. Penny and Nate seemed to take great pride in Chad's accomplishments and perhaps they had given him the love and guidance that helped him succeed.

Lucy knew that Friday afternoons tended to be slow in most offices, so she took a chance and called Zoe at work while she walked along Benner Road, which began in town as a straight road but once out of the town's grid pattern broke free and meandered along willy-nilly around hills and over humpy bridges. Zoe answered quickly, after only two rings.

"Hi, Mom. What's up?"

"Just checking in. Are you still the blushing bride-to-be?"

"Kind of a tired bride-to-be at the moment. It's been a long week."

"Any plans for the weekend?"

"Chad's got away games both days, so I'm going to do laundry and stream some *Succession* episodes I haven't seen."

"Sounds like a plan." Lucy stopped walking and leaned against a nearby tree. "I've been wondering about Chris, ever since the shower. Have you gotten to know him? Has Chad?"

"Not really. Chad only met him for the first time the weekend we got engaged, and he was pretty preoccupied with me."

"Understandable. But they came to the shower together, as if they'd been hanging out for a bit."

"Chad's actually been kind of disappointed, like he'd been hoping they'd become close, like real brothers, but they don't seem to have much in common. When you think about it, they grew up in very different circumstances. Chad's folks were always pushing him to succeed, not just in sports but in school, too. He's always been expected to work hard and do his very best, and you can see that. He doesn't just go to practices, he works out all the time. And he's a leader—he encourages the other guys on the team.

"Chris, on the other hand, at least the way Chad sees it, was raised by his grandparents and kind of spoiled. They indulged him, like he was a little prince or something. He's got that fancy sports car, he's got a cushy job in the family business that basically pays him a lot for doing nothing."

"What's he like?"

"He's okay, I guess. I know Chad thinks so but, well, I sense trouble ahead."

"What do you mean?"

"I get the feeling Chris can be kind of distant. And you saw him at the shower. He seemed shaky to me, as if he was coming down off a high. I'm afraid he needs some . . ." Her voice trailed off; she was talking to someone else. "Sorry, Mom, I've got to go. We've got a bit of a situation here."

"I hope it's not serious."

"Won't be, if I get ahead of it," she said, and ended the call.

Lucy tucked her phone in her pocket and looked up the road where she saw Samantha's home, a sprawling old farmhouse, perched on a hill overlooking the cove.

Lucy checked her watch as she walked back to town, her interview with Samantha completed. As she walked she began thinking about the story she would write, stringing remembered phrases together. What struck her most about the adorable Samantha wasn't her good looks or her considerable achievements, but her confidence. The sky was the limit to little Samantha, and good luck to her.

Lucy had never, not even for one day, felt that way. She tended to go where the fates dictated, hopefully finding time for her two top priorities: keeping up with the laundry and getting dinner on the table. Perhaps she'd sold herself short, she thought, pulling the office door open and setting the little bell jangling.

"ME's report came in," advised Phyllis, who was clearing her desk before leaving.

"Anything interesting?" asked Lucy.

Phyllis was sorting press releases by date and filing them

in a plastic bin containing folders; she paused and looked up. "Hetty was knocked unconscious before she was stabbed with the peavey. . . ."

"That's a relief," said Lucy, grateful for small mercies. "But still it must've been terrifying."

"It's horrible to think about," said Phyllis, picking up one of the releases and glancing at it. "The peavey was actually embedded in the floor."

Lucy struggled with this information. "It went through Hetty and into the floor?"

Phyllis dropped the release into the proper folder. "That's what the report says."

"Good God." Lucy dropped her bag on her desk, sat down, and opened her emails. The ME's report was at the top, and she quickly read it, feeling sicker with every sentence. She had to do it—she knew Ted would want a story posted as breaking news for the online edition—but it was definitely making her queasy.

Swallowing hard, she picked up the desk phone and called Sharon Oliver, hoping to catch her before she left for the weekend.

"I wasn't sure you'd be in," said Lucy, when Sharon answered.

"Summer hours don't start until July," she said. "Then I can leave at four."

"Well, I'm glad I caught you," said Lucy, noticing it was a quarter to five. "I've just got a few questions about the report."

"It's all there," sighed the examiner, sounding terribly sad, which Lucy realized was a first for her. She was usually absolutely professional as she reported the most gruesome details from automobile accidents, fires, and other mishaps.

"You noted that the killer must have been exceptionally strong, and I wonder if you think rage or maybe drugs might have been a factor."

"Possibly, especially if the killer was on amphetamines or steroids, something like that."

"Was the killer definitely male?"

"That does seem the most likely, but there are very strong females, too. An athlete, say, like a competitive swimmer, or someone who competes in track and field, like javelin or shot put. Those girls pack on some serious muscle." She paused. "I don't think we can rule out a female."

"Thanks for your time," said Lucy, noting that the clock was getting closer to five with every tick. She couldn't leave—she had to stay and write the story. She'd need a reaction from the DA, but was there time to catch him?

"Have a good weekend, Lucy," said the ME.

"No rest for the wicked, at least not yet," joked Lucy, ending the call and quickly dialing the DA's office. Phil Aucoin answered himself.

"Your secretary's gone for the day?" asked Lucy.

"And I hope to go, too. Make it quick, Lucy."

"I just want to know if you think the ME's report strengthens your case against Skye."

"It certainly makes a conviction more likely," he predicted. "Any jury that hears the details and sees the photos is going to convict."

"The crime is certainly horrendous," offered Lucy, "but what I'm asking is if the way the crime was committed fits with what we know of Skye's personality, his behavior."

"Lucy, you know just as well as I do that people are complicated. That nice, quiet guy who helps out his neighbors can one day come home from work and kill his entire family and shoot himself, too."

"But there are always signs, in hindsight. Are you finding those trouble signs in Skye's life? Because I've interviewed his family and there doesn't seem to be any there."

"I really can't talk about an ongoing investigation," said Aucoin.

"Off the record," coaxed Lucy.

"No way, Lucy. Now, if you don't mind, an icy cold gin and tonic is calling my name, if I can just get out of this office."

"Have a good weekend," said Lucy, wondering when her weekend would begin.

Left alone in the office, she quickly wrote up the update, choosing words carefully in order to avoid upsetting readers' delicate sensibilities. Ted would want more gore, of course, but he would have to wait until Monday, when he'd no doubt demand a more complete story for the print edition. After she'd sent the story, she started to get ready to leave. She was straightening up the accumulated mess of papers on her desk when she noticed Zebulon Logue's name, written in large capitals.

The Pine Tree takeover, she remembered, reaching for her mouse and Googling his name. The first thing that popped up was the Logue Log Homes website, which included a brief, laudatory history of the company, which, Lucy learned, began as a logging operation in 1913. That, Lucy recalled, was the same year as the takeover. The logging was only briefly mentioned, however, as the focus shifted to the company's present-day activities as a manufacturer of log homes, and more recently, prefab homes. Lucy knew this pattern was fairly typical for small logging operations that couldn't compete with the big corporations that had bought up the enormous timber stands in the northern part of the state. Reading between the lines, which did not mention Pine Tree at all, Lucy figured the company had somehow managed to get hold of that last stand of old growth timber and when that was exhausted, had segued into construction. It was a smart move that allowed the company to continue to exist; most of the other small outfits, she knew, had simply disappeared.

But what about that link with Pine Tree? That date. The company was formed in the same year that Pine Tree was taken over by the state. Was there some sort of collusion? Or was Logue simply the successful bidder, who'd gained the land with the old growth trees when the state put it up for auction? It was certainly an intriguing question, but one that would have to wait for another day, she decided, logging off. She wasn't a fan of gin and tonic, like Aucoin, but she did have a bottle of chardonnay chilling in her fridge, and it definitely knew her name.

Chapter Fifteen

On Saturday morning, Lucy had a long list of errands she wanted to accomplish, starting off at the post office, where she was mailing a package to her grandson, Patrick, containing some of the comic books his father Toby had left behind. Toby's collection was rather large, occupying a long, narrow storage carton that filled most of the tiny guest room closet, and the comics themselves were individually sheathed in protective plastic cases and stored in the proper sequence. She understood they had some value to collectors, but Toby had not only moved to Alaska, he'd moved on from this particular youthful phase, and had rebuffed her frequent pleas that he please, please take them off her hands. She'd lighted on this solution when Patrick discovered the box during his last visit and started reading the series, beginning at the beginning. Now, every couple of weeks, she counted out ten comics and sent them to him.

She was making real progress, she thought, congratulating herself on reaching the halfway point of the collection. The post office was always busy on Saturdays, and when she got in line she checked out the other customers, recognizing most of them. Noticing the two customers who were already being helped at the counter, she spotted Ellie Martin, who was buying stamps. When Ellie completed her transaction and turned to leave, Lucy greeted her. "How's it going?" she asked.

"Not great, but I'm hoping to see Skye today." Ellie seemed to have aged overnight; there was no sign of her usual smile and she hadn't bothered with lipstick.

The line was moving along, Lucy was next, but she really wanted to talk to Ellie. "Do you have a minute?" she asked.

Receiving a positive reply, she made the decision to sacrifice her place in line and stepped aside, following Ellie outside so they wouldn't be overheard by curious townsfolk.

"What do you want to know, Lucy?" asked Ellie, as they sought the shade of a big maple tree. She seemed terribly tired, overwhelmed by Skye's mounting troubles.

"Well, first off, I don't believe for a minute that Skye killed Hetty and I'm doing everything I can to help."

"The power of the press?" asked Ellie, somewhat skeptically.

"I know, there's only so much I can do, but I am going to shine a bright light on the case and make sure Aucoin plays fair and square. And I'm doing a bit of digging into what Hetty was researching, which maybe you can help me with."

"Anything, ask me anything, Lucy," she said, sounding resigned, clutching at straws.

"Well, I do have some questions about the state takeover of Pine Tree. What do you know about that? Because I checked with the state archivist and there's no record of any such thing. Malaga, yes. Pine Tree, no."

Ellie took a step back. "I really don't see the connection, Lucy. What does this have to do with Skye?"

"I'm not exactly sure, but something doesn't seem right about it and I think maybe Hetty figured that out and that's why she was killed."

Ellie was doubtful. "Hetty got killed because of something that happened in 1913?"

"I know," admitted Lucy. "It does seem far-fetched, but right now it's all I've got."

"Well, it was way before my time, it was over a hundred years ago, Lucy, but my grandmother told me about it. She heard stories as a child, from her mama, so I don't know what's actually true. These family stories can get twisted through the years. But according to Grandma, who wasn't even born yet, the story went that the men from the state came, wearing big hats and badges that glittered in the sunlight. Grandma always repeated these details when she told the story. Then they nailed up notices on all the houses, condemning them. People had to leave by a certain date, or they would be forcibly removed. That's what they were told, so they all packed up and went. Some had relatives in other parts of town who took them in. Great-Grandma's people had a little farm way out of town on Gilead road and that's where they settled. Others weren't so lucky and had to go farther afield, even to Portland and Boston to find work. And there were rumors that some people simply disappeared. They were taken to reform schools and mental institutions, but I don't know if that's true."

"What happened after that?"

"They came in with bulldozers and knocked the houses down. Pretty soon, she said, there was nothing left except the meetinghouse."

"Who were these men with the hats and badges? Was the sheriff involved?"

"I don't know, Lucy," said Ellie, a bit exasperated. "Like I said, it was such a long time ago, long before I was born. And Grandma, well, she wasn't the most reliable storyteller. She tended to embellish things, like the time she said we were descended from George Washington himself."

"Not impossible, I suppose," said Lucy, chuckling.

"Well, I wouldn't bet any money on it," said Ellie.

"Probably wise," admitted Lucy. "What bothers me is that there should be a paper trail, and there isn't. I checked with both the state archives and the AG's office. There's a lot about Malaga but nothing about Pine Tree." Lucy paused. "I wish I knew what Hetty found. A warrant maybe, or a photo . . ."

"Oh, I have photos," said Ellie, delivering news that practically knocked Lucy off her feet.

"You do?"

"Yeah. There's this box full of family photos. Somebody had a camera, even back then. It's kind of frustrating because none of the people are identified. Nameless ancestors, plus a couple of guys in big hats and badges, just like in the story."

"Could I see them?"

"Yeah, I'm on my way to visit Skye, but soon as I get home I'll dig them out. I'll stick 'em in your mailbox tomorrow on my way to church."

Lucy could hardly wait. "Thank you, thank you," she said, giving Ellie's arm a squeeze and letting go. "And tell Skye I'm thinking of him and doing everything I can to help."

"I will, Lucy," said Ellie, hurrying off. Lucy pulled the mailer containing the comics out of her bag, preparing to go back inside the post office, but noticed that the line had grown and people were now standing outside the door. There was no rush—Patrick could wait a day or two longer for the comics—but she had to get to the grocery store or there'd be no lunch or dinner.

Lucy was humming a little tune and putting her groceries away in the kitchen when her phone rang. She couldn't immediately locate it, finding it under a pile of empty reusable bags, and swiped up just in time. She knew from the screen that the caller was Zoe, but her daughter didn't respond to her hello. Terrified something was the matter, like maybe she was kidnapped and desperately signaling to her, Lucy listened intently, picking up sniffles. "Is everything okay?" she asked, getting sobs and gasps. Zoe was in tears. She knew that her daughter was changeable and tended to ride an emotional roller coaster, euphoric one moment and plunged into despair the next, but this was extreme, even for Zoe. Yesterday, she recalled, Zoe had been relaxed and cheerful, looking forward to the weekend. Today, she was practically hysterical.

"Slow down," said Lucy, taking a seat at the golden oak table that stood by the window. "Take a deep breath and tell me what's wrong."

"The wedding!" sobbed Zoe.

Lucy's heart stopped. Had Chad changed his mind? Had Zoe? "What about the wedding?" she asked, fearing the worst.

"Taylor called, just this morning. . . ."

"She can't do the wedding?"

"Not can't, won't. I mean, she's supposedly the planner, but she gave me this huge list of things to do. Things she says only I can do. Like looking at dresses and choosing invitations and picking a DJ. She's given me suggestions and options, like the printer she likes and a couple of dress shops, in Connecticut, thank you very much! But she says the wedding won't be my wedding if I let her do all the choosing."

"Well, do you care? Why not just tell her you've got confidence in her taste?"

"I don't think so, Mom. I mean, the shower was great and all, but really? I felt stupid, sitting there opening all those presents and playing those stupid games. I'm going to have to take control if I don't want to be a puppet in some sort of farce."

"Then you might as well get in the spirit and enjoy it. I'll help."

"And when, exactly, do you think I'll come up with time to do all this? I've got a new job, I can't afford to make mistakes, it's a lot of pressure. Like last night, I was all ready to leave when one of the players called; he'd been arrested for OUI and needed a lawyer. I didn't get home until nearly midnight. I couldn't get the team's attorney so I ended up going to the station myself to post bail. Then there was the whole matter of preparing a statement in case the press caught on, which they haven't yet, but it's just a matter of time." She let out a big breath. "When am I supposed to do all this wedding stuff when I can hardly keep up with my job? The days are too short, I can't get everything done so I bring work home and I'm up till all hours working on press releases and player bios and prepping for presentations. I actually stood up an advertiser the other day, completely forgot the meeting. He was nice about it and rescheduled, but I can't make mistakes like this or I'll be in big trouble. I need to be on my game."

"Do you think Taylor's overreacting? I mean, what's the rush? The wedding is more than a year away."

"Oh, Mom," moaned Zoe, allowing Lucy to picture the eye roll she'd seen so often. "That's what I thought, but I was wrong. According to Taylor, most weddings are planned for a couple of years. She says we're on the fast track!"

An idea was beginning to take shape in Lucy's mind, but she thought the chance of success was about fifty-fifty. "Do you think Sara would help?" she asked.

"Sara!" scoffed Zoe, answering her question.

"Well, you're probably right, but I'll give her a call. All I can do is ask."

"Good luck," growled Zoe, who had moved on from despair to anger.

"And good-bye to you," muttered Lucy, to a dead line.

Nothing ventured, nothing gained, thought Lucy, tapping the little button beside Sara's name in her phone's list of contacts. Sara answered right away, sounding bright and cheerful.

"Zoe's having a fit," she told her.

"Typical."

"I know, but she's absolutely losing her mind. Taylor gave her a list of stuff to do for the wedding and she says she doesn't have a spare minute, she's overwhelmed with her new job responsibilities and . . ."

"And she wants me to help?" asked Sara, with a distinct lack of enthusiasm.

"Well, it's more me. It was my idea. I think you might enjoy tasting cakes and picking fonts. . . ."

"Fonts?"

"For the invitations."

"Oh, *those* fonts."

"Mostly emotional support. I don't think it actually involves all that much. It's just that she's overwhelmed and panicked."

"Hard to imagine Zoe being panicked," observed Sara, stifling a giggle.

"Don't be sarcastic," chided Lucy. "You are the maid of honor, after all. You do have some responsibility for supporting the bride and making sure the wedding of the century goes off without a hitch."

"Now who's being sarcastic?"

"Guilty," admitted Lucy, with a laugh.

"Sure, I'll do it. Jodi's here, urging me on. She thinks it will be a blast."

"I'm really beginning to like Jodi," said Lucy.

"She's great," declared Sara. "We went to Boston Calling last night. It's a rock festival, and guess who we saw?"

"Ed Sheeran?" Lucy had seen the concert mentioned on the morning news.

"Well, yeah, he was there, but I was thinking of Chris, Chad's half brother."

"It's a small world. . . ."

"Get this, Mom. He was really high on something, must've been because he was stripping off his clothes and dancing and then he got in a fight with someone and they kicked him out. Bouncers actually grabbed him and took him away."

"Are you sure it was really Chris?" asked Lucy.

"Oh, yeah. Because earlier in the evening he actually spoke to me. He was there with another guy, and that guy offered me some pills. Meth, I think."

"Oh, no. That stuff's evil! You didn't?"

Sara was laughing. "No, Mom. Of course not. We're high on life. And besides, Jodi is an EMT and sees overdoses all the time. She's not about to let me risk my life by taking some fentanyl-laced drug."

Lucy felt her heart lifting; this relationship was clearly a good thing for Sara. "You know, I never got a chance to talk to you after you came out that night to tell you how happy I am for you. I've got to admit it was a big surprise to me. Everyone else in town seemed to know but it never crossed my mind."

"You and Dad are hopelessly heterosexual," said Sara, chuckling. "That's why I never said anything before. I was worried you wouldn't understand, or approve."

Sara's admission hit Lucy hard. "Oh, Sara, that makes me sad. We love you, no matter what, absolutely unconditionally, and whether you're gay or straight doesn't matter to either of us one little bit. And I'm so happy for you, that you've found someone special. Dad and I can't wait to meet Jodi."

"She's right here," said Sara. "Do you want to talk to her?"

"Sure," said Lucy, feeling a trifle anxious. What if she said the wrong thing?

"Hi, Jodi here," came over the phone. She sounded upbeat and confident.

"It's great to hear your voice," said Lucy. "I hope we'll meet in person. . . ."

"Hey, let me switch to a video call. . . ." The phone went dead, then rang, and there was Jodi, with a round face and short hair gelled to stand up. Sara was beside her, beaming.

Lucy held up her phone and smiled back for all she was worth. "Well, it's very nice to meet you in two-D. I hope to get three-D real soon."

"Same here," said Jodi. "So what's this about Zoe? She needs help with the wedding?"

"She's got a huge to-do list and I was hoping you two could help her. She mentioned cake tasting and picking out the save-the-date cards and invitations. . . ."

"I don't know much about stationery but I'm a whiz on cake," said Jodi. "You can count on us."

"That's great," said Lucy. "And thanks. Why not give Zoe a call and get that to-do list?"

"Roger Wilco," said Jodi, as the screen went black.

Roger Wilco? wondered Lucy. Where did that come from?

Ellie was true to her word and, when Lucy went out to pick up the Sunday paper, which the carrier had tossed into the driveway, she checked the mailbox and found an envelope with a couple of photos inside. They were black-and-white, printed on paper that had grown brittle over time, but did indeed feature three very impressive officials, all dressed according to the custom of the times in dark suits complete with vests and tightly knotted neck ties, standing in front of the clearly recognizable Indian Meetinghouse. One was tall, with a large mustache, one had a pair of wire-rimmed eyeglasses perched on his nose, and the third sported an impressively large belly that was adorned with a thick watch chain. They were all wearing big black hats and each had an oversized star-shaped badge pinned to his lapel. No wonder, she thought, that the hats and badges were remembered, even years later.

Walking slowly back to the house, Lucy decided to send copies of the photos to both the AG's office and the state archives, to see if those oversized badges corresponded to those of any state officials. Once in the kitchen she spread them out on the golden oak table and snapped photos with her camera, which she immediately sent on. She had just finished when Bill came down the back staircase, looking for coffee.

"What're those?" he asked, seating himself and taking that first swallow.

"Some photos I'm using for a story," said Lucy, who had seated herself beside him, also with a cup of coffee.

"Funny how people in old photos look so silly," he said. "Those guys are certainly impressed with themselves."

"Someday people will be looking at pictures of us and wonder what we were thinking, going around looking the way we do." Lucy took a sip of coffee. "Especially leggings. They will definitely scratch their heads over leggings."

"Definitely not for everyone," agreed Bill. "But some girls carry them off pretty well."

"They're not for your viewing pleasure, you know," snapped Lucy.

Bill wisely decided to change the subject. "Got any plans for today?"

Lucy thought for a moment, then groaned. "Afraid so. Hetty's funeral."

"Do you have to go?" asked Bill. "I was thinking we could take a drive up the coast, check out the new Wyeth exhibit at the Farnsworth."

"Maybe next weekend," suggested Lucy. "It's not just work. I've been friends with Hetty for a long time. She was one of the first people I profiled for the paper."

"I understand," said Bill. "How about I make some bacon and eggs? You'll need your strength."

"Sounds great," said Lucy, giving his hand a squeeze.

What with Bill's delicious breakfast—crisp bacon, cheesy scrambled eggs, and blueberry scones, not to mention the thick morning paper and a fresh pot of coffee—Lucy was running late. She arrived at the Baptist Church when the service was well under way and slipped into a back pew. The church was almost full, which Lucy guessed was not the usual case. Hetty was a well-known and even beloved local figure and a lot of folks wanted to pay their respects. The service, led by Reverend Wilkes Henderson, was in the evangelical mode, which was in stark contrast to the nondenominational services Lucy occasionally attended at the Community Church. That church had formed when the Methodist Church's tall steeple, the tallest in town, was hit by lightning, which resulted in a huge fire that completely destroyed the church's century-old sanctuary. Rebuilding was not feasible considering their dwindling membership, so the Methodists joined with the Congregationalists, who were also seeing their membership shrink, and were struggling to maintain their handsome church with the second-tallest steeple in town. The handful of elderly Unitarians who continued to attend their church, a decaying carpenter Gothic chapel, were also invited, and thus the Community Church was born. Reverend Marge had her hands full, managing these diverse factions, and sometimes complained that the only thing they all agreed upon was the Ten Commandments, and the Unitarians took issue with some of them.

Reverend Henderson ended the service by sending Hetty to join the heavenly host in unending praise of the Lord, they all sang "Nearer My God to Thee," the coffin was carried out of the church, and the mourners got down to business in the parish hall, where a generous collation was provided by the Baptist Church Women.

Before entering the parish hall, however, the mourners had to pay their respects to Hetty's family, and the line moved slowly as hands were clasped, eyes were wiped, and expressions of sympathy were offered. While she waited her turn in the hallway, Lucy's attention was taken by a newly arranged display of photos and documents on the wall under the heading "One God, One Family." Each was chosen to memorialize the history of the church decade by decade, beginning in 1810 with a reproduction of the original gathering document. The following decades were illustrated by facsimiles of newspaper articles mentioning the church, including meetings of abolitionists in the years preceding the Civil War. After the war photographs began to appear and two in particular caught her eye. They were group photos of the entire congregation taken in 1900 and 1910 that included a number of people of color. At that time, it seemed the congregation was quite diverse, which was not the case in later years, when the photos indicated an almost entirely white congregation. Lucy wondered what had happened, where did all the black and brown people go? Was this a result of the takeover of Pine Tree?

Then, suddenly, she was face to face with Hetty's daughter, and her sister, and a smattering of grandchildren. "I'm so sorry for your loss," said Lucy, repeating the phrase to each one and wishing she could come up with something more original, something that represented her true feelings. But that would involve mentioning the unmentionable, the horrible way Hetty died. And then there'd be the need to speak about the accused murderer, and the upcoming trial, and that was indeed a slippery slope. She couldn't imagine what Hetty's daughter was going through, or her sister, or even what the kids were feeling. So there it was, Hetty was gone, they'd lost someone they loved, and that was really all you could say.

Duty done, Lucy moved on to the buffet table, where she encountered Franny Small. Franny was the town's current selectboard chairperson, whose family roots went back to the first settlers of the area. She was also the town's richest resident, having turned a sideline making jewelry out of hardware into a major corporation that she sold to an international conglomerate for an undisclosed, but presumably very large, amount. "Hi, Franny," began Lucy, picking up a plate, "sad day indeed."

"Oh, my yes," agreed Franny, plucking a mini sandwich from an overloaded platter. "So very, very sad." Franny's gray hair was in a neat pageboy style, and she was wearing a black-and-white print dress, accented with a handsome string of pearls that Lucy suspected was the real deal.

"I never know what to say to the family at these things," confessed Lucy, hoping for guidance from an older, wiser woman. She was about to be disappointed, as Franny's attention was firmly fixed on the collation.

"Not nearly as nice as George Johansen's," observed Franny. "They had lobster rolls."

"The chicken salad looks good," said Lucy, reaching for one of the mini rolls. "With cranberries. I like it this way."

"The salad, Lucy," whispered Franny. "It's just lettuce, nothing else. And"—Franny paused, after surveying the drinks table—"there's no wine. Just coffee and tea."

"Well, this is a Baptist church," offered Lucy, in defense. "I don't think they approve of alcohol."

"Or much of anything else," snorted Franny. "They're big on disapproval." Having filled her plate, she moved on to one of the tables that had been set up in the hall.

Lucy followed, noticing the little bouquets of garden flowers on each table. Seating herself beside Franny, she speared a piece of bread-and-butter pickle. "Homemade," she said, with a nod of approval.

"They had Seafood Newburg at Audrey Winfield's memorial service," said Franny. "Those Episcopalians over in

Gilead do it up right. They had red and white wine and even a pitcher of Manhattans. In honor of Audrey. It was her favorite drink."

"My goodness," said Lucy, rather impressed. Or maybe not. Was it really appropriate to serve Manhattans at a memorial service?

"They called it a celebration of life," said Franny, answering her unspoken question.

"Well, then, I guess Manhattans were okay," said Lucy, as Emily Miller joined them, lowering herself with a huge sigh into a chair.

"My lumbago is acting up," she said, wincing as she reached for a fork. "Pretty paltry offering if you ask me," she said, digging into her potato salad. "Nothing like Audrey's."

Lucy couldn't help smiling. Emily was one of Miss Tilley's oldest and dearest friends, proof that she didn't tolerate any nonsense and always spoke her mind. Emily leaned forward, whispering, "Baptists! No fun at all."

"What do you know about them?" asked Lucy, hoping to tap into Emily's prodigious memory. "I was struck by the photos on the wall. There used to be a lot more members, and quite a few Blacks and Indians were in the early pictures of the congregation."

"The Baptists split into two parts, years ago. Now there's Black Baptists and White Baptists. Martin Luther King Junior and his father were Baptist preachers, you know."

"Why did they split?" asked Lucy.

"I don't know exactly what happened, but I suspect it was simply a parting of the ways," said Emily, moving on to a mini sandwich that she devoured in two bites. "As for this church, they're really down to just a handful of old folks." She shrugged her shoulders and smiled mischievously. "Like me."

"Are you a member?" asked Lucy, thinking that would be a surprising turn of events.

"Oh, no. I'm a nonbeliever. I don't believe in heaven or hell. Maybe there's a higher power, but if there is, he or she or whatever it is ought to start paying attention. Because, if you ask me, things are not going well. The planet's heating up, a lot of folks are misbehaving." She looked around, lighting on the dessert table. "Lucy dear, since my lumbago is acting up, would you mind bringing me some dessert?"

"Not at all," said Lucy. "What would you like?"

"Just a little bit of everything," said Emily.

On the drive home, Lucy smiled to herself, thinking of Emily Miller. She was so used to thinking of food as a temptation that needed to be strictly controlled so she wouldn't gain weight that she'd forgotten what a pleasure it could be. It was probably, she thought, one of the few pleasures that remained for someone as old as Emily. Good for her, thought Lucy, recalling the enjoyment with which Emily had tucked into her assortment of desserts, devouring a mini cream puff with special relish.

She was pulling into the driveway when she heard her phone's ring tone. She parked the car next to Bill's truck, and dug in her purse for the phone, which indicated the call was from Sara. "Hey, what's up?" she asked, climbing out of the SUV.

"News from the front," began Sara, as Lucy mounted the porch steps and seated herself in one of the rocking chairs. "Leanne and her buddies are under the impression that they're going to be bridesmaids."

Lucy was surprised by this turn of events, doubting that Zoe would have chosen them. "Did Zoe ask them?"

"No!" exclaimed Sara. "She wants me, Elizabeth, and

Molly, that's it. But now Leanne, Lexie, and Jenna think they're bridesmaids, too, which makes six. Zoe doesn't want that many, and frankly, she's not really all that close with any of them."

"She and Leanne were best friends. . . ."

"Until Leanne dropped her like a stone when she wanted to move into the fancy loft with Lexie and Jenna."

"She said things are different now that she's in the building, too."

"I'll say they're different. They've started a campaign. They've taken her out to lunch, they bombard her with texts and tweets, Jenna even stopped by at her office in the stadium with a latte. She doesn't even like lattes!"

"I know she's under a lot of stress with her new job," said Lucy.

"Yeah. So all this is the last thing she needs. It's driving her crazy. Like they're talking about colors and showing her pictures of dresses and suggesting certain players on the team for ushers. . . ."

"Oh, my," said Lucy, laughing.

"It's not funny. . . . Okay, it is funny," admitted Sara. "But it's really awkward. She's so busy, she has to keep putting them off, and the more she does that the harder they press."

Lucy sighed. "I'll talk to Taylor and ask her to call them off," said Lucy. "She can explain that Zoe just wants family, which is pretty reasonable. I would think her number one job is to keep the bride happy."

"You'd think so," replied Sara, sounding doubtful.

"So have you and Jodi been able to help Zoe with the planning?"

"Oh, yeah," exclaimed Sara, whose happy voice indicated she was smiling. "Zoe had an appointment at a bakery this morning, so we went in her place and tasted cake samples! Yummy!"

"What did you pick?"

"It was harder than you'd think to choose because we tried a lot of different kinds, but in the end we went with a traditional white cake, but with white chocolate and raspberry filling. It was close, we really loved the carrot cake, but that didn't seem right somehow."

"I think you made the right choice," said Lucy, thinking that Emily Miller wasn't alone in her love of sweets. "I better go and call Taylor before I chicken out."

When she ended the call a text message from Penny popped up and she decided to read it before calling Taylor. Penny had been pretty quiet so far and Lucy was curious about what was on her mind. It was bridesmaids, of course. The Wedding-Industrial Complex had been busy behind Zoe's and her back. Penny was thrilled about Zoe's decision to add Leanne, Jenna, and Lexie. **All such pretty girls, and fun, too,** read the message. **They're all so excited about supporting Zoe on her big day.**

Lucy decided she'd better take a moment to collect her thoughts, and began rocking her chair. Back and forth she went, taking deep breaths and gazing out over the driveway to the woods beyond. In the sky, an osprey was circling. Soon the fish hawk was joined by another and they seemed to be playing with each other, circling high in the sky. Lucy watched until they flew off in the direction of the cove, where they'd hunt for a dinner of fresh fish.

Feeling somewhat calmer and definitely more collected, Lucy decided to avoid speaking directly to Penny and Taylor and decided to message instead. "Zoe has chosen three bridesmaids, all family members, which is our tradition," she texted. This was stretching things a bit, but she thought it sounded good. "In keeping with that tradition her friends, Jenna, Leanne, and Lexie, will be invited to the wedding as guests and not as bridesmaids. Thanks for your understanding."

Duty done, Lucy checked her watch, learning it was only three o'clock. Oh, well, she thought, it's five o'clock somewhere, and it was a very warm day. She went inside, helped herself to one of Bill's beers, and grabbed the Sunday magazine. Heading out to the deck on the back of the house, she plucked a pencil from the vintage Dundee marmalade jar on the counter and went outside, where she settled herself in a cushioned lounge chair. That first sip of cold brew was delicious. She sighed and opened the magazine to the puzzle page. Hmmm, she thought, perusing the clues. "Angler's basket" caught her eye. Five letters. "Creel" she wrote, pleased to get off to a good start.

Chapter Sixteen

Lucy woke early on Monday morning and decided to take advantage of the early hour to get some work done when she had the office to herself. She was a bit behind on her assigned stories and hoped to knock off a couple before Phyllis, but more importantly Ted, arrived. Those plans went awry when she opened her computer and found an email from the state historian waiting for her. The historian had sent a short note, explaining that her request had caught her interest and she'd looked into it over the weekend. She went on to say that the badges in the picture Lucy had sent had not been issued by any state office but appeared to be the sort of insignia issued by local sheriffs to deputies. She noted that the state health department at that time relied on local physicians to mandate quarantines, condemn property, and enforce involuntary commitments, a practice that was discontinued because it was sometimes abused for personal motives. Moving on to the attachments, Lucy found an eye-opening collection of scholarly studies about the first decades of the twentieth century that concerned Ku Klux Klan activities in Maine, as well as several accounts of the tar and feathering of

Black individuals. Much of this activity, according to one article included in the attachments, was in response to the growing labor movement and the flu epidemic of 1919, as well as the influx of Southern Blacks moving North as well as foreign immigration. "Whites feared the loss of jobs and status," explained the author, who was a professor at the University of Maine.

Somewhat shocked and disturbed, Lucy shelved her plan to write up her interview with Samantha and decided to look through the old papers collected in the morgue, wondering if this sort of activity had surfaced in Tinker's Cove. And if so, was the Pine Tree takeover part of this nativist movement? She started with the issues dating from 1912 but didn't find any reference to Pine Tree at all. When she reached 1929 she noticed a laudatory front page obituary for Dr. Thomas E. Logue. Reading further she learned that in addition to being an "esteemed local citizen" he was a partner in Logue Logging and a proponent of eugenics who believed in the superiority of European bloodlines. But what really captured her interest was the photo of Dr. Logue, who strongly resembled one of the badge-wearing figures in the picture taken during the Pine Tree takeover. Fearing she was jumping to conclusions, she carefully compared the two photographs. There was no doubt at all. Dr. Logue and the man in wire-rimmed glasses were one and the same. Dr. Logue had participated in the takeover of Pine Tree, an action that would have most certainly benefited his family and himself.

"Yoo-hoo," called Phyllis, announcing her arrival. "You're here early," she observed, peeking into the morgue. In honor of Pride month Phyllis had added a rainbow-striped tee over her black leggings and bright pink Crocs.

"Look at this," said Lucy, pointing to the photos. "The

state didn't take Pine Tree, it was this guy, Dr. Thomas Logue and his buddies. They put on deputy sheriff badges and stuck up some phony official notices, convincing everyone that they had to move so they could grab the land for Logue Logging."

"I think you may be jumping to conclusions," said Phyllis. "Ted isn't going to like this. Logue Log Homes is a big advertiser."

"What aren't I going to like?" asked Ted, appearing behind Phyllis. "Nice outfit, Phyllis," he added, with an approving nod.

"I just thought since Sara's come out, it would be nice to show some support."

"Much appreciated," said Lucy, with a smile. "Thanks."

"So what have you discovered that I'm not going to like?" asked Ted.

Lucy explained the email from the state historian and showed him the photos identifying Dr. Logue as one of the phony health inspectors, stressing the word *phony*.

"But, Lucy, if local doctors were empowered to enforce health regulations, isn't it possible he was acting legally?" asked Ted.

Lucy chewed her lip. "It's still a clear conflict of interest if he abused that power in order to grab that land for Logue Logging. Remember, it included a stand of old-growth pine that they immediately cut down."

Ted looked over her shoulder, reading the obituary, and studying the photos. "I wonder who these other guys are," he said.

"I can try to find out," said Lucy, sounding hopeful.

"How are you doing on that Rotary Club kid?" he asked.

"I'm almost done," said Lucy, which was a huge exaggeration. "I'll finish it up and then how about I do an investigative report on Pine Tree?"

"I don't know," began Ted, only to be interrupted by Lucy.

"C'mon, Ted. This could be big. It's got corporate greed, White nationalism, corrupt officials. What's not to love?"

"It's old news," he protested. "Who's gonna care?"

"That's good, right. The bad guys are all dead, and I can write the story in a way that shows we've come a long way since these bad things happened. We don't tar and feather people anymore."

"Tar and feather?" asked Ted.

"Yeah." Lucy trotted over to her desk and showed him the story on her computer, which included a photo of two young Black men, stripped and covered with feathers.

"This happened in Maine?" asked Phyllis, incredulously.

"Yup," said Lucy. "Little known history, but the Ku Klux Klan was active back then right here in Maine. However, they used hot molasses instead of tar, which was a nice local touch. And this Logue guy, he was a big proponent of eugenics, which is a nice word for racism. They considered Whites superior to everybody else."

"Okay, Lucy," said Ted, wavering, "see what you can dig up. But I get final say on what gets printed. We don't want to ruffle anybody's feathers." He winced, glancing at the photo on the computer screen. "My bad. Bad choice of words. But first, I want that feel-good Rotary Club story. ASAP."

"You got it, boss."

Lucy put some extra effort into the story, including calling the local Rotary Club president, Mallory Monaco, who simply couldn't stop talking about the amazing Samantha. "She's gorgeous and smart and got into every Ivy that she applied to! Talk about girl power!" Confident that Ted would be impressed by the feel-goodness of the story, she moved on to investigating the story she really wanted to write about Pine Tree.

She spent much of the afternoon in the morgue, closely reading the papers from the early 1900s, where she found accounts of speeches that Dr. Logue delivered on the subject of eugenics and the supposed superiority of northern European bloodlines. While Dr. Logue had plenty to say on those subjects, he didn't have anything at all to say about the Pine Tree takeover, which puzzled her until she discovered that Dr. Logue was actually the publisher of the paper at that time. There were, however, a few telling references to the "recent improvements" in town, which she took to be a coded reference to the takeover, and there was a front-page story about the financial benefits that newly established Logue Logging would bring to the town. The story named the company's management team and she noted the names down, suspecting the other "inspectors" might be among them.

She then began poking around on the internet, beginning with Google and moving on to the state and university websites. Local Winchester College had a treasure trove of photos that included images of Pine Tree and its residents, most often depicting family groups. There were shots of smiling folks piled into a two-seated wood glider, a young kid proudly showing off a prize-winning heifer, two girls standing arm in arm with Gibson girl hairdos and shirts with billowing leg-of-mutton sleeves. Some were pictured on the porches of their houses, which appeared to be modest but well-kept clapboard affairs. All, of course, were Black or Indian, and some seemed to be mixed race. Taken together, the photos presented a fairly typical working-class community of the time; she had an old family album herself that included similar pictures.

Armed with the information she'd gathered, she put together a rough first draft that included areas she needed to research further, such as finding photos of the Logue company executives, two of whom she suspected were among the deputies who condemned the village. Looking it over, she thought she was off to a good start, and presented it to Ted. She watched closely as he studied it, noting that he seemed to be nodding along in approval. When he finished reading he handed it back to her with a smile.

"This is really promising, Lucy. Good work. Of course, you've got to get a reaction from Zebulon Logue," he told her. "It's his business and he clearly benefited from his ancestor's behavior." Ted paused. "It seems that what Dr. Logue did was actually legal, although perhaps immoral. It's a murky area. Looking back, it seems quite corrupt, but it's not clear that people at the time thought of it that way."

"Something's been worrying me," confessed Lucy, thinking of the growing animosity toward Skye in the town. "If Skye knew about this, some folks might think it was a motive for killing Hetty. I don't want to give the prosecution, or anybody else, ammo against him."

"Good point, Lucy. I'll clear it with Bob Goodman, you get a reaction from Logue. Then we'll reassess. Fair enough?"

Lucy nodded, feeling the weight of the story. People were going to react, it was going to touch sensitive nerves, and she wanted to be on solid ground and absolutely sure of her facts when it ran. Back at her desk, she took a deep breath and called Zebulon Logue.

"Mr. Logue, this is Lucy Stone at the *Courier.*"

"Ah, Lucy, nice to hear from you. I've been meaning to call and tell you what a wonderful daughter you have. It's thanks to her that I've reconnected with my daughter and gotten to know my grandson, Chad."

Lucy was taken a bit off guard. This was completely unexpected. "Well, I think that's really due to Chad," she said. "He was the one who wanted to reach out to you."

"But it was the engagement, starting a family with Zoe, that gave him the idea." He paused. "And I have to say it's been a real blessing at my advanced age. It takes a load off my shoulders and I'm feeling quite positive about my family's future."

Okay, thought Lucy, here was her opening. "That's wonderful, but I'm actually calling you about the past. I'm working on a story about Pine Tree. Does that ring any bells?"

"Can't say it does."

"Well, it was a little village in the town of Tinker's Cove, populated by Blacks and Indians. It was razed back in 1913. . . ."

"My, that was a long time ago."

"Yeah. The thing is, your company stands on the very land that used to be Pine Tree, and it was taken over under the direction of your ancestor Dr. Thomas Logue. All the people, the residents, were ordered to leave, their homes were bulldozed, and the land became the property of Logue Logging."

"That's all news to me, and it took place long before my time," observed Zebulon. "I only know about Dr. Logue from a painting in the company office, and I have to say he's always struck me as a rather tough-looking character."

"Well, it's kind of murky. Dr. Logue had the power to determine if the village was a public health risk."

"Was there evidence of that? Some sort of typhus outbreak or TB?"

"Not that I can find."

"And you've been researching all this so you can write about it for the paper?"

"We're considering it. We wanted to get your reaction first."

There was a pause and Lucy waited with bated breath. Finally, Zebulon spoke. "I don't know that I have a reaction. The past is past. Dr. Logue died long before I was born, and the company's been out of the logging business for nearly a century. Nowadays we buy logs from other outfits in the northern part of the state and make log homes for folks. I'll be interested to read your story. I'm a bit of a history buff and I enjoy learning about the past."

Lucy let out a big sigh of relief. "Can I quote you on that?"

"Absolutely."

"Thank you, it's been lovely talking to you."

"Same here. And I look forward to meeting you."

"See you at the wedding," said Lucy, ending the call.

"So?" asked Ted, who'd been listening in. "What did the old coot say?"

"He said he'd be interested to read the story because he's a bit of a history buff and enjoys learning about the past."

"Okey-dokey, then," said Ted. "I checked with Bob Goodman and he just learned today that all charges have been dropped against Skye."

Lucy couldn't quite believe what she was hearing. If this was true, it was wonderful news, but hard to understand. One minute Skye was the prime suspect, the next he was innocent? "What happened?" she asked.

"That's for you to find out, Lucy. You're the investigative reporter around here."

"Right, boss," said Lucy, once again reaching for her phone and calling the DA.

Phil Aucoin was in a meeting, which Lucy figured was his way of ducking awkward questions from the press. His secretary promised to send a press release as soon as it was ready.

Stymied for the moment, she put in a call to Officer Sally Kirwan, at the Tinker's Cove Police Department, who had become a reliable source. Sally wasn't as tight-lipped as other members of the department. She was pretty much Teflon-coated since her uncle was police chief Jim Kirwan, and Officer Todd Kirwan was a cousin. While those two most likely disapproved of Sally's willingness to share department information with Lucy, they were answerable to the family matriarch, Dot Kirwan, and Sally was her favorite grandchild.

Lucy was well aware that Sally was playing a long game, and had her eye on becoming the town's first female police chief, after Uncle Jim retired, of course. As much as Lucy considered Sally a valuable source, she knew their relationship was a two-way street. She was courting Lucy, keeping her close, in the expectation of positive press coverage. To that end, Sally had given Lucy her cell phone number and that's the number she called.

"Hey, Lucy, what's up?" asked Sally, sounding upbeat.

"Big news. The DA's dropping all charges against Skye Sykes. Do you happen to know anything about this?"

"News to me, Lucy. What does Aucoin have to say?"

"Nada. He's in a meeting. They're putting out a press release later in the day."

"Don't quote me on this, it's completely off the record," began Sally, in typical fashion, "but I bet it's because of this new video that turned up. It's from Liz Brogan—you know she has the home day care right opposite the Pratt house. She's really into video, has a fancy surveillance system and doesn't open the door to anyone who's not authorized. It's for the kids' safety, you know, what with all the craziness these days."

"Have you seen the video?"

"No. But I know it was sent to the DA."

"Interesting," said Lucy. "I wonder if she'll talk about what she saw."

"Don't tell her I gave you her name," cautioned Sally. "You could just say you've been wondering if she noticed anything, since she lives right across the street. Okay?"

"You got it, Sally. Thanks."

Liz Brogan was home, she was always home due to the nature of her business, and she was pleased to get a call from Lucy. "An adult, you're an adult, right? I haven't had much adult conversation lately."

Lucy chuckled in response. "I remember those days. I'd talk to anyone, the mailman, the guy delivering oil, the water meter reader."

"I do see the parents," admitted Liz, "but they're always in a rush. They don't even want to know if Ella peed her pants or Ryan ate his lunch."

"Well, I don't care about that, either, but I do wonder if you saw anything suspicious at the Pratt house the day Hetty was murdered."

"Hey, that was really something, right? But I was completely unaware. That weekend I had Kayla and Nicholas because their mom is a nurse and gets different shifts, and those two keep me real busy. Nicholas is three and can be a handful and Kayla was fretful, she's teething. Thank goodness I've only got one baby right now."

"I wonder, do you have any sort of video camera? It

would make sense, considering how you're responsible for the little guys."

"Oh, that. Yeah. I swear I'm regressing, getting dumber by the minute. I did have a problem with my doorbell camera, I had to update the feed. It's complicated, but the video gets stored on my computer, and I don't know what exactly was wrong, but when the guy came to fix it, I happened to notice I actually had footage from the day of that awful murder. I was just curious, you know, and I took a look. It wasn't terribly clear, kind of fuzzy, but I definitely saw a figure going into the Pratt house, a guy, but that's about all I could make out. He went in and left about five minutes later, and then that Indian guy came. I did recognize him from the day of the protest 'cause he's got that long hair. He stood on the steps, he rang the bell, after a few minutes he kinda put his hands around his eyes to look in, he rang again and waited a bit, then he left. He never went in."

"Goodness. I'm sure the police would be interested in something like that. You might have video of the killer, you know."

"I know. It makes me sick, just to think about poor Hetty. I thought the police ought to see it, so I asked the repair guy to put it on a thumb drive and I took it to them. I don't know what happened after that, but I hope it helps them catch that guy."

"Me too," said Lucy. "This is news, Liz. Is it okay if I put your name in the paper?"

"Oh, gosh. No! I don't want my name connected to any murder. No way. It would ruin my business. People wouldn't trust me with their kids."

"I understand," said Lucy. "You're officially an anonymous source."

"That's me. Anonymous."

"You did the right thing, Anonymous. You've probably saved an innocent man from a possible murder conviction and maybe even helped them find the killer."

"All in a day's work for Wonder Woman." She laughed. "I'll go put my crown on. The kids love it when I wear my crown and golden cuffs." She paused. "But it's really for me. Makes me feel like I can make it until three-thirty when Kayla's mom picks her up."

"Well, thanks again. Have a great day."

Lucy wrote up the story, citing "possible new video evidence that cleared Skye Sykes," and Ted posted it immediately on the online edition as breaking news.

"It's a scoop, Lucy. We got it before anyone," he chortled, pleased as punch. He pushed himself away from his desk and stood up, stretching. "Well, I think I'll head over to Gilead," he said, slapping a cap on his head and marching out the door. Lucy immediately decided to take advantage of the moment to follow up on her investigation of Pine Tree and slipped away from her desk into the morgue.

There she searched for obituaries of the other members of the Logue management team, which included VP Frederick Andrews, Treasurer William Snowdon, and Secretary Zachary Barker. Only one was accompanied by a photograph, but Frederick Andrews was shown with a most impressive mustache. So she'd found a second "inspector" who was connected to Logue Logging. In one last desperate move, she Googled both of the other men. Much to her surprise, good old Google produced a photo of Zachary Barker, pictured with his fraternity buddies in the class of '02. The photo had been included as part of a look backward in a recent online issue of the *Harvard Crimson*.

Lucy dug out her magnifying glass and compared frat

brother Zach with suspected "inspector" Zach and was pleased to see they appeared to be one and the same. Then, realizing she'd been overlooking the obvious, she pulled up the Logue Log Homes website. There, in grainy black-and-white, she found all four of the original principals of Logue Logging, posed stiffly at a ribbon cutting, and three of the four could be matched to the photo she had of the health inspectors. Considering their ties to Logue Logging, it seemed clear proof that those men had conducted what she believed was essentially a land grab using their powers as deputy sheriffs to condemn the homes in Pine Tree, determining them all to be threats to public health.

Lucy spent all of Tuesday working on the story, fact-checking every point, and fussing over the wording to eliminate any hint of bias. It wasn't her job to write a sermon; she was simply reporting the facts as she'd found them. What she didn't know was whether or not Hetty had made the same discovery, and if that knowledge had precipitated her murder. She had her suspicions, for sure, but kept them to herself. Finally satisfied with her work, she sent the story to Ted and anxiously awaited his response. After an hour or so of suspense, he called to congratulate her on her good work but said he wanted to "sleep on it" before deciding whether or not to run it.

On Wednesday morning, when Lucy was frantically pounding away on other stories in order to make the noon deadline, he finally came to a decision and told her the story was a go and he was going to put it on the front page. She was pleased, but also nervous about how readers would react. Some would be interested by this look at the past, but others might feel uncomfortable, or even threatened by their ancestors' behavior. Denial would be a natural response, and some would no doubt be angry. She suspected it was going to be a tough couple of days until some new story caught readers' attention. The one thing that comforted her was Zebulon Logue's reaction. He was the person most involved and he'd offered no objection whatever.

All that changed on Thursday, when the paper came out. The phone was ringing off the hook, angry emails were flooding in, advertisers were threatening to pull their ads and readers were canceling their subscriptions. Worst of all, Zebulon Logue had called and had a long talk with Ted, informing him that he had been advised by legal counsel to consider a lawsuit.

To his credit, Ted seemed to be taking it all in stride. "No such thing as bad publicity," he declared, humming a little tune to himself. "People are talking about the *Courier.* We're not just reporting news, we're making it. What seems to bother most people is the way the story ran right next to the one about charges being dropped against Skye Sykes. People seem to think the two are related, like Skye was simply charged because he's Indian. One lady got all huffy, she actually said, 'There's a clear implication that this sort of thing still happens.' "

Lucy found herself chuckling. "But racial bias certainly does still exist," she said.

"Maybe in those other parts of the country, but definitely not in Maine," said Phyllis, her voice dripping with irony.

That got Ted laughing, too. "That's classic. It's not us, it's them."

Lucy had fallen silent, worrying. She knew her story was factual, so she didn't fear Zebulon Logue's threat of a lawsuit, and she knew that readers and advertisers tended to bark rather than bite. What bothered her was her suspicion that the Pine Tree takeover could very well be the "something incredible" behind Hetty's murder. She could have been killed because somebody wanted very badly to keep it quiet. What would that person do now that it was out in the open?

Chapter Seventeen

Lucy was still fretting about possible repercussions to the story when she left work that afternoon and stopped at Macdonald's farm stand to buy a box of their home-grown strawberries. They were insanely expensive, but she justified the cost by comparing the sun-ripened and bursting with flavor goodness of the locally grown berries with their pale counterparts on sale in the IGA. There was really no comparison, she thought, lifting a box of Macdonald's berries and inhaling their flowery fragrance; she could practically taste them. And what better way to enjoy them, she decided, but with some of Macdonald's fabulous cream, fresh from the cow and sold in adorable little glass bottles. Expensive? You bet! But it was only once a year. . . .

She was heading to the checkout, thinking that she might need a second mortgage, when who should she meet but Penny and Nate Nettleton. Right, she thought, belatedly remembering that they had rented a place for the summer, a VRBO, somewhere in town. "Why, hi there, Lucy," said Penny, delivering air kisses on either side of her face. "Those strawberries are sooo delicious, aren't they,

Nate? Why he ate a whole box yesterday, naughty boy! Didn't leave a single one for me! So today, these are all mine. I'm going to dip them in white chocolate and make him watch me eat them!"

Lucy didn't quite know what to say, so she gave Nate a smile. "And you're all right with that?" she asked, in a light tone of voice.

"Whatever Penny wants," he said, smiling back. "I didn't know she was saving them, you know. I saw them on the counter and ate one and then another and before I knew what I'd done, they were gone."

"They are a real treat," agreed Lucy. "Are you enjoying your summer so far?"

"I'm only here for weekends," said Nate. "Long weekends, and I fly in to make the most of my time, but I've got to tend to business back home. Penny's having a good time, though, what with the wedding plans and all."

Oh, no, thought Lucy. Time to beat a retreat. But the line at the counter was moving slowly, if at all. She was trapped, and Penny wasted no time before launching the inevitable attack.

"Oh, Lucy," she began, in an *isn't it a shame* tone of voice, "poor Leanne is so upset. And Lexie and Jenna simply don't know what to think. Why doesn't Zoe want them? They're all such good friends, and six is not a large number. Not really. So much more fun for them all, and Chad tells me that all the boys on the team want to be ushers."

"Zoe doesn't like a lot of fuss," said Lucy. "She likes to keep things simple, and I think she wants to be with Molly and her sisters, girls she's really comfortable with."

"Oh, my, it's not as if Leanne and her roommates are difficult. They're lovely girls and they're so eager to support Zoe on her big day."

What was going on with this line? Something about a credit card that was declined? Really? Lucy was running out of patience and it showed in her tone of voice. "It's Zoe's wedding after all and she knows what she wants," she said, a bit snappishly.

"Well, as much as I simply adore that daughter of yours, it's not really all about her, now is it?" countered Penny. "A wedding is a social event, and it reflects upon both of our families. And I would be so mortified if it seemed, well, cheap. Nate and I want to let the whole world know how proud we are of our Chad and his beautiful little bride."

So now, thought Lucy, it was Chad's big day and Zoe was his *little bride*. Well, of course, he was the groom, but weddings were really all about the bride. The groom just had to show up and smile. And, last she knew, the groom's mother was supposed to wear beige and keep her mouth shut. Fearing that she was close to losing her temper, Lucy checked her watch. "Oh, my! Is that the time? I really have to get moving. I'm just going to put these things back. . . ."

"What a shame! And, oh, look, the line is finally moving!"

So it was. "Oh, good," said Lucy, resigned to her fate. "Bill does love these strawberries."

"I'm so happy we had this little talk," said Penny. "It's best to get these little kerfuffles out in the open. I'm sure if you explain things to Zoe, she'll reconsider."

"You don't know Zoe like I do," responded Lucy, attempting a little joke.

"Well, what I know," began Nate, in an end-of-the-matter CEO tone, "is that I'm footing the bill and I say my Penny should have as many bridesmaids as she wants."

Okay, thought Lucy. Have it your way. "Well, in that case, Penny, you have a voice and a phone. Perhaps you ought to talk to Zoe." She glanced at her watch again. "I really have to go," she added, turning and carefully replacing the box of berries in the display and returning the cream to the refrigerator case. It was a small price to pay, she decided, to escape Penny, and worse, Nate.

Lucy was still fuming about her encounter with the Nettletons as she drove home without her strawberries. Sacrificing the strawberries in order to escape the pair was bad enough, but she felt worse about siccing Penny on Zoe. It wasn't as if Zoe didn't have enough on her plate and now she'd have to deal with Penny's fake charm. Lucy could just imagine how Penny would tell Zoe she was only thinking of what was best for her when she was actually undermining her. She was jolted out of this train of thought when she turned a corner and spotted a police cruiser ahead with its blue lights flashing. She immediately slowed down as she passed, looking to see who the cop had pulled over. She wasn't actually all that surprised when she recognized Chris's sporty little convertible, with him at the wheel. About time, was her thought, remembering the roar of the engine when he'd zoomed away from the shower.

As soon as she got home she got on the phone to Zoe, to warn her about incoming missiles from Penny. Zoe reacted to the news by bursting into tears. Horrified, Lucy hastened to reassure her daughter that she could handle whatever Penny dished out. "But it's not only Penny," wailed Zoe. "I'm really at the end of my rope. It's just constant pressure. There's no break. I'm bringing work home every night, the emails alone take up hours. And then the girls will drop by, Leanne and her roommates, wanting to talk about the wedding. Taylor calls at all hours, with ideas and suggestions, demanding decisions. Everything is a crisis with her, it's now or never, she needs a decision right away. And Penny, she's the worst. Honestly, if I hear that voice with her phony Southern accent one more time I'm going to jump out the window. It's like somebody told her you catch more flies with honey than vinegar so she couches the craziest stuff in this sickly sweet, cloying tone of voice." She took a long, quavering breath. "Honest, I'm this close to calling the whole thing off."

"What about Chad? What does he think?"

"Oh, Chad." Zoe let out a long sigh. "Nothing seems to bother him; he thinks everything is great."

"Have you told him how stressed you are?" asked Lucy.

"Actually, he's the one causing the most stress, because when I tell him I've got so much work to do he just takes the papers away and starts kissing me, and before I know it I've lost an hour I could've been working and I'm more behind than ever."

Lucy smiled. "Well, he's got a point. You've got to take care of your relationship with him. That's number one."

"I know, Mom." Zoe began sniffling again. "Honest, I don't know why he puts up with me. I'm such a mess."

Alarmed, Lucy was quick to reassure her daughter. "You're not a mess, Zoe. You're strong and beautiful and loving and he's lucky to have you."

"I wish I could believe that," said Zoe. Lucy heard voices in the background. "Hey, he's back with the laundry. I gotta go."

Somewhat reassured—after all, Chad had apparently done the laundry—Lucy sat at the kitchen table and stared out the window, thinking. Then, acting on impulse, she called Sara.

"I just spoke with Zoe," she began. "I'm really worried about her. What do you think?"

"I'm glad you called," replied Sara. "Mom, she's fading

away. She's losing weight, and she's got these dark circles under her eyes." She paused. "I think she's losing her hair."

"Ohmigod," exclaimed Lucy. "Are you sure?"

"Yeah. I was over there last weekend and I was shocked. Jodi too. We're trying to think what to do. Like stage an intervention and drag her off somewhere. Jodi's looking into this yoga place in the Berkshires. But I think Zoe'd throw a fit if we suggested a getaway, she's so into her work. But I kinda think the problem isn't so much the job as her. I think she's so distracted and panicked she can't think straight and get control of things. It seems to me she just goes over and over the same stuff, she never gets it done."

"I'll check with Rachel," said Lucy. "Maybe she'll have some ideas."

"That's a good idea, Mom. Make sure she knows how serious the situation is. I'm really worried about Zoe."

Rachel didn't hesitate for a second when Lucy called; she immediately called for a meeting of the four friends, suggesting they meet for pizza at Four Brothers. Husbands would simply have to fend for themselves and eat whatever they could find in their respective refrigerators for dinner. In Bill's case, Lucy suspected, it would be beer and a meatloaf sandwich.

When Lucy arrived at Four Brothers, which was an upscale pizzeria that offered wine and beer and even had an outside terrace overlooking the parking lot, she found her three friends were already there. Pizzas had been ordered and they were sharing a bottle of Chianti, sitting at an old-fashioned wood picnic table with attached benches.

"Thanks for doing this," said Lucy, sinking into the vacant spot beside Sue on one of the benches. "Zoe's close to having a nervous breakdown. Sara says she's losing weight and her hair's falling out."

"Not as unusual as you might think," said Rachel, patting Lucy's hand. "Stress can take a toll on your body as well as your mind."

"It's her mind, too. She can't seem to concentrate, goes over and over the same things."

"What's at the root of it?" asked Pam. "It can't be the wedding. Weddings are fun."

"The wedding's definitely part of it," said Lucy.

"Yeah, a wedding is fun if it's what you want, but it sounds like Zoe is being forced into a dog-and-pony show that she really doesn't want," suggested Sue.

"Exactly," chimed in Lucy. "She never made any bones about it, right from the start. She wanted to keep the engagement a secret. They were going to go slow, enjoy getting to know each other. It doesn't seem like she feels ready for marriage. She wants to focus on her new job. She's so proud of her promotion and really wants to impress her boss. All this wedding stuff is a nonstop distraction. She says she's constantly bombarded with questions and demands from girlfriends, from Taylor, and worst of all, Penny."

A server arrived with a huge pizza, Sue ordered another bottle of Chianti, and they all turned their attention to the pie. After they'd each finished one piece, and were started on a second, Rachel floated an idea.

"What if we got everyone together to work out a win-win solution," she suggested. "An intervention."

"Everyone?" asked Sue. "All together? Sounds like a giant cat fight."

"More like ripping off a Band-Aid," said Rachel. "Get everything out in the open. Let them all understand what they're doing to Zoe."

"It sounds crazy," said Lucy, putting down her half-eaten slice on a paper plate. "But we're at a point where I don't think it could possibly make things worse and might, maybe, make things better."

"What do you have in mind, Rachel?" asked Pam. "A sort of encounter session?"

"Sort of," said Rachel, speaking slowly. "A casual gathering, like a social event, a tea, maybe. And I could steer things, be a facilitator. Let them know, either from Zoe herself, or from you, Lucy, or Sara, what's actually going on. Then ask them for some solutions."

"We're never going to get them to agree to an encounter group," scoffed Pam. "I mean, Penny is such a hypocrite. There's not a genuine bone in her body."

"That's just the Southern accent. . . ." began Sue.

"My point exactly," declared Pam. "She grew up right here in Maine. How did she get a Southern accent?"

"We can fake her out," said Sue, with a mischievous gleam in her eye. "Like Rachel suggested, we'll have a champagne luncheon. I'll host—after all they robbed me of the shower I wanted to give. And Penny's such a social creature, she'll be the first to accept, and she'll make sure the others will fall in line."

"I think it's a great idea," said Lucy, buoyed by her friends' concern. "But it's got to be soon, before Zoe completely collapses."

"A point well taken," said Pam, who had fresh memories of her son Tim's recent emotional breakdown.

"We can do it the weekend after next," said Sue. "I'll send out evites tomorrow. They have some really cute ones, and people RSVP online, so we'll know who's coming."

"Wow, I feel so much better," confessed Lucy, who had indeed felt a load taken off her shoulders. "Want to pass that bottle?"

* * *

When Lucy arrived at the office on Monday, she'd already heard from Sue that all the invitees had accepted her invitation to the champagne luncheon. Lucy had immediately shared the plan with Sara, and Sara had convinced Zoe to come. They were going to work on a statement together that Zoe would present, if she felt up to it. If not, Sara would do the talking for her.

With that item ticked off on her mental agenda, Lucy settled down at her desk and powered up her computer, ready to get to work. Phyllis was just coming in, togged out in red, white, and blue for the approaching July Fourth holiday, when the computer finally delivered Lucy's email. The week's police log was top of the list and Lucy opened it up.

Right on top was Christopher Logue Taylor, Chad's half brother, for a traffic stop. It was really none of her business, she told herself, moving on to the rest of the list. It included the usual assortment of suspicious activity reports, 911 requests for emergency assistance, traffic stops, and numerous OUIs.

Satisfied there weren't any leads that indicated follow-ups for possible stories, Lucy opened up the file containing the week's story budget. It was not inspiring: selectboard meeting, planning board meeting, tourism update, and a feature on a Revolutionary War battle reenactment. Notably absent was any mention whatsoever of the investigation into Hetty's death. That seemed to Lucy to be a good place to start, so she called Officer Sally.

"Hey, Sally," she began, "now that Skye's no longer a suspect, I wonder if there are any new developments in the investigation."

"I've been waiting for your call, Lucy," teased Sally. "There's been quite a lot, thanks to your story."

"Which story?" asked Lucy, puzzled.

"The Pine Tree story."

"What's that got to do with Hetty's murder?"

"This is absolutely off the record, Lucy, but they're looking at Chris Taylor."

"Chris?"

"Yeah. He was involved in a traffic stop and when the officer reviewed his bodycam he thought he noticed a resemblance to the guy in that video I told you about. He's Zeb Logue's grandson, you see, and as it happens, Franny Small came in and claimed that some documents have been stolen from the historical society's collection, including a first-person account of the Pine Tree takeover. The thinking is that Hetty caught Chris stealing the documents. . . ."

"But I spoke to Zeb about the story before we printed it. He'd never heard of Pine Tree. He told me to go ahead and publish it."

"So he said, but maybe he wasn't worried because Chris had grabbed the evidence."

"No, he would have known I already had the information and was naming names, including his grandfather."

"Well, he may have changed his mind. Or maybe the kid thought he was doing his grandpa a big favor. Logue's hired a bunch of big-shot Boston lawyers to defend him."

Lucy's immediate thought was that this was a big, a huge story. But Sally had insisted it was off the record. "So there's nothing official yet?" she asked. "No charges against Chris?"

"They've interviewed him, but thanks to the lawyers it was pretty much a dud. They wouldn't let him answer any questions and they've whisked him off into rehab."

"What about the video evidence?"

"Not conclusive. There's apparently a lot of sun glare,

and it kind of distorts the image. It's a person, that's about all they can make out."

Lucy was discouraged. In her mind there was nothing worse than having a story she couldn't use. "Well, keep me posted," she pleaded.

"Will do," promised Sally. Fat lot of good it would do her, thought Lucy, ending the call and immediately getting another.

This time it was Ted, calling from the paper's office in Gideon with bad news. "Sorry to tell you this, Lucy, but Zebulon Logue is threatening to sue us for defamation. Says the story slanders his family and business and he wants to see the evidence you based it on."

"It's because the police are investigating his grandson for the murder," said Lucy, explaining the stolen documents as a possible motive.

"That's a hell of a story, Lucy," he exclaimed. "Write it up!"

"I can't," wailed Lucy. "I got it off the record."

Ted's reaction was succinct. "Damn."

Chapter Eighteen

There was more than one way to skin a cat, thought Lucy, putting on her thinking cap. She couldn't quote Sally about the missing documents that investigators believed linked Chris to Hetty's murder, but she could ask Franny about them. Once she had that information, she realized, she could call Aucoin for an update on the investigation. She had to cover the selectboard meeting later that morning anyway, and she could chat with Franny afterward.

The selectboard met in the town hall's basement meeting room, which was a rather grim affair with concrete block walls painted a sickly shade of green, gray linoleum tiles on the floor, and folding metal chairs that were notable for being remarkably uncomfortable. A long table set on a dais awaited the five selectboard members who would sit behind plaques with their names. Franny's plaque was front and center, flanked on one side by those identifying long-time member and IGA owner Tony Marzetti and banker Bert Cogswell. On her other side were former chairperson Howard Wilcox and the board's newest member, Zach Starr. Zach, a biker who owned a controversial vape shop, had taken advantage of the fact that no one else had stepped forward to run for an open seat and filed papers. There had been much concern among the old guard, but they couldn't find a willing candidate, so Zach was elected with a mere eleven votes, which was a new low.

Selectboard meetings were not well attended and when Lucy entered the rather dank and chilly room she found only Natalie Withers, the town's self-appointed watchdog, sitting there. The meetings were televised on the local cable station, so presumably Natalie Withers was not the only citizen who was keeping a critical eye on the board's behavior. Lucy decided to sit beside her, just in case Natalie had discovered something going on in town hall that deserved further investigation.

"I wonder if that Zach Starr will even show up," hissed Natalie, by way of greeting. "It's an absolute scandal, elected by eleven votes."

"He ran unopposed, Natalie. You could have put your papers in. You would have beat him. Your dog would have beat him."

"If I only had the time," said Natalie, who Lucy knew was retired. "Everybody thinks you've got time on your hands when you retire, but I've found I'm busier than ever."

"Ah, here they come," said Lucy, as the board members filed in.

Spotting Zach, Natalie fumed. "Look at that, he's wearing a Hell's Angels T-shirt."

"He only does it to annoy people," said Lucy, who knew that Zach was really a mild-mannered fellow who cooked up oatmeal overnight in a slow cooker for his breakfast. It was that oatmeal, he swore, that gave him the energy he needed to roar around town on his huge Harley.

"I'm calling the meeting to order," declared Franny, with a tap of her gavel. And they were off, debating the taking of a private road, approval of emergency funding for a leaky water main, and opening discussion of the renewal of the cable TV company's annual license. That last item got Natalie's attention.

"If you don't mind, I'd like to say something," she said, raising her hand.

"If the board has no objection," said Franny, receiving none. "You may proceed, Natalie."

Natalie stood up and began reciting a long list of complaints that included unreliable service, exorbitant rates, and damage to children's developing minds. When she ran out of steam and sat down, Zach called the question, which was unanimously approved by the board.

The meeting was adjourned, but Natalie wasn't through. She was determined to convince Lucy that an investigation of the cable company was urgently required. Seeing Franny slipping away, Lucy quickly disengaged and followed her, catching up to her on the stairs.

"Franny, have you got a sec?"

"Sure, Lucy." She turned, halfway up. "What's on your mind?"

"I understand you've discovered some of the historical society's papers are missing. Can you tell me about that?"

"Well, it was Lydia who made the discovery when they took the crime scene tape down and she could get inside. It seems that Hetty had completed a pretty thorough inventory of everything they had back to 1900, and when Lydia compared the actual documents to the inventory, she discovered that everything related to Pine Tree was missing."

"Was there a lot?" asked Lucy.

"I'm not sure. You'd have to ask her."

"I'll do that," said Lucy. "Thanks."

Now that she had the confirmation she needed, Lucy decided to confront the DA in his office since her last few attempts to contact him by phone hadn't been successful. She knew he usually kept his office door open, the better to keep an eye on his receptionist and the comings and goings of the assistant DAs, so there was a good chance she could catch him in situ.

As it happened, Aucoin was just returning from court when she arrived in his office, and in addition was pleased as punch with whatever had taken place there. "C'mon in, Lucy," he said, with an expansive gesture. "I understand you may be facing a defamation suit from Zeb Logue, that's if the scuttlebutt is correct."

"No fears on that count," said Lucy, voicing confidence she didn't actually feel and giving his receptionist, Betsy Barker, a big smile as she followed him into his office. "You know what they say: If it's true, you can't sue, and my story was based on solid research." She sat down in the visitor's chair and waited for him to take his seat behind his very large desk.

Phil propped his elbows on his desk and tented his hands. Looking over his fingers, he asked, "So what brings you here today, Lucy?"

"Just doing a little follow-up on the investigation of Hetty Furness's murder," she said. "Do you have a new suspect now that charges against Skye Sykes have been dropped?"

"Well, Lucy, you know I can't comment on an investigation. That would violate a potential defendant's rights."

"I understand," said Lucy, who was well aware that Aucoin wasn't always that scrupulous about protecting suspects' rights. "I'm thinking more of motive. I heard that a number of the historical society's documents are missing that might be linked to Hetty's death. Is that something you're looking at?"

"Again, Lucy, I really can't comment on that except to say that in cooperation with state and local police we are exploring a number of leads as we vigorously continue to investigate Hetty Furness's murder. This was a heinous crime and we fully intend to bring the perpetrator to justice."

"Any idea when you might bring charges?"

Aucoin bristled at this, placing his hands face down on the desk and leaning backward, narrowing his eyes. "When that happens, Lucy, you'll be the first to know. Now, I am a busy man. . . ."

Lucy took the hint. "Well, thanks for your time." Leaving the office, she noticed that the receptionist's desk was empty. She checked the ladies' room on her way down the hall, but found it empty. The court employee's break room was in the basement and Lucy bopped down a couple of flights of stairs, following the scent of coffee. The door was open and Betsy was sitting at the table, working on a Sudoku while she drank her coffee.

"Hey, Betsy," said Lucy. "Got a minute?"

"Sure, Lucy. There's a fresh pot."

"Thanks, but I'm good. I just talked to your boss. . . ."

"And he didn't give you anything," said Betsy. She was in her thirties, a bit overweight, with rosy cheeks and a little turned-up nose. She always dressed professionally, today wearing a flowery print top and an A-line skirt that skimmed her knees.

"He says there's a 'vigorous investigation' underway in Hetty's death. . . ."

Betsy shook her head. "If only."

"I heard they were looking at Chris Taylor," suggested Lucy. "He's Zeb Logue's grandson, and there are documents about the Pine Tree takeover missing from the historical society, and that takeover benefited Logue."

"That's interesting," said Betsy, chewing on her pencil. "The cops may be looking at him, but nothing's come to us here, no referral."

"Well, I'll let you enjoy the three minutes that are left of your break."

"Three! That's just what I need." Betsy completed the Sudoku with a flourish. "Thanks, Lucy."

"Anytime," said Lucy, deciding to head back to the office to write up her recap of the selectboard meeting. This week it looked as though they'd be devoting most of the paper to the upcoming Fourth of July celebration.

July Fourth was the kick-off for the summer tourist season and Tinker's Cove made the most of it. Main Street was decorated with red, white, and blue bunting, and the Chamber of Commerce always organized a parade and fireworks. Local organizations pitched in: the Lions Club held a frank 'n' bean supper, the fire department hosted a pancake breakfast, the Community Church had a massive, town-wide rummage sale, and the Garden Club had a plant sale that relied heavily on daylilies culled from the members' overcrowded flower beds.

Lucy loved covering the parade, which was definitely a home-grown community effort that drew a big crowd that packed the Main Street sidewalks. Everybody in town was either in the parade, or watching it, but it also attracted lots of tourists. It always began with a color guard made up of veterans wearing their old uniforms. Some were a bit snug while others hung on their increasingly frail owners. They were followed by the high school band, struggling to march together and keep to the tune. Local businesses and groups entered floats into the parade, vying for prizes for "most original" and "best overall." Folks who had antique cars proudly showed them off, honking their horns as they waved to their friends and neighbors. There was usually a contingent of Shriners, in clown costumes, along with a mini car, or two, and a group of "Ancient Mariners" who dressed as pirates and fired off a mini cannon that frightened the dogs and babies. There were always lots of kids on bikes, and plenty of dogs, but Lucy had noticed that the once dominant black Labs had now been replaced by pit-bull mixes and French bulldogs. The arrival of the town's fire trucks signaled the end of the parade, horns tooting and sirens wailing. Then, for a brief half hour, there was actually a traffic jam as folks hurried to get out on their boats, or to gather at family picnics.

This year, however, Lucy found she was struggling to get into the holiday spirit. She found she couldn't get over Hetty's death; the facts of the brutal crime cast a gloom over everything. How could such a thing happen in this little red, white, and blue coastal community? It simply didn't fit. And on top of that she was worried about Zoe. While Sue was excited about the champagne luncheon, the very idea made Lucy feel terribly anxious. How were they going to pull this off? Chances were, she thought, that it would either be a super-polite, ladylike affair, pinky fingers in the air, or would degenerate into a giant cat fight. Neither one would be helpful, and wouldn't do a thing for Zoe. So when the big day finally dawned, Lucy had a bad case of nerves.

"I love a sunny Sunday," said Bill, who was cooking up

eggs and bacon when Lucy came downstairs. "Sunny side up?" he asked, holding up the spatula. "Or should I flip them?"

"I don't think I can eat a thing," said Lucy, forgoing her usual mug of coffee and collapsing onto a chair. "I'm terrified. What if it all goes wrong?"

"I thought you said Rachel has everything under control. . . ." said Bill, loading up his plate and joining her at the kitchen table.

"Bill, she's not actually a therapist. She was a psych major in college, and that was quite a while ago."

"Hmm." Bill chomped down on a piece of bacon. "You can count on Sue. She's the hostess with the mostest, and you know she'll keep the champagne flowing."

"That's what I'm worried about. Too much booze can loosen tongues and inhibitions. This thing could turn into a giant free-for-all, which is not what Zoe needs right now."

Bill was thoughtful, digging into his eggs. "Maybe that would be for the best. At least she'd know where she stands with Penny and can move on from there."

"That's what I'm afraid of, Bill. What if she decides to call off the wedding?"

Bill shrugged. "Better sooner than later."

"Wow." Lucy let out a long breath. "I didn't know you felt that way."

"I'm not against the marriage," said Bill, giving her hand a squeeze. "I'm neutral, I'm fine either way, but I want Zoe to make the right decision for her and Chad. Nobody else matters."

Lucy decided she felt better. Maybe she could manage some coffee and an English muffin. Some time later, dressed in the Tinker's Cove summer uniform of sandals, white jeans, and a colorful tunic, Lucy parked in front of Sue's house.

The street was already lined with cars, indicating that the party was well underway. Lucy walked down the driveway to the backyard where Sue had set up a rented tent, unwilling to bet on Maine's unreliable summer weather.

As it happened, it was a perfect summer day, and Sue's backyard was at its best, bursting with color from foamy spirea bushes and masses of blooming daylilies. A long table had been set up under the tent, set with Sue's best china and crystal. A parade of small bouquets marched down the center of the table and little wrapped presents did double duty as place cards and favors.

Most everyone was gathered around Sue's prized wine-tasting table that she'd bought in France and had shipped home at huge expense. A half-dozen bottles of champagne were chilling in an enormous antique china punch bowl and several petite silver Revere bowls were filled with nuts and cheese straws. Spotting her, Sue immediately passed her a flute of champagne and informed her that all the guests had arrived.

Fortified with the champagne, Lucy began making the rounds, greeting everyone, beginning with her girls. Noticing Sara and Jodi were deep in conversation with Zoe, Lucy joined them, giving them all hugs. "We finally meet!" she exclaimed, giving Jodi an extra hug.

"It's great to meet you, Mrs. Stone," said Jodi. In contrast to Sara, who was peaches and cream with blond hair and struggled with her weight, Jodi had olive skin, dark hair, and a runner's lean body. She was dressed in a short, tight skirt and a sleeveless white shirt cut high at the shoulders to show off her toned and tanned arms. When she smiled, which was often, her cheeks dimpled.

"Lucy, call me Lucy. Please." Lucy glanced around at

the gathering. "And thanks so much for helping Zoe, and coming here today."

"Well, emergencies are kinda my thing," she said, dimpling.

"Sara said you're an EMT. That must be a tough job."

"Yeah," she admitted, with a twisted little smile, "that's what I thought until I got involved in this wedding. Weddings are way tougher than CPR."

"Never thought of it that way, but you're right," said Zoe.

"Well, it's good to know you'll be on hand in case resuscitation is required," joked Lucy.

"Absolutely," said Jodi, grabbing Sara's and Zoe's hands. "We're in this thing together."

"I'm very grateful," said Lucy, moving on to Rachel and Sue, who were chatting with Janice Oberman and Penny, and then approaching Leanne, Lexie, and Jenna, who were admiring Sue's table setting.

"This is exactly what I'd like to have," said Jenna, casting an envious eye on Sue's collection of tableware.

"What exactly?" asked Leanne. "The plates? The silver? The linen?"

"All of it," exclaimed Jenna. "It's so perfect. It's like in a magazine or something."

"Imagine washing it all," suggested Leanne, who was a practical sort of person.

"I bet she's got help," whispered Lexie. "There doesn't seem to be any lack of dough."

"You're right," agreed Jenna, doing an appraisal that included the antique captain's house, the generous property, and all of Sue's displayed possessions. "I think the chairs came from France, and they all match."

Spotting Sue approaching with a bottle of bubbly, she raised her empty glass. "Having a nice time?" asked Sue, and the girls, startled, began giggling. "We were just saying how lovely everything is," said Lexie, as Sue topped off their flutes.

"Sue always gives wonderful parties," said Lucy.

"And I think it's time to get this show on the road," said Sue, whispering into Lucy's ear. Raising her voice, she declared, "Now that everyone's here, I think we can sit down. À table, everyone!"

While the guests searched out their places and seated themselves, Sue and Pam began bringing out the food: big bowls of salad, platters of assorted sandwiches including mini lobster rolls, potato chips, bread-and-butter pickles, along with several passes of the champagne bottle. When conversation resumed, indicating everyone had eaten their fill, Sue tapped her glass with a spoon.

"Let's take a little break before dessert, and open your favors." Bows were untied, paper unfolded, and boxes were opened revealing little silver wedding bell keychains engraved with Zoe's and Chad's initials. Everyone seemed delighted; there were plenty of oohs and aahs. That was when Rachel seized the moment and went into action.

"Zoe," she said, in a super-casual tone, "are you excited about the wedding?"

All heads turned toward Zoe, who began speaking nervously, sharing a prepared statement she had put together with help from Sara. "Well, actually, I'm finding it all very overwhelming and stressful," she began, which was not what her listeners expected. Surprised, they waited for the little joke that would surely follow, the bit of levity that preceded her "but, of course, I couldn't be happier."

They were going to be disappointed. "I was thrilled when Chad proposed, I knew he was the one, I knew right away. But, as it happened, I'd just received a big promotion at my job, only days before we got engaged. This is the job I've always dreamed of and I'm determined to make a success of it, but it's very demanding. If I'm going to succeed, I really have to give it my all and Chad understands that. He's doing the same thing, really, working very hard to fulfill his dream of becoming a major-league player. So that's where we are and it's not easy. Nothing worthwhile is, but we're willing to do the work and make the sacrifices that we need to build the careers that we want.

"As Taylor knows, planning a wedding is a full-time job. It's every bit as challenging and demanding as my real job, and I'm finding it very difficult to do both. If I take time from work to make phone calls to DJs for example, then I end up having to bring work home. Most nights I'm up very late trying to catch up with the work I was unable to get done when I got calls from all of you about wedding details. It's very stressful, I've lost weight, I'm even losing my hair, and the irony of the situation is that I never, ever wanted a big, fancy wedding."

"You don't?" asked Jenna, clearly struggling to understand. "I thought every little girl grows up dreaming of a beautiful wedding."

"Not me," said Zoe. "Not at all."

Getting a nod from Sue, Pam began pouring more champagne as Rachel went into action. "I think we're all a little surprised by Zoe's explanation, but if we take a moment I think we can all sympathize with her. Taylor, you're the pro. Do you find that other brides struggle with the demands a big wedding poses?"

"Well," said Taylor, "to be honest, I think it's not that unusual. I always try to find out exactly what the bride and groom want and what their expectations are so I can make their wedding perfect for them. Unfortunately, it's not always that simple because other members of the family"—and here she glanced at Penny—"may have different ideas. In this case, well, there was a little bit of that here. . . ."

"Well, I never!" exclaimed Janice, taking offense where it wasn't intended. "I was just looking out for your interests. You need to build your business, your reputation as a top-tier wedding planner, and thanks to Penny and Nate, you had an unlimited budget. Penny told me herself that she'd spare no expense on her son's wedding, isn't that right?"

Penny, who had been hitting the champagne hard, didn't mince words. "I sure wanted to show all those mealy-mouthed hypocrites in Tinker's Cove how well I've done since they practically drove me out of town. You know, I could buy this dinky little town if I wanted to, and I want them all to know it."

"Weddings, all social events, send various messages," observed Taylor, attempting to smooth things over.

"Is that really what you want?" Rachel asked Penny. "To retaliate at some folks who hurt you a long time ago?"

"Well, of course not," said Penny, realizing she'd made a faux pas. "This is Chad and Zoe's wedding, and the truth is, my Chad's been telling me, well, he's asked me to back off. He's been worried about little Zoe and, well, I thought he was exaggerating, that it was nothing more than jitters. Now it seems that maybe I was a teensy-weensy bit pushy and the time's not right for either of them."

Lucy could hardly believe what she was hearing, but Penny seemed entirely sincere as she got up and walked a bit unsteadily around the table to Zoe. "I'm sorry," she said, scooping Zoe up in a big hug.

"Damn!" exclaimed Jenna. "Does this mean the wedding's off?"

"Not off, but maybe different," said Zoe.

"What does that mean?" demanded Lexie. "Aren't we going to be bridesmaids?"

"Yeah," agreed Leanne. "We really wanted to be bridesmaids. . . ."

Rachel interrupted. "Why did you want to be bridesmaids?" she asked. "Really?"

"Why? Because we figured Chad's teammates would all be there! A whole team of hunky guys."

"That's crazy!" exclaimed Zoe, starting to laugh. That brought down the house; all was merry as Sue announced that coffee and dessert would be served inside.

The women began moving into the house, where Sue was offering an assortment of cookies and other baked treats in her comfortable family room, as well as carafes of coffee and decaf (actually half-caff in light of the expected consumption of champagne). As she sipped her coffee and nibbled on a lemon bar, Lucy thought the atmosphere had definitely changed for the better. The women were no longer engaging in polite small talk, but had relaxed and become more themselves. Tight shoes were slipped off as they settled onto couches and easy chairs, conversation was livelier as funny stories were shared.

"You did it," said Lucy, joining Rachel and Sue in the kitchen, where Pam was refilling a plate with brownies. "I can't believe it."

"It went well," said Rachel. "Taylor is already arranging with Zoe to meet and rethink the wedding plans."

"And, Sue, I can never thank you enough," said Lucy. "This was absolutely over the top."

Sue shrugged. "I love to throw a party. . . ."

"Well, you did a magnificent job," said Penny, bustling in. "I've just got to give you a hug, Sue. You are truly a woman after my own heart."

"I'm glad you enjoyed it," said Sue, displaying her Yankee reserve.

"Now, honey, tell me, where did you find that gorgeous wine-tasting table?" asked Penny.

"Why, in France," said Sue, warming to a favorite subject.

Hearing the doorbell chime, Lucy went to see who was there, expecting perhaps Nate or one of the other husbands. Instead, it was Officer Barney Culpepper and Officer Sally Kirwan, in uniform, looking very serious.

"Is Penny Nettleton here?" asked Sally.

"Why, yes," answered Lucy, puzzled. What could the police want with Penny?

"I'm afraid we have some bad news for her. Could you get her?" asked Barney.

Sally was looking through the hall, which led to the living room, presently unoccupied. "Maybe we could talk in here?" she suggested, leading the way.

"Okay," said Lucy, leaving them and continuing through the dining room to Sue's family room, actually her remodeled and enlarged kitchen that now included a dining table and a large seating area complete with a sectional sofa. Finding Penny still in conversation with Sue, discussing the advantages of various French flea markets, she tapped her on the shoulder. "Sorry to interrupt, but there are some police officers who want to speak with you."

"Me? Whatever for?"

"I don't know," said Lucy, showing her the way. Reaching the living room, Lucy stepped back, giving Penny the privacy the situation seemed to call for. She had just stepped into the family room when she heard an ear-piercing, heart-rending scream. Turning on her heel she rushed back, finding Penny collapsed on the sofa, sobbing. She sat beside her and began rubbing her back. "What . . ." she began, looking to Barney and Sally, who were standing awkwardly in front of the fireplace. Barney was a big man who seemed almost too large to fit indoors, and Sally was crisp and efficient in her blue uniform. "What happened?"

It was Barney who answered. "Terrible situation. Her son overdosed. . . ."

Lucy panicked. "Chad?"

"No. That's not the name. It's Chris. Chris Taylor," said Sally.

"Rescue came, gave him Narcan, but it was too late," said Barney, looking more mournful than usual. "He was DOA when they got to the hospital."

Chapter Nineteen

Penny's scream had attracted the other guests, who wanted to know what had happened. Janice was in the forefront, leading the charge, followed by Taylor; Leanne, Lexie, and Jenna were hot on their heels. Zoe, Sara, and Jodie lagged behind, looking around uneasily at this unexpected turn of events, followed by Pam, Sue, and Rachel. "She's had some bad news," said Officer Sally, blocking their entry. Observing Penny in tears on the sofa, they were all reluctant to leave, and clustered in the doorway, reminding Lucy of a flock of clucking hens.

"Maybe Rachel could help," suggested Pam. "She's a trained caregiver and knows how to give comfort in these situations."

Barney and Sally summed up the situation, a nearly hysterical Penny on one hand and a number of nosey women on the other. "Good idea," said Barney. "Rachel, c'mon in. The rest of you, move along. Give the woman some space."

"I'm her best friend," declared Janice indignantly, stepping forward. "At least here in town," she added, as a qualifier. "I should be the one to help."

Rachel, who had been working her way through the gathered group in the doorway, paused in the doorway. "Fine with me, Janice," she said, stepping aside to let Janice bustle her way into the room.

"Let's all go back to the family room," suggested Rachel, stretching her arms out if she was herding a bunch of sheep. "I'm sure everything will be explained in due time."

Lucy was more than willing to yield her seat to Janice, who immediately plopped down and wrapped her arms around the sobbing woman. "There, there," she crooned.

The guests began moving away, leaving room for Sue, who was bringing a box of tissues. Lucy took it and set it on the coffee table, where Janice immediately began plucking them out and passing them to Penny. Rachel and Sue then followed the others who were slowly making their way back to the family room, whispering to each other. Lucy was about to join them, but hesitated, noticing that the police officers were in no hurry to leave. She suspected they had some questions they wanted Penny to answer and were waiting for her to collect herself, but it didn't seem as if that was going to happen any time soon, considering her condition. Penny's sobs and cries seemed to be growing worse, rather than better, despite Janice's tender ministrations. Lucy began to wonder how much of Penny's tearful reaction was actually genuine, but was immediately ashamed of the thought. People grieved differently, everyone in their own way, and she wasn't in a position to judge. It was undeniable, however, that Penny had hardly seemed the least bit interested in her firstborn on the few occasions when Lucy had seen them together. And the fact remained that Penny certainly wouldn't be the first woman who had attempted to use a crying fit to avoid, or delay, talking to the police and answering possibly awkward questions.

Barney was beginning to grow restless and he gave Sally

a nod, prompting her to seat herself on Penny's other side. "Would you like me to call a doctor to give you something to help you calm down?" she asked.

Barney turned to Lucy, who responded with a questioning look. "What can I do to help?" she asked, not entirely without self-interest. Helping would give her an excuse to observe what she knew would be a big news story.

In response he pulled out a notebook. "Want to take me to the guests?" he asked. "They might be able to share some information."

"Zoe's here. She knew Chris, and Sara and Jodi ran into him at a concert in Boston."

"Okay." Barney nodded and Lucy led the way to the family room, where all conversations suddenly stopped as they all waited expectantly for Barney to tell them what was going on. "Ahem," he began, clearing his throat and holding his hat in front of him. "It's a real shame to interrupt this nice social occasion with sad news," he began, taking in the scattered coffee cups, crumpled napkins, and plates of food. "I'm very sorry to inform you that Chris Taylor has died of an apparent drug overdose."

Expressions of shock and dismay were heard as everyone tried to understand and process this news. *Chris was so young, it was a terrible thing when a young person died. His poor parents, poor Penny. What a shame. Drugs were everywhere, everyone knew that. What had the kid been thinking? He lived with his grandfather, didn't he? He wasn't terribly close with his mother, was he? Of course, she's still his mother, it has to be awful. Just imagine losing one of your kids. Terrible.*

"Umm, I understand some of you knew the young man?" began Barney. "I'd like to have a word with anyone who has information about him."

Lucy noticed that Zoe was already deep in conversation

on her phone, and from her sad expression concluded that she was most likely sharing the terrible news with Chad. Sara nudged Jodi and together they approached Barney.

"We didn't know him well," began Sara.

"But we did see him at a concert in Boston," added Jodi.

"He was really high on something," said Sara.

"He was with another guy who offered us drugs," continued Jodi.

Barney was definitely interested. "Do you know this guy? Could you identify him?"

Sara and Jodi both shook their heads. "It was at a concert; we were in a big crowd. It was real noisy . . . if he told me his name I didn't get it," said Jodi.

"Me neither."

"If you think of anything else, give us a call," said Barney, giving them each a business card. He then went over to Zoe, leading her out through the French doors to the deck, where they could speak privately. The conversation was brief. Barney came back inside, leaving Zoe, who seated herself on a deck chair. He stood by the door, surveying the room, but nobody made any attempt to catch his attention or approach him. He clapped his cap on his head, hoisted up his service belt, and departed. He'd no sooner left the room when the buzz of conversation resumed. Lucy went outside to be with Zoe; she suspected her daughter would be more upset than she seemed.

"I'm so sorry," began Lucy. "How's Chad taking it?"

Zoe glanced at the phone she was holding in her hand. "I don't know where to begin. He's angry, he feels he's been robbed of a relationship with his only brother, and he feels guilty, wishing he'd done more to help him. We knew he was on drugs, but there's only so much you can do, right? Chris didn't see it as a problem. He'd just laugh when Chad said maybe he should stop, you know?"

"Did Barney give you any details?" asked Lucy.

"Not really. He said Chris was home and his grandfather found him in a bathroom and called nine-one-one. That's it." Zoe stroked her phone, subconsciously reaching out to Chad. "He wasn't surprised," she added, indicating Chad with a tap on her phone. "He thinks it was probably fentanyl."

"Why does he think that?"

"'Cause it's everywhere, dealers mix it in with other stuff to give a stronger high. He probably had no idea that what he was taking could kill him."

"I thought he was in rehab," said Lucy.

"He was. He just got out. His grandfather made him go. After he got questioned by the cops about Hetty's murder the lawyer advised it. Chris resisted, but finally agreed to do a seven-day detox at a place in New Hampshire; the plan was he'd get clean and come back home for outpatient treatment. That's the idea now, that people do best when they get treatment in the environment where they abused drugs. It seemed like it was working. He was faithful about going to therapy and group meetings. Chad was, I guess you'd say cautiously optimistic, last time he spoke to him; he said Chris was really into the whole program." She paused, staring ahead into space, then bowed her head. "It didn't work, but that's no surprise. Opioid addiction is pretty much impossible to beat." What neither one said, but what they were both wondering, was how this tragic news would affect the wedding.

Driving to work on Monday morning, Lucy found her mind wandering, going over the events of the weekend. Chris's death loomed over everything because it was so senseless, so pointless. He had had his whole life ahead of him but had thrown it away trying to get high. And he wasn't alone. Lucy had been covering the drug problem for years and it only seemed to get worse. Last year she'd written a piece about how the county was offering support and treatment for rescue squad workers who were experiencing post-traumatic stress syndrome from the number of overdoses, including many fatalities, that they were now dealing with on an almost daily basis.

Braking at the stop sign at the bottom of Red Top Road, Lucy took a moment to count her blessings. Coming up with five blessings was a practice she'd adopted to remind herself that even though the world seemed to be going to hell in a handbasket, as her late mother often observed, she was one of the fortunate few who had plenty of things to be thankful for. Making the turn onto Route 1, she counted her first blessing: none of her children were addicted to drugs. That was big. Number two, she had new tires on the car. Three, of course, the success of the champagne luncheon that cleared the air and would hopefully relieve some of the stress Zoe had been struggling with. That led to number four: her wonderful friends, especially Sue, who had pitched in to help. Five, five, what was five? How could she forget? It was Bill! Always there for her, and still as passionate, well, almost as passionate as he'd been when they were first married.

Feeling somewhat more cheerful, Lucy parked in front of the office and went in, ready to face the day's challenges, which she expected would include writing up Chris Taylor's death. She got started right away, using the official statement provided by the police, which was brief and to the point. Since she happened to know that his father, Sam Taylor, also died at a young age in a construction accident, she added it to the story as a tragic coincidence. Ted was very big on tragic coincidences, which he claimed readers loved. Not only one tragic death in the family, but two! And even better if these tragic events happened to befall one of the richest and most influential families in town: Tinker's Cove royalty. It only went to show that wealth and position did not provide immunity to life's difficulties, or even guarantee happiness.

Those thoughts came into the forefront of Lucy's mind at the burial, which took place the following weekend. The ceremony was limited to family, which Lucy discovered she and Bill were now considered to be, thanks to their daughter's engagement to Chad. The small group that gathered at the town's oldest cemetery included only Lucy and Bill, Zoe and Chad, Penny and Nate, and Zebulon Logue; a memorial service was planned to take place sometime later.

The cemetery was typical of many old New England cemeteries, with stones that tipped this way and that, and others that had fallen to the ground. The oldest graves dated from the 1700s, some carved with death's-heads. The 1800s brought fancier gravestones that included obelisks and even angels, some remembering lives lost in the Civil War. Those flights of fancy ended in the 1900s when stubbier, more solid stones were chosen, many adorned with badges and American flags denoting veterans of foreign wars, continuing up to the present day. Yankees didn't go in much for wreaths or floral tributes, but some stones were accompanied by clusters of tiger lilies. As they made their way to the open grave, Lucy was struck with the cemetery's stark and somber appearance under a sunless, milky white sky.

Reverend Wilkes Henderson was officiating, reminding mourners rather pointedly that all earthly things were transient, before going on to assure them that Chris, sinner that he might be, was loved by God and would most surely be welcomed at the pearly gates. Penny was barely able to stand and had to be supported by Chris and Nate. Zoe had taken it upon herself to support Zeb as he tottered a bit walking on the uneven ground in the cemetery. His wrinkled face with his hawklike nose reminded her of the Old Man of the Mountain, a stone outcrop that had long been a New Hampshire landmark until erosion took its toll and it fell down.

After they'd each dropped a handful of earth into the grave, the part that never failed to bring tears to Lucy's eyes, she turned and encountered Zeb, looming over her. She was taken aback, aware of the threatened libel suit, and fearing he might attack or insult her. He did neither, instead giving her a weak smile, clearing his throat, and congratulating her on her lovely daughter.

"Sad day indeed," he began, with a nod to Zoe, "but your daughter has been kind enough to help an old man like me."

"I am very sorry for your loss, for all our loss," said Lucy. "I know Chad was so happy to have a brother and was looking forward to a long relationship."

"Yes, yes. Chad and Zoe have given me . . ." He paused, taking a moment to regain control of his emotions, then continued. "I wonder if I might one day soon have a talk with you. There are some matters I would like to settle."

Lucy wasn't sure that she wanted to settle matters with Zeb, whatever that meant. And she wasn't sure that Ted—or Bob, who was his lawyer—would approve of the meeting. Zeb, however, didn't seem especially threatening, especially when he reached out and took her hand. She noticed his was shaking slightly due to a tremor.

"It would mean a great deal to me," he said, rather gravely.

"Of course," said Lucy, fearing the old boy was on his last legs. "I'll call in a day or two and we can set a date."

"Thank you," he said. "I'm most grateful."

Reverend Henderson, who had been talking quietly with Penny and Nate, now took Zeb aside for a few words of consolation. Zoe had joined Chad, who was standing with his parents, which left Lucy and Bill by themselves. "Do you think it would be okay if we left?" asked Bill, who had only attended because Zoe had insisted.

Lucy looked around and concluded that the others were involved in conversations that did not include them. "I think this is our chance," she said, taking his hand. They began walking slowly toward their car, studying the old gravestones in the ancient cemetery as they went, occasionally commenting on a particularly noteworthy one.

"That fellow had four wives, all buried beside him," said Bill.

"They probably all died in childbirth," said Lucy, noting a number of small stones memorializing very brief lives.

"Lost at sea," said Bill, sadly, observing a neighboring stone.

"I should really do a feature on the cemetery. I bet I can find a lot of information about these folks in the old papers in the morgue," said Lucy, as they reached the car. She was just reaching for the door when Nate surprised her by grabbing her arm.

"What?" she cried in surprise, whirling around to face him.

"Who do you think you are?" he demanded. "Digging up family secrets for that stupid rag of a newspaper."

"I don't know what you mean," said Lucy, genuinely puzzled.

"Sam Taylor! That's what I mean!" he snarled.

"That's not a secret. Lots of folks around here remember him."

"Did you stop to think about how Penny would feel? He was her first husband! And now Chris! What you call a 'family tragedy' is her life. But you don't care! It's just a story to you!"

This was a problem Lucy struggled with every time she wrote about local people who were touched by tragedy, because she did care. Fires, car crashes, and accidental deaths were news, but she always tried to remember that real people were involved and struggling with terrible loss. She was about to say that she understood and sympathized even while she had a difficult job to do, which was to report the news, when Bill spoke up. "Listen, buddy, this is not the time or place—"

"Whaddya mean!" Nate puffed up his chest and began flexing his fists, as if preparing to fight with Bill.

"I mean that you're out of line here," said Bill, studiedly calm. He glanced over at the car where Penny was sitting in the passenger seat. "Your wife's waiting for you."

Nate looked over, then made a decision. "Okay. But don't think this is over." He glared at Lucy and stabbed toward her with a pointed finger. "If you know what's good for you, you'll leave our family alone! You've done enough damage!" With that final word he turned on his heel and marched off to join his wife.

"What a jerk," muttered Bill, watching him go.

"That makes two, I guess," said Lucy, pulling the door open.

"Hey! I'm your husband. It's my job to defend you."

"I don't need anyone to defend me," said Lucy, sliding into the passenger seat. "I can take care of myself." She looked toward the Nettletons' car. "Besides, he was right. Airing people's troubles is a dirty business."

Bill snorted, starting the car. "He had no cause to confront you like that," he said, rolling his eyes.

"I'm used to it, it's part of the job," said Lucy, with a shrug. She looked at Bill, who she knew wouldn't hesitate for a second to leap in front of a runaway truck to save her, and reached for his hand. "I forgive you this time," said Lucy, with a little smile. "What do you say to lobster rolls for lunch?"

"Sounds like a plan," said Bill. "That place in Thomaston?"

"Yeah," said Lucy, brightening. "I think they have beer and wine?"

"I think they do," said Bill, shifting into drive and proceeding along the narrow dirt track that ran through the cemetery and led to the road.

Lucy fell silent, thinking about Chad's family, the family that Zoe and now she and Bill were part of. "I'm confused; I simply don't get it. Penny abandoned Chris as a baby, she made absolutely no attempt to have any sort of contact with her own child for twenty-odd years, and now all of a sudden, she's overwhelmed with grief? I mean, when I saw them together, she treated him like a stranger, barely even spoke to him."

"Well, it would be awkward, after all that time," suggested Bill. "And maybe she had a guilty conscience."

"Maybe she does," said Lucy, wondering if Penny was struggling with guilt, or grief, or both. Actually encountering Chris, all grown up after all those years, must have been an emotional earthquake, especially since it was followed so quickly by his death. And Lucy knew how dealing with one loss often brought back memories of other losses. Perhaps that's what Nate meant, when he attacked her for writing about Sam Taylor. He'd accused her of revealing family secrets, which made her wonder if there might be more to that particular story. What if Sam Taylor's death was suspicious in some way and the family had insisted it was accidental to prevent a scandal of some sort? Suicide came to mind, or even murder. Was that the secret the family wanted to hide?

Later that afternoon, when Lucy was sitting on the porch attempting to finish the Sunday *Times* crossword puzzle and Bill was mowing the lawn on his tractor, Zoe and Chad stopped by. They all gathered on the porch and Lucy served cookies and lemonade from a vintage set that included a pitcher painted with lemons and matching glasses.

"Thanks for coming to the service," said Chad, before lifting his glass and draining it in one go.

"Of course. We're very sorry," said Lucy, standing and refilling it from the pitcher.

"A real shame," said Bill, joining them and grabbing a chocolate chip cookie. Lucy knew he was still fuming about Nate's confrontation with her.

"Your mom seems to be having a difficult time," said Lucy, quickly adding, "and it's no wonder. Losing a child is just about the worst thing that can happen to anyone."

A gloom fell on the group as everyone pondered this difficult thought and nibbled on cookies. Lucy broke the silence, asking Chad, "And how are you doing? I know how excited you were about finding your half brother."

Chad leaned back in the rocking chair and set his lemonade glass on the nearby table. He stared out at the driveway, thoughtfully studying his Jeep. Finally, he spoke. "I feel real bad about it. I don't know what I was thinking. I should've let sleeping dogs lie, that's what Dad said. But instead I went ahead and I was really excited when I found Zeb and I couldn't believe I really had a brother." He paused. "When I was a kid, all I ever wanted was a brother. All my friends had brothers and sisters. They seemed to have so much fun, but in our house it was just me. So I think I kind of went bananas when I discovered Chris." He picked up his lemonade and took a big swallow. "I was excited, yeah, especially at first. But the more I got to know Chris, well, I didn't like what I was seeing. You didn't have to be a genius to know this wasn't going to end well." He shrugged apologetically. "And now Mom is all upset, Dad's pissed at me, and I don't blame him. I opened a big can of worms."

One big question remained unanswered by Chris's death, and Lucy could not resist asking Chad for his opinion. "Do you think Chris had anything to do with Hetty's death? The police did bring him in for questioning, but his lawyer didn't allow him to answer, citing his right to remain silent."

Chad rocked forward and clapped his hands on his knees. "Absolutely not," he answered, in a firm voice.

"That's right," said Zoe, speaking up for the first time. "He was a mess, but it was all about hurting himself. He would never have attacked an old woman like that. It simply doesn't fit."

"Like OJ's glove," said Lucy, offering a comment that flew right over Zoe's and Chad's heads.

"Uh, right," agreed Zoe, pulling an envelope out of a tote bag with a coastal print design that Lucy had immediately noticed.

"Cute bag," she said. "Is that new?"

Zoe beamed. "It was a present from Chad. A surprise."

He smiled at Zoe. "No special occasion, just because I felt like it."

"Good work," said Lucy, casting a meaningful glance at Bill, getting a scowl in return.

"I've got these photos I want to ask your opinion about," said Zoe, passing the envelope to Lucy.

"Yeah, we're considering a wedding website," explained Chad. "Mom was pushing us to do it and now, well, after everything that's happened, I'm thinking maybe it would kind of cheer her up."

"Yeah," agreed Zoe. "We could go with black and white, or color. We're just not sure."

"A wedding website?" asked Lucy, thinking that perhaps it was a bit too soon after a death in the family.

"Everybody does them," said Zoe. "It's a way to keep your friends and family involved in the process. . . ."

"And it would reassure Mom that the wedding's still on," added Chad. "It would give her something to look forward to."

"But I thought you were overwhelmed and wanted to have a simpler, smaller wedding," said Lucy, remembering Zoe's frantic phone calls. "And now, after Chris's death . . ."

"Well, the wedding's not for a year, and now that Chris has, um, died, well, I think even Penny will agree that smaller is more appropriate," said Zoe.

"We can't put our lives on hold because of Chris," said Chad, with a decisive nod. "It's like when you lose a game, real bad. You can't dwell on it. You've got to pick yourself up and work harder to win the next one. The world doesn't stop because one guy misses a fly ball or makes a bad decision."

"And all we have to do for the website is supply some photos," said Zoe. "The designer does the rest."

"With the proviso that we get the final say," added Chad.

"So, Mom and Dad, what do you think about the photos?"

Lucy opened the envelope and withdrew the photos, smiling at the one on top that showed Chad and Zoe mugging for the camera. "Did you have a professional photographer?" she asked.

"Nope. They're all from cell phones. Sara took that one. A lot were posted on social media and we printed up the ones we liked."

"I like the black-and-white," said Bill, looking over Lucy's shoulder as she flipped through the pile.

Lucy paused at one, of Chris and Chad standing beside Chris's sports car. There was something about the photo that gave her a sense of déjà vu as she studied the two brothers' faces. "This one looks so familiar," she said, passing it to Chad. "Like I saw it before."

"I forgot about this one," said Chad, glancing at it before stuffing it back in the envelope. "I don't think we'll use it."

It seemed to Lucy that Chad was packing up the whole Chris episode and moving on. "I think I like the color ones," she said.

"Me too," agreed Zoe. "The black-and-white are a little too artsy, like we're trying too hard."

"I'm glad we got that settled," said Chad, standing up and glancing at his chunky Rolex watch. "I've got a game tonight, so we better get going."

"Thanks for stopping by," said Lucy, taking Zoe's arm to stop her as she followed Chad across the porch. "Before you go, I just want to make sure you don't forget to send Sue a thank you note."

Zoe rolled her eyes. "Already done, along with an enormous bouquet of flowers. And I sent the same to Rachel, for facilitating."

"I'm impressed," said Lucy, who had always had to practically imprison her children to make them write thank you notes.

"Of course, Mom. The luncheon was amazing; I couldn't believe you all would do that for me. And it's made such a difference. I feel so much better now that everything's out in the open. It's a huge relief."

"Same here," said Chad. "I'm really grateful for everything you and your friends did. And now, babe, we gotta get going."

"Safe drive," said Lucy, taking Bill's hand and watching as the couple made their way to the car and drove off. "They're a cute couple," she said, squeezing Bill's hand. "I just hope—"

Bill cut her off. "Everything's going to be all right," he said. "Everything."

Chapter Twenty

Lucy only wished she could share Bill's optimistic view. The fact of the matter was that very little was actually right. Sure, Zoe seemed to have gained control of the wedding, but Lucy feared it was only temporary. Penny was out of the picture for the moment due to Chris's death, but there was no telling how long that situation would last. It was possible she would truly be overcome with grief and guilt for some time, but it was also possible that she would rally and look to the wedding as a way of assuaging her grief. She might even become more determined than ever to give Chad a lavish wedding as a way of compensating for the loss of Chris. And her BFF Janice would be more than ready and willing to encourage her in that direction.

Truth was, while Chad was determined to move on after his half brother's death, Lucy suspected others would not be so eager. Like a pebble dropped in a pond that sent ripples across the water, his loss would affect many people in town who had known him for his entire short life. In addition to his friends, neighbors, and teachers who had personal connections to him, the fact that he died of an overdose meant that the community at large would feel a sense of responsibility. There was a small universe of police, social workers, clergy, and media that would be motivated to renew their efforts to address the ongoing problem of drug abuse. And then there was his grandfather, Zebulon Logue, who had raised the troubled young man and was the person most deeply affected. And why, she wondered, had he made a point of speaking to her at the burial, asking for a meeting?

That meeting gave Lucy pause. She always found it difficult to deal with people who had suffered a tremendous loss; it was the part of her job that she found the most challenging. Interviewing survivors of house fires or devastating accidents never came easily, and even writing up obituaries for ninety-year-olds who had led happy and fulfilling lives was challenging. And then there was the threatened lawsuit in Zeb Logue's case, which definitely complicated the matter.

Ted was already at his desk when she got to the office on Monday and she turned to him for guidance. He was immediately suspicious. "He wants to talk to you? Alone?"

"I think it's just family stuff," said Lucy, hoping that was true. "Bill and I were at Chris's burial yesterday. Zeb made a friendly overture and said how much getting to know Chad and Zoe had changed his life." Seeing Ted's skeptical expression, she added, "For the better. And then he said he wanted to meet with me."

"Sounds like he's playing the sad old man card," said Phyllis, from her corner behind the reception counter. Today she was wearing a roomy magenta muumuu dress embroidered with green, blue, and purple flowers. Apparently deciding it wasn't quite colorful enough, she'd slathered on a lot of purple eye shadow, which made her look as if she had two black eyes.

"Well, he is definitely old and of course he was sad," declared Lucy. "He'd just buried his grandson. A kid he raised from birth. And he's a widower, too. He's all alone now."

"He's also a canny Yankee businessman who's threatened to sue us," said Ted.

Some matters I would like to settle, remembered Lucy. That didn't sound like he wanted someone to hold his hand while he reminisced. He definitely had something on his mind, probably the lawsuit. And he might have thought Lucy would be a soft touch, easy to manipulate for his own ends. Maybe, she thought, he was right. "So what should I do? Should I meet with him?"

While Ted scratched his chin thoughtfully, Phyllis shook her head no.

"I don't think I can blow him off," said Lucy.

"No," agreed Ted. "You have to go."

"I bet he's planning some kind of ambush," said Phyllis, narrowing her eyes, which disappeared into a purple haze. "He'll probably have a bunch of lawyers there. I've seen it on TV. They call it *discovery*. They put you on the hot seat and ask embarrassing questions, force you to admit all sorts of damaging stuff they can use against you in court."

Lucy looked to Ted. "What should I do?"

"Give him the benefit of the doubt. Maybe he does want to talk to you about Zoe and Chad and whether or not he'll have to rent a tux for the wedding. That's how you should approach it. If he starts talking about a lawsuit all you have to do is say you can't discuss it. Tell him to call me."

"And if there's half a dozen lawyers sitting there?"

"Turn around and leave, immediately."

"Okay," said Lucy, reaching for her phone. She dialed

his number, then took a few calming breaths while she listened to the ring. Maybe, she thought, after it had rung five or six times, he wasn't going to answer. Then he did.

"Hello?" His voice was strong; he sounded like a much younger person.

"Hi, Mr. Logue. This is Lucy Stone. We spoke yesterday and you mentioned getting together for a meeting. I'm just wondering if you'd like to set a time. . . ."

"How about now? You could come right over. You know where I live?"

A rhetorical question for sure. Everyone knew the Logue house. "I do," said Lucy. "Do you want to see me right now? Like this minute?"

"If you're free," he said. "No time like the present. After all, I don't know how much longer I'm going to be around."

He was shameless, she decided, definitely playing the old man card for all it was worth. But what could she do? Might as well get it over with. "Okay. I'm on my way."

"See you then." He snorted. "Mebbe."

Hanging up, Lucy saw that Ted and Phyllis had been listening in. "At least I'm getting it over with," she said.

"*Via con Dios*," said Phyllis.

"What's with you?" demanded Ted, noticing Phyllis's makeup for the first time. "You look different. Your eyes are all weird, like you've got allergies or something. And since when do you speak Spanish? Have you been watching spaghetti westerns or something?"

Time to go, decided Lucy, grabbing her bag and heading for the door. She'd just pushed it open when she heard Phyllis say, "*Sí, señor*," and continued on across the sidewalk to her car. She could only imagine Ted's reaction.

Driving along, Lucy switched on the radio and concentrated on singing along to the oldies. Weird, she thought, how she knew all the words to songs she didn't know she knew. It was a great distraction, but all too soon she reached the long private driveway that led to Zeb Logue's home. Everyone called it the "Logue house," but it was actually an imposing four-square federalist-style mansion complete with a widow's walk on the roof that overlooked a hidden cove. Zeb didn't have to worry about neighbors intruding on his privacy since he owned every bit of land within sight of the house.

There was a large circular drive in front of the house and Lucy parked a polite distance from the front door. She'd no sooner climbed out of the car when the door opened and Zeb himself greeted her.

"You made good time," he said, with an approving nod. "Come on in."

Lucy followed, impressed by his brisk pace, as he led the way through a spacious hall to a bright sunroom that overlooked the manicured back lawn that swept down to the cove below. The room was furnished with an enviable assortment of vintage wicker with flowery chintz cushions. Numerous plants filled the open windows, which admitted a refreshing breeze. Lucy noticed with a sense of relief that there were no lawyers.

"What a pretty room," said Lucy, seating herself in an armchair.

"My late wife had a good eye," said Zeb, easily seating himself on a similar chair. Zeb didn't hesitate to talk about his advanced age and its implied decrepitude, but from what Lucy observed he seemed to be in remarkably good health. His walk was a bit stiff, to be sure, and while he'd been a bit unsteady on the uneven ground in the graveyard, he zipped right along indoors and was able to seat himself easily without grasping the arms of the chair.

"Thank you for coming." He cocked his head inquisitively. "Would you like some coffee or tea? It's no trouble, I have a very helpful housekeeper."

"None for me, thanks," said Lucy, deciding to skip the small talk and get to the matter that was foremost on her mind, despite Ted's advice. "I have to admit I'm not at all sure why you want to see me. My boss thinks it's something to do with the lawsuit." She paused, thinking it best to clear the air. "Are you still planning to sue the paper?"

Zeb shook his head, which boasted a thick thatch of white hair. "My lawyers tell me I wouldn't have a chance in court. They say it's not libel if it's true, which it apparently is."

"I have learned the hard way to check my facts, twice," said Lucy, who felt as if an oppressive burden had been lifted from her shoulders.

Zeb propped his elbows on the armrests and tented his hands, enormous hands, in front of his chin. "These days a lot of us old folks are having to reckon with questionable things our ancestors did. They didn't know they were doing bad things; they were simply acting according to the accepted values of the time, but those values have changed. People like me, who grew up in the North and were taught that our ancestors fought in the Civil War to free the slaves, well, it never occurred to us that a lot of those sea captains we're so proud of were commanding ships engaged in the notorious triangle trade that brought slaves from Africa. And a lot of our early settlers had slaves, too. Not hundreds, like the Southern plantations, but we know they had them because they were listed in wills, along with the teapots and bedsteads and all the other property they bequeathed to their heirs.

"In my case, I'm not aware of any ancestral activity in

the slave trade, but I have to admit that thanks to your article I am revising my opinion of Dr. Thomas Logue." He smiled. "I am willing to give him a small benefit of the doubt, due to the fact that a lot of scientifically minded people accepted the theory of eugenics, and his actions in Pine Tree were within the scope of his lawful powers, but that's as far as I'm willing to go. Seizing the property for himself was clearly unethical, even if it was legal, and my family clearly benefited from it. That seizure was the foundation of my family's wealth, and that was something that my grandson Chris found deeply troubling."

Listening to this, Lucy thought that Zeb Logue was indeed a man who had undergone a conversion, which was certainly unusual for someone his age. She was impressed that he had the courage to examine his preconceptions and was willing to change them, and gave him an encouraging smile.

"That article of yours really shook him up and he was even talking about reparations in the days before his death," he said, continuing, "and while I'm not sure that's advisable, or even possible, I do think there's a need for folks like me who clearly benefited from our ancestors' dubious behavior to make amends."

Lucy found herself struggling to process this new information, which contradicted everything she'd assumed about Chris and his grandfather. "Uh, how do you plan to do that?" she asked. "To make amends?"

"I discussed this with Chris, you know. He was all for reparations; he wanted to give everything away, but soon realized that would be impractical. Instead, we agreed it would be better to fund a Winchester College research study of the Metinnicut people with an eye to eventually setting up a Native American Studies Department." He paused and cleared his throat. "I'd also like to establish a scholarship in memory of Chris."

"That's a wonderful idea," said Lucy, warming to the tough old guy.

"I can't take credit. It was my grandson Chris who suggested the plan. I'm just . . ." He paused, staring out the window for a long moment before continuing. "I'm just carrying on for him, doing what he wanted to do."

"Really," said Lucy, somewhat surprised, considering the little she knew about Chris. "I am so sorry about what happened. You must miss him very much."

Zeb was silent, studying the view he saw every day as if he'd never seen it before, and Lucy wondered if she'd said the wrong thing. It was so hard to know what to say to a bereaved person, especially a stiff-upper-lip Yankee like Zeb who preferred not to indulge in displays of emotion.

"The boy was troubled," he said, speaking slowly and definitely not making eye contact. "There's no two ways about it, and I suspect I bear a certain amount of responsibility for his difficulties. My wife simply adored him. She would never believe he ever did anything wrong, and that was a big mistake. We spoiled him, never held him to account for any of his bad behavior. Until now. That police interview was quite a shock, to him and also to me. I had no idea he was abusing drugs. I thought he was perhaps overdoing the booze, but I knew nothing about these opioids. I'd heard of heroin, sure, but that was a big city problem. I would never have believed there were drug dealers in Tinker's Cove and that my grandson was a customer, or that his drug habits were known to the police, who apparently suspected him of murder. Nonsense, of course, but still. . . ."

"I'm sure it's not much consolation, but he wasn't alone," said Lucy. "It's a big problem here and everywhere."

Zeb finally looked at her. "Chris was determined to make a fresh start after the detox program. They put him on a maintenance drug, something called sub . . . sub . . ."

"Suboxone?" asked Lucy.

Zeb's rather impressive eyebrows shot up in surprise. "You know of it?"

"I'm a reporter. I write about these things." She bit her lip. "I have to say I'm a bit surprised he didn't go into a residential program. A lot of rehabs are for twenty-eight days, and you could certainly have afforded the cost."

"That's what we wanted, but we couldn't find a bed. Just getting him into any detox was a challenge. But he did have a support group, that's what it was called, and he went every day." He paused to take a long, long breath. "It seemed to be working. . . ."

"Recovery is a long, slow process," offered Lucy. "Users often relapse and fall into old habits."

"They said he took something called fentanyl."

"While he was taking Suboxone?" asked Lucy, finding this very surprising indeed. She knew that anyone on a maintenance dose would most definitely have been counseled that taking any opioid could be deadly. That meant he had either decided to throw caution to the wind and risk everything on a hit, or had taken the drug intentionally, planning suicide. "Did he give you any hint that things weren't going well?" she asked.

"No. He had a program and he was following it. He got up early every morning and went for a long run, he asked Mrs. Spencer, she's my housekeeper, to make special foods for him that were especially healthful, like kale and broccoli"—he paused, making a grimace—"and he had a bunch of vitamins and supplements, that's what he called them, that he took religiously." He looked down at his large hands that were lying, idle, on his lap, and his voice broke a bit as he said, "He looked healthier and seemed happier than he'd been in years. And he'd found a purpose, researching and making amends to the Metinnicuts."

"We never really know what other people are dealing with," said Lucy, speaking softly. "What demons they're wrestling with."

Zeb quickly recovered his composure. "Truer words were never said." He clapped his hands on his thighs. "Well, that's really all I wanted to tell you. That boss of yours doesn't have to worry about a lawsuit and I'll keep you advised of progress on the Pine Tree Project." He stood up. "That's what I'm thinking of calling it. What do you think?"

"Not the Chris Taylor Memorial?" asked Lucy.

"Nope." His answer was immediate. "It should be about the people who lost their homes, their community."

Lucy was impressed. "Good choice."

"I'm setting up a team, lawyers and folks from the college and the Tribal Council. I think we'll have a statement for the public relatively soon," he said. "In the meantime, remember you're always welcome here."

"Thank you, I hope to see you soon." He then walked her to the front hall, where a number of framed photographs on the wall caught her eye. "I saw a similar display in the Baptist Church," she said.

"A bit of family history," he said, with a rueful expression. "I used to be proud of them, but now I'm not so sure."

Lucy took a closer look, seeing pictures of a logging camp as well as men balanced on logs that were floating down the river. There were also images of the sign going up on the newly constructed Logue Logging headquarters, followed by the replacement of that sign by the new Logue

Log Homes sign. Mixed in, there were a number of studio portraits of Logue ancestors, including Dr. Thomas Logue. The photo of the logging camp caught her eye and she leaned closer, the better to see the faces of the workers who were indeed a heterogenous group that included people of varying complexions. As before, she felt a sense of déjà vu. Well, of course. She'd been looking at a lot of old photos lately, and they shared a number of similarities. They were black-and-white, or sepia, the people were dressed in old-fashioned clothes, and they rarely smiled. She turned to Zeb. "A glimpse into the past," she said.

"I've spent too much time looking back without seeing the truth of what was actually going on," he said, casting a disdainful eye on the photos. He nodded his head decisively. "Now it's time to move forward."

"Forward? You're sounding like JFK," teased Lucy, pretty sure that Zeb was a rock-ribbed Republican who loathed the Kennedys and all Democrats, every last one of them.

"Heaven forbid!" he declared, in mock outrage, causing her to smile. "Now, you drive safely," he advised, opening the door for her. He remained there, standing in the doorway, and waved her off.

As she drove away it seemed to her that despite his brave front, the recent events in his life had shaken him to his core. She suspected that Phyllis was right and this hale and hearty old fellow was, in truth, quite a sad and lonely old man.

Chapter Twenty-one

As she was driving back to the office, Lucy realized Zeb had presented her with a dilemma. He'd given her a big news story, but wasn't ready to go public. That meant, in effect, that the time she'd spent with him was wasted. Ted would be pleased for sure to learn that he no longer had to worry about a libel suit, but he'd soon forget that little point when adding up her hours and finding no story. Remembering the photos that had caught her attention, however, she thought she might use them for a nostalgic pictorial feature story. She didn't want to go back and bother Zeb, but she was, she realized, quite close to the Indian Meetinghouse. She knew there were old photos there, too, and impulsively decided to take another look.

When she arrived she found Bear at his office desk behind a pile of old, yellowing documents. He greeted her with a smile. "Hi, Lucy. You're just in time. I was getting ready to chuck this stuff in the dumpster!"

"I don't think that's a good idea," cautioned Lucy.

"No. No. Just joking. But my neck's getting stiff and I need to move around."

"Well, maybe you can give me a tour of that Pine Tree photo exhibit."

"I thought I already did," he said, looking puzzled.

"I mean an in-depth tour. For a feature story."

"Okay," he said, rising heavily to his feet. Once up he scrunched up his shoulders and stretched his neck, slowly moving his head in a circle. The movement was clearly painful, if his expression was anything to go by.

"Feel better?"

"Uh, no. Growing old ain't for sissies, and that's the truth."

"I wouldn't know," said Lucy, teasing.

He gave her a skeptical glance, then followed her out of the office into the main room. "Photos didn't really come into play until around the Civil War," he said, "so most of these date from the late eighteenth century up to 1913, when Pine Tree was taken."

Lucy walked slowly through the exhibit, studying the photos. Many were group photos that matched those at the Baptist Church, obviously taken to celebrate the church membership. She thought of the annual town photo that was taken every New Year's Day at the Quissett Point Lighthouse that brought the whole community together. There were also other photos taken of Pine Tree residents going about their daily lives, posing on their porches or in a rowboat. A lot of the photos included an animal that had won a prize at the county fair, including a huge hog and a very fancy rooster with feathers that curled. There were also photos that celebrated family events, one or two even pictured deceased children. Lucy studied each one carefully, hoping for the déjà vu feeling, but she wasn't prepared for the frisson of recognition she experienced when she encountered one of the wedding photos.

She stopped in her tracks and leaned closer, studying the faces that looked back at her. The bride was a beautiful young Metinnicut woman, dressed in a long, white dress with a dropped waist, decked in lacy ruffles, topped with a long string of pearls. Her hair was cut in a nineteen-twenties bob and she was holding an enormous bouquet of white roses. It wasn't the bride, however, who caught her attention; it was the groom.

Standing beside her, a good head and shoulders taller, was a handsome young white man dressed in one of the loose-fitting suits that were the fashion of the time. What actually stood out to her, however, was the fact that the groom was the spitting image of Nate Nettleton, if Nate was about thirty years younger.

"Who are they?" she asked, pointing to the couple.

"That's Little Rabbit," he answered, smiling. "She was my grandma's sister."

"She's beautiful," said Lucy, "but who is the groom?"

"Not sure. Looks as though he was white, not a member of the tribe."

"He actually bears a strong resemblance to someone I know. Nate Nettleton."

Bear carefully removed the photo from the display and turned it around, reading the label on the back. "That's because the groom's name is Arthur Nettleton. Some relation I guess," he said, shrugging, and replacing the photo.

"Do you know anything about them?"

"My grandma used to get letters from Little Rabbit from time to time, and always Christmas cards. I think she lived somewhere near Washington, DC. She didn't call herself Little Rabbit by then, she was Aunt Laura. She was always pressing my grandma to bring her kids to come visit and see the sights—it would be educational, she said. It seemed she and her husband were doing very well."

"Did they ever go?"

"No. There was no money for travel."

"Did Little Rabbit have a family?"

"I think so. There were cousins. Mom was a pen pal with one for a while when she was a kid, but I think it petered out after a bit."

"What did your family think of the marriage? You know, marrying a white man?"

"I think my mom was a little envious of her pen pal, to tell the truth. She loved my dad, but he was a janitor and we had a big family. A lot of mouths to feed, you know, so she was pretty stuck here. I don't think she ever left Tinker's Cove except maybe to go to Rockland a couple of times. I don't think she ever made it to Portland, much less Washington, DC."

"The racial thing didn't matter?" persisted Lucy.

Bear shrugged. "We're a pretty motley crew," he said, with a shrug. "I don't think you could find a single Metinnicut who is one hundred percent Indian. And there's been a steady drift away from Tinker's Cove for years, it's nothing new. There's not a lot of opportunity for young people here, period."

"I wonder what Arthur's family thought. Do you think they accepted Little Rabbit?"

"I imagine she could pass for white. If her picture wasn't in this tribal history exhibit, would you have identified her as Metinnicut?"

"I guess not," admitted Lucy. "But what about her heritage? Would she just give all that up and adopt a white lifestyle?"

"Probably without batting an eye," replied Bear. "Remember the times she lived in, all the pressure to give up traditional ways. Our language has largely been lost; our kids were forbidden to speak it in school. They had to cut their hair, too, and couldn't even wear moccasins."

"Shameful," said Lucy, shaking her head. She was thinking of the abuse piled on the Metinnicut people for centuries, the relentless tide of white settlement that pushed them aside as their land and even their culture were stolen from them.

"It is what it is," said Bear. "No sense carrying a grudge. What I'm trying to do is to recover what I can, and hopefully instill some pride in the generation that's coming along. I want them to have a future that both honors their heritage and allows them to thrive and succeed here in their traditional home, and I don't care if their DNA is one percent Metinnicut, or a hundred percent." He paused, chuckling. "You know Ellie makes dolls?"

Bit of a detour, thought Lucy. "Sure. They're works of art."

"Well, she made a Little Rabbit doll that illustrates the dual nature of Metinnicut identity these days. It looks to be a sweet little Metinnicut girl, with black braids and a deerskin dress, but when you flip it over and lift the skirt it turns into a White girl with blond hair and a cloth dress. It's a Little Rabbit/Laura doll."

"That's very clever," said Lucy. "I'd love to see it."

"That's a problem," he admitted. "She loaned it to the historical society, but it seems to have disappeared."

"That's terrible. I suppose someone stole it—those dolls are valuable. Collectible," said Lucy. "I could have used it for the story."

"So you're definitely going to write a story? A feature?"

"If my editor goes for it," said Lucy, hedging her bet.

Bear looked disappointed. "Of course. It's just we could use some publicity." He gestured to the room, empty apart from them and the pictures. "We're not exactly getting any crowds."

"I'll see what I can do," she promised.

Back in the car, she again wished she could have told Bear about Zeb's plan. He'd seemed so discouraged and she knew it would have given him a boost. But a secret was a secret, right? Not that she was especially good at keeping secrets, not for example, like the Nettletons. That family had managed to keep their Native American ancestry a very deep secret indeed, considering Nate's racist comments about Matt Rodriguez. She smiled to herself, wondering how Nate would react if he knew he wasn't one hundred percent White.

Acting on impulse, she pulled off the road and reached for her phone to call Chad. The phone was in her hand, but her finger hovered over the call button. She was having second thoughts about making the call. What if he didn't know he was partly Metinnicut? How would he react? What was she thinking, anyway? It was none of her business, right?

She'd just have to play it by ear, she decided. She would be tactful and polite, she promised herself. She would not deliver any bombshells. She pressed the button.

He answered immediately, in a cheerful voice. "Hey, Lucy. What's up?"

"I heard the traffic going south was terrible yesterday. How was your drive?" This was a safe bet; Sunday afternoon traffic was always bad as vacationers headed home.

"No problems," he answered. "Just a bit slow here and there."

"That's a relief," she said. "And how are you holding up? After the funeral and all?"

"Well, I'm not going to lie. It's been a bit rough, but I try not to think about it." He paused. "And I've got the game, you know? That's what I'm focusing on. Baseball and Zoe."

"Sounds like a plan," said Lucy, thinking that this conversation wasn't going as she'd hoped and she wasn't going to get the information she wanted. "Well, have a good—" she began, intending to end the call.

"Before you go, I've got big news."

Lucy figured he'd been scouted by the majors. "Good news?"

"Zoe's over the moon over it," he said. "It turns out that I'm part Indian. Native American, you know?"

"Really?"

"Yeah. Chris discovered it. It's not the Logue side of the family, it's through my father. It seems there were Nettletons here in Tinker's Cove for ages, until they branched off and moved to Virginia."

"Does your dad know he's not one hundred percent White?" asked Lucy. "I got the feeling he's not really into multiculturalism."

Chad laughed. "No. It might explain why he's into White nationalism, right? Like those guys who are so fiercely against homosexuality but are really gay. It's an extreme form of denial, I guess."

"When did this all come out?" asked Lucy, thinking Chad was really a bit of a gossip. Who knew?

"Grandpa Zeb had the whole gang over for dinner a few days before Chris died. He wanted to make amends to Mom and Dad for keeping Chris. He told them he knows it was wrong, and it was because he disapproved of their marriage." He chuckled. "You should've seen my dad's face. I thought he was going to explode."

"Because of the affair?" asked Lucy.

"That was big, of course. Grandpa's big on morality. But also because he knew about Nate's grandmother being Native American. She was called Little Rabbit! And when Nate showed up at the church and joined the choir, Grandpa's old relatives remembered the Nettleton family, and that Arthur had married an Indian. It seems that's actually why the Nettletons relocated to Virginia. They felt shamed, I guess, and wanted a fresh start."

"So Zeb was racist? That's why he wanted the guardianship? He disapproved of Nate because his grandmother was Native American?"

"Yeah! Big time. But when Chris started poking around in all this local history and after your story about Pine Tree, he had a change of heart. Right is right and wrong is wrong, and taking Pine Tree was wrong. Chris said it took the old guy a few days to process the information, but he ended up deciding he needed to make amends for the way the Logue company treated the local tribe. The Metinnicuts, right?"

"Yeah. He invited me over and told me all about his plans. He's setting up a foundation to provide scholarships and even a Native History department at Winchester College."

"I think he was hoping Chris would head it up as part of his recovery, but now it's a memorial." Chad's voice broke on the last word.

Lucy jumped in, changing tracks. "So how did it end. Happy family?"

"We-e-ll, not quite. Dad was pretty pissed, but Mom was really happy. She and Grandpa had a big hug, and they were both teary. It was pretty emotional. She told Chris there wasn't a day that passed that she didn't think of him and how she finally had two sons now."

"Silver linings," said Lucy.

"Up to a point," he said. "As you can imagine she's pretty cracked up now, and what's more, her good buddy Janice has dropped her."

"Oh, no!"

"Yeah. Turns out they weren't really soulmates, it was all about the big paycheck for her wedding-planner daughter, Taylor."

"Wow."

"So now she's pretty lonely. Janice was taking up a lot of her time."

Lucy took the hint. "I'll reach out to her," she promised.

"That would be great! She really misses Janice."

"Well, I can't replace Janice. . . ."

"No one could," joked Chad.

"But I can ask Penny to lunch."

"Great!"

Chad seemed to be succeeding at moving on, concentrating on Zoe and baseball, thought Lucy, putting her phone away and switching on her blinker before pulling out into the road. If only she could do the same, but she knew only too well that life was full of twists and turns. Sometimes she felt that for every step forward she took one back. Which turned out to be the case when she walked in the office and Phyllis handed her a pink "While You Were Out" slip.

"Rachel called, said she couldn't get through on your phone," she said, by way of explanation.

"It seems Miss Tilley's in the ER."

Lucy's jaw dropped, and her heart skipped a beat. "What happened?"

"She took a fall."

"That doesn't sound like Miss T. She does yoga every morning."

"It was a medication mix-up. She took one of her evening sleeping pills thinking it was her morning calcium."

"I guess I better get over there. Give Rachel some moral support."

"Yeah. I bet the old bat's really pissed," said Phyllis.

"That's one way of putting it," admitted Lucy, turning on her heel and pushing the door open. What next? she wondered.

Chapter Twenty-two

Lucy didn't have far to go; the Tinker's Cove Cottage Hospital was located just outside town, on a piece of prime real estate offering the patients spectacular views of the cove. The cove wasn't visible, however, from the ER, which is where Lucy found Rachel. She was sitting on one of the chairs in the waiting area, which was about half full, looking miserable.

"How's she doing?" asked Lucy, taking the chair beside her.

"Hi, Lucy," said Rachel, looking up from her study of the floor tiles. "Thanks for coming."

"Of course," said Lucy. "What's going on?"

"They took her to be X-rayed for a possible hip fracture."

That didn't sound good to Lucy. "Really?" she asked, in a concerned voice.

"Just to be on the safe side. To be honest, I think she reacted more to the shock of the fall. I don't think she's really hurt, but she didn't put up much of a fight when I said I was calling the rescue squad and told her not to try to get up."

"That doesn't sound like her," observed Lucy.

"I know. That's why I'm worried."

Lucy took Rachel's hand and they sat like that for a few minutes. Lucy glanced around the waiting area, curious to see if she recognized anyone. Most of the people seemed to be tourists but there were a few familiar faces, though no one she knew by name. Locals tended to avoid the ER if at all possible during the summer, when wait times were longer than usual. She and Rachel didn't have to wait long, however, as a nurse approached and told them they could see Miss Tilley. "She's giving us a bit of trouble," the nurse told them as they stepped through the swinging double doors. "The doctor is hoping you can get her to see reason."

"That's unlikely," said Rachel.

The nurse pulled a curtain aside and Miss Tilley was revealed, sitting upright in the hospital bed. A young doctor in scrubs was standing beside her, consulting a computer notebook.

"What's the diagnosis?" asked Rachel.

The doctor turned to face them. "Are you her daughters?"

"I'm her caregiver," said Rachel, introducing herself. "And this is a friend, Lucy Stone."

The doctor turned to Miss Tilley. "Do I have your permission to share your information with these women?"

"Only if you tell them the truth," declared Miss Tilley, indignantly. "That I'm perfectly fine but you want to keep me overnight anyway!"

"Her hip is okay?" asked Rachel.

"There was no sign of a break," he reported, "although she can expect to have some considerable bruising. And I would like to keep her overnight for observation considering her advanced age. It's a good idea, just to make sure everything's tickety-boo."

"Tickety-boo!" scoffed Miss Tilley. "What the hell does that mean?"

Rachel gave her a warning look. "They want to make sure that shriveled up heart of yours is still ticking."

Miss T laughed. "It must be, since I don't appear to be in a coffin. Not yet," she added. "There's no telling what might happen if they keep me here and poke me with wires and do tests and things. No, there's no two ways about it. I'm going home. I'm not going to be a human guinea pig for their experiments."

Lucy went beside the bed and took Miss Tilley's hand. "You were lucky. Anyone else would have broken something."

"Don't try to butter me up," warned Miss T, snatching her hand away. "I know what you're up to and it's not going to work. I'm going home." Miss T flipped the covers back, revealing her scrawny legs protruding from the hospital-issue johnny, and started to swing those legs off the bed.

"Not so fast," said Rachel, grabbing the blanket and replacing it. "If you go home you're going to need someone to stay with you twenty-four/seven, and I can't manage that. I've got commitments I can't break including a dinner party for some of Bob's clients."

"I'll be fine on my own," declared Miss T.

"I'm afraid I can't release you unless you have a caregiver for at least the first twenty-four hours, preferably forty-eight," said the doctor.

"Well, you're no fun," snapped Miss T, pouting.

"Maybe we could do shifts," suggested Lucy, turning to Rachel. "I can stay tonight, you can do your regular shift tomorrow, and Pam or Sue could come tomorrow night. Do you think that's feasible?"

"It would be a big help," answered Rachel, looking to the doctor. "Would that be okay?"

The doctor rolled his eyes. "I have other patients, you know. You ladies can figure it out and tell me what you decide. I'll need names and phone numbers before I sign off." With that he stalked off out of the cubicle; they could hear his footsteps slapping against the tile floor as he went.

"Good riddance to him," sniffed Miss T.

Lucy and Rachel shared a glance, then got to work on a schedule. It only took a couple of phone calls to sign up Pam and Sue, and Lucy produced her reporter's notebook and wrote up the schedule, which she ripped out and took with her in search of the doctor. She found him at the nurses' station, probably regaling them with Miss T's uncooperative behavior.

"Okay," he said, glancing at the schedule before tucking it in his pocket. He then produced a computer notebook and scrawled something loosely resembling a signature. "I'll be in touch," he said, making serious eye contact with Lucy.

"Great!" said Lucy, expressing enthusiasm she didn't actually feel. "So Miss Tilley is free to go?"

He nodded.

"Thanks for everything," she said, smiling to the assembled nurses and the doctor. "We'll be out of your hair."

Back in the curtained cubicle, Lucy found Rachel helping Miss T dress. "I've got this," she told Lucy. "I'll take her home and you can take over at six. Okay?"

"You got it," said Lucy. "And you," she added, pointing a finger at Miss T, "please try to stay out of trouble."

Miss T shrugged her bony shoulders in a gesture of helplessness. "A tiger can't change its stripes," she said, baring her rather yellowed but still perfect bite.

"See you later, Tigger," said Lucy, laughing as she made her exit. Checking her watch, which read four o'clock, she figured she had two hours in which to complete a day's worth of stories.

The hands on the antique Willard clock on the wall seemed to think they were in a movie, rotating at top speed to indicate the passage of time, because six o'clock came a lot sooner than Lucy expected. She was alone in the office, Phyllis having left at five on the dot, so she closed the windows for the night and locked the door behind her. She was ten minutes late when she got to Miss Tilley's little Cape-style house, where she found Miss Tilley enthroned in her favorite wing chair in the living room with a cotton summer blanket over her knees. "You're late," snapped the old woman, by way of greeting. Lucy ignored her and continued on to the kitchen where she found Rachel.

"How's the patient?" asked Lucy, meaning her psychological rather than physical condition.

"A bit testy. It seems the fall is my fault."

"I suspected as much," teased Lucy. "What's for supper?"

"I'm afraid it's a bit on the light side. I heated up some canned clam chowder and there are some blueberry muffins warming in the oven. I think that's more than Miss T will want, but if you need something more there's salad fixings in the fridge and fruit on the dining room table."

"We'll be fine. You should go."

"Thanks for helping out, Lucy."

"No problem," said Lucy, smiling as she dug in her bag for her phone, which was playing its little song. "It's Bill," she said, checking the screen.

"Probably wants to know what's for dinner," said Rachel, leaving through the kitchen door.

"Did you get my text?" asked Lucy, speaking into the phone. "I had to work late and now I'm at Miss Tilley's. She had a fall."

"Is she okay?"

"Seems to be fine. The doctor didn't want her to be alone tonight, so I'm staying."

"I guess I missed your text. What's for dinner?"

"Check the fridge for leftovers. I think there's still some chili."

"You're staying there all night?" he asked, sounding like a toddler who'd just learned mom was leaving him with a babysitter for the evening.

"You'll be fine, honey," she assured him. "I'll be home in time for breakfast."

"Okay." He didn't sound happy.

"I'll bring donuts," she said, thinking that men were really children.

"I like the Boston creams," he reminded her, sounding a bit more cheerful.

"You got 'em," said Lucy, hearing Miss T calling her. "I gotta go. My patient is ringing." She tucked her phone into her pocket and went into the living room, where Miss T was sitting by the fireplace, now occupied by a lush Boston fern.

"What were you doing? And where's my dinner?" she asked, fretfully.

"Coming right up," said Lucy, as inspiration struck. "Would you like a wee glass of sherry?"

"Better make it a double," snapped Miss Tilley, sounding as if she was bellying up to the bar.

Lucy filled a stemmed glass with a moderate amount of sherry and delivered it to Miss T, hoping to buy some time to get dinner on the table.

"I suppose this will have to do," complained Miss T. "I was hoping for a more generous pour."

"That was the last of the bottle," lied Lucy, heading

back to the kitchen. When everything was ready she went into the living room and offered to help Miss Tilley out of the chair. Her efforts got her a sharp look and a snort as Miss T popped up and trotted into the dining room. Lucy followed, intending to pull out a chair for her, but was too late as Miss T yanked her usual Hitchcock chair out from beneath the table and plopped herself onto it.

She'd no sooner spooned up some chowder than she launched into an explanation for her fall. "It was all Rachel's fault, you know," she said, smacking her lips. "Did you warm the muffins?"

"They're nice and toasty, just the way you like them," said Lucy, passing the basket. As soon as Miss T plucked out a muffin, Lucy put the basket on the table and quickly passed her the butter.

"Mmm, a blueberry muffin does require a healthy amount of butter." Miss T drove her knife into the butter, grunting with satisfaction. "Room temperature," she said, with an approving nod. "The refrigerator is no place for butter."

Lucy nodded, breaking open a muffin. "How was your fall Rachel's fault?"

"There's two bottles, that's all I take, you know. I have my morning calcium tablets, for my bones, and the allergy tablet I take at night." She bit into her muffin in a move that reminded Lucy of a snapping turtle. "I don't have allergies, of course," she continued, as if such a thing was a thoroughly preventable condition, "but they do make me a bit drowsy and help me sleep better."

"How did you happen to mix them up?" asked Lucy.

"They were in the wrong place," declared Miss T, indignantly. "The allergy pills are always on my night table, and the calcium is in the bathroom. They must have been switched."

"I don't think Rachel would do that," said Lucy, stirring her chowder with one of Miss Tilley's inherited silver spoons.

"She's always fussing about, cleaning, and moving things from where they ought to be." Miss T's tone was confiding, as if Rachel were indulging in some rather dubious activities.

"She's like that," said Lucy, smiling to herself. "This chowder is really good."

"Canned!" scoffed Miss T. "As if I couldn't tell the difference!"

Lucy was growing tired of Miss T's attitude, which reminded her of a spoiled two-year-old. "Rachel works hard to make sure you can stay here in your home," she said. "If it wasn't for her, and me, and Pam and Sue, you'd be eating a lukewarm dinner off a hospital tray."

"I suppose you're right," said Miss T. "Is there anything for dessert?"

After they finished eating and Lucy cleared and washed the dishes, she suggested that Miss Tilley might like an early night. "Nonsense," snapped Miss T. "I don't usually have company in the evening and I want to make the most of it. Let's get out the Scrabble."

So Lucy dutifully played Scrabble, getting absolutely demolished as she knew she would when Miss T happily grabbed all the triple-word spaces and counted up the points. Lucy was yawning and could barely hold her head up when her old friend finally called it a day and toddled off to bed. She insisted she didn't need any help, and Lucy was frankly too tired to offer any. Tired as she was, after she put on a borrowed nightgown and sank into the antique spool bed in Miss T's guest room, she had trouble falling asleep. Her mind was awhirl, wondering how she was ever going to find time to do her job, help out with

Miss T's increased needs, not to mention spend time with Penny. That last, she thought as her breathing slowed and she finally felt sleep creeping up on her, well, she couldn't say that being with Penny was something she . . .

Next morning, Lucy woke earlier than she would have liked. A glance at the clock on the night table indicated it was barely five, so she flipped her pillow over and rolled onto her other side, determined to get at least another hour or two of sleep. It was not to be, and after fifteen minutes she gave up and got up, padding into the kitchen on bare feet to make a pot of coffee. While the pot did its thing she went into the bathroom, where she noticed that the bottle of calcium pills was in its proper place on the glass shelf over the sink vanity. Opening the bottle, she peered in and was reassured that the large white tablets were identical to those in the bottle in her medicine cabinet, exactly like the ones that she frequently forgot to take.

Hearing the coffeepot ding its announcement that it was finished brewing and was now ready, she went back to the kitchen and filled the largest mug she could find, one that the Association for the Preservation of Tinker's Cove had sold as a fund-raiser and featured the outline of a great blue heron. Miss T didn't have anything as vulgar as an actual outside deck, but she did have a little area paved with bricks that was furnished with a couple of Adirondack chairs and that's where Lucy took her coffee. She leaned back in one of the chairs and took that first delicious sip of coffee, then checked out the weather. So far, so good, she thought, observing that the sun was rising into a cloudless sky. It was already hot and humid, but a pleasant sea breeze promised a relatively comfortable day.

Her thoughts turned back to that bottle of calcium tablets in Miss T's bathroom, the bottle that she claimed had been switched. Had Rachel, or Miss T herself, replaced it in its proper place, or had the notion of the misplaced bottle been a fantasy? An excuse even, for a slip and fall. That was the sort of accident that frequently happened to older people, especially those as old as Miss Tilley. Lucy knew that Miss T practiced yoga faithfully, and was remarkably supple and sure on her feet, which she often bragged about. "I don't want to move like an old person," she often said. "I like to move right along and keep up with you young people."

That, thought Lucy, was the rub. She knew herself from experience that overconfidence was responsible for more falls than any lack of fitness. She'd taken a tumble herself quite recently when she marched out onto her deck to shoo some turkeys and hadn't noticed it was slippery with dew. Her legs went right out from under her and she landed on her fanny, which she had to admit was lucky because it was the body part with the most padding. She didn't break anything, but she knew it was just luck. If she'd landed differently she might well have had a broken arm instead of a bruised bottom.

Her thoughts were interrupted by Miss T herself, who was standing in the kitchen doorway, looking rather a fright with her hair sticking out all around her head and wearing a white granny gown that was at least three sizes too big. "Good morning," she sang out, in a cheerful voice. "I made it through the night!"

"How do you feel?" asked Lucy.

"Right as rain! And hungry as a bear coming out of hibernation."

"Let's see what we can do about that," suggested Lucy, hoisting herself out of the Adirondack chair. She joined Miss T in the kitchen, where two places were already set at the kitchen table. Miss T poured herself a cup of coffee and took a seat. "Rachel always makes me eat oatmeal," she complained. "Do you think I could have something a bit more exciting?"

"French toast?" suggested Lucy.

"Just the thing!"

So they were just polishing off their servings of French toast, topped with plenty of maple syrup, accompanied by several rashers of bacon, when Pam arrived to take her shift. "Oh, my goodness!" she exclaimed, taking in the scant leftovers. "Bacon and French toast! What won't you two naughty girls get up to?"

"Just for that I'll let you do the cleaning up," said Lucy. "I'd like to go home and get showered and dressed before I go to work."

Pam sighed. "I'll get rid of the evidence," she promised, speaking to Miss Tilley, "but don't think I'm going to continue this sort of reckless behavior. I'm under strict instructions from Rachel to give you salad for lunch."

"Chicken salad?" asked Miss Tilley. "I like it with mayo and those dried cranberries."

"Lots of delicious greens, topped with a few bits of lean chicken."

"I think I'll go back to bed," said Miss T. "There's no sense getting up for that."

Lucy shook her head. "I'll leave you two to it. I've really got to get a move on." She smiled at Pam. "You know how Ted hates for me to be late."

"Go, go," said Pam, shooing her off. "I've got things under control here."

"That's what she thinks," muttered Miss T, popping up from her seat and refilling her coffee cup.

"Let me do that," protested Pam, reaching for the mug

and causing Lucy to smile to herself as she made her way back to the guest room. There she quickly made the bed, and put on yesterday's clothes, leaving the nightgown neatly folded on the foot of the bed. She stopped in the kitchen to make her farewells, then headed for home. The dashboard clock indicated it was already almost eight and she wondered where the time went.

Luckily Ted was not in the office when she showed up a half hour late. "How's the Wicked Witch of the North?" inquired Phyllis, meaning Miss Tilley.

"Feisty as ever. She claims Rachel mixed up her calcium with her allergy pills and that made her fall, but I have my doubts." Lucy noted with interest that today Phyllis was togged out in a red T-shirt featuring a green Christmas tree, and had mini tree ornaments dangling from her ears. "Uh, Christmas in July?"

"Right the first time!"

"Is there a prize?" asked Lucy, making her way to her desk, where she sat down and powered up her computer.

"Well, I do have a fruitcake left from last Christmas. . . ."

"I'll pass," said Lucy, digging in her bag for her phone, which was ringing. Glancing at the screen, she saw Penny's name and reluctantly swiped up. "Hi, Penny," she said, trying to sound cheerful.

"Hi, Lucy. I hope I'm not disturbing you at work. . . ."

"Well, it is deadline day. What's on your mind?"

"I don't want to keep you. . . ."

"It's all right, really." Lucy was already scrolling through her emails.

"Well, if you say so."

"No problem." *Please get on with it,* thought Lucy, impatiently.

"I know you're busy with your job and all, but Chad

said you enjoy walking and so do I, and he thought maybe you could show me some interesting trails."

"Of course," said Lucy, remembering her promise to Chad. "Not today, but maybe tomorrow. Thursdays are slow news days."

"That would be great. Morning or afternoon?"

"Well, it's cooler in the morning," said Lucy, who was studying the police log. "Do you have any preference? Woods? Shore?"

"I do love lighthouses," confessed Penny.

"Hmmm," said Lucy, who was wondering what exactly the suspicious activity on Sea Street was and whether it warranted further investigation.

"You know that lighthouse you see on the other side of the cove?" persisted Penny.

"Quissett Point. There's a nice trail there. What say we meet there at nine? Or is that too early?"

"Nine's okay. How do I get there? I'm afraid I'll get lost."

The woman sounded pathetic, which irked Lucy, who then felt guilty about being annoyed. "It's easy, you just take the road right after the hospital, it goes straight to the lighthouse."

"Are you sure? Maybe it would be better if you picked me up?"

For Pete's sake, thought Lucy. "That won't work for me," she said, rather snappishly. "I have a job and I don't have unlimited time. . . ."

"Maybe another day then. . . ."

"Okay," said Lucy, who knew when she was beat. "Nine it is. At your place."

"Thanks, Lucy. Now have a nice day, you hear?"

Lucy didn't hear; she was already on another line, calling the police department. "Hi," she said, when the dispatcher answered. "It's Lucy at the paper. Any idea what the suspicious activity on Sea Street was, you know, it was listed in the log."

The dispatcher chuckled. "Turned out it was Colin Rodgers rooting through the trash bin because his mother threw out his favorite T-shirt."

"Not a suspected identity thief hunting for old bank statements?"

"Who has paper bank statements these days?"

"Point taken," said Lucy, ending the call.

Chapter Twenty-three

Thursday was usually Lucy's decompression day, which she looked forward to after the pressure of the Wednesday noon deadline. That had been the situation when the *Courier* was a weekly known as the *Pennysaver*, but now that Ted had bought the *Gilead Gabber* and combined the two papers into the *Courier*, and added an online edition, Thursdays weren't quite as relaxing as they had been. Instead of one weekly deadline, Lucy was expected to post breaking news whenever it happened, twenty-four/seven. She still clung to the fiction that Thursday was a slower day, however, and usually tried to grab a few morning hours for herself. Today, of course, she was devoting those precious hours to making nice with Penny.

"The things we do for our kids," she muttered to herself as she pulled into the drive at the modest ranch on Shore Road that the Nettletons' had rented for the summer. The typical one-story house was a survivor from earlier days and was now dwarfed by huge McMansions that filled the road, which boasted ocean views. Penny had been looking out for her and popped out of the front door and hurried across the lawn to hop into Lucy's compact SUV. "Thanks for doing this," she said, settling herself in the passenger seat and fastening the seat belt.

"No problem," said Lucy, admitting to herself that it really wasn't. She would have had to drive to the point anyway, and detouring onto Shore Road didn't really add any time to the trip. "How are you liking it out here, so close to the ocean?" she asked.

"The surf is noisy, that surprised me, but I'm getting used to it." She gazed out at the enviable view. "I do feel a little bit ashamed to have the smallest house on the street, but it's only for the summer," admitted Penny.

"Have you been getting to know the neighbors?" asked Lucy.

"Oh, yes. There's Corney Clark, she's very friendly," said Penny, naming the executive director of the Chamber of Commerce who had bought years ago, before real estate took off. "But most of the others kind of come and go . . . they're not really here much. These are all second homes, I guess. A few are VRBOs, which people only rent for a week or so. There's one family, the McCarthys, they're also renting for the whole summer, but they have a bunch of kids, some quite young, so the mom is really too busy to socialize."

"It's a shame," observed Lucy, driving past the gray-shingled monster houses with sweeping Dutch gables. "All these empty houses, while working people can't find places to live that they can afford."

"I never really thought about it," said Penny.

Lucy couldn't think of a response, so the two fell silent for the remainder of the trip. When they arrived at the lighthouse, however, Penny gasped in surprise. "Wow, it's really tall," she said, as Lucy parked the car. "Thanks for suggesting it. I never would have guessed there were trails here."

Lucy glanced at the sign that clearly said "trails" and reminded herself not to get pissy. "Haven't you seen the lighthouse? Up close I mean."

"No. Only from a distance," said Penny, getting out of the car and studying the structure. "It's quite impressive, isn't it? When you're below it, I mean. It looks so tiny from across the cove."

"I think it is one of the tallest," said Lucy, wondering why Penny didn't remember the lighthouse from her childhood. She'd grown up in Tinker's Cove, after all, but it seemed as if she'd purposely suppressed all memories of her life before Nate came into it. Weird, she thought, but probably not something she should bring up. Better to play along with Penny's Southern belle fantasy and stick to small talk. "It's been decommissioned and there's a group of people working to raise funds to maintain it."

"But what about the boats? Won't they crash on the rocks?"

"They have LORAN, it's a modern navigational system that uses satellites. They don't need the lighthouses anymore and the government doesn't want the expense of maintaining them."

"That's sort of sad," observed Penny.

"Times change," said Lucy, with a shrug. "The trail is about a mile and a half long. . . ."

"I wore my walking shoes," said Penny. "I put on sunscreen and bug spray, I'm ready. I even have water and a hat," she said, clapping a Sea Dogs cap on her head.

Lucy couldn't help smiling. "Then we're off," she said, leading the way. The trail wound through some piney woods, then circled back along the cove, which offered scenic views of the village, and the picturesque harbor filled with colorful boats. "I can't imagine this is the summer you were hoping for," began Lucy. "How are you doing?" she asked. Lucy hardly expected Penny to open up and bare her soul in response, but that's what she did.

"Well, I sure didn't know what I was getting into, that's for sure. I just wanted to be here for Chad, and the wedding. But he got in touch with my father and Chris," she said, letting out a big sigh. "I thought I'd moved on, but, well, what is it they say, karma's a beast? I guess what goes around comes around. You know I left Tinker's Cove under a cloud because I was having an affair with Nate. My parents disowned me, they threatened to take me to court claiming I was an unfit mother for Chris, and I caved. I knew I didn't have much of a case; I really hadn't even tried to hide the affair. The fact that my first husband died in rather suspicious circumstances didn't help."

"I thought it was a construction accident," said Lucy.

"Well, a company truck was involved, which made for a convenient explanation that it was an accident, but he drove that truck straight into a bridge abutment."

"It was suicide?" asked Lucy.

"I think so. He'd been depressed for some time. Everyone put it on me, that I wasn't supportive enough." She paused, studying a little downy woodpecker that was climbing a tree trunk. "I don't know if you've ever lived with someone who's suffering from depression, but all I can say is it's not easy. It's a lot for anyone and I was young and immature. I wanted to party." She shrugged and smiled. "I can't say I regret what I did. Nate's fabulous, and look at Chad! He's my pride and joy! And when he said he'd found the right girl and was getting married, I thought I was riding pretty high, everything was great and I could finally come back to Tinker's Cove in triumph, show everybody that I'd done just fine. Better than fine."

She stopped in the path and took a drink of water. "I didn't for a minute think—I guess I thought that Chris would be all grown up, just like Chad, and we'd have an adult relationship. It never occurred to me that he'd be so immature and troubled, so unstable. I simply wasn't prepared for what happened."

"Nobody could be prepared for that," said Lucy, as they continued walking along the trail, which was well-trodden. She noticed clumps of orange tiger lilies that were evidence of earlier homesteads, now abandoned. She knew that if you wandered off the trail you could find old cellar holes, lilac bushes, even apple trees planted by the former residents. "Chad is a terrific guy," she finally said, in an effort to lighten the mood. "You have every right to be proud of him."

"Of course, but I can't help but wonder if Chris might have turned out differently if I'd fought to keep him." She paused to wave away a gnat that was flying in front of her face. "I rationalized leaving him by thinking Mom and Dad could give him advantages that Nate and I couldn't. Things were tight when Nate was just starting out, you know. But as things turned out Chad's been so successful while Chris had all that trouble. Nate says my folks spoiled him, but I think that maybe being older, they just didn't realize he was using drugs. Kids today face a lot of challenges that we didn't, you know?"

"I know," agreed Lucy. "Zeb does seem pretty old-fashioned."

"You have no idea what he was like as a father. He was very moralistic, very stern, everything was black and white. Church attendance was compulsory, and you would have thought we were royalty or something. Mother and I had to sit in the front pew and behave perfectly . . . we had to set an example."

"I can see why you fled," offered Lucy, pausing to point out a beachy section littered with old bricks. "Ballast from ships," she said. "But of course, you grew up here. You know all this stuff."

Penny laughed. "Believe me, I put a lot of effort into forgetting. Nate says I was born out of place here in Maine; he says I'm a natural Virginian. He's right. I did take to Virginia. I like the slower, more relaxed way of life." She sighed. "We go to an Episcopalian Church there. It's nothing like the Baptists, you know. They're not judgmental; they accept people as they are. But just before we left to come here our rector gave a sermon about the Prodigal Son and I was beginning to think about somehow trying to repair my relationships with Dad and Chris, and then Chad went and found them and started the ball rolling. It's thanks to him, and your lovely Zoe, that I got the courage to reach out to them." She gazed out over the water, her eyes tearing up. "I am truly grateful to Chad and Zoe, especially because of the way things turned out, you know? I at least got to know Chris before he. . . ."

"Let's sit for a bit," suggested Lucy, pointing to the conveniently located trunk of a fallen pine tree.

"Good idea," agreed Penny, brushing away her tears and then taking off her cap and fanning her face. The two women sat side by side and sipped on their water bottles.

It was peaceful on the little beach where gentle waves lapped at the shore. Gulls wheeled overhead, and a heron high-stepped through the water, hunting for a fishy breakfast. Lucy found herself not only sympathizing with Penny, but admiring the way she was dealing with her troubles. "This has been a real roller coaster of a summer for you," she began. "The wedding, reconciling with your father and Chris, and now. . . ."

"Yeah." Penny nodded.

"I really admire the way you're coping," said Lucy, meaning it.

"Don't think I'm doing it on my own, not for a minute," said Penny, adding a rueful chuckle. "Nate's a pharmacist, remember? I'm highly medicated."

"I had no idea," said Lucy, who hadn't. As one who resorted to an occasional Advil for pain, but preferred to do without if she could possibly manage to do so, she hadn't given much thought to the idea that life's emotional ups and downs could be eased by pharmaceuticals.

"Nate's a pharmacist, you know, and he's got something for everything," said Penny, with a smile. "In fact, he was very interested in Chris's rehab and the maintenance drug he was taking. Sub-something. He was worried that there might be some residual damage to his organs, you know, from the stuff he'd been using, and he compounded a special mixture of vitamins he said would help with recovery. He offered to give him some Valium, too, but Chris refused that."

"Really," said Lucy, as the wheels began turning in her head.

"I know," said Penny. "A little Valium never did any harm, take it from me. But Chris was adamant, said he wasn't going to take anything that might mess with his sobriety."

"Zeb told me he was really committed to staying sober. . . ." began Lucy, only to be interrupted by Penny.

"Zeb! Have you been talking to Zeb?" she demanded, in a sharp tone.

"For work," said Lucy, sensing she'd wandered into uncharted territory and needed to tread carefully. "He asked me to come over because he had something he wanted to tell me. Kind of a heads-up. He said he wasn't ready to go public just yet, but he was working on a project in Chris's memory."

"That Indian thing of Chris's?" Penny's tone was dismissive.

"Yeah. He said Chris was real interested in making restitution to the tribe for the taking of Pine Tree by his great-great-grandfather? I think that's right, a couple of greats anyway. So he's looking into setting up a Native American department at Winchester College in Chris's memory."

"He never said anything about that to me or Nate," said Penny, sounding hurt.

"Well, it's not a done deal. It's just in the beginning stages. And maybe he thought you wouldn't approve," said Lucy, sending out a little feeler.

"Well, Nate certainly doesn't!" declared Penny. "He was furious when Chris came up with all that stuff about Little Rabbit being his grandmother. He absolutely refuses to believe it. He remembers his grandmother, Laura, as the sweetest, most genteel Southern lady imaginable. She was a keen member of the garden club, known for prizewinning flower arrangements. And he goes on and on about her biscuits, says mine are good but can't compare to hers!"

"One thing I've learned is that you can't compete with memories. Grandma's cookies were much better than mine, at least in Bill's recollections."

"So Nate's not the only one with fond memories of his grandmother's cooking," said Penny.

"Not at all, it's a common affliction," said Lucy.

"Shall we head back?" suggested Penny, checking her watch. "I have a hair appointment in about an hour."

"And I need to get to the office," said Lucy, standing up. The two women mostly walked in silence back to the parking lot, occasionally commenting on the view of the harbor on the other side of the cove, or the heat, which had risen steadily during their walk. Lucy was beginning to think she'd been wrong about Penny; maybe she wasn't the superficial drama queen that she'd thought. Under that puffy hairdo and behind that artificial Southern accent it seemed there really was a thoughtful person. Lucy wasn't entirely convinced, when they reached the parking lot, but resolved to give her the benefit of the doubt.

"Thanks for showing me the trail," said Penny, as she arranged herself in the passenger seat. "You can drop me off at the Cut 'n' Curl."

Lucy felt her hackles rising at Penny's tone of voice. She was apparently no longer Penny's confidant, but a chauffeur. Too bad, she thought, reverting to her original opinion of Penny, with one modification. It seemed she was quite a good actress, manipulative and adept at presenting herself as what others expected and wanted to see. Today she'd cast herself as a sorrowful and regretful woman who'd made some bad choices, and Lucy realized she'd fallen for it.

"The Cut 'n' Curl," said Lucy, making a decision and changing her plans as she shifted into drive. Instead of heading back to the office, she had some questions she wanted to ask Zeb. As soon as she'd dropped Penny at the salon, she pulled her phone out of her bag and called Zeb, asking if she could come over. Getting a yes, she drove straight to his house.

He met her at the door. "What brings you back so soon?" he asked. "Not that I mind. I'm delighted to see you again."

Lucy smiled. She'd grown somewhat fond of Zeb, who reminded her of the grandfather she'd only known for a short while as he died when she was six or seven years old. Like her grandfather, as she remembered him, he was tall and wiry, with a stiff sort of walk. He was invariably polite, as was Poppop, and they even dressed similarly in chino slacks and pressed sports shirts, often, as today, with a jaunty bow tie. "I hope I'm not imposing," said Lucy, suddenly remembering her manners.

"Not at all, my dear. Come inside, it's cool in the sunroom, and we can have some iced tea while you tell me what's on your mind."

"Thank you," said Lucy, as he stepped aside so she could enter the hall, then led the way to the sunroom. "Mrs. Spencer," he called, as they went, "could you bring two iced teas to the sunroom?"

"Right away," came the answer, from a distant room.

"This is difficult," said Lucy, seating herself in one of the wicker chairs. "I don't quite know where to begin."

"At the beginning," advised Zeb, taking the opposite chair.

"You should take what I'm going to suggest with a grain of salt," admitted Lucy. "My editor would say that I'm letting my imagination run away with me."

Zeb smiled. "Now I'm curious."

"Well, it started with my old friend, Miss Tilley. She fell the other day and insisted it was because her calcium vitamins got mixed up with her allergy pills. The allergy pills make her drowsy, she says, and that's why she fell."

"I suppose that could happen," said Zeb, as Mrs. Spencer arrived with a tray containing a glass pitcher of iced tea and two tall glasses filled with ice. There was also a sugar bowl and a dish of lemon slices, as well as a plate of shortbread cookies. "Thank you so much," said Zeb, smiling at her.

"Would you like me to pour?" she asked.

"If you would," said Zeb. Once Mrs. Spencer had supplied him and Lucy with tea and cookies, he turned to Lucy. "As you were saying . . ."

"What happened to Miss Tilley got me thinking about how meds can be switched, and then I went for a walk with Penny this morning. . . ."

"My Penny?" asked Zeb, before biting into his cookie.

"Yes. Chad asked me to take her under my wing, since she's been through so much this summer, so when she asked me I agreed to take a walk with her." Lucy paused and gazed out the window at the sparkling blue water beyond Zeb's manicured lawn. "We went to Quissett Point."

"And she said something that upset you?" prompted Zeb.

"Not exactly upset. More like it got me thinking. Thinking thoughts I don't want to think."

"Ah," said Zeb. "And these thoughts you don't want to think about concern me?"

"Actually Chris," said Lucy, "and how everybody said he was doing so well with rehab, but then he went and overdosed, which didn't make sense. The thing is, Penny said that Nate gave him vitamins to help with his recovery, but. . . ."

"That's true. He was very concerned about Chris's recovery."

Lucy finally got it out. "He's a pharmacist, you know, and it would be easy enough for him to doctor those vitamins. I mean, we all get drugs from the pharmacy, prescriptions. . . . We don't know what they really are, but we take them because they're supposed to be good for us. But what if they're not. If there's a mistake, or even—" She let out a big sigh, then took a long swallow of iced tea. "But why would he do that? Why would he want to kill Chris?"

"Two reasons I can think of," said Zeb, speaking slowly. "The obvious one is to stop the genealogical research Chris was doing. He was definitely not on board with that."

"Penny said he refuses to acknowledge that his grandmother was Metinnicut."

"He certainly didn't seem to welcome the idea," admitted Zeb, "but I think the second reason is actually a much stronger motivation. I think he might have wanted to eliminate Chris from the picture so Penny would inherit my entire estate." He reached for another cookie. "You see, after Penny came back and we reconciled I changed my will so that the great majority of the estate, after some charitable bequests, will be divided between mother and both grandsons. Before that everything went to Chris." He nodded and bit into the cookie. "Eliminating Chris would give Penny and Chad pretty much the whole kaboodle."

Lucy was struck by this rather detached explanation and wondered if it was typical of the way wealthy people thought about their legacies. As for her and Bill, they just hoped to make it through the month. "It's really just a wild guess," said Lucy, getting back on track. "Pharmacists take oaths, right? There are codes of conduct. Do you really think he would do something like that?"

"Easy enough to check," said Zeb, polishing off his cookie. "The vitamins are still here. Nothing's been moved, and nobody's used the upstairs hall bathroom since Chris died. It's just as he left it."

"Didn't the police check for drugs after he OD'd?"

"No. He was still alive when the EMTs came and they rushed him to the hospital where he died. It was obvious that he'd overdosed, so there was no autopsy or investigation. I think it's about time there was." He reached for the phone, an old-fashioned black Bakelite version with a rotary dial. "Do you know the number of the police department?"

"By heart," said Lucy, rattling it off and watching as Zeb painstakingly inserted his finger in the appropriately numbered hole and dialed. "Zeb Logue, here," he began. "I wonder if you could send an officer out to the house. I may have discovered some evidence related to my grandson's death."

When Zeb Logue wanted something done, it usually happened, at least that's how it seemed to Lucy, who was amazed at the department's quick response. "Someone is on the way," he said, hanging up.

"Perhaps I should just take a look," suggested Lucy. "So I can point the officer in the right direction."

Zeb nodded. "I wouldn't want to be like the boy who cried wolf," he said, "but don't touch anything. Just take a look, upstairs, second door on the right. As I remember, they were on the sink vanity."

Lucy's emotions were in a bit of a tempest as she began climbing the lovely floating staircase that swept around the circular hallway. It was the sort of staircase you pictured a lovely girl descending, like Scarlett O'Hara, in a hoop skirt. But she wasn't descending, anticipating a party or a dance, she was climbing, intending to search for something she was pretty sure she didn't want to find.

Reaching the carpeted hallway, which was hung with paintings and dotted with tables holding plants and flowers, she walked slowly to the second door on the right. She paused, thinking that perhaps she shouldn't touch the knob, which might retain incriminating fingerprints, then noticed that she wouldn't have to. The door was ajar, so she gave it a nudge. It opened slowly, revealing Nate, big as life, standing in front of the vanity, holding the Little Rabbit/Laura doll, which he quickly whisked out of sight, behind his back.

Chapter Twenty-four

"Oops, sorry," said Lucy, quickly withdrawing and pulling the door shut. What was he doing in the house? And what was he holding in his hand? Why did he have the doll? It was supposed to be at the historical society.

The door opened and Nate stepped out. "Your turn," he said, bowing and gesturing with one hand that she should enter, along with a smile that would do a shark credit.

Lucy's heart was pounding as she stepped inside, playing it cool and pretending she simply needed to use the bathroom. What was going on? Did he sneak into the house, unknown to Zeb? Or was Zeb himself playing her for a fool, knowing all along that Nate was upstairs? Had he sent her upstairs to confront Nate? Or did he even believe what he'd said about Nate's possible motives for doing away with Chris? Maybe he'd simply led her on and expected Nate to set her straight. Could she really trust the old guy? Was he merely hoping to gain her sympathy as he embarked on a program to rehabilitate the Logue name? Her mind was working overtime and she needed to sort out her thoughts, so she flipped the top of the toilet seat down and sat on it.

Yoga breaths, she told herself, breathing in through her nose and out through her mouth. Get a grip, Lucy. Nate's presence wasn't a coincidence, she decided. He knew that Penny was going to walk with her, and probably figured it would be wise, while Penny was occupied with Lucy, to remove the vitamins, if that's what they were. He'd been to the house several times before and certainly knew how easy it would be to sneak inside unobserved, given the home's large size and numerous doors and windows, many left open to catch cooling breezes. What she couldn't quite figure out was how the doll figured in all this.

Still puzzled, but now feeling rather more in control of her nerves, Lucy decided to take a look at that cluster of vitamin bottles on the vanity. It was the usual assortment of nutritional supplements you could buy in any drugstore or grocery and might find in anyone's house: a daily multivitamin, calcium and vitamin D for strong bones, vitamin C in case you felt a cold coming on, and some B vitamins for whatever B vitamins did, even magnesium, which she'd heard was the latest mineral we don't get enough of. What she didn't find was a prescription bottle containing the special mixture Nate had compounded for Chris.

If it actually existed, he could have pocketed it. In fact, that's what he would have had to do because the bathroom didn't have a window. But this was all a lot of guessing, based on little more than hearsay and her own suspicious mind. The police were on the way. If she could find him and somehow delay him, they could search him and find the drugs. They would need probable cause, of course, and an accusation from her would most likely not be enough. It would be her word against his. If Zeb also spoke up, his claims would have more weight, but it was hard to imagine a Tinker's Cove police officer conducting a body search without a very strong reason. Of course, maybe they already had some other evidence she was unaware of. Maybe he was already a person of interest. It was worth a try, she decided, standing up and heading for the stairs.

What if he decided to hide himself, or the drugs, somewhere in the house? It was certainly big enough, and she had to admit a police search of the property, which was owned by an extremely respectable and influential citizen, was probably out of the question. She was well aware of all those constitutional protections that required a warrant in order to conduct a search. And even if the police did agree to set up a perimeter and go room to room, it would take time to organize, time in which Nate could slip away. Or he could simply go to the front door, step outside, and pretend he'd just arrived, planning to visit with his elderly father-in-law.

It all seemed pretty hopeless, she thought, as she began descending the stairs. Nate's quick action had prevented her from finding any evidence, and now Zeb would just have to tell the officer that there'd been a mix-up and apologize for making the call. That was her thinking when she reached the curve in the staircase that allowed her to see down into the hall, where Nate was at the door, ready to leave. The doll, she noticed, was nowhere to be seen, and she wondered if she really had seen it. Nate turned to give her a smile and a wave, then opened the door, which revealed one of the Tinker's Cove Police Department's blue and white squad cars parked right outside.

He did a double take at this unexpected sight, then quickly stepped back inside, slamming the door shut. He leaned against it for a moment, considering his options. "It's probably just a wellness check," said Lucy, improvising, as she continued down the stairs. "They regularly check on old folks, making sure everything's okay."

"Small town life, hunh?" asked Nate, sounding somewhat doubtful.

"Yeah," said Lucy, hoping she didn't look as nervous as she felt. She crossed the hall and looked out the sidelight beside the front door at the squad car where Todd Kirwan was seated behind the wheel, apparently talking on his communicator.

"What's taking him so long? Why doesn't he come in?" he asked.

"You know. Checking in with the department, probably. Something like that. I think it's routine."

"I don't like it," said Nate, who Lucy noticed was breathing rather heavily.

"Nothing to worry about," said Lucy. "It's only Todd Kirwan."

"You know him?" He kept patting one of the pockets of his cargo shorts with his right hand, as if he wanted to make sure whatever was inside was still there.

Lucy wondered if it was the prescription vitamins, or something else, like a gun, and hoped she wasn't going to find out. "Sure. I'm a reporter," she said, with a casual shrug. "I have a lot of contact with the local cops."

His hand now remained in the pocket. "Go on out," he said. "Tell him Zeb's okay but he's resting and doesn't want to talk to him today."

"He'll think it odd. After all, why would I be here if Zeb was resting and didn't want to see anybody?"

"I'm sure you can think of something," said Nate, wiping his forehead. "Like you're leaving because Zeb's a bit under the weather."

"But then he'd definitely want to check on him; he

might even call the rescue squad." Lucy could see that Todd had now exited the squad car and was doing a visual survey of the property. "He's coming. Do you want me to answer the door?"

Nate hesitated, as if confused, then came to a snap decision. His hand came out of the pocket, holding a small automatic handgun, which he waved at her. "Nobody's answering the door. We're going in the living room. Where's Zeb?"

Lucy went rigid, staring at the gun, thinking it was amazing that she was still alive because it felt as if her heart had stopped beating. "I—I don't know," she finally said.

"Move!" he ordered, waving the gun, and Lucy obeyed, scurrying out of the hall and into the living room. "Where did you see him last?"

"I left him in the sunroom," said Lucy, who knew there was no point in arguing with a man holding a gun.

"Get him!" he ordered. She started to move just as the doorbell rang, and Nate gave her a hard shove, propelling her toward the adjacent sunroom. "Get Zeb!" he snarled.

"Okay, okay," said Lucy, rubbing her shoulder.

"Now!" he growled, hurrying over to the windows where he pulled the long drapes shut.

Lucy went to the sunroom doorway, where she found Zeb dozing in his chair. She hesitated to disturb him, but Nate was right behind her, waving that gun. "Zeb, you've got to get up," she said, giving his shoulder a gentle shake.

He suddenly opened his eyes, startled. "Hunh?"

"Nate wants you to go into the living room."

"Why? What's going on?"

Lucy tilted her head toward the doorway, where Nate was standing big as life, with the gun in his hand. "Okay," Zeb said, pushing himself up by pressing his hands on the chair's armrests, wavering a bit as he stood. Lucy took his arm and together they walked toward the living room. Nate backed away from the door, keeping a beady eye on them. As soon as they were in the darkened living room, he ordered them to sit back to back on the coffee table. While Lucy helped Zeb lower himself onto the low table, Nate yanked at the curtain cords, all the while keeping an eye on them. When he finally freed the cords he tossed them across the room to Zeb and yelled at him to tie up Lucy's hands and feet. Zeb wrapped the cords rather loosely, but Nate wasn't fooled and made him tighten them. He had finally done the job to Nate's satisfaction when the doorbell rang again. The grandfather clock in the hall began ringing the hour and she felt a terrific pain in her head and everything went black.

Next thing she knew, she had a terrific headache and she was trussed up tightly and bound to Zeb, who now also had his hands and feet tied. It was all extremely painful, especially since Zeb was leaning against her for support. "How long was I out?" she asked, with difficulty. Her mouth was dry and she had trouble finding her voice.

Nate was looking outside, peering through the crack in the curtains. "I'd say about two squad cars and an ambulance ago."

So Nate was really going through with this hostage situation, realized Lucy, who had covered a few during her career but had never actually been a hostage. Two squad cars and an ambulance meant the situation was still in the hands of the local Tinker's Cove PD, but if it went on much longer, units from neighboring towns would be called in for mutual aid and everything would escalate. The clock in the hallway chimed once, indicating the quarter hour; it was still early in the process. Then a horrible thought occurred to her.

"Where's Mrs. Spencer?" she whispered.

"Gone to the grocery store," Zeb whispered back, getting a warning look from Nate.

"Shut up!" he snarled.

Lucy let out a sigh of relief; at least Mrs. Spencer was safe. Now if Nate would untie them and let them go, saying he was sorry and temporarily lost his mind, there was a chance they'd all get out alive. Not likely, she decided, watching as he paced back and forth, peeking out the window and then approaching them, waving his gun as if to remind them he could shoot unless they obeyed him. Lucy had covered hostage situations in the past, and she knew that they never ended well for the hostage-taker, and rarely for the hostages. She figured her only chance, their only chance, was to convince him to let them go before things escalated further.

"Nate, I know you're scared, but you don't have to do this. We're on your side, we know you didn't do anything wrong, and that's what we'll tell the officer. Whatever it is, it's a big misunderstanding . . . that's what we'll tell him and send him on his way with a donation to the Police Benevolent Society."

"Shut up!" snarled Nate. "Keep quiet!"

"I think you've seen too many movies," said Zeb, in his scratchy, old-man voice. "You're acting like a criminal and you don't have to. We can work this out."

"Time's not on your side," said Lucy. "You've got to get this sorted before—"

Lucy's little plea was cut short by the squeal of a bullhorn, followed by an amplified male voice. "Police! Nate Nettleton, come out with your hands up!"

"Before it escalates? Is that what you were going to say?" demanded Nate, as his cell phone began to ring.

"Answer it," urged Lucy. "Talk to them, it's your best option."

Instead, Nate ignored the phone and smacked Lucy across the mouth. "I said shut up!" he growled, as her head snapped back, right into Zeb's, and she blinked back tears from the pain. Outside, she could hear the sirens of approaching police cars and knew there must be half a dozen or more by now. An ambulance was probably already standing by and a fire engine would also be at the ready in case the hostage taker decided to burn the house down. The SWAT team would have been called and were on the way.

If only she could convince Nate that continuing down this road would only lead to a dead end, she thought, tasting blood in her mouth. Once the SWAT team arrived, it would soon be over. Nate would most certainly be dead, and she and Zeb might be, too. But why was Nate acting like this? He was risking everything and it didn't make any sense. Why was he so jumpy? Even if he did have a bottle with his pharmacy's label, and if that bottle contained opioids instead of vitamins, it was hardly conclusive evidence. Chris himself could have made the switch. He was a known user and relapse was common, often leading to overdose and death. Just ask any EMT.

Nate was pacing back and forth, certainly very agitated. He'd hurry to the window, peek out, then whirl around to make sure she and Zeb were still tied up, then back to his observation post. She had to get him to calm down, she realized, wondering how she could possibly do that. An idea occurred to her, but she knew that talking presented a risk to herself, and also to Zeb. Then again, keeping quiet didn't guarantee safety, either. She swallowed hard and said, "I wish you'd think of Penny. She really loves you."

Nate didn't react. He was standing at the window, motionless, staring out. Encouraged, Lucy continued. "When we were walking, honest to God, she couldn't stop singing your praises . . . she told me you're fabulous. That's the word she used. And she's so proud of you and of Chad. She'll stick with you, whatever happens, Nate. Maybe you should call her. I'm sure she'd beg you to give yourself up. . . ."

"So she can visit me in jail?" asked Nate, in a sardonic tone. "I don't think you know Penny very well if you think she'd set foot in a prison."

"You might be surprised," said Lucy, as the grandfather clock chimed three times, a quarter to the hour. Had this really only been forty-five minutes? It seemed an eternity.

"Don't forget Chad," said Lucy. "I've been so impressed by him. At first I thought he was just a really good-looking guy out for a good time, but he's deep. He really is. He's got a charitable outlook, always looks for the best in people. He understands that people make mistakes. Think how he reached out to Chris and tried to help him. He wants you alive and in his life. Don't let him down."

"I think maybe you should shut up and mind your own business," snapped Nate. "I've got kind of a lot going on right now."

"Yeah," agreed Lucy. "Zeb's not doing too good," she said, realizing he'd lost consciousness. His head had fallen forward, onto his chest, and he now was leaning away from her, pulling against her and causing her to strain to remain upright. "He needs medical help."

"Do you think I care about the old coot? I hope he dies and rots in hell." Something outside caught his eye, then he continued. "This is all his fault. That's what you can tell St. Peter when we're all standing there at the pearly gates."

"There's no need for that, nobody needs to die," said

Lucy, alarmed. Had he seen the SWAT team? "You can give yourself up, probably get a plea deal, go to jail for a year or two. . . ."

"That's what you think."

"What could they possibly have on you?" she asked, as the image of the doll popped into her head. The doll that had been loaned to the historical society. How did he get it?

"Plenty," he answered. "I don't think they're out there with every cop in the county if they think I'm innocent."

Lucy felt a tugging on the cords that bound her to Zeb, and he raised his head. "You're good for nothing," he said. "Killing Chris was a big mistake. You were never going to get a cent. I'm leaving everything to the Metinnicuts."

"So now you're some kind of Indian lover? What about all those years you claimed my grandmother wasn't white. You called her a squaw, I seem to remember, and you said I was a half-breed."

Suddenly Lucy understood. "You killed Hetty," she said. "She found proof that your grandmother was Native American. . . ."

"All I wanted was that doll, that was all, and the stupid bitch wouldn't give it to me. Said it wasn't hers to give, it belonged to the whole damn town, to our shared heritage, and she was going to put it on display for everyone to see."

"You killed her over a doll?"

"Yeah. It was vile. It was actually labeled *Little Rabbit/Laura*, like it was my grandmother." He snorted. "I'm the victim here. She made me do it, actually grabbed it out of my hands."

"What did you do with it?" asked Lucy.

"I was going to burn it, but thanks to you. . . ." He turned and took another look out the window, then came to a decision. "Okay. It's like this. I'm going to use you two as a shield, got it?"

Lucy nodded, indicating she understood. He bent down to untie the cords around their feet, and Lucy felt the entire binding loosen. This might be her chance, but the gun was still within Nate's reach, right on the floor by his foot. Maybe she could grab it, she thought, wiggling her wrists in an effort to free her hands, when suddenly Nate crumpled to the floor, out like a light.

"What happened?" she asked, incredulous.

"He's an incompetent fool," declared Zeb, revealing the bronze sculpture of an Indian warrior he'd used to conk Nate on the head.

Just then the door opened and the SWAT team burst in, all in black with helmets, shields, and guns ready to shoot. "Everybody okay?"

"All except him," said Zeb. "What an idiot. Couldn't even tie a decent knot."

Nate began groaning, indicating he was coming to, and the team went into action, surrounding him and removing the gun. He was soon handcuffed and patted down, revealing the prescription pill bottle Lucy had suspected he'd taken. Lucy and Zeb were freed from the remaining cords. Lucy was stretching her arms when Officer Todd Kirwan and a couple of EMTs entered to care for the hostages, as well as Nate, who had been seated in a chair. An EMT was applying an ice pack to his head when Todd asked him to identify himself. "Are you Nate Nettleton?"

Getting a nod, the officer recited his rights. "Nate Nettleton, you are charged with the murder of Hetty Furness and you have the right. . . ."

"You might want to add the murder of Chris Taylor," suggested Lucy. "I think you'll find that those pills aren't vitamins, they're fentanyl, which he gave to Chris knowing they'd kill him."

Todd's eyes widened and he gave Lucy a nod, indicating that he would follow up on her accusation. Then he hauled Nate to his feet and began leading him out the door resuming the rights recitation that Lucy had interrupted "You have the right to remain silent. . . ."

Chapter Twenty-five

As soon as Nate was led away the EMTs went into action, tending to Lucy and Zeb. Zeb was fine, but they were concerned about Lucy, who was obviously bruised and complained of a bad headache, so she was transported to the hospital, despite her protests, with a suspected concussion. Concussion or not, Ted wanted the story and managed to bull his way into the ER where Lucy was awaiting a visit from a neurologist.

"Now, Lucy, I'm not going to pressure you," he began, waving his phone in front of her face, "but if you can remember what happened. . . ."

"I remember everything, Ted," said Lucy, who was still coping with that headache. "I went for a walk with Penny Nettleton, Chad asked me to kind of befriend her, and she mentioned that her husband—you know he's a pharmacist, owns a big compounding pharmacy, that's how he's so rich—anyway, he mixed up a batch of vitamins for Chris that were supposed to help him in recovery after detox. And Miss Tilley, well, you know she had that fall and she blamed a pill mix-up. . . ."

"Uh, Lucy. I think you may be a bit confused," suggested Ted. "What does all this have to do with Nate Nettleton taking you hostage?"

"It's the reason I was at the house, Ted. It occurred to me that maybe Nate had substituted an opioid for the vitamins so that Chris would OD, and I wanted to see if I could find the pills."

"Right," said Ted, slowly, as if speaking to a demented aunt. "And why would Nate want to kill his stepson?"

Lucy rolled her eyes. "Because Chris had discovered that Nate's grandmother was Metinnicut. Which made Nate himself part Native American, and since he's a racist and deep in denial he didn't much like that or want people to know, and Chris was doing all this research into local history and was all keen on making reparations for Logue Logging taking Pine Tree. And that's why he killed Hetty, too."

Ted scratched his head. "Chris did kill Hetty after all?"

"No. Nate. Nate killed her because she'd found evidence that his grandmother Laura Nettleton was also known as Little Rabbit. There was a doll, a Little Rabbit/Laura doll that Ellie Martin made that they were going to exhibit, and when Hetty wouldn't give it to him he got furious and killed her."

"Allegedly, Lucy. He's innocent until—"

"Well, the fact that he took me and Zeb hostage seems pretty good proof. Why would he do something like that if he didn't have a guilty conscience?" She paused. "And besides, he pretty much admitted everything to me and Zeb. He was going to use us as shields to escape."

"Do you think he knew the police were investigating him?"

"I think so, Ted. They had DNA from the peavey, remember, that they thought implicated Skye Sykes. They might've done some genealogical sleuthing and discovered the link through Little Rabbit to Nate. All the Metinnicuts and the Baptists knew that she married a white man and moved to Virginia."

"Wow," mused Ted. "That's ironic."

"Or karma," said Lucy, flashing back to her conversation with Penny as a woman in a white jacket stepped into the cubicle.

"I'm Dr. Santos," she said, introducing herself.

"And I'm out of here," offered Ted. "And, Doc, I sure hope you give Lucy a clean bill of health, because she's my best reporter and she's got a hell of a story to write."

"I can't make any promises," answered the doctor. "But you can be sure we'll take good care of her."

Lucy still had a headache when she was released that evening, but it was gone when she woke the next morning and learned that the DA was holding a press conference. She was sitting front row center as he recounted the various steps of the investigation that led to charging Nate Nettleton with Hetty's murder.

"It was DNA and forensic genealogy that led us to him," he announced, smugly. "It turns out we have quite a number of amateur sleuths here in Maine who volunteer to conduct this research, which would be prohibitively expensive otherwise."

Lucy was still tired, but perked right up hearing this. Amateur forensic genealogists? Seemed like a good subject for a feature story.

"And when Chris Taylor died of an overdose, interviews with people who knew him well, including his therapist, led us to conclude we had to consider his death as a possible homicide, perhaps connected to Hetty's murder. This was confirmed when Nate Nettleton was taken into custody and we found he had in his possession a vial from his pharmacy that was labeled as containing vitamins but actually contained fentanyl. He knew his stepson was taking a maintenance drug that would cause him to overdose if he also took fentanyl. I would add that yesterday's hostage taking provided additional proof of his guilt. . . ."

Other reporters began shouting questions at Aucoin, but Lucy sat silently, suddenly overcome by memories of what had happened. She remembered Nate's expression as he confronted her in the hallway, the way he'd attacked her, the way he threatened them. Would he really have shot her and Zeb? She liked to think his decision to use them as shields indicated he'd decided against it, but she wasn't sure. Maybe he was hoping he'd succeed in escaping. Maybe he was hoping they'd all go down in a blaze of gunfire. Maybe at that point he really didn't care.

She realized she suddenly felt quite chilled in the overly air-conditioned basement meeting room in the county courthouse, which was crowded and noisy, so she made her way outside. The old granite building was surrounded with a bit of lawn and she seated herself on a sunny bench to warm up. It was over, she thought, wishing she could feel a sense of relief. But it wasn't over, she decided, because Zoe was going to marry Chad and she would be forever tied to his parents, the in-laws. Or the out-laws, she decided, with a rueful chuckle.

Considering the situation, Zoe and Chad decided to get married sooner rather than later and settled on Columbus Day weekend for a small, family affair in the house on Red Top Road. That meant that Elizabeth, Toby, and Molly had to act quickly to get their travel plans together, but they had all promised to come. Lucy was most excited about seeing her grandson, Patrick, who was also coming with his parents. Arrangements had been made with Reverend Marge to conduct the ceremony and Lucy, with Sue's help, had arranged for a catered lunch and ordered flowers. She was at the office one day in late August, telling Phyllis about the plans, when Zoe called.

"Mom, I don't know what to do. Penny's decided she won't come to the wedding if Zeb is there."

Trust Penny to throw a monkey wrench into the gears, thought Lucy. "But I thought they'd reconciled. . . ."

"That's over. Penny's absolutely convinced that Nate is innocent and has somehow decided Zeb had masterminded some sort of plot against him. It's really crazy, but she's dragging up all this old family history about how Zeb never liked Nate, and he disapproved of her, and even though he'd seemed to change, he was really conspiring against them all along."

"You've got to be kidding me," said Lucy, hoping that was the case.

"No, Mom. It's true. She's in denial. She won't admit that Nate is guilty, so she's created an alternate universe in which he, and she, are victims of her father's evil machinations. She's insisting that we uninvite Zeb, and the whole thing is killing Chad, who's having a hard time himself dealing with his father's guilt and the loss of Chris. Zeb's been terrific; he's been coming to the games to see Chad play and he's given us a honeymoon cruise to Bermuda, as well as a big check, so it's really awkward. Chad really wants his mom at the wedding. He loves her even though she's so difficult, but he's grown awfully fond of Zeb, too."

"That is awkward," admitted Lucy.

"Zeb's been so good to Chad and me; he says he's finally got a family again. I know he's tried to reach out to Penny, but she won't even talk to him. I think Nate's poisoned her against him."

"That wouldn't surprise me. So what are you going to

do?" asked Lucy, putting the stress on *you*. She had a bad feeling that Zoe was hoping to involve her and wanted nothing to do with it.

"Well, that's why I called you, Mom. I'm hoping you could talk to Penny and bring her around."

Lucy was determined to be firm. "Oh, no, this is not my problem."

"I know, Mom, but I don't know who to turn to and Chad says that if anyone can get Penny to see sense, it's you. He thinks the world of you, you know. He's so impressed with your career and your independent attitude."

"That is really low, Zoe," said Lucy, who wasn't the least bit fooled by her daughter's flattery.

"Desperate times, Mom. Desperate times."

"Well, I'll give it a try, but don't get your hopes up."

"Thanks, Mom. I owe you big time. Bye."

Lucy let out a long sigh. If she only knew, but of course kids never really know how much their parents do for them. With any luck, she and Chad would have kids of their own—grandkids!—and Zoe would come to appreciate her and Bill.

There was no point putting it off; she might as well give Penny a call and get it over with. Another walk, perhaps? Penny was all for it, and the next morning Lucy found herself back at the Quissett Point parking lot, waiting for Penny. She arrived fifteen minutes late in the Mercedes, which seemed to have developed a problem as it made a weird noise. Penny seemed oblivious, however, to the ominous knocking that continued as she stepped out of the car and gave Lucy a big hug, collapsing against her.

"This is so kind of you, it really means a lot to me," she said, brushing away tears. "All my friends seem to have deserted me."

Lucy figured that's what happened when your husband was indicted for two murders, but didn't say so. "I'm so sorry for your trouble," she said, instead. "What you need is a bit of exercise and a change of scene to clear your head."

"If only," moaned Penny. "It's overwhelming. Poor Nate, locked up in that horrid county jail, and his lawyers aren't very encouraging, but they're happy enough to take our money."

"Maybe he should consider taking a plea deal?" suggested Lucy, as they set off toward the path.

"And admit he's guilty? Never!"

"The DA's convinced he's got a strong case, but he'd probably be willing to go for reduced jail time if it meant saving the trouble and expense of a trial."

Penny stopped in her tracks. "Don't you see, Lucy? Nate's completely innocent. He would never do the things they said he did. . . ."

"Enough, Penny. He tied me up and held me hostage, along with Zeb. We could all have died that day, so don't tell me he's not guilty."

"I don't expect you to understand," said Penny. "There's a long history of family problems, and my father, well, he's not the nice old man he pretends to be. He's mean and vindictive and he'd go to any lengths to hurt me and Nate. No . . ." she continued, shaking her head, "he's still up to his old tricks. Take that honeymoon he's giving the kids, just when Nate and I have all these lawyer bills and can't afford to do anything for them. Not a thing. And instead of throwing his money away on a lavish cruise that they'll spend in their lavish stateroom and won't even remember, he could be helping me and Nate!"

So it's all about you, Penny, thought Lucy. "So I don't suppose I can convince you to come to the wedding?"

"Not if Zeb is there, and that's my final decision," said Penny, with a self-righteous little nod.

Lucy's phone indicated a text had arrived and she checked it, noting that Sue was telling her about a big end-of-season sale at Carriage Trade. "Oh, dear," she said, seizing on this opportunity to escape. "I'm afraid I've got to go. Breaking news."

"But we've only started the walk," protested Penny.

"I know," said Lucy, turning around and heading back to the parking lot. "It's really too bad, but there's no arguing with Ted."

"Of course," said Penny, nodding acquiescence and following along the trail. When they reached the parking lot she once again embraced Lucy. "We girls have to stick together," she said, adding a little sniff.

"Sure do," said Lucy, "and if I were you, I'd get that car in for service. It doesn't sound right."

"I don't know what to do. Nate always took care of my car. 'A dirty old garage is no place for a lady like you,' he'd say. What on earth am I going to do?"

"There's a mechanic right on Main Street, Greg's Garage. Just take your car and hand it over to Greg. He's very nice and he'll take care of you."

"Thank you, Lucy. You're a doll."

What about that doll? wondered Lucy, as she got in her car and gave Penny a wave. Had it turned up? Only one way to find out. She was going straight to Zeb.

She caught Zeb and Mrs. Spencer just as they were loading a beautifully restored woody station wagon with suitcases, obviously setting out on a trip.

"I don't want to hold you up," apologized Lucy. "I see you're getting ready to leave."

"It's my annual vacation," said Mrs. Spencer, with a smile. "The last week of August and the first week of September. I've been taking it for years. I go and stay with my sister at Mackinac Island."

"Sounds lovely," said Lucy. "Does Zeb go, too?"

"Oh, no," he said, shaking his head. "I go off to this camp in the Adirondacks with some old buddies. We spend all day fishing and play cards all night."

"So you're going to be gone right through Labor Day?" asked Lucy.

"Yup." Nate banged the rear gate shut, clearly eager to get going.

"The reason I came was to talk to you about the kids' wedding. . . ." said Lucy, tagging along as he walked to the front of the car.

"I know. Penny's being a spoiled brat," admitted Zeb, kicking the tire.

"Would you be upset if the kids took advantage of your vacation to get married? That way Penny could come and it wouldn't look like you gave in."

"Whatever they want is fine with me," said Zeb, settling himself behind the wheel of his woody. "The sooner the better!"

He honked the horn and Mrs. Spencer hurried to climb in beside him. She'd barely managed to get the door closed before he started the classic car rolling off down the driveway. "Wait! Wait!" Lucy yelled, running after them.

The car slowed and Lucy ran up to the driver's side door. "I have a question. Did you happen to find the Little Rabbit/ Laura doll?"

Zeb shrugged and shook his head. "I don't know what you're talking about."

"A doll with two heads?" asked Mrs. Spencer. "It was an Indian maiden, but if you flipped the skirt around, instead of legs it had a white girl? Is that what you mean?"

"Yes," said Lucy. "Nate didn't want the historical society to display it; that's why. . . ." She paused, thinking she didn't really need to go into it. "Did you find it?"

"It was in the umbrella stand in the hall."

"What did you do with it?"

"I tucked it away. I was going to give it to my granddaughter."

"It was made by Ellie Martin and belongs to the Metinnicut people," said Lucy. "It's also evidence in Nate's trial."

Mrs. Spencer immediately climbed out of the car and hurried back to the house, unlocking the door and going straight to a mahogany lowboy that served as a hall table. She opened a drawer and withdrew the doll. "Can you take care of her for me?" she asked. "Give her back to her rightful owners."

"Absolutely," said Lucy, taking the doll. She followed the housekeeper out to the porch, holding the doll while Mrs. Spencer locked the door and hurried back to join Zeb in the woody. She waved them off, then walked slowly to her car, examining the doll. It was beautifully done, typical of Ellie Martin's work. Little Rabbit had black hair in two braids and was wearing a dun-colored dress decorated with beads and fringe. When you flipped her over, the white girl appeared, with blond hair and blue eyes, in a white eyelet dress with a blue silk sash. If only she'd named the doll something else, thought Lucy. Maybe then Nate wouldn't have made the connection, maybe then everything would have been different. Maybe, maybe, she thought, setting the doll beside her on the passenger seat. Before she took her to the DA, she had something she needed to do. She took her phone out of her pocket and called Zoe.

"How do you feel about getting married Labor Day weekend?" she asked. "Not Columbus Day."

"Fine with me. At this point I just want to get it done, but why Labor Day?"

"Because Zeb will be on vacation in the Adirondacks."

"He doesn't mind if we . . . ?"

"Not in the least. I just spoke with him. So go for it."

"Okay. We will." Zoe paused. "You know that means Toby and his gang and Elizabeth won't be able to come, right? Are you okay with that?"

What with everything on her mind Lucy hadn't realized that and it took a moment to sink in. "They're coming anyway for Columbus Day," she said slowly, rearranging her thoughts. "I guess the question is more whether you're okay with it."

Zoe sounded thoughtful. "I think so. It really means a lot to Chad to have his mom at the wedding, and we can video the whole thing and do a replay when everyone's together."

"Okay," said Lucy. "Sunday of Labor Day weekend. It's a date."

It was a small group that gathered in the Stones' family room in preparation for Zoe and Chad's nuptials. Reverend Marge was there, of course, and so were Lucy and Bill, Sara and Jodi, Chad's buddy and best man Joe Zapata, and Penny. She was clutching a lacy hanky and kept dabbing at her eyes, overcome with the emotion of the day.

Elizabeth was there, too, arriving the day before to everyone's surprise. "How did you manage it?" asked Lucy, hugging her eldest daughter when she suddenly, miraculously, walked into the kitchen when Lucy and Bill were grabbing a quick lunch.

"Well," began Elizabeth, with a sly smile, "it just so happened that Monsieur Loiseau at the hotel was attending a manager's meeting in Boston this weekend, so he gave me a lift in the company jet." Elizabeth was a concierge at the very posh Cavendish Hotel in Paris, one of a chain of international top-market luxury hotels. Dressed for travel in flats, trim black pants, and an oversized fisherman's jersey and bright red lipstick, she seemed to bring France right along with her. "I rented a car and here I am."

"I can't believe it," said Lucy, hoping to settle in for a long chat to catch up with her daughter, but Elizabeth had other plans. "We'll have plenty of time to catch up later," she said, giving her parents quick hugs. "I have a few things I want to do before the wedding." Then she was off, leaving her stunned parents behind.

"Typical Elizabeth," was Bill's comment.

There was no clue as to what Elizabeth had been up to when she returned, and when questioned she merely pressed her lips together and said all would be revealed in good time.

Lucy was still wondering what sort of surprise Elizabeth had in mind as they waited for the ceremony to begin. Chad was handsome, in an open shirt and blazer, and was patiently allowing his mother to adjust his boutonniere and pick imaginary fluff off his jacket. All the preparations had been made, all the participants had gathered, and the ceremony could begin as soon as Zoe came downstairs. Lucy checked her watch, realized it was later than she thought, and decided to go and check on Zoe. Was it a matter of last-minute nerves? Or maybe just a stubborn button?

She whispered in Bill's ear that she'd be right back and slipped away. She was in the kitchen, headed for the back stairs, when she caught a glimpse of something out of the corner of her eye. Turning to see what it was, she made out a rather grimy, bug-spattered camper van in the driveway. To her horror, the driver gave the horn three beeps.

Thinking it was a car full of lost tourists seeking directions, she stepped onto the porch, intending to get rid of them as quickly as possible. But when the driver's side door opened, it was Toby who stepped out, followed by Molly and Patrick. Unable to believe her eyes, Lucy stood there amazed, as Patrick ran to her and threw his arms around her. Soon all four were engaged in a big family hug.

"How on earth did you get here?"

"We had the whole thing planned; we just moved it up a couple of weeks," said Toby. "We were always going to drive, make an adventure of it, because Molly won't fly anymore." He grinned at his wife.

"Not since that door fell off the jet. No way! And actually, this was better timing for us. I was a bit worried about the weather in October, there's often snow," said Molly, who was raising her shoulders one by one and stretching her back. "We came through Canada."

"Yup," said Toby, sounding like they'd popped over from neighboring Gilead, "took a sharp right in Montreal."

"Long drive," said Bill, who had come into the kitchen to investigate the hubbub. He was grinning broadly as he shook Toby's hand, gave Molly a fatherly hug, and high-fived Patrick. "What is it, five thousand miles?"

"Four thousand nine hundred and ninety-seven," said Patrick. "I kept track."

"I can't believe how tall you are," said Lucy, studying her suddenly gangly grandson, with long arms and legs.

"Well, come on in," said Bill, leading the way.

Zoe was just coming down the stairs when they all got in the kitchen, so there were more hugs. "So you're really doing this?" teased Toby, after wrapping Zoe in a big embrace. "Getting married?"

"That's the plan," said Zoe, all smiles and pink cheeks.

"Well, let's get on with it," said Bill, leading the way to the family room where the newcomers were greeted with more exclamations of joy and lots of hugs. Elizabeth, after sending a quick text on her phone, tapped a glass and the ceremony began.

Chad was every bit the handsome bridegroom and Zoe was beautiful in a flowery little tea dress with a wreath of asters and daisies in her hair. Like the wreath, her bouquet had been picked in the garden earlier that morning. A bottle of champagne was chilling in a bowl of ice on a nearby table, beside a homemade layer cake, ready for a celebratory toast and cake cutting.

They all gathered in front of the fireplace, which held a lush Boston fern in honor of the occasion, and Reverend Marge conducted the simple marriage ceremony, which was over in fifteen minutes, ending by pronouncing them husband and wife. The happy couple kissed, Penny was overcome and collapsed against Joe, everyone else clapped, and all of a sudden the familiar strains of the wedding march blared out at top volume.

Not part of the plan, thought Lucy, startled.

"What's going on?" asked Zoe, as Elizabeth opened the curtains on the French doors leading to the deck, revealing a backyard that had been transformed, decorated with paper lanterns and twinkling lights. The picnic table was covered with food, flowers, and a huge wedding cake; all of the Stones' friends were there, along with some of Chad's teammates and Zoe's old school friends. Everyone was clapping and applauding, glasses were filled, toasts were pronounced, and finally the happy couple cut the cake.

Noticing that Lucy was sniffling a bit, Bill wrapped his arm around her waist. "They're going to be fine," he told her.

"I know," said Lucy. "I'm just a bit overwhelmed. It's been quite a day," she said, glancing around the backyard, filled with friends and family. Everyone seemed happy, except for Penny, who was nowhere in sight. "Oh, my gosh, I forgot all about Penny."

But there she was, still clinging to Joe as she wobbled across the yard with an empty wineglass, clearly headed for a refill. Lucy caught up with them, expecting to find Penny dissolved in tears, but instead got the distinct impression that she was actually flirting with Joe, who was at least thirty years her junior.

"So tell me all about the team," she was saying, hanging on to his arm and batting her eyelashes at him. "Do you have to practice a lot?"

"Well, yeah," he said, looking as if he wanted to join his teammates, who were gathered around the grill, beers in hand.

"C'mon, Penny," invited Lucy. "I'm sure you want to freshen up a bit."

"Thank you, Lucy," said Penny, grabbing Lucy's arm with her free hand as if she were grabbing a life raft. "You know this is all so, so emotional for me, and I'm having to do it all alone. If only Nate could be here, but you know the judge was quite unreasonable and absolutely would not agree. . . ."

"I do understand," said Lucy, leading the way inside the house. "But at least we're ending this horrible summer on a happy note. That's something to be glad about, right?"

"I suppose," said Penny, leaning heavily on Lucy's arm as she made her way across the grassy lawn in her high heels. "But I just don't know what I'm going to tell Janice. There was no DJ, no dancing, not even a theme!"

"You're wrong," said Lucy, supporting Penny as they

climbed the steps to the deck. She paused and surveyed the backyard, which was filled with all the people she loved most. Elizabeth, who admitted she was the instigator of the surprise reception, helped by Sue, was seated with Jodi and Sara, engaged in animated chatter; Bill and Toby were throwing a Frisbee around with Patrick; Sue and Pam were freshening up the buffet; the baseball players were clustered together, teasing each other; and Rachel was talking with Zoe and Chad, probably giving them relationship advice. She thought of her own wedding and the life she and Bill had created together. She thought of Zoe and Chad, who were just starting out. Then she smiled and turned to Penny. "There's definitely a theme; the theme is love. True love."

"Ouch!" screamed Penny, collapsing on the steps and holding her ankle. "I think it's twisted," she moaned. "Probably sprained. Maybe even broken."

"I'll get you some ice," said Lucy, with a resigned sigh. Could in-laws get divorced, she wondered, reaching for the freezer door, or was she stuck with Penny for, well, forever?